Pamela Longfellow is th
of a nightclub singer an
an actress, a model, a
owner. She lives in Ve

By the same author

China Blues

PAMELA LONGFELLOW

Chasing Women

Grafton

An Imprint of HarperCollins*Publishers*

Grafton
An Imprint of HarperCollins*Publishers*
77–85 Fulham Palace Road,
Hammersmith, London W6 8JB

Published by Grafton 1993
9 8 7 6 5 4 3 2 1

Copyright © Pamela Longfellow 1993

The Author asserts the moral right to
be identified as the author of this work

A catalogue record for this book
is available from the British Library

ISBN 0 586 21025 3

Set in Times

Printed in Great Britain by
HarperCollinsManufacturing Glasgow

To Vivian, for all the gaudy times

Contents

Paper Chain

The alley smells like rubber and hot bananas. Thick blue smoke, crazed with black specks, cracks in the close night air. In a garbage can against a brick wall, the children of Times Square burn whatever they find: cigarette packs, old clothes and burlap stiff with human sweat, bus tokens, theatre tickets, banana skins – trash.

Small ragged shapes of innocent violence, city urchins with bittersweet eyes, dance beside the can, its dented metal sides thinner, dull red with heat.

'This too! Burn this!' screams a kid with the piping voice of an altar boy, the face of a gunslinger and singed eyebrows. He whips away a sleeping tramp's newspaper blanket to toss it on the fire.

The wind steals a page. A sudden gust snatches it before it burns, front page and back, flipping it over and over, cartwheeling the printed paper up the alley's sooted wall, over the roof of the Loew's State Theater, down the white glow of the marquee – John Gilbert in *His Glorious Night* – driving it north up Broadway. The sheet of newspaper becomes a white window on the dark blue air, then – pressed flat in a slip-stream – becomes a paper carpet, skimming two feet above the busy evening pavement. Big city wind, ambitious wind that smells of hotdogs and soft fat pretzels, charcoaled chestnuts, steam heat and gasoline, takes it on a corkscrewing ride through dark trousered legs, light silken strides, the snap and miss of a fox terrier's teeth, past the bright lights: drug stores, automats, florists, soda fountains, funeral parlours, small sour hotels – theatres. The paper – now violet, now rose, amber, a low hellish green – caught in a swift side-street eddy, twists up to the black after-hours window of a pawnbroker on the first floor, on the second a show-business agent and a shady lawyer, on the third, a cut-rate dentist and a ten-dollars-a-day gumshoe.

Crossing against the light on Forty-sixth Street, the fleeting page dervishes with candy wrappers in the hissing white steam from a manhole cover. Blown back by the passing of a clanging Broadway trolley, it wraps itself around the sleek legs of a woman in a moleskin coat reading the poster in front of the Palace Theater. Startled, the woman highkicks like a chorus girl, sending the paper back up – straight into the face of her escort wearing a sedate bowler hat. The gentleman whacks it with his walking stick. Jerking, almost alive, the newspaper gains the sixth floor of an eight-storey walk-up before plunging down into a crater, a huge bulldozed hole in the bedrock of Broadway that intends to be a skyscraper by spring. Rolling on its edge, the sheet spins across Forty-eighth Street, clings for a moment to one of hundreds of ruby light bulbs spelling ROSELAND, rips neatly in half, front page spinning north one block to Lindy's. Folding and refolding in mad origami, back page skips next door to the Silver Slipper, winks past the angry heads of Jack Eagels and Teddy O'Rourke, climbs the brittle iron fire escape above the Slipper, sails up and up and over – to disappear east beyond the rooftops of Tin Pan Alley.

It's a Saturday night in early November. For over a week New York City has been close and warm and cloudy – and it keeps raining at the oddest times. Sudden downpours that scrub the dirty air and soak the unwary.

Teddy and Jack have just tumbled down the stairs from their shared third-storey walk-up – arguing the whole way – when a broken bolt of sizzling white cracks open the brittle sky and thunder drumrolls down Broadway. The words they've used against each other, harsh words with hard edges, wash away in the sudden bustle of the Great White Way.

Almost the last thing Teddy says to Jack is, 'Where's your coat?' Hers is a thick grey drill that reaches her ankles. Her red hair is crammed into a soft grey fedora she's pulled down over her furious ears. And her teeth are clenched.

The last thing Jack says to Teddy is, 'Lost it somewhere. Don't need it.' But he shivers as he speaks, dodging drops of fat rain.

'Crap,' says Teddy.

Leaning on the wet wind, the two feuding reporters walk from 1600 Broadway to Madison Square Garden on Eighth Avenue between Forty-ninth and Fiftieth Streets – one of them going to work, both wearing trousers, and both simmering in hot silence.

1

Shadows, Boxing

'Ladies! aaa-nd gentlemen! Winner by uuu-nanimous dee-cision, Tiger Bink!'

Madison Square Garden booed, threw programmes, wads of chewed gum and lit cigars into the ring as the far-carrying tenor voice of the Garden's announcer, Joe Humphries, bawled the result of a short and unsatisfactory skirmish between boxing flyweights Kid McDoddle and Tiger Bink. The squat referee, trousers held up by yellow braces, toupee on his head flapping up at the front, scurried around sweeping it all back out again. Dazzled in the white light, Tiger Bink, a pallid one hundred and four pounder from Pittsburgh, looked like a skinned lizard. He blinked his bruised gooseberry eyes at the hissing mob and grinned.

'Fook youse!' he yelled, straight into Humphries' dangling mike.

For this, the crowd warmed to him – and threw whatever they had left. The referee was pelted with everything he'd just swept out.

The ugly arena of the concrete Garden – no longer on Madison Square and hardly in flower – was packed with a palpitating mass of excited men, its smoky air laced with the hot stink of cheap cigars and hair tonic, cheaper hooch in hip flasks. Holding on to her hat – press ticket tucked in the band – Teddy O'Rourke squeezed into her usual seat ringside. Crouched on her left, cigarette stuck in his face, typewriter wedged somehow between his knees and the edge of the ring, was Damon Runyon, disdainer of women – especially women on newspapers, even more especially women on newspapers working sports.

12

Finishing a rapid flurry of two fingered typing, Runyon leaned over and hissed in her ear, 'What? You're some kind of precious; a dame who only shows up for the heavyweights?' 'Speaking of precious,' she hissed back, 'I'm surprised you're here at all.'

Puzzled but pacified, Runyon – turning his small sour head – caught sight of Jack. 'Hey, Eagels! still taking a back seat?'

Jack Eagels, squashed behind O'Rourke and Runyan, shook rain out of his tie, took the cigarette out of Damon's mouth and stuck it in his own. He gave Runyon one of his slow, sweet, rumpled smiles.

'Fook youse,' said Jack.

Teddy turned and glared at him.

Jack glared back. 'You too, Red.'

With the swift, economical flick of a finger, Teddy flipped Damon's cigarette out of Jack's mouth. 'Go away, you goddamn Indian – beat it before I climb over this seat and belt you one.'

Jack leapt from his chair, dukes up, thumbing his nose. 'Come on, lady, come on. I dare you. Put 'em up! And it's *half* a goddamn Indian.'

'The both of you! Sit down and shut up!' snapped Runyon. 'I came for the pros.'

'You said it, mister!' agreed the guy on Jack's left.

Up in the ring, Humphries was yelling at the top of his voice. 'Madison Square Garden is proud to announce the last and *main* event of this momentous Saturday evening – November the second, Nineteen Hundred and Twenty-nine. An elimination bout to determine one of the final two contenders for the now vacant title of Heavyweight Champe'en of the World!'

Humphries, beaten back by a roar, hung on to his mike; to the ref's relief, no one threw anything. While Runyon used the opportunity to jerk a thumb at Jack, toss a barb at Teddy. 'Make that featherweight, sister – you two would be in with a chance.' Bathed in brash light,

13

Humphries swung his arm, pointed at the far corner of the ring, and bellowed. 'Let me introduce to you! All the way from Germm-anny! At two hundred and thirty-three pounds, Maaa-x Schuldner!'

Max lumbered onto the canvas: six foot one, blond hair cropped to mere stubble, tiny eyes like raw eggs with blue yolks, the rest of him a blotched and mottled pink. In a floppy pair of baby-blue trunks, Max hopped around the ring throwing shadow punches.

'Go back to Krautland, ya bum! Say, you gotta jaw like my sister's! Hey, stupid!'

The last crack made Teddy glance up from her scribbling – a personal O'Rourke shorthand no one but she could decipher. Stupid? What slug in a beanie said that? She'd just written: *Max looks awkward, powerful, and as stupid as an eighth-grade bully. But Schuldner isn't as stupid as he looks. A veteran of thirty-eight professional bouts, Max is a winner by KO in thirty-three.*

Humphries, now turning a full 160 degrees, hollered, 'And from the Yew-nited States of America! New York City's very own! Weighing in at two hundred and seven pounds, Joe! Bri-ight!'

The Garden went loopy. Through bedlam, Jack leaned forward and poked Runyon. 'Look to your left,' he said. 'There's Killer Madden with some of his sportier boys.'

Teddy narrowed her eyes. Four hours home with Jack, four hours of bitching, and now he was ignoring her? Should she be grateful? Or hit him with her hat? She'd look at Madden; Jack, she'd hit later.

Owney Madden, New York's prime hijacker and racketeer, sat behind Westbrook 'Bud' Pegler, another sporting scribe. Madden was flipping raisins up into the smoky air and catching most of them on their way down. Those he missed went into the brim of Pegler's hat. Even with his famous temper, Bud had a nice sense of survival. The raisins stayed where they landed without a word out of him.

'Holy shit!' whistled Jack, poking Runyon again. 'If it isn't Tom Channing.'

Runyon, lighting another cigarette, spat. 'Jesus! This is some night; *all* the hard guys are here. Wonder who Tom's got a bet on?'

Teddy's head jerked up. Tom Channing! Where?

Madden tickled Teddy's baser curiosity, as all America's gangsters tickled America. But Tom Channing? Unusual things happened around Channing – mainly on the bad side. The darling of the tabloids, indicted for extortion, trafficking and sale of illegal drugs, five times for murder – but never convicted; shot up by both sides of the law – but never dying; Channing walked around with more lead in his system than the composing room of the *New York Trident*. A cocksman with a gun in his pocket, a gunman with a tender smile, Tom Channing would be someone worth seeing. If she could find him. The confusion of faces in the Garden was like a painting on the ceiling of a Wild West saloon: crude and writhing with life. Loud men getting up from their seats or making their way back. Drunks climbing over each other, making passes at a few crusty dames – ladies who tossed these efforts back in their laps. Stylish women who'd come to the fights ever since '21 when the Frenchman 'Gorgeous Georges' Carpentier gave boxing a heavy dose of sex appeal. Shady men in the aisles placing side bets. Where the hell was Jack looking?

Runyon was having the same problem.

Jack pointed. 'Over by Bright's corner. Two rows back of Dempsey and Winchell. The guy who looks like he smells good.'

She didn't know about Damon, but it took Teddy a few more seconds to spot anyone in this rowdy crowd who looked like they smelled like anything but high-octane sweat. When, suddenly, there he was: New York's bad boy, its desperado with charm – the notorious Tom Channing. She shaded her eyes and stared. Was he pretty? The boys on crime called him pretty. Under the hat, who could tell? Under that hat, he might be as pretty as Gary Cooper or as ugly as Bela Lugosi. All she could see: a dark suit, a showy white shirt with a high collar, the suit had a small red flower in its buttonhole, the tie was oddly green against the dark waistcoat. But there was a certain tilt to the head, a way of holding his – oh hell, who was she kidding? All she really saw was his taste in clothing. And that Mr Channing had to be the only quiet person in the Garden. Especially now.

Strolling down a wide centre aisle flanked by a couple of millionaires, a commissioner or two, and a squad of sweating, red-faced policemen, all tall and all Irish, the one-hundredth mayor of New York City was making an entrance. Gentleman Jimmy Walker looked like he smelled swell. Flagrant disdainer of Prohibition, married – yet escorting a pretty actress to every show on Broadway, penning ditties that were sung around pianos in half the nation's parlours, vacationing in Europe at the drop of a top hat, Walker was perfect – from the set of his hat to the shine on his shoes.

Whistles and cat-calls followed his jaunty walk. New York loved its handsome Beau James. 'Hiya, Mayor!' 'Who ya bettin' on, Jimmy?'

Walker, always a showman, was never stumped for an answer. 'Why, who else? The underdog from New York, of course.'

'Say! Jimmy!' called a girlish voice from somewhere in the crowd. 'Who's gonna beat Fiorello?'

Mayor Jimmy doffed his hat to the distant lady. 'Need you ask, Madam? I am – naturally.'

Two may be company, but a crowd is a moron. It howled with approval.

Jimmy's party settled in Jack's row, Jimmy right on the aisle for a quick getaway. He grinned at Eagels and Runyan, threw a kiss to O'Rourke, and sank back gracefully for the main event. His police escort stayed where he'd left them – in the aisle and standing.

Tensed forward, nerves cracking in the weighted air, the sweating crowd forgot Jimmy as they watched the boxer now ducking through the ropes.

Six foot two and one half inches tall, twenty-one years old, and the delicious colour of wet liquorice, Joe Bright held up a gloved arm and grinned. Madison Square Garden erupted in boisterous welcome. Jimmy's 'underdog from New York' might be a nigger but, goddammit, he was an *American* nigger.

Scraping his boots in the resin box, Bright danced across the ring. Circling the planted German, rolling his shoulders, throwing playful jabs at shadows, Joe was fresh, wild, intense, explosive. Max swivelled his enormous head on his enormous neck, pale Anglo-Saxon eyes squinting through pale blond lashes – if looks were blows, the coloured kid was already pulp. And the little ref with the flapping toupee, baggy pants and yellow braces followed Joe in person, reading out the rules in a high thin voice.

Teddy O'Rourke, watching Joe, forgot her troubles with Jack Eagels, forgot Channing and Madden, the idiot crowd. This was her boxer; after Dempsey, the one man in the game she admired. After all the brutes, the sluggers, the grunting pea-brained 'hit-and-be-hitters', beautiful black Joe had come along: light on his feet as the dancing Astaires, catching punches out of the air, *making* his fights, breathing poetry into the sport she loved. *If* boxing was a sport. Or just show business with blood.

Hunkered over her note pad, blocking out her column, Teddy pushed her hat to the back of her head. Not all boxers were stupid – but few were smart. How smart was Joe Bright? How long would he last? Tonight's story on Joe must be her – what? – fifth or sixth in the last two months. Week after week, word after word, shoving him under the public's nose. Two Sundays before she'd written: *This guy Bright is as game as Mickey Walker, as lethal as Jack Dempsey, as stylish as Benny Leonard, better looking than Georges Carpentier, more dignified than Gene Tunney, blacker than Jack Johnson, and as graceful as a taxi dancer.* That was the column that did it. Sporting America now called him Dancing Joe. Teddy O'Rourke of the *New York Trident* wasn't *all* that put him up there in the ring tonight, but she was a lot of it.

O'Rourke was writing faster than Runyan could type, already sure of the outcome. Against Schuldner, Bright couldn't lose. On her right, a few seats down, a radio commentator confided to his bulky mike.

'There's the coloured boxer now, hop, skip and jumping around the ring. I don't know what to make of this, ladies and gentlemen – and neither does the big Hun. He's just standing there, his gloves like two cannonballs swinging on the ends of his powerful arms. My bet is that a few taps with those things and Mr Bright will stop his dancing.'

Teddy snorted, saying to no one but herself, 'What a chump. Joe, stop dancing?'

Behind her, Jack laughed. 'You tell 'em, slugger.'

Halfway round in her seat, Teddy's heated response died on her lips; the opening bell snapped her head back. Three seconds later, she was on the edge of her chair. Joe Bright was losing – from the moment he'd dodged his first punch. Schuldner, galumphing about the canvas like Paul Bunyan's ox, kept going forward; Bright kept going back. Tonight, Joe – so light on his feet, so instinctive he was almost psychic – was a second too slow, an inch too close, uncertain, unsteady. Tonight, Joe wasn't the same fighter Teddy had waved like a bright black flag in America's red, white and blue face. Two minutes in, she was sure of it. What the hell was going on?

By the end of round one, Max cut open the skin over Joe's left eye, marring the stretch of white canvas by three scarlet patches of blood – all Bright's. One second before the bell, Schuldner, his bullet head sinking into his

18

massive, pink shoulders, swung his huge arm in a powerful arc and brought his glove down on the top of Joe's head. Dancing Joe's knees buckled.

The bell went with a reverberating *clang!*

'Did you see that, Jack!' Twisting in her seat, Teddy got all the way round before remembering who she was asking.

Jack, canted over somebody's lap, was talking to Walker.

Typical. If the idiot was even watching, all Jack would see was a coloured kid getting his brains rearranged.

Round Two.

Round Three, Four. Her stomach churning, her fingers dead, Teddy couldn't believe what she was seeing. This wasn't a fight; this was murder. Only heart kept Joe moving, heart dragged his mind and body forward – taking Schuldner's punches, easy blows that made him reel – heart alone forcing him back for more.

Around her, the crowd grew gradually quieter, became sullen, slowly turning against its man, but not yet willing to accept the German. So it just sat there.

In the fourth, Teddy heard the commentator say, 'I hate to see even a coloured boy take this kind of punishment.' She felt like biting him.

By the fifth it was just too much. The Garden rocked with groans of frustrated rage. They'd come to the fights to feel like second-hand champs. US vs the Krauts. Instead, like Dancing Joe, they were getting their expectations beaten out of them.

Teddy cupped her hands to her mouth. 'Joe! Joe, for God's sake – Joey! Dance!' she yelled, her ears stunned from all the other yelling going on around her.

'Glass chin! You're all through, ya dirty bum!'

Teddy whirled round in her seat. One of those voices was Jack's.

The bastard winked at her. 'You call this dancing, Red?'

19

'No, redman! *This* is dancing.' Teddy jumped up, swinging with her right.

Ducking, Jack held up a hand. 'Hey, calm down, Tiger – it's just a fight.'

'*Just* a fight! Is that all you see, hotdog? Where the hell are you looking!'

'Sit down, lady! A window, you ain't!' yelled a guy in a bowler hat behind Jack.

Teddy sat.

Right over her head, Schuldner had Joe against the ropes. Pounding at his gut, his kidneys, rabbit-punching. Max grunted with effort, Joe with pain. Teddy flinched. Flecks of baby oil, ammonia, rubbing alcohol, rank sweat – the sweat mixed with Dancing Joe's blood – coloured the words in her notebook. What was the goddamn ref doing? – letting flat-footed Max slam his gloves over and over into Joe's hunched body, that's what he was doing. Bright slid slowly down the ropes, crumpling over, his leg bent back under him, his beautiful, bloodied face distorted, a foot in front of hers.

Leaning forward, Teddy gripped the ropes. 'Joey? What's the matter with you? Joey, can you hear me?'

No recognition in Dancing Joe's eyes – the ref standing over him now, counting: three! four! five! six!

Clang! went the bell – ending the fifth round and, just for this moment, saving Joe's black skin.

Shucks Spooner jumped in the ring. Helped his boxer back to his corner.

Runyon shook his head. 'Ker-ist! Some boxer you got there, O'Rourke. I think I'm gonna puke. That cotton planter, the coloured kid's manager, what's his name? – Dixie Fiske? – should throw in the towel. At least his trainer ought to know better, what's the matter with Shucks?'

By now, Jack hung over the back of Teddy's chair. He whipped off her hat, rumpled her red hair, slapped the hat back on again – crooked. 'I know you love the guy, hooligan, but this is a hard way to make a living. Give me a nice clean gangland killing anytime.'

Seething, Teddy straightened her hat. Men! Were they blind? Or just basically born stupid? Something was sour here; something stank. Joe was out there fighting on heart alone. If he were hers, would she stop the fight? This was Bright's chance at the title. If Fiske called it off, would Joe get another? Hell, no. New York'd heave a fat sigh of relief: no nigger for champ. In Fiske's place, what would she do? She'd do just what Shucks Spooner was doing now. Arguing. But with whom? Joe's trainer wasn't yelling at Dixie Fiske. Shucksie was yelling at Dancing Joe. *Hot*damn! It was Joe who wouldn't quit.

The sixth round: Max, pumped with pink confidence, strode to the centre of the ring – black Joe came slowly. And it started all over again.

'Oh hell,' moaned Jack, climbing over the guy next to him. 'I'm getting out of here, Red. Meet you home after the slaughter.'

Chewing her bottom lip, pencil cracking between her fingers, forgetting to write, Teddy forgot to listen. Jack loped, unnoticed, up the aisle and out of the overheated Garden. The radio commentator, glossy with sweat – his face, like Teddy's, flecked with Joe's blood – gibbered into his microphone.

'Watch Schuldner go to work on Bright. A punishing right and left combination, an uppercut to the body, then a right to the head. I don't know how he's staying on his feet. Bright is desperately trying to last out this round. Wait a minute! Oh my God! Oh *my* God! Ohhhh! – *my* good God! What's happening? Joe's back! Dancing Joe is coming back! – '

Teddy stood up. With a deafening roar, everyone in the Garden stood up. The whole place screaming, 'Joe! Joe! Joe!'

' – You hear that out there in radioland! That roar is for Joe Bright. This is incredible! Can he keep it up? After five and a half rounds of gruelling punishment, Bright is suddenly in control of this tremendous fight! He's broken the German's nose – blood is pouring down the German fighter's face! I wish you could see this! What! Are my old eyes deceiving me? Schuldner is down! Max Schuldner is down and, ladies and gentlemen, I assure you – he won't be getting up! I can't believe it! I simply *cannot* believe it! What a turnaround – what a fight!'

Teddy watched Dancing Joe's knock-out punch on her feet, her whole body pushed forward into the ropes. Joe hit Max with a short sharp shot, a left hook that kissed the German's nose like a blood-red rose. Max went down like a bull brained with an iron mallet.

'You see that, Jack! I told you he'd win! Jack?' In triumph, Teddy spun round. No Indian. 'Jack!'

And then – she couldn't keep track of everything that happened next. Joe was hustled out of the ring by Spooner and Fiske, barely waiting to have his arm raised victoriously into the unholy air of chaos. Sports reporters scrambled for typewriters, hats, pads, pencils, racing in a mad dash for Joe Bright – Teddy in the lead. Photographers with cumbersome cameras and blinding flash explosions were getting in everyone's way. But the crowd stayed on its feet, yelling in happy delirium.

Teddy got to Bright's dressing room first – and found the door locked. No amount of yelling and pounding, by her and everybody else a second later, could open it. Why not? Publicity was life's blood to the 'sweet science' – it created million-dollar gates. Bud Pegler pushed past chilly-eyed Runyon. Angry as usual, Pegler pounded the loudest. 'Hey! What's all this shit!' The others, eager for their stories, carbonated with adrenaline after what they'd just seen, agreed with this eloquent thought. 'Yeah!' they added in one loud, indignant voice.

Teddy wasn't angry; she was confused. The more she thought about it, the less enlightened she got. The fight was wrong, the fighter was wrong, now *this* was wrong. What the hell was going on here? And hotdamn! – was there a story in it for Teddy O'Rourke? She'd bet her sweet butt there was. One look at the faces of the men around her, famous sports reporters, cynical bastards all, and she knew it. It was hers – and hers alone – because not one of them knew there was a story at all. As for Jack, he was strictly front page; no sports for the *New York Trident*'s star reporter. Unless Babe Ruth assassinated President Hoover, her redman wouldn't touch it. And the rest? They'd be writing about a fighter who figured that with one brilliant, come-from-behind wallop, who needed the press? Another uppity nigger. Another flossy Ace of Spades like Smilin' Jack Johnson – thumbing his nose at America, flaunting a string of white wives, beating the living crap out of white boxers and doing it with a big wolfish grin on his big black face.

Baloney. That wasn't Joe. Joe was a gentleman. What did Shucksie call him? An 'up-an'-up fella'. Whatever was happening tonight, was happening to him. And whatever that was, Teddy O'Rourke, writer of the *Trident*'s SNAPBACK and the only woman sports columnist in the goddamn business, would be the first to know. Starting now.

Leaving everyone still pounding on the door, Teddy ran for a phone – and connected not with rewrite or her sports editor, Hype Hohenloe, but with George Bache.

'George! What are you doing in sports?'

'Just passing through,' said Bache.

Swell! George might be a drama critic but he'd still know a good story when it sat on him. Bache was Teddy's closest friend on the *Trident*. He was Teddy's closest friend, period. Not counting Jack. Right now, Jack didn't count. Speaking of which: where the hell *was* Jack? Off again – just when she needed him. *Damn.*

'You got a pencil, George? Take this down – '

23

'Forget the pencil, Teddy – for you, I'll write in blood.'

Before Teddy could get more than 'Dancing Joe won' out of her mouth, Connie Mezinger cut in. Connie Mezinger was her editor-in-chief; he was also loud, vulgar, fat, bald as a cue ball and almost short enough to qualify as a dwarf.

Connie, grabbing the phone off Bache as soon as he heard it was O'Rourke, hollered, 'Where's that Indian!'

'Get off the line, Mezinger!' Teddy hollered right back. 'I got a story to get in!'

'What story?'

'Joe Bright just won his fight with Schuldner by a knock-out. The Garden's in an uproar.'

Mezinger snorted, a horrible honk that went right down the line and practically popped her eardrum. 'That's a story? Sport sells a lotta papers, girlie, but it ain't no story. America isn't interested in reading where a coloured kid is the hero. *This* is a story! A white cop's been killed up in Harlem. Get Eagels's pink ass back here!'

She held the phone at arm's length; Connie Mezinger's normal holler now reduced to a hollow buzz. How does one kill from a distance? Her enraged mind tore at the idea. By mail, of course! Send the sawnoff bastard poison by post. While she wallowed in gleeful revenge, the buzzing stopped. Silence. No high-pitched insults from Mezinger, no click of the receiver put back in its cradle.

Choking on fury, Teddy jerked the phone up to her hot ear. 'George?' she whispered. 'You still there?'

'Sure am. Mezinger's just trotted off on his chubby little legs to yell at someone else.'

'What's that runt doing in sports at this time of night?'

'Same thing I'm doing – looking for Jack. The story broke less than half an hour ago. Our demented dwarf's

24

got runners out all over New York. Better get your fellow in. No time for temper now.'

'Sure, George. We all need Jack Eagels.'

Teddy slowly hung up, slowly turned from the wall – and was slammed into a giddy state of romantic terror. Four phones down . . . his back to her and talking low into his own receiver . . . stood Tom Channing. No armed, flat-nosed thugs to guard him, no gum-chewing moll wrapped in fur on his arm; in fact, no one around at all. No one but Teddy O'Rourke of the *New York Trident* and Tom Channing of the New York underworld back here in this dingy Madison Square Garden corridor. Teddy, finding her mouth ajar, shut it. Plans for the killing of Connie, for the next hard round with Eagels, fled somewhere dark and unimportant; sharing a bank of Garden phone booths with a thief, a gambler, a notorious New York City outlaw was suddenly much more compelling than a couple of newspapermen – even if they were bastards. With a newsie's instinct, she shrank back into a corner of her own booth. Seen from behind, and with only the barest hint of his face visible – here she jigsawed hurried words in an effort to explain Channing away, to make him fit into the barred and locked sanity that passed for living – there was a shine to him, a black-edged radiance that threw reality, poor dim creature, into shadow. Oh yes, and a scent, a smell so raw, so heavy with risk it made her heart race. Who was he talking to? What was he saying? She caught only the tag end, '. . . *so it didn't go right, so calm down, I'll take care of Joey. Yeah, Bernie too, the stupid donkey.*'

Joey? What didn't go right with Joey? The fight? Of course, it was the fight, what else could Channing mean? What else was happening around here? With Tom leaving his booth, Teddy popped out of her own. Only to pop back in when Dixie Fiske darted round the far corner of what was starting to be a very crowded corridor. Overdressed, understuffed, overwrought, Dancing Joe's manager barely missed crashing into a fire bucket. He also looked sick with fear – even before he saw Channing. After – skidding to a stop in front of Tom – he looked worse. Whatever Dixie expected to find by the phones, it wasn't Tom Channing. Teddy watched as Tom said something to Dixie, as Dixie whined something back, as the gangster walked away and was gone – leaving the corridor somehow less alive, less significant – and Dixie Fiske mumbling to himself. Until Teddy tapped him on the shoulder, and found herself locked into his quick brown eyes, eyes sunk deep in sagging pockets of discoloured flesh. The long nose rising between them quivered.

'Miss O'Rourke!' shrieked Dixie Fiske in a southern accent – not one that would have come from Charleston or New Orleans; one right off the red Georgia clay. 'Perfect. Why didn't I think of you!'

That stumped Teddy. Think of her for what?

'Listen, sports lady. I'll give you an exclusive, you do me a favour?' Without waiting for her answer, Dixie ran off the way he'd come.

Teddy, quick on the uptake, followed the big orange checks of his carpetbagger's suit out of a side exit.

Joe Bright, weakened – a weakness that came from much more than six rounds of pounding – was in the back seat of a steel blue sedan, head down, big hands covering his face. The sedan was parked and idling on Fiftieth Street. Beside Joe sat a small black woman in a small cloche hat, one hand gripping Joe's huge arm, her head turned towards Teddy. Teddy took a minute to place her. Ah, yes, she remembered. This was Miss Jesse Bean, a dancer up in Harlem, the wordless woman with the unremarkable face who sat by Bright's corner for all of his fights – Joe's woman. Now she was looking at Teddy, her small, close-set eyes dark with worry. Why was everyone so afraid? O'Rourke's newsprint blood tingled, hungry for a story.

26

Dixie clucked his tongue. 'You saw the fight, Miss O'Rourke. You got to call it shameful.'

All Teddy saw was a complete mystery. But shameful? What did Fiske mean by that?

His face a grimace of intense sincerity, Dixie grabbed Teddy's arm, moved her away from the car. She wasn't sure of the sincerity, but the intensity was real enough. 'It ain't safe for us to stick around here, not even to collect what we're rightly owed. You collect the purse, OK, lady? I know you'd do that for Joey. I gotta get my fighter to a doc.'

Why? Who? How? What in hell was going on? Dixie Fiske was so nervous he bounced on the balls of his feet. Looking over her shoulder, over his, keeping a lookout for – what? Who? For Tom Channing? Why? Who was here but Fiske and herself and a big silver-haired man in a pearl-grey fedora chewing gum as he leaned up against the Garden? A man who didn't seem a tenth as interested in Dixie as Dixie was in him.

Was there a story here or wasn't there? Hotdamn, was there! Something bigger than a fight, even a *fixed* fight. Something she'd get out of somebody – or eat her notebook trying. Dancing Joe's purse was more than an ace-in-the-hole; it was an ace-high flush.

Teddy smiled. 'OK. Then I get the story, right?'

Dixie grinned back. From Teddy's point of view the grin was there and then it wasn't. It was over so fast she wasn't sure if she'd seen little pointy teeth behind the sudden grin or not. 'Sure thing, as soon as I know Joe's OK.' Then Dixie was in the car; the car exploded away from Madison Square Garden's side entrance, speeding west on Fiftieth Street, fishtailed around the corner at Ninth Avenue, scattering wet, windblown trash, and disappeared in the dark.

O'Rourke was back in the Garden fast, using the bank of press phones again.

'Mezinger? Goddammit, listen to me! There's a story here. A good one. *Will you please listen!* – '

'That you, O'Rourke? You haven't left yet? I need Eagels and I need him *now*. We got a cop murder breaking back here. Move your butt! Sports reporters! Dames! Damn!'

This time he hung up on her.

2

Words in a Box

That, said Teddy to herself, is a wild and faulted mess of a man. At the time she said this she was looking at Jack, and looking at Jack brought to mind Bluff O'Rourke, and Bluff gave an Irish lilt to her thoughts. *'Jack'*, her daddy once said over the rim of a full shot glass, *'is a wild red bloom of a man.'*

Three feet and a mile away, Jack himself stood in the echoing lobby of the *New York Trident* Building, big useful hands shoved deep into the pockets of his brown leather jacket, a jacket with the elbows worn thin from a few spectacular falls off his old Harley motorcycle, in his mouth a cigarette he hadn't swiped off Runyon burning down to the stub, on his dark curly head a battered hat, on his embattled chin a two-day stubble. And these things were only on the outside. Inside, Jack was in much worse shape. Her redman – Jack Eagels: poet, newspaperman, the pride of the *Trident*, writer of a damn good book about the war, Bluff's wild red bloom of a man – was coming apart. The drinking was only a part of it. He wasn't sleeping, he wasn't eating, he hadn't touched her in days. But worst of all, Jack wasn't laughing. Jack Eagels without laughter was like sun without heat. And for the life of her, she didn't know why. Waiting for Sally's elevator to take them up to the twenty-third floor and the horror of Cornelius Mezinger, Teddy thought she might weep over the loss of what her half Indian once was – how long ago now? Only a month? More? And just as she thought that, Jack looked up, seemed to read her mind, and grinned. A wild and faulted mess of a grin on a wild and beautiful face. It made Teddy want to throw her arms around what he still was – and hold on.

29

'Jack?'

Eagels hunched his shoulders. An evening of Teddy's mouth made him nervous. 'What?'

'Spit out the cigarette.'

'Why?'

'Just do it, please.'

Jack, shrugging at the unknowableness of women, turned, ditched his butt in a cylinder of lobby sand, turned back – and slowly, Teddy began to unzip his leather jacket. 'I won't fight with *you* anymore if you won't fight with *me* anymore. It's a deal?'

When Red slipped her hand inside his jacket, Eagels sucked in his breath – and held it there. 'I can have that in writing?'

'You can have it bound in calfskin.'

Jack exhaled. 'Oboy,' he whispered.

'Up?' said Sally as the doors to his elevator opened with a thrilling whoosh. O'Rourke and Eagels fell in. Red-faced with mortified delight, Sally leaned back to enjoy another ride with his favourite *Trident* reporters. They made a guy's job interesting; gave him something to dream about on a long winter's night.

The *Trident* made its home in a skyscraper. Not just any skyscraper – its very own twenty-seven-storey tower of light. Built nine years before by its far-ranging absentee owner, the odd, terminally rich and perpetually ailing Alva T. Thorp, it stood between Seventh and Eighth Avenues west of Times Square. Thrusting up in one god-almighty whoop! from the south side of Forty-fourth Street, Thorp's monolith was capped by a dazzling copper dome, cornered by massive stone gargoyles from the twenty-first floor up, and entered by carved bronze doors wide enough and tall enough to steer a tramp steamer through. Over the huge doors flew three huge flags: one for America, one for New York, and one for Thorp. On a stone scroll beneath the flags were the words: 'Here Lives the Truth.' That was Alva's idea.

Surrounded by a sudden surfeit of midtown granite and steel – no longer awed by much – New York was still impressed by its new skyscraper. Thorp, somewhere in Switzerland seeking a cure for whatever he'd caught this time, heard the applause and was satisfied. Unlike William Randolph Hearst, who bought newspapers for personal power, or hand-me-down tycoons who bought them as playthings, Alva bought anything merely to own it. Steel mills, a seat on the stock exchange, coffee plantations, a shipping fleet, a Midwest manufactory of hot-air balloons, four wives – though not all at the same time – mistresses in every capital in Europe, a few magazines, a publishing house, the *Trident*. Then forgot about each one of them. Owning so much, maniacally buying more, suffering from everything, what was a newspaper to Alva T. Thorp?

Especially the *Trident* newspaper. When Thorp picked it up for a measly few hundred grand it'd been bumbling along for years – and dying on its back. Crammed into what had once, long ago, been a pickle factory, the *Trident* was a warren of mouldering newspapers dating back to the Civil War, poky holes lit by bare bulbs, and fifty years of dust. When lunch was doled out, rats were first in line. Badly managed, out of step, scorning pictures, laid out like a turn-of-the-century *London Times*, the *Trident*'s circulation was down to a few die-hards: old birds in stuffy clubs who used it to snore under. Until Alva had the good luck to trip over the man who would become his editor-in-chief. And it *was* luck. Thorp simply hired the first guy who showed up for the job.

Cornelius Mezinger blew into New York from Chicago the very day Alva needed his editor. Only one week earlier, Connie was still the feisty, outspoken editor of the erratically brilliant *Chicago Globe*.

It took a bullet to prise Connie loose from the windy

city. Not *at* him; with Capone running things in Chicago, Mezinger was used to being shot at. It was Connie's own handling of a gun that made him leave the paper he'd sweated blood for, pushed, shoved, and shouted into Chicago's beefy face. The day Mezinger barricaded the *Globe*, armed himself with a ten-dollar pistol and took potshots at Al Capone was the day Mezinger called it quits. Squeezing off rounds with his eyes closed, he hadn't hit a damn thing but an old lady's Pekingese.

Alva hired Mezinger on a Tuesday and left for Europe on Wednesday. On Wednesday afternoon, Connie rubbed his fat hands, smiled to himself, and quickly established another fuming dictatorship of personal mania that filled his new city room with invigorating panic. In New York his editors dreaded him, his writers tolerated him, the financial department hated him, the guys down on the presses laughed up their sleeves – but they had to admit: Connie Mezinger picked up the *Trident* and shook it. To prove he could, he took the circulation up to a dizzy million, then dropped it to less than half that by making the paper intelligent, politically independent, irreverent, gave it a lightness of touch, even wit. Connie did all this by hiring talent. He did it by giving his readers some of what they wanted, and a lot of what they ought to have, like it or not.

Never quiet, never satisfied, always sweating, always in one uproar or another and always the cause of them; vulgar, bigoted, insensitive: in spite of all this – Mezinger was a reasonably honest man. And he ran a reasonably honest paper. Verbally abrupt, linguistically crude – crude? Mezinger could make a pile-driver blush – a man who barely made fifty-eight inches in a good pair of shoes, Connie was afraid of nothing. He'd be damned if his paper would know fear.

'Out,' said Sally.

Before Jack, his arm around Teddy's shoulders, stepped

32

three feet into the busy city room on the *Trident*'s twenty-third floor – a city room that took up nine more – Connie practically broad-jumped out of his office and collared him. Mezinger's round face was ripe persimmon with rage.

'What the fuck took you so long!'

Long used to Connie's winning ways, Jack flipped his hat off his head and tossed it neatly on a nearby hat rack – where it stuck, spinning. It won him a round of tepid applause: two guys from composing and a late-working cartoonist.

At midnight, Thorp's skyscraper thrummed. A frantic, electric stir that lifted loose paper on desktops, put a crackle into human hair, made a writer's fingers itch. Jack strolled to his desk – trailed by a still steaming O'Rourke and the squat little editor dancing with nerves – and sat down. Which put Jack's face on a level with Connie's.

'Never mind the cute shit with the hat, Eagels. Get out of here. That cop got found dead way over an hour ago and where the hell were you?'

By now, Jack was head-down in his open desk drawer and rummaging in the clutter: old markers blotted with coffee cup rings, a pistol with a busted clip wrested off a hood in Little Italy, short stories begun but unfinished – and finally found the bottle of bootleg bourbon he was looking for. 'Where Teddy was, where else?'

'Teddy?' Connie's tone held as much interest as a slammed door. For a minute he was stumped. Teddy who? Roosevelt? His quick brown eyes swivelled up and found O'Rourke – who was still standing, still in her long, grey tapering coat, slacks and slouch hat, and still over a head taller than he was. O'Rourke? What about her? O'Rourke was one of the biggest thorns in his side. First: she was a redhead. All redheads were unreliable. Second: she was a female. Fuck me! What editor hired a girl to report on sports? Connie had, that's who the fuck who. Which came from listening to Bluff O'Rourke, skin his Irish soul. If Bluff's brat hadn't turned out so versatile: covering boxing, baseball, football, the big races; if her column wasn't so full of humour; SNAPBACK so popular; if the time ever came when he'd have to pay her what he paid the men – he'd fucking fire her ass. But she was, and it was, and it hadn't – so he didn't. Thinking all this in the blink of an eye, he dismissed her. It was Eagels he wanted to yell at. He'd get to O'Rourke later.

'Oh, her.' Resting his eyes on Teddy for exactly one second, he said, 'Forget O'Rourke.'

Tapping her square-tipped fingers on Jack's typewriter, Teddy stared at the top of Mezinger's bald and bobbing head. Wondering where to bore for the most damage, biding her time. As Connie yelled, 'Goddammit, Eagels, get out of that desk! Every sheet in town's got their best men up in Harlem already – and who the fuck have I got? I've got fucking Brennan!'

The bottle firm in his hand, Jack popped back up with interest. 'You sent Billy?'

'Who the hell else! Who else did I have? I sent a copy boy, some kind of a relative of Thorp's, pat my fanny if I didn't. To cover a major killing! *You* think it's crazy? How the fuck do you think *I* feel! But at least Goetz was around to go for the pictures.' Connie swept his short fat arms around the city room, releasing waves of fresh sweat into the printed air. When the waves got to Teddy, she gagged. 'The biggest story since Wall Street and where is everybody? Fucking around, that's where they are, wasting time watching sports. If the *News* scoops us on this, it's your ass, Eagels. Your ass! Grab a pencil and beat it.'

Teddy stiffened at Connie's description of what she did for a living – *'wasting time watching sports'*? Jack stayed where he was. But over Connie's bald head they looked at each other – and smiled. The smile said: good grief, not again. The *Daily News* was Mezinger's bugbear, his affliction, his curse. As it had once been the *World*, now the *News* was his torment: it might beat him to a story, find an angle he hadn't found, make contacts he couldn't make, hire a writer he couldn't hire, or – horror of horrors, steal one away from him. The tabloid *News* drove Connie to frenzy because it sold one million three hundred thousand copies a day. Which meant that there had to be one million three hundred thousand bozos in the city of New York. The thought made him crazy, or ill, or both. At least once a day. Like now.

'Eagels! Why the fuck haven't you moved?'

Jack propped one long leg up on his desk, picked up a letter opener, fiddled with it. 'Aren't you forgetting something, Connie?'

'What! for crying out loud?'

'What's the story? Where am I going?'

Mezinger hopped from one foot to the other, rubbing his hands. 'I was coming to that.' Then he drew a deep breath, paused –

And Teddy jumped right in. 'Speaking of stories – '

At the first word out of O'Rourke, Mezinger flinched. From Teddy's vantage point way above his head, it looked like a short seizure. He jerked his pink and porcine face up at hers. 'You still here? Why aren't you writing up the fight?'

Sure of what she'd seen, intoxicated holder of a high card called Tom Channing, Teddy rushed him. 'That's just the point, Connie. If you'd been at the Garden tonight, you'd know what I mean. What I saw wasn't a fight, it was – '

'Murder,' finished Jack.

She kicked him on an available ankle.

'Ouch!' yelped Jack, and, spooked, Connie jumped straight up in the air. High enough to put him, for less than a second, eye to eye with Teddy.

Jack rubbed his leg. 'Why'd you do that?'

'You're lucky, redman, I don't wear cleats. Listen,

35

Connie, it wasn't murder, and it wasn't a fix. At least, I don't think it was a fix. Tell you the truth, I don't know what the hell it was. But I do know one thing for sure, some damned interesting people are mixed up in it, people like – '

'O'Rourke, what the fuck are you blithering about?' Connie flapped a pudgy hand, waving her away. 'It was a fight, girlie. Butt out and write about it. I'm busy here with Eagels. Can't you see we got a big story on the boil?'

Teddy looked at Jack who wasn't looking at her. He was playing with the letter opener. Casually flipping it over the back of his wrist, picking it up, flipping it. Like lightning in a field of dry wheat, she sent him a beam of such intense outrage it ought to have scorched a track through his hair.

Yawning, Jack used the opener to prise off the top of his bottle.

The wave of irritation passing through Teddy's slim body at that moment made her knees lock and her teeth grind. A big story? Mezinger wanted a story? Holding on to Jack's desk for balance, she spun her own hot yarn. Composing it quickly and smoothly behind a fine, freckled forehead, steaming under a heavy cap of blazing auburn hair. '*Looking deep into her victim's eyes, the killer rubbed her gun. Savouring the fear she saw there, tasting this moment of complete control. No one had ever been as perfect as the fatman, none so worthy of murder. And why? Immaculate revulsion, that's why. She brought the gun up slowly, sighting along her arm. And fired. Three sweet shots. Point blank. In grisly extravagance, the head exploded; the body dropping like a clubbed pig. To lie twitching at her feet. Like dazed maggots, pink brains oozed out of the fatman's blasted skull. The girl with the gun regarded the mess that was her own unique creation with a casual surprise. Brains? It was the first time she knew he had any.*' Teddy was making

36

herself sick. Her index finger ached from its real grip on an imaginary trigger. Stop it, O'Rourke. Get hold of yourself. Dropping like a clubbed pig? God! Where were these ideas coming from? The vivid image of Schuldner's ponderous crash to the canvas an hour before, that's where. And where were her thoughts taking her? Up the River. If Sing Sing welcomed women.

Skipping Mezinger – Connie was strictly an ice cream man; for some reason Eskimo Pies calmed him down – Jack shoved the bottle at Teddy. 'Have a slug of this, Red. I get the feeling you need it.'

Stunned by her own thoughts, Teddy grabbed the bourbon and bolted a mouthful. Surprised, Jack grabbed it back.

While Connie talked the only way he knew how. Fast, furious and crude.

'So the body of this white cop, and get this, Eagels – he's not just *any* cop, he's a fucking police lieutenant – the body gets found by some black tootsie at the Cotton Club. She trips over it and falls flat on her face. The body's in an alley back of the place, right? Near one of the doors the coloureds have to use. All she sees besides that was the back end of a light coloured car, maybe yellow, maybe not, speeding out of the alley.'

Sipping bourbon, Jack asked, 'This cop, what was he, shot?'

'Doesn't he wish. Knifed in the throat. Knifed? Christ, filleted, more like. Stripped of his wallet and dumped.'

'A robbery?'

'That's what the cops think they were supposed to think.'

'But they don't?'

'Fuck no. The coons at the Cotton were scared stiff. Though they didn't know the dead guy was a cop, they sure as hell knew he was white – outta uniform and inna tuxedo.' Connie's brown eyes went a sly shade darker. 'But that ain't all. That wasn't just any white cop back of the Cotton, it was Mayor Jimmy's *pet* cop, the one he and Police Commissioner Whalen just awarded for bravery. Shit, Eagels, think about it. Only last month I went to the fucking dinner they gave for him. Sat between District Attorney Tuttle and that woman judge, what's her name? You know – Mrs Norris. A goddamn *woman* judge! Holy jumping – '

Jack sat up, bottle halfway to his mouth. 'For pete's sake, Connie, forget Mrs Norris. Are you talking about Bernt McTaggart, Cawley's son?'

'That's him. Dead as dead can be. Deceased, gone to glory, booted into eternity, drop-kicked to God. In Harlem, for Christ's sake.'

Blowing a soundless whistle, Jack put down the bottle. 'Bernie McTaggart. Jesus, that'll shake a few folks up.'

Visions of mayhem still in her head, Teddy picked the bottle up and bolted down a shot. Then suddenly choked. *Bernie? The dead cop's name was Bernie? What!*

While below her, Connie beamed. 'Jimmy Walker's cop gets knifed. Right as he's running against La Guardia for re-election, a fucking week and a half before Election Day. Can't wait to hear his reaction. Come to think of it, can't wait to hear La Guardia's reaction. If I know our fathead Fiorello, the little flower'll hit high C. Say, we could lose our piano-playing, philandering leader on this one. Just think of it, Eagels – what if there's a connection?'

'Holy shit!' said Jack. 'Is there?'

'How the hell do I know! *You* find out. What the fuck do I pay you for?'

Teddy listened to all of this – but heard none of it. What she heard was her own busy brain chattering away in her own head. Newspapers hired women – then expected them to work like men, behave like ladies, get treated like children. When anything important happened – a war, a murder, politics – a woman got shoved out in the cold. Patted on the fanny. Not now, cutie. Wait in the wings. Knit something small. We're not playing house here; we're shooting craps with life. Men's work. Toddle off. Do what you're good at. What she was good at! Maybe not a reporter like Eagels was a reporter, but she was still a writer, and a goddamned good one. One who could tell one end of a story from another. And, what do you know? The end she was holding led right back to Jack's story – the killing of a white police lieutenant in darktown Harlem. What had Channing said? *I'll take care of Joey and the idiot, Bernie.* Who the hell else was Bernie if he wasn't Bernie, as in Bernt McTaggart? And was Teddy O'Rourke going to be small enough to keep this information to herself? A swift glance at the top of Connie's retreating head and the answer almost blew her off her feet. She sure as shit was. Wasn't Dancing Joe a piece of the puzzle? He must fit in somewhere. And wasn't Joey a boxer, and weren't boxers her exclusive territory? My God! O'Rourke, you're holding your first front-page story in the palm of your hand. She knew it, felt it, could taste it. Too busy with the Bernt McTaggart killing, too busy to listen to O'Rourke, Jack and Mezinger were off and running. Jack to get his hat back off the hat rack, Connie to yell at someone else. The presses were acting up again.

Which left Teddy exactly nowhere. Except with herself and a story no one but she was interested in. Which was only to be expected around Mezinger – he hated women. But Jack? So much for the argument before the Bright/Schuldner bout: a lover came before a story, he'd said. But *whose* story? That was obvious. Hers. Not his. He wanted a home, he'd said, with her *in* it. More than once a week. Teddy began walking back to Sally's elevator, the racket of her thoughts drowning out the rattle of typewriters, teletype machines, pneumatic tubes, sub-editors. Jack wanted a home? He had one. Right in her apartment. And she *was* in it. Sometimes. Though, more often than not, when she was, he wasn't. But that's what came of the both of them working for a newspaper. So, what did Jack want? That she should quit? Teddy stepped up her pace. Was he crazy?

Cutting across the humming city room, bottle in his jacket pocket, Jack was heading for the elevator, passing her on the trot.

Keeping her voice low and light, Teddy gave it one last shot. After all, no matter how much she'd like to knock him on his tall Indian ass, Eagels could come in handy. She'd never followed anything but sports before. A sports murder might pose some problems; on her first shot at one, she was willing to share the kill.

'Jack?'

She made Jack slow down but she didn't stop him. 'Not now, Red. Got to get to Harlem. See you when I see you.'

Hands balled into fists, Teddy rode with a silent Sally down to the seventeenth floor. Strode across the sports department, and slammed into her very own chair. Her own chair, her own cubicle, her own desk, her own lead, her own story. But if this was all she had, it was enough. No support from her paper, no support from Jack.

Teddy O'Rourke might as well have been a ghost, haunting without effect. Still in hat and coat, she switched on a lamp, wound a sheet of yellow copy paper into the typewriter, and went to work. Rattling off a steaming piece about Joe's come-from-behind win. Punching out the words. Feeling the thud of gloves on flesh as she typed. Wishing it was Connie's, or much better – Jack's.

Finishing, she stood up. And gazed out of her tall corner window right down into the hard heart of Broadway. Times Square was dirty, crowded, busy, beloved, and – home. Home – on her cocksure island in the dying days of the dollar decade.

Broadway. Lit lurid by the light of the hard sell: Coca-Cola, Planter's Peanuts, Sunkist California Oranges. So many marquees: the dazzling neon names of Ziegfeld, the Shubert Brothers, Earl Carroll's Sketch Book, George White's Scandals, Billy Minsky's undraped Rosebuds, the George M. Cohan Theater, the Selwyn, the Paramount, the Roxy, Capital, Globe, Rivoli, Astor, Central, Colony, the Palace – all jostling for room, all pitched to a neon shout. Eight blocks uptown Teddy could skate at Iceland, one block west and five north see a wild-west rodeo at Madison Square Garden, merely cross the road to the Forty-fourth Street Theater and laugh at the Marx Brothers in what was left of Kaufman & Ryskind's *Animal Crackers* after Groucho and Chico and Harpo got through with it. Right under her nose were an even dozen side-street whorehouses, within sight a thousand speaks.

Straight ahead, the revolving Motogram over on the Times Square Tower was sending its last message of the evening. Linder and Torpey, the two guys who worked the Motogram's thousands of light bulbs, had spelled Bernt McTaggart's name wrong. Bernt, in letters five feet tall, came around the triangular building without an 'r'. Looking up and east, Teddy caught the silver flash of the new Chrysler Building as the moon came out from behind the dark sour cheek of a cloud. The Chrysler was a building she could believe in. Rising like the future above a city that was drunk on more than illicit booze – New York was drunk on itself. High times, fast times. While far away across the sea Europe gathered round itself the red robes of fascism, America was a world of paper: stocks, bonds, shares, magazines – newspapers. In her city alone, dozens of dailies: morning, evening, late editions – newsboys on street corners calling, 'Ex-tra! Ex-tra! Read all about it!' The mighty and vigorous press – never was so much newsprint squandered on so little – filled with smut and smugness, a murder every other day,

41

a scandal on the hour, the titterings of a silly Café Society side by side with the dubious glamour of a lot of healthy ethnic gangsters. So many writers, so much paper. It was enough to make Teddy's blood sing in her veins.

She lived in a city gone tilt, when the world was spinning nowhere as fast as it could. A week after the latest and greatest Wall Street crash and people were still spending money they would never have. After seven years of unparalleled plenty, seven fat years of sipping a heady cocktail of crime and sex and money, the underworld and the stock market had taken every sucker in sight. It was a mad, bad, sad time when everyone was tap dancing in the dark. Standing at her window high and giddy above it all, Teddy hugged herself. She was at the top of her field, at the top of her form, working for a paper that meant something. Could she ever be happier than she was right now? Or unhappier? God, how she loved New York City. God, how she loved Jack Eagels, and God! – how she hated him. Brown-eyed, red-skinned, black-hearted Jack.

Like last week's market of flimsy paper, Teddy came crashing down.

George Bache's very tall, very Jewish, shadow fell across her desk.

'Hark,' he said, 'the voice of the crackpot is heard in the land.' George dusted the seat of Teddy's spare chair before lowering himself into it. 'Guess what that grumpy little man over in Germany called me.'

Teddy, thinking of little men right here in New York, was only half listening. 'What grumpy little man?'

'Hitler.'

'Who's Hitler?'

'Please, Teddy. I ran into Walter Winchell today. There's only so much ignorance I can take. *Adolf* Hitler, the biggest tick in Hindenburg's hide. Adolf called me a mushroom. Right out loud in that book of his, said Jews were eternal mushrooms of humanity. Speaking as a Jew,

I am, of course, offended, but speaking as a man of words, that's not bad. Mushrooms.' George shifted in his chair, trying to get his lanky frame comfortable. 'I've just been chatting about Nazis with Phelps on the Foreign Desk – he says they're spreading like bacteria in a culture. It occurs to me, there's a spoke loose somewhere in the cartwheel of the world. Maybe more than one. Hell, maybe they *all* are. All getting ready to pop off when we're not looking and drop America, bag and baggage, right in the mud.'

By now, George had Teddy's attention – not much, but some. 'What are you talking about?'

'Mud.'

'Ah,' sighed Teddy. 'Mud.'

'Think of it. In Italy, Mussolini parades his blackshirts, in Russia, Stalin has Trotsky in a headlock, in Germany, that very unfunny Chaplin of hate spins web within web, and here in our own land – what have we here?'

'What?'

'I quote from an Eagels piece: *A dentist who calls himself the Imperial Wizard of the Ku Klux Klan leaves offerings on southern trees, Huey Long is busy whipping up Louisiana, home-grown fascisti plot in the backrooms of pizza parlours, Father Coughlin's Christian Front march behind a cross of fire, and everywhere, Teutonia Clubs goose-step down Main Street – while America plays miniature golf.*' George suddenly shut up, stood up, and extended his hand. 'You're not listening, are you?'

'What?'

'How about a late supper? Tell you what, I'll let you talk about the 1927 Yankees.'

Out of the corner of her eye, Teddy caught Leonard Lamont heading their way. Leonard, wasp-waisted and wasp-tongued, was the *Trident*'s gossip columnist, the guy who wrote 'Tattle on the Town', the snoop who'd been giving that weasel Winchell a run for his money. On unstoppable and wicked impulse, she made a grab for Bache's still offered hand, used the strong grip to haul herself out of her chair, and threw herself into George's arms. To kiss him right on his thin literate mouth.

George wasn't the least bit flummoxed. He pulled her off her feet, kissed her back harder than she was kissing him, then dropped her on the floor. Teddy missed her footing, went backwards, and landed in her own desk chair with a startled flump.

'Does that mean you accept?' said George.

Leonard stopped three feet from the door to Teddy's cubicle, hand to his shocked mouth, his slack eyes bulging. One sniff of the wind for Lamont and he spun on his pointed toes, heading for his typewriter.

That'll get back to Jack, thought Teddy. But not letting herself think what she'd just done was mean, low, was cruel. George was her best friend. And though he'd never said so, he loved her. 'I can't, George, I'd like to – but tonight, I've got to do a man a favour.'

'Fine,' said George. 'Come to think of it, so do I.'

George Bache went back to the fifteenth floor – the floor above advertising where Connie kept the trivia, like the tricks and jokes department, like theatre, movie, and book reviewers – looked through his files and found the name of one of the few women he knew in New York who hadn't asked him to marry her. He'd take that one to a late dinner. Picked up the phone, listened to the operator's 'Number, please', hung up. Who was he fooling? He wasn't hungry.

Catching a cab on Forty-fourth Street fifteen minutes later, George silently laughed at himself. If there was a man on the isle of Manhattan who had more women than he needed, George Bache was that man. Women crawled over George like theatre producers after a hit play. He was forever peeling them off. Why? Because he was good looking? No. Because he was rich? No. Because he could get them an aisle seat on opening night? No, not even that – though it helped. George didn't know why – not that he was complaining – but the women could have told him. Because he was funny, that's why. Because he was kind and thoughtful and honest and – funny. Funny was sexy.

So? Now he was in a yellow cab laughing at the breaks.

Why does a man always want what he can't have?

Why should a kiss, given in anger, a kiss that was someone else's slap, taste so sweet?

3

Black Cotton

In 1929, New York was America's entertainment – and Harlem was New York's. The Negro was in vogue.

In the twenties, Harlem was not a ghetto, not yet a slum. From Morningside and St Nicholas Avenues to the Harlem River, from 116th to 155th Streets and spreading, it was a green, leafy suburb. For one short decade its broad streets and sturdy houses saw the rise of the finest black neighbourhood in America.

At the turn of the century, property speculators, quick to spot a buck, intended Harlem for high-class whites. Wealthy whites who were being squeezed out of downtown and midtown Manhattan by the huge increase in European immigrants, lured north of Central Park by the spanking new elevated. But the speculators built too fast, built too much, outpacing the market, over-reaching themselves. Frantic, they scrambled for a way out of their own greed – and found the only market they could. To save their fiscal butts, they sold Harlem to the Negro. Unable to stop them, the upper-class whites, having just moved in, moved right back out.

And Harlem turned black. It became a Mecca, a magnet for every Negro in America. By the mid-twenties, Harlem had become an American myth. It was a myth you could strut through.

They called it the Harlem Renaissance.

One bug-eyed look out of the window, and the cabbie sunk down in his seat. 'Say, mister! What's happening here? Jungle bunnies look kinda restless.'

Jack was sitting in a taxi on Lenox Avenue and the taxi was sitting in traffic. All around him, Harlem was alive with the smell of death. North of 140th Street, Lenox, a broad, still-elegant avenue, was jammed with police. In cars, on steaming horseback, revving motorcycles, standing around grim-faced and impressive, New York's finest had shown up for the messy murder of one of their own.

Above the rooftops, Harlem's sky growled – potbellied with rain. Below, its streets shimmied with neon and body heat. All its dark shining people massed on Lenox and 142nd Street: black bluebloods from Brooklyn, the working classes up from the Tenderloin and old San Juan Hill, poets and artists, musicians and writers, and, of course, the poor. Once hemmed in by Manhattan's Hell's Kitchen, enslaved down South, impoverished in the West Indies – now, all come to the Promised Land, each hopeful in Harlem. Perched on open window sills, hanging off fire escapes, clinging to street lamps – they held a curious wake for a white man. Except for the cops, no one was mourning.

Eagels counted heads, stopped when he got to fifty. Over a thousand, more on the way. A drifting film of rain settled over the crush, running on hot black skin as the crowd pushed north to the Cotton Club.

Uneasy as the uneasy white cops, Jack lit the cigarette he was holding with the scratch of a match on his thumbnail. Cupping his hands to the flame, his tired face glowed a quick eerie red. The killing of Bernt McTaggart wasn't what bothered him; poor old Bernie wasn't even what he was thinking about. Women, that's what bothered him. Jack loved women and they drove him crazy. The worst times in his life always had something to do with women.

Could he pick them, or couldn't he? Did he get the worst of it, or didn't he? What about that girl back in Chicago, the sculptress who lived on the roof of his apartment building in Towertown? Covered in granite dust and waving a baby that surely wasn't his in the lobby

47

of the *Chicago Globe* – for pete's sake, the kid was a towhead with ice-blue eyes. Or the high-class maniac from the Gold Coast who said she was rich enough – well, Daddy was anyway – for the both of them. Daddy said there wasn't any real money in writing, all that was a lot of hot air for eggheads; why waste his time writing boring old books, chasing the news? When she got him a job working up ads for Daddy's sausage-packing company, Jack knew it was time to get up and go. High time to accept his old editor's plea to come east.

A big man with a man's rough beauty in his face, Jack Eagels was an Arapaho Indian. Or, half of him was. At least that's what Charlie Eagels said. Jack was never sure Arapaho was *all* Charlie was. The old man's face was neither broad as a basket nor sharp as a hatchet; only one eye was brown, the other a dreamy hazel. Though he spoke three languages, Montreal French, Reservation English and Platte River Arapaho, it was the tongue of 'Our People' Charlie tied in knots. But Charlie insisted he was full-blood, and, hell, who was young Jack to argue? As far as Jack Eagels was concerned, if the old man died thinking he was a top-to-toe Indian, then he *was*.

Jack grew up on the flat plains of eastern Wyoming. Wyoming, where the wind blew cold and bitter; Wyoming, where America banished what his father said were his people. Not an eloquent man, no recaller of things past, old Charlie Eagels told his son no stories. Charlie was a full-time drunk; Collette, his common-law wife, a French orphan from Cheyenne. When Jack was six, Collette ran away with a baggage-car handler from the Union Pacific Railroad – leaving Charlie and Jack flatter than the plains of Wyoming. Charlie settled down in a tumbledown shack to drink his life away. The shack was by the tracks leading south out of Cheyenne. Until he was thirteen, Jack thought he was Huckleberry Finn. Until he was thirteen, Mark Twain's Huck was the only person besides Charlie he loved. That was the year he got a job sweeping out the offices of the *Cheyenne Star*. And at the *Star*, he had a revelation. Jack Eagels was a newspaperman. At fourteen, his head bursting with words and the love of words, Jack ran away as well. To the blue mountains of Colorado and the land of 'Our People', now cluttered with the white man's mile-high cities: Denver, Boulder, Greeley.

In Denver, he wrangled his first job on a newspaper.

Printing its headlines in red, fitting exactly twenty-one stories a day on the front page, each headline over each story in a different typeface, the *Denver Post* gave the folks of middle America a show that knocked their hats off. With scandals, giveaways, stunts and promotions, the *Post* was a fevered education in slam-bang journalism, a madhouse of hard-living newspapermen. It was 'the most lunatic paper in America'. Jack Eagels was home at last.

From Denver, Jack went to San Francisco and the *Call*, from the city by the bay to the *Los Angeles Times*, from the city of the angels to France. Enlisting as soon as war was declared, fighting with his division on the British front, coming back four years later unbowed, but not unscathed. Mules and mud and star shells bursting over his head – over all their heads – like some mad, inverted Fourth of July; Jack, half white and half red, thought the whole thing stank. His first job home: the *Chicago Globe*. In Chicago, he ran headlong into Connie Mezinger – and Connie put the polish on Jack Eagels. In Eagels, Connie found the reporter of his dreams: unschooled, yet somehow a scholar, erratically read, yet a poet. Any city room Jack was in was crowded with Jack. With his laughter, his gaudy talent. In his spare time – which was never much – Jack wrote his only book. In it he poured all his feelings about war, about sitting in the cold mud of a strange land waiting to die. The book won him a few prizes, a few critics waited for what he would do next. What Jack did next was go east.

In New York, Connie walked into a plum of a job and spent the first few years of it luring Eagels with money, fame, freedom – but it was a towheaded baby in the lobby of the *Chicago Globe* and the Wienie King's daughter who gave Jack the hardest push. Mezinger hopped on the twentieth century over a Pekingese; Jack over women. Besides, everyone else was leaving the city of sausages for New York: Ring Lardner, Charlie MacArthur, Ben Hecht, Sherwood Anderson, anybody who could rub two brain cells together. If Jack had stayed, it would have wound up with just him and Carl Sandberg. That thought alone could get a man moving.

Now there was the newspaper lady, his very own redhead with the smoky grey eyes. Grey eyes flecked with hard gold – gold flecks like coins bet in a cool crap game. The lady with the slender body, long slim legs, upstanding breasts, an ass like an inverted heart, and every bit of it dusted with freckles. Jack groaned. What had Ambrose Bierce, that cranky old Frisco newsman, said? 'Ah, that we could fall into women's arms without falling into their hands.' But the lady was as smart as he was, as fast, as talented, much better looking, and three times as stubborn. A lady he loved more than the ladies of the northern lake had loved him. Jack coughed. He was starting to shiver. Coming down with a cold at the age of thirty-five; just what he needed. Three winters here now, three colds. He finally got himself to New York and there they were – waiting for him. Chest colds and women. Millions of women. And who runs smack into the brightest of all? Jack Eagels, of course. Who else would get hooked up with Bluff O'Rourke's daughter? Who else could stand the pace? He used to think he could. The question wasn't: did he love Teddy O'Rourke? The question was: did he love her *enough*? And the answer? Yes. No. Hell, Jack Eagels didn't know the answer. So, he was drinking a little more than he should to cushion the question.

Two years ago, even two months ago, he thought he could cope with a girl who was a raving individual. A girl who not only worked on the same paper as he, but reported on the rich and racy sporting world. A girl who hung out in locker rooms, hobnobbing with sweaty boxers and gum-chewing baseball players, with preening racetrack jockeys and collegiate football squads. Speaking their language – all five hundred words of it. One of the boys. A girl who shot a better game of pool, played a better hand of poker – poker? Christ, she shot craps better than he did. A freckled-faced, snub-nosed Irish hooligan who dragged a guy into a public elevator and embarrassed the shit out of the elevator boy. A girl who was never home. Teddy was a woman. She ought to be doing something a woman did.

'Hey! Listen to this, willya!' His driver was twisting the knobs of a radio, filling the taxi and Jack's head with shrieking, high-pitched eeks! and whoops! 'Just got this baby installed last week, a radio right in my own cab. What say we try for some news, seeing as we're stuck here?'

The meter ticking over, Jack Eagels was still a block from the Cotton Club, getting nowhere. Nowhere was no way to write a story. Opening the door, he pushed a five-dollar bill at the cabbie and jumped out.

Dodging cops and the geometry of rain, Jack coughed as he ran. He still hadn't found his greatcoat.

Leaning his head out of the window, the cabbie called after him. 'You hear what they're saying! President Hoover is saying soon we'll have radios with pictures. Think of that, buddy!'

Jack thought he should have ridden his Harley to Harlem.

The Cotton Club took up the whole second floor of a big, boxy, two-storey building on the northeast corner of 142nd Street and Lenox Avenue. Starting out as a dance hall, it promptly failed. Rented to Smilin' Jack Johnson, the boxer turned it into a supper club. The Club Deluxe failed too. Whites hated Johnson; blacks hated his white wife. Except in a ring, the old fighter couldn't win.

With the advent of Prohibition, thoughtful New York eyes turned uptown. Smelling profit in the high-living whites' fascination with the low-living black, hoods of all nations moved on Harlem's clubs and cabarets, its theatres and speakeasies, muscled in on multimillion-dollar booze and policy rackets. Within a year the entertainment was black but the audience white.

Owney Madden moved on Jack Johnson and his Club Deluxe.

Once in, Owney changed everything. Madden called his new place the Cotton Club; after that, things went from sad to bad. But bad with a difference. Under mob management, the Cotton rapidly rose to become Harlem's premier nightclub – more popular with slumming New Yorkers than Connie's Inn or Small's Paradise or a hundred lesser cabarets. Owney Madden might be a thug, but he knew how to run a club. The Cotton gave eager, free-spending whites – in from the wilderness of Winnemucca, Nevada, or McKinney, Texas, or wind-bitten towns in the Dakotas – top black talent, red-hot music, the dark-green flavour of the jungle, and loads of exotic sex. It gave the slummers what they expected – primitive, happy darkies.

As the first shock waves of hard times to come shook the hard-working families of dark Harlem, the wages of booze and broads, gambling and dope kept the mobs on a high-roll. The Cotton Club was like rouge on the cheeks of a dying child.

Flashing his press card, Jack pushed his way under the club's marquee. Over his shivering head glowed the Cotton Club's electric come-on: TALL, TAN AND TERRIFIC! FIFTY SEPIA STARS! Before Jack could reach

52

the doors, he'd run a gauntlet of agitated police. But before the police, a skinny black hand attached to a skinny black body ending in a pair of dirty bare feet reached out and grabbed him.

'Do you have time?'

'Time?' Jack was looking down into the face of Harlem's self-proclaimed Messiah. Like any good prophet, barefoot Martin always knew where the action was. Under each baked eyehole was a crescent of ragged red. Cracked purple lips opened and coughed, spraying Jack with sweat and spittle.

'If the hand of the Lord is not upon you, I say unto you! Brother, you have no time.'

'Ah,' said Jack, and gently prised the hand from his sleeve.

'Doom,' tolled Prophet Martin.

'Doom?'

'Doom!'

'Jesus, let go, fella. We sound like a couple of bells.'

Upstairs, it was turmoil at Madden's joint. Normally, not Jack's kind of club. At the Cotton, they watered the jazz. And shut its doors to a black face. But tonight, Jack liked it fine. Perhaps Bernt McTaggart wasn't having a good time, but one quick look round, and Jack loved it. Heavily carpeted floors, terraced in a horseshoe and rising to corny theatre boxes, a small stage with a large railed thrust, fake palm trees hung with fake nuts and coy cupids blowing kisses on the powder-blue ceiling. And – just as he'd thought – Ted Husing from CBS over on the stage broadcasting live. Ted was there most nights, but tonight he got more than a Cotton Club radio show. He got a Cotton Club scoop. No wonder Harlem had come to the shindy. Radio could kill a newspaperman.

Jack missed a look at the body. Police Lieutenant Bernt McTaggart had already been tagged, bagged, gathered up off the back alley's warm wet pavement and taken away. But every cop left alive in the city of New York clogged up the Cotton – each jittery with outrage. Customers, mainly white, and entertainers: singers, dancers, comedians, all black, pushed and shoved on the tiny dance floor, babbling at each other. Waiters, busboys, cooks, dishwashers, bartenders, and a bobbing, weaving sample of hoods hugged the walls.

Smack in the middle of it all, seated at one of the many small tables, was one very calm crook. With his china-blue eyes and receding chin, dapper Madden was the centre of a hell of a lot of attention. Owney, who seldom showed up at the Cotton, who spent most of his time in his Chelsea penthouse counting his takings and shunning the limelight, was enjoying the place for a change.

As Eagels elbowed his way in, Owney called over the head of a cop with a busy note pad to 'Big Frenchy' DeMange. 'Anybody seen Dutch Schultz around lately?' Owney had the soft, sweet voice of a girl.

Frenchy, hulking over another table a few cops away, was also supposed to be answering questions. 'Say, right!' he hollered back. 'What about Dutch?' Frenchy had the voice of a tuba. He poked his cop on the chest with a forefinger the size of a German sausage. The cop and his chair reeled backwards. 'You guys ever t'ink a dat?'

Once a bootlegger and often a safecracker, six-foot-two DeMangè looked like a gangster's gangster, the kind of underslung goon with big, bushy eyebrows and that coal-blue stubble cartoonists drew to make themselves very, very clear. Unlike Madden, DeMange loved the limelight and the limelight loved him. Frenchy went down well with the Mink Set. He hung round the Cotton giving the place just what the tourists came looking for – the thrill of underworld panache. He poked at his cop again, who dodged just in time. 'What you t'ink, dummies? We'd go an' kill a cop on our own doorstep?'

This tableau warmed Jack's heart. Even shitting themselves over the killing of one of their own – if one cop could get himself cut down, *any* cop could – the police were handling Madden like they'd handle a performing cobra, with care.

While everybody yelled at everybody else, Jack found himself a booth by a fake marble pillar and sat in it. To the ears of a reporter come late, came the sound of blissful confusion. Dozens of conflicting stories worried the air. This kind of mayhem meant nobody knew what the hell was going on. The story was still clean as a blank sheet of paper. Full of fury and fear over McTaggart, the cops were getting nowhere and making a mess while they went. How pleased the fat man would be.

Jack lit a cigarette, leaned back and smoked it. Howling in a pack was no way to learn anything. All it gained a man was a damn sore throat. Ah, but by listening! The story so far: the cops thought maybe Madden knifed McTaggart. Why? They had no idea. His fellow scribes – he'd spotted the *World*, the *American*, the *Mail*, three bozos from the *Graphic*, a gentleman in evening clothes from the *Times*, the *Herald Tribune*, the *Brooklyn Eagle*, the *Mirror*, Jesus, why bother counting? Every newspaper in town was here. Shouting out questions, stepping on toes, baying at Madden.

Every cop and every newsie in the Cotton knew Owney was at Madison Square Garden all evening. But then again, who didn't know that? Not Jack. He was at the fights; he saw him. So how did Madden do it? Easy. The cops figured he'd ordered it done. But lawdy, here come dat old debbil again – why? Jack laughed to himself. Hell, *why* wouldn't be too hard to learn. They'd beat it out of somebody.

The only other suspects? Meyer Lansky – senior member, along with Bugsy Siegel and Lucky Luciano, of the Broadway Mob and not such a nice Jewish boy

– Dutch Schultz, Legs Diamond, how about every hood in New York? Schultz was Owney's choice. So no one listened. Except Jack.

Eagels looked for a place to get rid of his cigarette. From a tub of genuine sand sprouted one of those fake palms. He buried the butt in the tub and started moving, edging on past the clutch surrounding Madden and DeMange. Time to look for Billy Brennan – or much better, for the *Trident*'s best photographer, Gene Goetz. Billy was a klutz, Goetz was a pro.

Last Valentine's Day, Jack and Goetz were together in snowy Chicago counting holes in cold bodies in a cold garage on North Clark Street. (Bugs Moran's wasn't one of them. Al Capone must have been so disappointed.) In May, they got stuck down in Washington, DC, Jack hanging his head in shame as the United States Supreme Court denied citizenship to a Hungarian immigrant who was also a pacifist. In July, the *Trident* sent them to China. The Walled Kingdom had just seized the railroad that ran across Manchuria. When the story – pungent with the alluring stink of the orient – pounded out over the teletype, Connie clapped a sitting Jack on the back and said, 'The very man. You got three fucking hours to be our expert on Chinks. We got a plane leaving at nine. Go get that story – and make it colourful as hell!' Jack, Goetz right behind him, spent a month getting shot at by everyone – as he tried to make sense of Chiang Kai-shek's confused government, Mao Tse-tung's splintered communists, Japanese and Russian imperialism, and the traditional warlords. Noting that, as usual, the people were the ones who carried the can as the powerful squabbled amongst themselves. When Jack got back to New York after that one, O'Rourke was everywhere but – following baseball's Philadelphia Athletics as they played their way to their first pennant in fifteen years. O'Rourke was *always* everywhere but. Red was the only woman he'd ever known he was eager to get back to – and the only one who was never there.

Jack shook Teddy out of his head. Where the hell was Goetz? Or even Billy, for that matter? Before Jack could find either one, he ran straight into Simpson Caffey.

'Hiya, Eagels. Overslept? Thought I hadn't seen you round yet. Almost missed the show.'

'What's up, Caffey?'

'Up?' Caffey surveyed the chaos with disgust, and spat. 'A whole pile of dog shit.'

'Sims, when you talk, angels sneeze. How you write the way you write when you speak the way you speak, beats me.'

'Piss on it. This place stinks. Look around. Stupid looking trees, walls with colours could put your eye out, jazzy niggers leaning on horns, and a bunch of naked nigger showgirls young enough to be jail bait. Walker oughta close the joint.'

Jack tipped back his hat and looked – saw nothing but a great story. Until he got back to Sims. Simpson Caffey wrote for the *New York World*, a paper still heady enough to hold a topnotch reporter even after the loss of its one-of-a-kind editor, Herbert Bayard Swope. Swope was newsprint's original redhead and the reason Connie hated them to begin with. Swope was also the one man Jack Eagels would have worked for if he wasn't already working for Cornelius Mezinger. And Sims the one reporter in New York Jack felt threatened by – not that he admitted it to anyone, not even Teddy. But only when Caffey was writing. Doing anything else, Caffey was a pain in the butt.

Next to Sims stood a cop the size of a jockey in a pony race. Officer Handley came up to Jack's armpit. 'About time we cleaned up Nigger Heaven, huh, Eagels?'

'Not so long as the gods are white.'

'Yeah, there's that,' agreed Handley, staring at Madden and the corpulent Frenchy. 'Look at the size of that guy,

57

DeMange, bigger than you. He could rip somebody's head off with his bare hands.'

'You think he did?'

'I *hope* he did. If some dinge got Bernie McTaggart, it's gonna be like Chicago round here.'

'With the cops standing in for Capone?'

Handley squinted up at Jack, couldn't decide if he was OK or not – what nosy reporter was really a pal? – and shrugged. 'Maybe you just said something and maybe you didn't. Cop killers don't get away with it, not in this town. Snuff a woman, even maybe a cute little kid – but not a cop, not even a cop like Bernie.'

Noting the light in Jack's eyes, the quick pencil in Sims Caffey's hand, Handley held up a beefy palm. 'Say now, why am I talking to you guys? The wife's always saying I got a big mouth. Jumping Jesus, is she right. Don't print that last, print the other stuff where I said cop killers get caught, right?' Handley sprinted off to seek some quiet spot where folks were more his size – mentally.

And Jack offered Caffey a cigarette. 'What's the *World*'s angle, Sims? You think Madden did it?'

Caffey laughed – but took the cigarette. 'What? You're crazy? You think I'd tell you? Read it in the paper in the morning.'

'I don't have to wait, I already know.'

'Know what?'

'You're going for Mayor Jimmy on this, aren't you? You always go for Jim.'

Caffey shrugged. 'Can I help it if the guy's on the take, if McTaggart was his? Follow my stuff, Jacko. Whoever killed the poor sap, somehow it'll lead back to City Hall.'

'You can prove that?'

'Nope. I just know it.'

'Great reporting, Caffey – ever think of working with Winchell?'

'Up yours. I been chasing stories in this town since you were sucking your thumb on the back end of some squaw; by now, kid – I gotta nose.'

'By now, Sims, you got a bad cold.'

'You'll have to excuse me, Eagels. I don't know what *you're* doing, but I'm working here.'

Digging down into his pants, Caffey adjusted his privates, then sauntered off to do some deep breathing – as close as he could to a cluster of plucked blackbirds.

Jack spotted Goetz. Gene and a ton of photographic equipment had set up shop by the stage.

Sitting on the set of the Cotton Club's last number, Gene fiddled with a bulky flash. Behind him lurked plenty of big-leafed, nameless green things, lots of liana, a couple of stuffed lions, tom toms big enough for a dancer to dance nude on, and a rubber boa constrictor. It was all as African as Tarzan – but it made the hearts of the Midwest burn. Goetz greeted Jack as he did everybody. With a languid wave of his little finger and no hello.

Jack sat on the edge of the stage, chucking the snake under what must be its chin. 'Where's Billy?'

'Don't know. Last seen talking to a cutie the colour of a strong cup of tea.'

'Which means what?'

'Which means you'd better move your ass. The *Trident* ain't exactly represented in strength here.'

Falling back flat on the stage, Jack moaned. 'Oh God, I need a drink, I need a bath, I need – '

'*You* need? I need an hour with one of them chocolate cookies.'

Back up again, Jack thought about that need for a few seconds, got confused, and changed the subject. 'You learn anything yet?'

'Cops don't know the time of death. Body got found towards the end of the after-dinner show, around ten o'clock. Knifed right through his bow tie. Not nice, but clean and very effective. Husing got the news just as he was announcing Snakehips Tucker for the listening folks. It stopped the show – the news, not Tucker. That's about it. Teddy with you?'

'Red's in a snit.'

Goetz fixed Jack with a baleful eye. 'Don't tell me – you two are fighting again. Did I ever tell you you're a mug, Eagels? If I had me a broad like O'Rourke, I'd, why, I'd – '

'You'd what?'

'I'd figure it out. Damn, a redhead like that. First off, she's tall.'

'Not as tall as she thinks she is.'

Gene rolled his eyes. 'Sometimes, looking at her, I think of changing my beat, of working for Hohenloe. That way I'd share a sleeping car with a great-lookin', tall redhead, and to hell with you. Think of it! Stuck in an upper berth with O'Rourke, a dame who knows sports. What more could a man ask for?'

'Less lip?' offered Jack.

'There's that. But you gotta take the long with the short.'

'Lately, all I get is the short.'

'I know what you mean, my wife's drivin' me nuts – '

'Wife? What wife, Goetz! Since when?'

'Since forever.'

'That long? So, what's it like?'

'Norma? She's a good old girl. Cooks, irons my socks, knows to put things so I can find 'em, never asks for more dough than I feel like handin' over, never asks where I been – and complain? Nah, not my Norma. Of course, she don't know a goddamned thing about baseball. And boxing? Boxing makes her go all squeamish.'

'Then why is she driving you crazy?'

'She wants to go live in Florida. Ever heard anything so awful? Me, leave New York permanent? I start breathing all that clean air, it'd kill me. Gotta go. Snapped a few

60

pics of the body, but none of Madden. So far, haven't got near enough to smell him.'

So saying, Goetz gathered up the smallest of his collection of cameras, and clanked off, a tripod hanging from his belt.

Jack patted his snake. Goetz married? Jesus, you travel halfway around the world with a guy and he never tells you he's married.

Married, for crying out loud. And the wife's name is Norma. Norma who never complains, never asks questions. She cooks. Cooks? Since he'd known her, Teddy'd cooked – what? – a dozen times. Not bad either. Whatever Teddy did, she did well. How would she do as a wife? Put that mass of red hair in a net, lever her out of those slacks and into a housedress – Red? In a housedress? Teddy O'Rourke, a wife? Dreaming in pandemonium, Jack saw Teddy, her body, slender as a Colorado aspen, bent over a broom, saw her sweeping the floor, her sweet ass beckoning, saw himself taking her – whoa! Hold on a minute, Eagels. This is a wife we're imagining here. But whose wife? Yours? Mrs Teddy Eagels. Mrs Jack Eagels. Mr Jack O'Rourke. Marry Red? Turn a gambling, travelling fool into a wife? And himself – into a husband! Jack shuddered down the length of his spine. There's an idea that goes in a back pocket.

Up on the stage, Duke Ellington, sprawled on his piano stool, tuxedo'd legs stuck sideways, was doodling around on the black keys. Duke, playing the kind of jazz he didn't play for the slummers at the Cotton, was the only living soul in the joint who looked bored as hell.

Jack skipped Ellington, who was busy running chords anyway, and went for the stand-in saxophonist.

To get to Bubs Bailey, he had to climb over Sonny Greer's flashy collection of drums: timpani, chimes, a snare drum, easing by the vibraphone, banging into high-hats, saying hi to Duke's men. Bubs, hidden behind

Greer's drums, smoking a thin joint and laughing, watched him come.

'You are one determined snoop,' said Bailey and passed the joint.

Jack took it. 'Have to be. I'm late. Jesus, what's in this?'

'Secret. My momma rolled it.'

Jack gave it back. 'I see the cops think the big boss killed McTaggart.'

'People say things like that when they see the man. I dunno, there's something about him.'

'What do *you* say?'

'Cops don't know nothing.'

'And you do?'

Bubs shrugged his shoulders. 'Mebbe. Mebbe not. Tell you what, Eagels. It seems to me that if you want to know who killed the man, you know the man hisself.'

'And you knew him?'

'Sure. We all did. Since I been sitting in with the band, seems like that cop lived here. Every night a new sweetie on his arm. Broadway types, hoofers, chorines, whatever. McTaggart didn't act like no policeman I ever knew, crooked or straight. No uniform. Plenty of money. Always hanging out as near Frenchy as he could, sucking up to Mr Madden, asking for us to play songs. Mostly weepies. I'd try the girls if I was you.'

'What about Walker? You ever see the Mayor around here?'

'Sure, this is the Cotton, ain't it! – But then, what hot club don't? The mayor, he's a happy man. He don't hide his light under no haybale.'

'From now on, he might have to. Any of the other papers talked to the band?'

'In this place? Got too much tone for that. We been sittin' here like we was stones on a rocky beach.'

With a gratified grin and sudden dry cough, Eagels shook Bailey's hand. 'Thanks, Bubs. You seen Billy?'

Bubs jabbed a thumb backstage and down. 'That way. Fifteen minutes ago.'

Billy Brennan was in a basement dressing room – narrow, windowless, and dank – the one the Cotton provided for the girls. Littered with cartons of Chinese food, bags of knitting, holed stockings and stray sequins, it stank of spirit gum, Sterno, and the perfume of girlish sweat. But every night up in the alley by the back stage door, long classy limousines lined up like a taxi rank.

With Billy was a light-skinned girl of gentle beauty but little character – and that little, subdued. The beauty wouldn't age well. But for the moment, who cared? The girl wasn't more than nineteen. Until Jack showed up, she and Billy had had the place to themselves.

Billy's face lit up when he saw Jack. Brennan was the kind of kid who said the first thing that settled on his tongue – and lived to regret it. If he didn't, someone else did. He also said it in a very loud voice. Connie hired Billy because he was Alva T. Thorp's third wife's brother's boy. Billy was Mezinger's second – and last – concession. The first, of course, was Teddy O'Rourke. From the day Billy arrived on the paper, Connie had Jack babysitting him. Billy idolized Jack and Jack first tolerated, then grew to like, Billy. He couldn't help it. The kid was so lacking in vice, he was almost angelic – so dumb, he was brilliant. On the *Trident*, Billy bloomed. But only around Eagels.

'Mr Eagels! You're here. I got us something.' Billy pointed at the girl, who shied. 'Meet Hyacinth Henderson. She found the body.'

Much larger at the hip than the shoulder, eager and shy, Billy was suet soft and oddly angular all at once.

'I figured with everyone asking Madden and DeMange stuff, I'd try to think like you would. So I asked around for the girl who found the body – and here's

Hyacinth. Of course the cops'd already talked to her – but they didn't ask her much. Miss Henderson told me – '

Jack held up a hand. 'Hold on, Billy. Slow down. You're bending my pencil.'

Billy shut up and breathed loud.

Jack turned to Hyacinth. She was sitting on a chair stacked with fan magazines. The frozen face of Joan Crawford peeped out from beneath her petite brown butt. Aside from a feather or two and a strip of scarlet satin, she wasn't wearing a thing. She had big eyes, a small mouth, long, muscled legs, and thin arms. Hyacinth was hugging herself and moaning.

'I tolt the police and I tolt this boy. I talked an' I talked. I'm gettin' tired of talkin'.'

In a moment of unaccustomed insight, Billy softened his voice. 'This is Jack Eagels, Miss Henderson. He's all right. Tell him what happened.' The voice rose. '*Please.*'

Hyacinth sighed. 'Ain't much to tell. Went down to the alley after my last number for some air. Can't get air in this place what with everybody breathin' it all. It was dark but I saw a car leavin' real fast.'

'A yellow car?'

'Don' know. Could have been cream, could have been white, but it was prob'ly yellow. Anyway, I walked less'n a foot an' tripped over somethin' soft an' big an' cold. Landed right on it an' got right off.'

Billy beamed at Jack. 'Cold! Get it!'

Jack got it. 'You mean the body was cold?'

'That's right. Not all the way cold, but it sure wasn't warm. An' wet too. The man's head was bent like this – ' Hyacinth twisted her pretty head until it set on her pretty shoulders at a grotesque angle. ' – an' there was blood comin' out of his nose.'

'Did you know him?'

'Sure did. Came round backstage a few times to make a nuisance of hisself. That man thought women was mattresses. But that was before he started showin' up with those models an' left us alone.'

'What models?'

'From that Lady Snow magazine.'

'*Vogue*?'

'That's the one.'

'You ever meet any?'

Young Hyacinth looked at Jack with old eyes. 'Meet one of them? You shittin' me? They came here like they was going to a zoo. But tonight the man had two – '

'You saw McTaggart alive – tonight?'

Billy butted in. 'You didn't tell me that!'

'You didn't ask. But, sure – I saw him. Way before I fell on him though. Just after the first show, eight o'clock maybe. He had him a new girl, real dinky, seemed too young for him – an' then one of them models he hung around most times with showed up to give him some trouble. I remember both ladies' names because the man was sayin' somethin' like, "Now, Lulu, you calm down, an' Marlo, you shut up." The man, he was talkin' like his new one, this Lulu, was too delicate to hear what that Marlo was screechin'. *Her* too delicate. Man! My ears was burnin'!'

'Did you see him again after that?'

'Not 'less you count steppin' on him.'

The door to the dressing room swung suddenly open. With it came a blast of fresh air – and Herman Stark. Stark, no exception in the standard of Cotton Club management, was white, gruff, stout, chewed a cigar, and manned a machine gun during the war. Now he was the Cotton's stage manager.

'Whoever you two bums are, get the hell out of here. This show's over. Now we got our own show to put on. And Hyacinth? Shut the fuck up.'

4

Tap Dancing in the Dark

In a private office over Madison Square Garden, Albert Groat was perched on a chair made from the remains of Texas longhorns. Groat wore a herringbone suit that could have stood on its own, his watery eyes squinted through rimless glasses, long fingers fussed at a heavy watch chain, and what hair he still had was waving goodbye. Albert and the very odd chair were behind a desk that had once belonged to Warren G. Harding. On top of the desk was a stack of ledgers and on top of the ledgers was Theodore Roosevelt's cane. The cane was made of rhinoceros hide. Groat had inherited the desk, the cane, the ledgers, the chair, and the office, from his erstwhile boss, boxing promoter George 'Tex' Rickard. The longhorned cattle, ex-presidents Harding and Roosevelt, and Tex Rickard had one thing in common: they were all dead. Albert Groat was alive – but barely. At one o'clock in the morning, the throne of Rickard was killing him.

'Took you long enough to show up, O'Rourke,' said Groat, getting up from the hideous chair. 'Don't know why I'm doing all this for Fiske. Who's Fiske?' He slid aside a panel in the wall and worked the controls of a safe.

Standing at her second window in one night, waiting for Dancing Joe's purse, Teddy yawned. Fighting with Jack was wearing her down.

Groat's window looked out over Fiftieth Street. Across Fiftieth groaned the brick bulk of the Polyclinic Hospital. Three years back, Rudolph Valentino died over there. The death of the celluloid sheik sent thousands into a tizzy, but not Teddy O'Rourke. The death at the Polyclinic that bothered O'Rourke occurred almost exactly one year ago

66

– Arnold Rothstein's, king of the New York gamblers, banker of Broadway.

When the man who fixed the 1919 World Series died, it kept Jack away from home for days. Days Teddy had free: no story, no game, nothing to do but love Jack Eagels. Who wasn't there. Again. And if he was, she wasn't. Two reporters too busy for love. Teddy saw him for maybe an hour in two long days. What Jack said when he finally came home was, 'Rothstein died game.' What he meant was: Arnold wouldn't say who belly-shot him. The big-time crook lay dying for forty-eight hours, poked at by doctors, sniped at by police, but always 'Mum was da word.' Which made a certain kind of sense in Rothstein's world. The underworld hated intruders – like cops and newsies. What Jack also said was: 'I got into his room by dressing up like a Rabbi. It worked for three whole minutes before the cops threw me out – but hotdamn, little hooligan, I got my story.' What Jack didn't say was: 'I missed you.'

Staring from Groat's window into the windows of the Polyclinic, Teddy made a small, sad discovery; the day Arnold went off to his smoky backroom in the sky was the day New York's Governor Al Smith lost – and Herbert Hoover won – the presidency of the United States. It was also the day she and Jack had begun to die. It was only in the last few weeks she'd noticed. Maybe she ought to find Rothstein's grave, put flowers on it – how else could she mourn?

Meantime, Groat finally got Rickard's safe open. Tex – who thought Scotch aged better in the presence of money – had kept his supply in it. Albert pushed a few bottles out of the way and hauled out a suitcase that hadn't belonged to anyone before, shoved it at Teddy, then started a speech in a flat monotone that began slowly enough: 'Get this out of here, it's making me jumpy.' By then he was leaning into the words, dealing them out like a professional cardsharp. 'Phone's been ringing since the fight, everybody looking for Fiske. What do I know about Fiske? Who the hell is this Fiske? Some small-time southern cracker who calls me in the middle of the night about his darky's purse, says he wants me to give the money to you in cash, in cash! Holy mother of Mike, you got any idea how hard it is to get seventy-five thousand bucks in cash in the middle of a Saturday night? I said, you sure you want O'Rourke to have it? And he said he was sure. Whoever Fiske is, he's nuts. The money's all mixed up too. Some of it's those new bills, you know, the little ones the Treasury's making us use now, but most of it's the regular kind – big, like they should be.'

Dragging her thoughts from Arnold and Jack and a year of slow sliding grace, Teddy turned. Groat had gone green.

'All this money's burning a hole where I got it now, so you take it, get it away from me. If it weren't for that nigger of Fiske's, if the coloured kid didn't have so much potential, Dixie Fiske could take a running jump. I even had some guys here in person after the fight, guys you'd cross the street if you saw them coming, asking where he was. And I told them, how would I know? What's with this Dixie Fiske? I'm lucky Tex had a safe.'

For the first time since she'd walked into his office, Albert had Teddy's full attention. 'What guys?'

'I should know their names? Not the kind of guys anyone wants to see hanging around boxing is all I know.'

'Albert, you're talking about the *only* kind of guys who hang around boxing. They look like gamblers?'

'Like gamblers? What's a gambler look like? They looked like winners, like guys who eat losers.'

Teddy sympathized with Groat. Whether he knew it or not, by 'losers' he meant himself. Albert was trying to hold a far-flung promoting empire together with spit. For him, it wasn't easy. Not only had a pack of wolves gathered as soon as larger-than-life Tex was lowered into his eternal hole, but Albert Groat was no Rickard. Groat had only bluster; Rickard had verve. Teddy ought to know; Tex had chased her around Harding's desk for years.

'Was Channing with them?'

Like one of Ziegfeld's girls, posing in the kind of show where Flo got away with calling nudity 'Art', Albert stopped moving; only his lips left alive. 'Channing? You mean *Tom* Channing! The gangster that used to run with Madden? Why should he come here? Jesus Christ, O'Rourke, he don't own any of Dancing Joe, does he?'

Afraid Albert was about to fall down in a dead faint, Teddy backed away, gave him room. 'If he didn't before the fight, he probably does now.'

Albert surprised her, all he said to that was a soft, speculative, 'Damn.'

Teddy hefted the suitcase. It wasn't that heavy; like lugging a few New York telephone books.

'It's all here, isn't it, Al?'

Groat batted his thin lashes at her, pale hazel eyes watering behind an old man's glasses. 'Please, after a night like this, insults I don't need. Maybe I should ask you for a receipt.'

Taking the suitcase, Teddy headed for the door.

'Say, you – O'Rourke.'

Teddy turned.

'You in good with Joe Bright?'

'Why?'

'After tonight I could get that boy a bout with anybody, put him on easy street for life – especially if he got rid of that cracker manager of his, and even more especially if he was to lose.'

'Lose?'

'Sure. You don't think America wants a coloured boy for heavyweight champion? I'd be doing him a favour – make him some money before he gets tossed back into Harlem. Where he belongs. Of course, this is all supposing Channing ain't in the picture.'

'Bye, Al.'

'Say, what are you? His manager? You're just a writer, what the hell do you know?'

Carrying all that money, Teddy couldn't slam the door.

At one thirty in the morning Teddy went home, fuming. It took her less than ten minutes to walk from Madison Square Garden to 1600 Broadway, retracing the steps she'd walked with Jack three and a half hours earlier. One clenched hand shoved deep in a pocket, the other gripping Groat's suitcase, she listened to the tiptap of her angry heels along the wet and littered sidewalk. A spitting speech spiralled through her head, bumped into her skull – and careened off in fury. She was holding a conversation with Jack Eagels. Talking to Jack live was like fielding fast balls in a game that counted. But in the privacy of her mind, talking to Jack gave Teddy all the homers. She was feeding him lines, felling him with her own. Walking down the Great White Way, still clogged with shady types and painted ladies – what Damon Runyon liked to call his 'guys and dolls' – no one looked at O'Rourke twice. One glance at her freckled furious face and they wouldn't dare. No one, that is, but the big, gum-chewing man with the silvery hair. He not only dared, but shadowed her every step of the way.

Jack's Harley Davidson, grimed with carbon and oil, was propped against the brick wall of 1600. Which meant Jack could be home, that he wasn't out riding the city range, swapping his Indian pony for a motorcycle. Teddy steeled herself for her second match of the evening.

Teddy O'Rourke and Jack Eagels lived in a nine-storey brick building on Broadway; two New Yorkers who wrote for a living calling a small apartment home. The building housed the rowdy Silver Slipper on the bottom, a cooing kingdom of caged pigeons on the roof along with three potted ginkgo trees, and a thriving animated cartoon factory on the sixth floor. Right next door was the Roseland Ballroom. Lindy's restaurant and the Winter Garden Theater were a block further north. The cartoon factory was the Fleischer Studios. Over their heads, Ko-Ko the Clown lived in a bottle of ink and Betty Boop was in inky embryo. Beneath their feet, Broadway hopefuls danced with anyone for a dime. Sandwiched between, Jack and Teddy's place – all three rooms of it – was book-infested and lousy with newspapers. The ceilings were too tall, the gas log fire too erratic, the cockroaches too big and too sure of themselves, too many chorus girls came up to have a good cry, too many cartoonists came down for a cup of coffee, and the sagging sofa Teddy threw herself on when she finally climbed the stairs took up most of the living room. Jack's old rolltop desk took up the rest, the stories he wrote stacked on top, loose pages spilling onto the gramophone. The walls were covered in cartoon sketches: tap-dancing chickens, bees with a buzz on in cocked bowler hats, cats in boaty high heels, and, of course, Ko-Ko – with his ice cream cone hat.

The Harley might be home, but Jack wasn't. Which only made her angrier.

On the wall above Teddy's head were cartoon doodles of Jack and Teddy that looked just like Teddy and Jack. Eagels wearing his usual battered hat tipped back on his clever head, smoking his usual cigarette, note pad in hand, pencil behind his ear. Jack cocking an inquisitive eye at ladykillers, swagmen, well-fed Tammany Hall hucksters, anarchists aiming fat black bombs with fizzing wicks, raging hotel fires. Jack in a full-feathered Indian headdress jotting down the bloated wisdom of bigwigs – or under a bullet-pocked helmet, peering across the cross-hatched trenches of yet another somewhere war. O'Rourke in her usual unusual slacks, sometimes smoking, sometimes not, once with a cigar. Teddy sparring with boxers, down on

71

her knees and thumbing her freckled nose in a crap game, racing side-saddle in the Kentucky Derby way ahead of the field, blocking a tackle, batting in a home run – tidy ass stuck out, blowing a huge bubble of gum. Gifts from the upstairs neighbours, grateful to have a place that served free coffee and honest advice.

Teddy shifted around on the sprung sofa, looking for a position that didn't itch. How the hell did Jack manage on this thing? Lying on it was something he'd done a lot of in the past few weeks. Ever since he'd stopped sleeping and started drinking – and, of course, fighting with Teddy, who, of course, fought back. She dragged at a cigarette, watching the column of white smoke break into wild squiggles in the dark air, sneering at the cartoons of Jack above her head. Jack Eagels was a reporter. Teddy O'Rourke was only a sports writer. What Jack wrote made the headlines, all his copy above the fold. What she wrote made the back page, where they put the sports. If the front page, as Swope believed, 'was the mirror of the world in which a man lives', what did that make the back page?

Games. Men's games. Teddy O'Rourke's whole life. Christened Kathleen Ellen by a mother who'd died at her birth, but called Teddy by her hot-headed Irish father.

Teddy O'Tooth was the name of a long-dead bull terrier. Winning a bundle on a fighting dog paid Michael Francis O'Rourke's passage on a boat sailing west in the dead of night. Slipping away from the folded green mountains of County Leitrim to the grey geometry of New York, Michael Francis made straight for the lower East Side and the Irish district of Gas House, where he wooed and won a shy girl from County Roscommon, pretty Pegeen Molloy. Fathered a daughter instead of a son, and was left holding the baby. Michael Francis made do with what he had. Naming a kid after a dog, he'd dragged a quiet, grey-eyed infant, then a chubby freckle-faced little girl, and finally a slim young woman with fiery red hair, to every ballgame, every fight, every horse race, every floating crap game, every bit of sporting action he could muscle in on for twenty years. Raising her like his son – in ballparks and poolrooms, at the starting gates of America's racetracks, in grubby backrooms where men played serious poker and dingy boxing gyms where nervy street kids sometimes got turned into men.

Teddy wore no bows in her hair, no middies and brown stockings. Michael Francis let her wear what she pleased. Long pants, sloppy sweaters with turtlenecks, and a big cap – always on backwards and always green.

At three, Teddy's best friend was a bookie at Belmont, she could stack a deck by five, taught herself to read from racing forms by six, and to write by swiping library books. The ten-year-old son of the man who swept out Daddy's favourite Cherry Street saloon showed her how to spit through her teeth. The fat kid hawking the *Sun* on the corner gave her a white rat she named Snuffy and kept in a shoebox. Daddy's friends called her 'Pepper Pot', 'Bricktop', 'Red'; called Daddy first 'Ring', then 'Bucks', and finally, 'Bluff' O'Rourke. Bluff struck the fancy of Michael Francis – and he let it ride.

The fighters helped Shucks Spooner teach Teddy to box, the jockeys taught her to ride, the gamblers how to handle a gun. As she grew up, the littlest O'Rourke loved every minute of it. Until she turned twenty and fell in love with newspapers. Leaving Bluff for the world of the printed word, quick words quickly read – and forgotten. Bluff O'Rourke, happy with his handiwork, waved her a gay goodbye and booked passage for the Orient.

And Teddy settled down in her little apartment on Broadway where she'd spent less than a year in the nine years she'd had it. Thirty years old in a little over a month, her only domestic efforts: arranging her books. And raising one small sad plant. No dog, cat, canary, not even a goldfish since Snuffy the rat, Teddy had only a cactus. After losing a rubber tree, a spider plant, and an aspidistra, she'd discovered a cactus was about the only living thing that could take neglect.

Teddy kicked off her shoes and wriggled her toes. Mad, bad Bluff O'Rourke. She adored him. Everybody did. So where, when she needed him, was the bastard now? Hopping into the two-seater plane of a barn-storming friend, a friend almost as crazy as he was, disappearing into the blue of a western sky. That was two years ago. Last she'd heard, he was legging it across the Himalayas chased by some rich broad who, after a go-round with Bluff, wasn't so rich anymore. But that letter came three months ago. He'd probably outdistanced the lady by now and was placing bets on how many grains of sand there were in the Kalahari desert. And finding takers. Bluff could always spot a sucker.

Swinging her long trousered legs off the sofa and onto the carpet, Teddy stood up and paced. Criss-crossing the living room, dodging furniture. It took her less than a minute. After Jack and his rolltop moved in on her, there wasn't much floor space left. Cardboard boxes filled with his magazines: *Black Mask*, *Ghost Stories*, *Weird Tales*, *Tales of the West*. One with half a dozen copies of Jack's war novel, *Pay The Scarecrow*. Three boxes of short stories. Jack's own, stuff he'd been writing for years, most published. Stories of hard-boiled detectives, stories of the old west where the Indian wasn't always the savage, stories of horror. Jack turned his hand to anything. There was a deck of cards on the gramophone. She riffled the pack; the cards brand new, stiff. Of course! This was Saturday night. Jack ought to be playing poker. But last Tuesday, October the 29th, 1929, Wall Street – as *Variety* put it – 'laid an egg'.

Some egg.

The day Wall Street went down – the thousand faces on the floor of the New York Stock Exchange pale with panic – Jack calmly watched it all, making notes. While O'Rourke was sitting seven hundred or so miles away, watching Mickey Walker defend his Middleweight title against Ace Hudkins. Mickey won.

For two and a half years, ever since he'd hit New York from Chicago, Eagels played poker with a bunch of his more literate friends in an upstairs room at the Algonquin Hotel. Teddy attended twice. After the second clean sweep of the entire table, Jack's friends banned her. She never forgot what her redman said as she walked out of the door with everyone's IOUs. 'OK, boys, cut the cards. Now we can get back to what we usually do; pretending we're good at this game.'

But there was no game this Saturday. Jack's poker-playing cronies were all home counting what was left of their dimes.

So was Wall Street. The Market traded only half the day on Thursday, shut down completely yesterday and today. The bankers and brokers, the terrified thousands on margin: everyone sat home, licking their wounds. Somehow, thirty billion bucks – fifteen billion more than the entire national debt – had vanished into thick air.

Angry, restless, hungry, Teddy got a bottle of cream soda from the kitchen, fishing it out of a grumbling icebox with virtually nothing else in it. Levering the top off the bottle, she knew what she really wanted to do right now. Forget Jack. Forget Dancing Joe, Dixie Fiske, Jesse Bean's quasi-tragic mug, forget poor dead Bernie, even the alluring Tom Channing – instead, pop downstairs, slip her shapely behind onto a padded chrome stool at the soda fountain in Walgreen's, order a grilled cheese sandwich and a double chocolate malted. But more angry than hungry, she stayed where she was – and waited. Sipping cream soda, shuffling Jack's deck, she dealt herself a Royal Flush. Someone had to. Lately, life was all low cards.

The big man waited in a darkened doorway between Roseland and the Silver Slipper, paring his nails and chewing a wad of tutti-frutti gum. He wore a pearl-grey fedora, a dark blue overcoat, his favourite old Smith and Wesson .32 pulling down the left pocket, and a pearl-handled Colt dragging on the right.

He saw the small black Studebaker sedan before the two torpedoes in it saw him.

'Hey, CD, over here,' the big man hissed.

CD Durata, young, eager and willing, slid the sedan up beside him. 'How's it going, Mr Rosenbloom? By the way – this here is my cousin, Arch. Boss gave him a job.'

Solomon Rosenbloom put a spatted foot on the running board, bent down and looked Arch over. Swarthy, black-eyed and beak nosed as two young Turks, CD and his cousin were as alike as cubed carrots. Italians. Sol didn't like Italians. Too emotional, too stupid. But what the hell, if the boss wanted a couple of punk wops on the payroll, who was Sol Rosenbloom to argue? Not even if less than five hours earlier young CD had just pulled one of his dumber moves, what was Solomon Rosenbloom supposed to say about that? At least the kid was using the right car, was back in the Studdy like he belonged.

Sol tipped his big head towards the Slipper. 'The skirt's on the third floor. There's a back way over on Seventh but she won't think of using it. Never noticed me once. She's got the case. She comes down without it, one of you stay here. She comes down with it and she and the money split up, *you* split up. No losing either one of them, right?'

CD and Arch nodded together. 'Right, Mr Rosenbloom.'

'The rest of the boys found Fiske yet?'

CD grinned. 'Sure. No problem. Zipper put 'im in a box.'

Satisfied, Solomon Rosenbloom hailed a cab.

When Jack let himself through the third-floor door at 1600 Broadway, the apartment was dark. And thankfully

76

quiet. Teddy wasn't hiding behind the door to brain him. No cartoon rolling pins, no rusting kitchen knives, no scrappy screwy redhead to flatten him with fury. Using the Roseland's lurid sign to see by, red light leaking through half-closed curtains, he found his house bottle and poured himself a drink. Carrying both the bottle and the glass, Jack sought the sofa by touch. And collapsed on it. Might as well make himself as comfortable as he could on the damn thing. As usual, he couldn't sleep. He'd been soaked through four times during this long, wearisome day. Once in a field in upstate New York watching four Russian aviators bring in their tired plane, the *Land of the Soviets*, after a twelve and a half thousand mile flight from Moscow the long way. Him and his Harley almost getting run over in the mud by ten thousand eager transplanted Russians and a few thousand native communists. Drying off at his desk in the city room as he wrote up the Russian piece, only to get wet again greeting Teddy's train from Connecticut at Grand Central. Again, walking fast and mad to the fight at the Garden. Once more in Harlem. Now it was a few minutes past three in the morning and the apartment was warm, silent, and dim with Jack in a stew. Sipping bourbon neat, his head clear – who said an Indian couldn't drink?

Lying on the sofa drowning his talent in hooch, Jack had filed his McTaggart story. Eagels's front page coverage would read like any other paper's, except for style. He'd barely hinted that Police Lieutenant Bernt McTaggart was a little out of the ordinary, playing down Hyacinth Henderson's, Bubs Bailey's, even Handley's descriptions of the dead cop until he could dig up more – and better – information. Knowing how the police – and Sims Caffey – were going to sell McTaggart, a reporter had better know his stuff when he sold a different line. But he *had* mentioned suspects – both the cops' and the mob's. It was a long, illustrious list. Eagels liked to play fair.

Right at this moment, if Jack could wish for anything, he'd wish it was hours earlier. That instead of going with Teddy to Madison Square Garden, he'd bribed Hype Hohenloe to let her off for the night, assign a second stringer to cover the fight. Then, he should have taken her to the movies. John Gilbert's first talkie, *His Glorious Night*, was playing right down the street. Gilbert was Jack's favourite male movie star; his favourite picture: *The Big Parade*. After that, who knew? A midnight supper at Lindy's? Home? The Teddy he wished he knew in the bed he used to know? But he hadn't. And now? Something about that Joe Bright match soured Teddy – but what? Damned if he knew. Lately, damned if he *ever* knew. Red was getting to be a pain in the ass. Speaking of ass! Forget it, Jack old boy. You'll be lucky if you get a knee in the groin.

Sighing, he treated himself to one last nightcap. Turning back time was a hard trick to pull off. Even for a half-drunk half Indian. Jack gave it up and went to bed.

Where Teddy was waiting for him. My God! – he was in luck. His redhead was smiling.

In gleeful hope, Jack hopped around the bedroom pulling off shoes, pants, shirt – throwing the shoes on the floor, the pants on a chair, the shirt on the end of the bed. Teddy just lay there and watched him do it.

Lulling Jack into a false sense of safety. Buoying his heart. Maybe things were going to be all right. Maybe he'd get through this night intact. Sifting through his scanty stock of Catholic totems inherited from the long-gone Collette, Jack said a little prayer to the saint of the impossible. *Please, St Jude, don't let me sleep on the sofa tonight.*

Saying at almost the same time, 'I ran into Sims at the Cotton. The way I figure it is, the bastard falls asleep at his typewriter and then an elf sneaks in and writes its little

78

heart out. In the morning Sims wakes up, and hey presto! Another Pulitzer Prize.' Jack tried out a laugh. It fell at his feet and lay there, useless.

Teddy'd stopped smiling. Good Christ, what now?

Now – she talked. When her voice reached him, it was sweet and low; it was the kind of voice she used when she said things that hurt. Jack's laugh crawled under the bed.

'I've been thinking – ' she said.

Oh shit, thought Jack, and stood at the foot of the bed, one sock on and one sock off. Only one sock and unbuttoned briefs between him and a suddenly hostile world.

' – and what I've been thinking is this: get out of my apartment.'

'What?'

'You heard me. Go away, drive somebody else crazy with your moods . . . *he sees me, he sees me not* . . .'

'Is that it? He sees me not? Jesus, Red, *I* see you.'

'As Connie would say, *Bullshit*. Find some other dumb tootsie, dumber than me, to play footsie with. And wipe that surprised look off your face. We've been coming to this for weeks. Or more precisely, for exactly one year. It's our anniversary, Jack. One year since we fell out of the sky.'

'Pooey,' said Jack, took off his second sock, shook off his briefs, leapt into bed, and lunged for Teddy. Who, twisting like an eel, slid away and over the side with a speed that amazed him.

Now she was standing where he'd been standing, Jack was in bed, and she was saying, 'I get the feeling you don't think I'm serious.'

Jack sighed a long, theatrical sigh, found the pack of Luckies next to Teddy's cactus plant on the night stand, shook one out and lit it. 'OK, I'll listen. All ears. Shoot.'

'That's perfect. *Now*, you'll listen. Christ, I hate you.'

'That's OK. I love you.'

'Love me? Love me! What are you talking about? What the fuck do you mean by that, love me? Love what? This?' Teddy turned, flipped up the shirt she'd been lying awake in – one of his, of course – and slapped her beautiful white, freckled ass. Turned back. 'There's more to me than my butt, you half-breed half wit.'

Jack, still under the impression that things would turn out fine, said with real reverence, 'Dear God, you better believe it! Get back in bed, Red, and let me count the "mores".'

At which point, Teddy picked up his shoe and threw it at him.

Jack ducked and the shoe smashed through the window behind his head, sailing out over Broadway. 'Dammit, Teddy, that was half of my best pair of dress shoes.'

'From now on, you can hop.'

Jack scrambled round in the bed, stubbed out his Lucky in cactus dirt, opened the smashed window, leaned out. As he watched, a truck ran over his shoe. The truck was loaded with the early morning edition of the New York *Daily News*. Just below what was left of the window, a couple of nocturnal someones were fooling around with his Harley. 'Hey, you two!' yelled Jack. 'Leave that bike alone!'

Even from Jack's height, they both looked like kids, very young punks. The dark head of one jerked up, exposing a huge, beaked nose; he backed off from whatever it was he'd been doing. 'Sorry, mac, just looking. You break that window?'

'No,' said Jack, 'I did not break the window. A lunatic broke the window.'

The punk grinned up at him. 'I getcha. Lot of loonies in New York.'

'You said it,' said Jack, turning away from the window, tucking himself back into bed, out of the Broadway wind. 'All right, O'Rourke, that does it. You owe me nine dollars and seventeen cents, plus tax. What the fuck are you doing?'

'What does it look like?'

Teddy was dressed and packing, already on her second suitcase. How she'd managed to finish with one during the time he'd been having his pre-dawn chat with a big-nosed punk he couldn't imagine.

'It looks like you're going someplace.'

'Give the man a banana.'

'Oh, for Christ's sake. Where to now? What kind of goddamn sport is played at this hour of the night?'

'The only game you know, Jack.'

'Which means?'

'Yours. But deal me out. You won't leave – so I will.'

'That's it then. You're serious?'

'That's it then. I'm serious. When you move out, I move back in.'

A groundswell of anger surged past Jack's sense of humour, past his cold, into his head, turning the room red. What was going on here? What the fuck had *he* done? Nothing but love the flameheaded freckle-faced hothead; nothing but almost toy with the idea of marrying her. For *that* he was getting kicked out of 1600 Broadway at three o'clock in the morning? Without so much as a two-week notice? She wasn't coming back until he left? Fine. He'd take his time about moving. Wherever she was going, whoever she was going to – and he had an idea it was George – could put up with the blistering bitch until he had the time to leave, until he felt like leaving. Jack Eagels had had enough. His anger was wonderful. It made him believe it. 'Swell. Beat it. Take your Irish temper and your Irish ass and scram. I'm tired, I gotta get up in the morning and solve a murder. What do you have to get up in the morning for? A crossword convention?' Jack punched Teddy's swan's-down pillow, slammed his head into it and shut his eyes.

81

Teddy picked up both suitcases, walked to the bedroom door, turned and said, 'You're going to trip over your brains someday, Jack Eagels – they're way ahead of your heart.'

At the top of the third floor landing, Teddy made up her mind. If she was going to do something about Dancing Joe – *and* Police Lieutenant Bernt McTaggart – it might as well be now. And it might as well be Teddy O'Rourke who called the game. Alone. She picked up Albert Groat's suitcase, her own, tripped down all those stairs to Broadway, stood on the wet sidewalk in the shattered glass of her bedroom window, and whistled for a cab. She got one on the first ear-splitting blast.

Jack's shoe was halfway to Forty-sixth Street. Her cab ran over it. Less than a minute later, so did the Studebaker sedan.

5

Uneasy Money

At three thirty in the morning, Teddy was banging the palm of her hand on a fifth-floor door in the Dakota Building, New York's spookiest apartment house. Twelve feet over her buzzing red head brooded a scrolled and corniced ceiling. Thirty feet either side stretched the dim, dark-painted width of an echoing corridor.

Not soaring but squatting on its blackened haunches, curled round a courtyard of ominous slanted shadows, the Dakota had it all: copper green cupolas, dormer windows in pyramidal peaked roofs like the mystic eye on a dollar bill, hundreds of black, unblinking windows, iron fretwork marking mean balconies. Exotic drifting seed – caught in upper storey cracks – sprouted strange dark shapes, and the wind, once inside the yellow brick walls, was never free again. The Dakota, its trapped wind howling, awed both the city and its own proud residents. It was the stuff of nightmares. And lent its eerie bulk to whispered story, both fact and fiction. At the Dakota, *anything* looked like it could happen. And sometimes did.

One raw minute of Teddy's hard knuckles, and the peephole in the door flicked open. She put her grey eye up to it and yelled.

'Hurry up! Open the door, Dinah; it's dark out here. Not to mention scary.'

There was the metallic clunk of a deadbolt, then, creaking on its hinges, the big oak door swung back into gloom. Behind it, Dinah Bache, dainty as a barrel of cider in a high-necked dressing gown fussy with lace and ribbons, blinked frightened eyes in a face white with sleep. Like a tiara, a sequined sleeping mask was shoved to the top of her grizzled head. 'Vot? Vot? You got a problem, you kin't sleep?'

'Jack's in danger.' Teddy, grabbing her suitcases, dodged past George Bache's mother.

'Jeck?' Dinah gasped, covering her dismayed mouth with her fine-boned, trembling hand. 'Oh, dot poor Mr Eagels. *Vay is mir!* Vot kind denger?'

'My kind,' answered Teddy, swinging down the Bache's dim hallway. 'If I don't find somewhere to hole up, and quick – I'll kill him.'

George Bache, at the other end of the hallway, long, lanky, stooped and yawning, said, 'Let her in, Ma, or we're accessories.'

Teddy snapped her eyes open. It was pitch black. The jump-start left her heart somewhere down around her knees. And her reason ducking for cover. Where in the hell was she? All she knew was her lips were cracked, her nose had plugged up, and she was lying on her stomach in a hard bed with no blankets. Groping, she found a lamp. With a very dim bulb. Now she only knew that she was in a big bed in a little room, and that the rest of the furniture was enormous. There was a chest of drawers from the dark ages, a wardrobe that leaned to the left, and a dressing table made out of what looked like cement. What there wasn't, was air. Teddy peeked over the edge of the bed. The blankets were in a heap on the floor – and she was enveloped in a pair of what had originally been George Bache's pyjamas. Ah, George. Teddy was in the Dakota. And the pyjamas were hers – now.

By four in the morning, George had bundled his nervous mother back to bed with her hot water bottle, by four thirty Teddy had vented her anger and frustration over Jack and Connie to a patient Bache, by five she'd convinced herself, if not him, that Dancing Joe mixed up with the murderous Tom Channing was a hot story if there ever was one, and by seven she'd won the pyjamas, a copy of December 1926's *Black Mask* magazine – an issue with a Jack Eagels story in it – and sixty-three bucks off George at poker.

Teddy rolled out of bed and crawled to a curtain of heavy brown swag. Behind that must be the window. Getting to her feet and yanking at a worn velvet rope, Teddy got a look at a dirty brick air shaft – and across it, a window just like hers. Small, curtained, and closed. She also learned what time it was. Daytime. A weak sun had found its way into the shaft and was huddled in there, stunned.

Desperate to breathe better air, Teddy tugged at the window. Nothing doing. She almost lost a nail trying. The frame was nailed to the sill. At Dinah's insistence, no doubt. It came from living in the Dakota Building. But with the curtains pulled back, the room was brighter. Not much brighter – but at least she could see. Her suitcase was at the foot of the bed; Groat's suitcase in the closet. She hadn't packed much but she'd packed well. Grabbing her toothbrush, Teddy went looking for the bathroom.

Scrubbed, brushed, red hair and white teeth shining, Teddy found George lying on the living room couch and the air tainted with the faint, peppery smell of fresh newsprint. Both the couch and George were covered in New York's Sunday papers. Holding the *Trident*'s entertainment section with one hand, he was picking invisible lint off his trousers with the other. His mother, held up by whalebone and perched like a mantis, sat in an armchair across the coffee table from her son, crocheting or knitting or, well – she was doing some kind of sewing.

'Morning,' said Teddy.

'You vant tea?' said Dinah, holding up an empty cup. 'Or maybe a piece *Schwarzwälder Kirschtorte*? I got da cream.'

'Which paper?' said George.

A fat copy of the Sunday edition of the *Trident*, minus the section George had, glowered at her from the table.

'Tea, please. I think for now I'll skip the cake. Gimme the *Graphic*, George. I could use a laugh.' Teddy ignored the *Trident*, but she couldn't miss the picture. Lit with horror, dramatically framed, a grim shot of a bundled misshape, pathetic in death. Gene Goetz was very good at dead bodies. Or the headline – a four-column banner – JIMMY'S PRIZE COP MURDERED IN HARLEM. And slugged, *Police Baffled, No Real Leads To Killer. Mayor Walker In Shock And Seclusion. Police Commissioner Whalen Promises Swift Action.* The by-line? Jack Eagels's, of course.

Teddy plumped herself on the couch next to George. Compared to the sofa in Teddy's apartment, this one was luxury. Covered in soft loden green wool, buried under rainbowed pillows – Dinah had embroidered every last one of them – the couch didn't chafe, it didn't itch, and if Jack ever had to sleep on it, even he could have stretched out full-length. Jack didn't deserve a couch like this. Teddy stuck two pillows under her head, shoved one behind her back, kicked off her shoes, and curled her long trousered legs beneath her. The *Graphic*'s whole front page was devoted to a clever composite photo (what the *Graphic* called a 'cosmograph') of a hood – closely resembling Mr Owney Madden – standing over a dying body in a dark alley. The halo around Bernie – and the sneer on the hood's face – was a work of art, which, of course, was what it was. Above, the headline spat, WHITE COP CROAKS IN COONTOWN! Teddy chose another paper. But first she checked Ed Sullivan's sports column; no mention of anything odd about the Joe Bright/Max Schuldner fight. In the *American*, Runyon actually panned Dancing Joe, said his winning was a fluke. Slamming the paper back on the pile, Teddy swore under her breath. Fluke? Jesus! How would Runyon like a fluke stuffed down his throat?

George's mother bent forward and poured Teddy a cup of tea from a real samovar. The cup matched the saucer and the chair matched the couch – including the pillows. Dinah Bache had busy fingers. The tableau of couch and armchairs, curved coffee table between, was in the middle of the Baches' vast grey, silver and green living room overlooking Central Park. George and his mother were collectors. Silver pillboxes, Tiffany enamel, stamps, sheet music and theatre programmes, dime novels, musical instruments, and lethal weapons – George had a passion for pistols. Each gun oiled and loaded. What George collected was always the real thing. The guns, postage stamps, pillboxes, the penny whistles, ocarinas, bassoons, were stuffed in drawers, arranged on shelves, slipped between the pages of tooled leather albums, hidden in armoires, or under glass-topped tables. It was a room of hoarded secrets.

Aloud, George was reading his own review of *Meteor*, an out-of-town theatre effort in three acts preparing for Broadway: *'The Lunts are stars of the first magnitude – but the play? Not quite a meteor – more like a falling rock.'* Along with Brooks Atkinson of the *Times*, Burns Mantle over at Connie's hated *Daily News*, and Alexander Woollcott writing for the *New Yorker*, George Bache's presence in an aisle seat terrified producers – his written word could close a show on opening night. Eyes lowered, suffused with a suffocating love for her clever son, her *Shayner Yid*, Dinah went on purling one, knitting two.

And Teddy – Teddy looked at the funny papers, curling her toes with pleasure. It was heaven at the Baches'; it was *Mispoche* – family. It was what a Sunday morning ought to be like, what a Sunday morning *was* like, until Jack came along. Before Jack, Teddy had spent all her Sundays playing poker with George and Dinah. Dinah Bache, seventy-two years old, a one-time vaudeville trooper, and a past expert at mahjong, was the only person in New York who could beat her. Not always, but often. On a good day, Dinah was a whizz. On a bad day, she cheated.

But for the last two and a half years, Teddy'd spent her Sundays with Jack. That is, she'd spent them with Jack if he was home – or she was. When they were both home together, there had been times. Oh! There'd been some times all right. Teddy, remembering midnight in Sally's elevator, flushed, missed the point of Moon Mullins, turned the page for the Gumps. The comic strip Gumps were fighting again, a daily battle that was both funny and – deadly. Which only reminded her of Jack all over again; Eagels in his undershorts, ducking as his own shoe flew by his curly head. Teddy dug through the stack of Sundays until she found another Hearst paper – Willie owned three in New York City alone. Sunday was the only day George allowed any one of them in his home; on Sunday, *Krazy Kat* and *Ignatz* danced the dance of the brick on Coconino County's enchanted *mesa*.

George yawned, turned to the crossword puzzle, stared at it for a moment – then began filling in the answers at speed. Over the top of the funnies, Teddy watched him do it. She loved the *Trident*'s critic like a gun collector loves a hair-triggered gun – carefully. George Bache looked like the devil – if the devil looked like a demented moose. Tall, thin, ugly, walking with a slouch, horn-rimmed glasses stuck on his big nose, way past forty and Jewish – George had an air of impenetrable gloom and eyes the colour of raw bacon. He also had a head full of black hair, a thick sprouting shelf that drove Connie Mezinger crazy. Quiet, kind, thoughtful, unassuming; but when goaded, George could come up with one-liners that stopped people in their tracks. But only the people who deserved it. He was a truly witty man.

George was also phobic. He had a horror of human contact – for fear of catching something (though he'd risk it if the human was female), of travel – he got physically sick if he left the island of Manhattan, of failure – a critic himself, any criticism aimed towards him could wound. This was all thanks to Dinah. She'd spent his childhood and her motherhood teaching him to be afraid of things, including life. Dinah not only sewed, she reaped. George was in worse shape than Jack. But he was her best friend, her pal. Before – and after – Eagels. She tapped him on the knee.

'You've noticed, Georgie? No mention of Channing in a single paper.'

'I've noticed.'

'It's my story.'

'To each his own.'

Dinah rose in a slow rustle of brown taffeta and a racket of stays. 'I been only vaitink you should vake up, Teddy. Vot you vant for lunch? Zoup?'

'Lunch!'

'Sure, lunch.'

'George! What time is it?'

George glanced at a French clock under its shiny glass dome in full view on the mantle. 'Almost four. I don't know about Dinah but I've been up for hours. Two of them, to be exact.'

Teddy swallowed her tea in one gulp. 'Four! Holy Macaroni! I thought I was waiting for breakfast. Can I use your phone? I've got to hide seventy-five thousand bucks today.'

Teddy was off the couch – and dialling, before the Baches could say yes or no – or, *how* much?

Dinah blinked. 'Vot you t'ink, George? She's stayink for lunch?'

'Only if she's buying,' is what George said. What he didn't say, though he wanted to, Lord, did he want to, was, 'I hope so. I hope she's staying for lunch and for dinner and forever.' George's love for Teddy O'Rourke was like a wound that had formed a very thin scab. At the age of forty-six, he'd learned not to pick. But over poker she'd told him she'd left Jack. Teddy could be flighty, she could be whimsical, impractical and unrealistic – but she said what she meant and meant what she said. What did all this mean for George? That Jack Eagels, the first guy he'd ever liked who wasn't New York City born and bred, a naturally charming man, and a fellow he just plain felt good about (he could number those on the fingers of one hand), *that* man was going to lose the lady George loved? A tune he'd heard for the first time only an hour ago on Dinah's radio tuned up in his mind; 'Happy Days Are Here Again'. Should he help things along? The way they were behaving – pigheaded the both of them, it wouldn't be difficult. A wise man, George put it out of his head. As for the story Teddy thought she'd found – who knew? Maybe there was something to it, and then again, maybe there wasn't. George put his money on O'Rourke.

Teddy wasn't stupid. She caught a yellow cab to Grand Central Station as soon as she hit Central Park West. Stashing the suitcase in the station was a much safer bet than sitting around the *Trident* with it while she waited to find out what she was supposed to do next. As usual, Albert Groat hadn't impressed her, but his talk of unsavoury visitors had.

Entering the main concourse of the new Grand Central, its powder-blue dome painted with half the constellations of the zodiac going the wrong way, its dusty, sun-shafted air echoing with the name of a high-shouldered, west-bound train, Teddy went looking for her favourite redcap. She found the old black man under an enormous clock that ticked off time over the hot hubbub of restless New Yorkers, charmed him into storing the case in a special lock-up behind the parcel room and giving her a receipt.

Below her feet, deep underground, rumbled the hiss and rattle of locomotives, the squeal of great metal wheels on metal tracks. Tucking the receipt away, Teddy's thoughts slipped into the rhythm of the wheels.

Less than twenty-four hours earlier, Jack met the incoming train from New Haven. The one Teddy O'Rourke came home on. Teddy stepped onto the lower level platform with hope, praying that the last miserable, quarrelsome weeks she'd spent with Jack Eagels would be over, whatever was wrong with them settled. She'd see Jack's face under its crumpled hat just as she'd seen it for the very first time – on 21st May, 1927, the day she'd been sent by Mezinger to meet the train from Chicago, Connie yelling, 'Get your fucking tail over there, O'Rourke. I don't care if you're Miss America, beat it! I need someone to meet that goddamn Indian and I can't spare a reporter!'

Teddy O'Rourke went in fury to greet Connie's imported Chicago hotshot. In fury, stood tapping her feet on the grey and red carpet of platform 34, a carpet woven with the name of the Twentieth Century Limited.

At that same moment, wheels propped behind chocks in a muddy field out on Long Island, the Spirit of St Louis was waiting for the wind to die, the rain to stop, the fog to clear. Charles Lindburgh paced beside his spidery crate, blowing on his hands, dreaming of Paris. Connie had got it into his head: Jack Eagels, his best reporter from the old days on the *Chicago Globe*, would cover what would turn out to be the story of the decade. Before Eagels could find a hotel, see his new typewriter at the *Trident*, before he could brush his teeth, he'd be standing in the mud watching Lindy pace. What went on in Connie's head usually happened outside it. Teddy O'Rourke met Jack Eagels's train.

They hated each other on sight. Argued over Connie's orders as they strode down the platform, sniped in a taxi as it crossed the Fifty-ninth Street Bridge, bickered over Blackwell's Island, sulked the width of the borough of Queens, started all over again as the exasperated cabbie threw them out at Roosevelt Field. Stood bitching in the wet cold mud of dawn, and froze while a bashful

American kid with a cowlick got ready to make America proud of itself again.

Shamed after so many years of Capone; after the steaming revelations of Teapot Dome, ever more murky, ever juicier with scandal; after all those tears over the sudden death of its president, Warren G. Harding, enough tears and enough money to build Warren a Memorial Tomb in his old hometown, Marion, Ohio – then finding itself too embarrassed by Teapot Dome to dedicate the thing; after the intolerant violence of Attorney-General Palmer's great witch-hunt and red-scare which was leading to the lengthy killing of Sacco and Vanzetti, America needed this gangling, dopey boy.

Standing side by side, gradually drawing nearer for warmth, two strangers settled for common sense, and huddled together to keep from freezing solid. And when The Spirit of St Louis bumped uphill across the sodden field, when it lurched and shuddered, made a heart-stopping pass at the sky, Jack Eagels had thrown his hat in the air, grabbed Teddy O'Rourke in his arms, swung her round and round, laughing – the love of one man against the odds in his brown Indian eyes. Teddy, clinging to this big, curly-haired madman, fell in love with the cocky sonofabitch from Chicago. It was the intelligence in this stranger's face, the light in his eyes, that got to her, made her flush from the bottom up.

At the age of twenty-seven, Teddy suddenly knew what sexy was. Not a tight butt or a jutting chin or being bent backwards over sand in a sheik's gauzy tent. Brains and talent and laughter, that was sexy. After Lindy was up and away, she took Jack on a tour of her town, a spiky city of swank and mayhem. The two things he most wanted to see: Park Row where Archy the cockroach banged typewriter keys with his head, and – any place where he could buy a Harley Davidson motorcycle. By then, the *Trident* was on the streets, its headline shouted from street corners, Jack Eagels's headline, his first goose up the backside of New York: LINDY LEAPS FOR THE SKY!

Teddy smiled at the memory, a fleet and fading effort that never made it past her lips. Fading – like their relationship. No, not fading. Eagels and O'Rourke couldn't fade. They could only implode.

Over by the Lexington Avenue exit she spotted a candy counter. Behind the counter was a guy with a nose like an eggplant.

'An envelope and a stamp, please. What the hell, I'm starving. Gimme a Hershey bar too. Two Hershey bars.'

Teddy wrote her own name and the Baches' address on the envelope, slipped in the redcap's receipt, sealed it – then licked the stamp.

The guy at the counter ogled her. 'Wish't that was me.'

'Excuse me?'

'The stamp. Right now, I wish't I was a little stamp.'

On her life, Teddy couldn't think of a response. Is this what having a bad time with Jack Eagels had done to her? She'd lost her snappy come-backs. So she stared the guy down. It didn't work. The candy man licked his lips and panted. He won. And savoured the winning until a little fellow with five kids, a wife, a mother-in-law, and a large dog getting dragged on a leash, doggy nails squealing along the station's tawny marble floor, saved her. The candy man forgot about stamps.

Next to the candy counter was a newsstand. Like the Baches' coffee table, the stand bristled with rabid headlines. Commander Byrd and his snow shoes messing up Antarctica, Jimmy Walker's sudden shyness when the subject was the murder of Bernie McTaggart, Henry Ford cutting the price of his new Model A by up to two hundred bucks, everyone assuring everyone else that prosperity was unhurt, that the market was beginning to steady.

Munching Pennsylvania chocolate for lunch, Teddy couldn't help it; she had to look. Wiping Wall Street's crash and the belated trial of George McManus for the killing of Arnold Rothstein the year before off the front pages, McTaggart made them all.

Surrounded by press, New York's District Attorney, Isidor Force Tuttle III, had his grim, harried mug on everybody's front page; according to Izzy the third, New York City was outraged. Quickly scanning competing copy, Teddy gathered that Police Lieutenant Bernt McTaggart had been, as of yesterday, Mayor James Walker's handpicked crusader for the public good, personally responsible for the arrest and conviction of some of the city's most interesting and wanted citizens. Bernie had been young and noble and honest and white and brimming with good deeds. Reading all this at a skim, Teddy thought the way they were going Cawley McTaggart's late son would be a myth by Wednesday, canonized by Christmas – and Gentleman Jim might be out on his butt by the end of November. Sims Caffey of the *World* was blatting for an all-out investigation; Fiorello La Guardia bloomed.

The papers were calling it a 'revenge' killing by persons unknown. But any New Yorker worth his cheesecake would know who these 'persons unknown' would have to be – mobsters like Madden, Dutch Schultz, Meyer Lansky, Lucky Luciano danced daily through the press. But today? Where was the intriguing Tom Channing today? Not a printed whisper. Teddy smiled a happy little smile.

Then gave up the struggle to avoid Jack and bought a two-cent copy of the *Trident*. The one she'd ignored at the Baches'. There was no snubbing a man who wrote for a major paper, not if a girl was curious – and literate. So she read Eagels's copy. Damn him. Jack Eagels wrote with a vital economy that could jolt with its perceptions. His stuff was so good: tidy, punchy, fair, salt and peppered with unique observations and unusual turns of phrase, recognizable as Jack's even without the by-line. And more than that, informed. Eagels knew his stuff: the whys, wherefores, why nots and how comes of it all. Except this time. This time it was Teddy's turn. Still, confronted only with Jack's talent, he was a hard man to get rid of. But she was working on it.

Freckled nose in the paper, snap-brimmed hat slanting down over one grey eye, her long grey coat flapping in the wind, Teddy wandered through Grand Central's Lexington Avenue exit. Across the street, bristling with stainless steel hubcaps, hood ornaments and workmen on the last girders seventy storeys straight up, the almost complete Chrysler Building blocked out Manhattan's cloudy November sky. Belittling the steep slender Chanin, the Chrysler – shimmering in Deco, sixteen feet higher than the Woolworth Building – was now the tallest building in the world. Though, a few blocks south, they were tearing down the old Waldorf to make way for something even taller: the Empire State Building. For Teddy, nothing diminished the Chrysler. Below it strolled theatre people anonymous in loud colours, grizzled old men hawking fruit and phlegm, pigeons dodging feet, a young, almost feminine, kid with a huge hooked nose leaning on the blunted black nose of a parked Studebaker sedan, another, who might have been his twin, opening the door on the driver's side, Sunday couples – holding hands, laughing, whispering in the wind. A gritty impish wind that smelled of kisses and coal. No one was jumping out of windows.

Reading, Teddy walked right up the back of a young man and his girl.

'God, I'm sorry.'

'Gee, that's all right, lady,' said the boy. 'Where these shoes come from, there's plenty more.'

The girl dimpled up at her man. 'You said it, Charlie. Lots of plenty.'

Fresh out of Yale or Harvard or a mail-order business school, the boy wore a patterned brown muffler wrapped up to his ears, a heavy muskrat coat dropping to the top of his shoes, slicked back his hair straight from the forehead. The girl, with a sweep of caramel yellow feathers cupping her pretty painted face, wore a slender blue coat tight at the knees and a small, head-hugging hat. Gripping the arm of her fellow with slim nocturnal fingers, she batted huge, gay nineteen-twenty-nine eyes at Teddy. Hot eyes that saw nothing and understood everything and forgot it all in the morning. The boy saw everything and understood nothing.

With plenty, thought Teddy, who cared? Wasn't everyone saying the Market would recover? Hadn't it all happened before? Prices yo-yo'd for months; little crashes in June and December of '28, again in March of '29. It was a bear now, prices still dropping day after day – but things would be bully again. America was still on a roll.

Roll on, Wall Street. Bring that easy money back.

The boy and the girl linked arms, skipped away up Lexington like children, laughing at plenty.

Watching them go, Teddy somehow knew they were the last of their breed. How she knew, she'd never be able to say.

Back in her paper, Teddy was reading between Jack's lines. Jack didn't say Bernie was noble and honest and a hell of a swell guy, but he did say he was young and white and handpicked by Beau James. More than any other paper, Jack went into McTaggart's background. Teddy knew Jack. And she knew what he was hinting at. Something wasn't quite kosher about Bernt McTaggart.

The first sharp shivers of drizzle went down the back of Teddy's neck. She dumped the *Trident* in a trash can, dropped the envelope with its receipt into a mailbox, and hopped on a crowded Forty-second Street bus. Then hung by a swaying strap under cute little ads for Odo-ro-no and Listerine – *Oh no! Halitosis!* – and a picture of Jack Dempsey raising his arm in victory as he said, '*No ducking O'Rourke's SNAPBACK in your daily* Trident –

it's a knock-out! The best back page in New York!' Teddy kept her eyes on her shoes. It hadn't been easy earning that ad; it took years. How long would it take to get a splash across the front page? Worse than how long was 'how'. What should she do now? Bag Channing? Ask him if he killed Bernie, and when he said, 'Sure, lady. What's it to you?', ask him why? Jack knew every big-time crook in town from Madden to Schultz: a lot of them owed him favours. Who owed her anything? Dixie Fiske? Dixie'd promised her an exclusive. So where was he? If she couldn't find Dixie, how would she find Tom Channing?

Teddy went back to the Thorp building. To sit by her phone. To hear from Fiske or Joe Bright. To fuss and fidget and – hopefully – to find out what the hell was going on before Jack did. To make sure that Kathleen 'Teddy' O'Rourke, somewhat son of Bluff and famed New York sports writer, wasn't making a damn fool of herself.

Stepping out of Sally's elevator onto the seventeenth floor, Teddy had her first inspiration. Her story was where Dancing Joe was, where Fiske was. A reporter didn't sit by a phone and wait to be found; a reporter went looking. And the only person this reporter could find for certain was Miss Jesse Bean, which was surely a good start.

Connie Mezinger, eating what he was always eating, an Eskimo Pie on a stick, caught up with her as she was stabbing with a rigid thumb at the elevator 'down' button.

'You! I been looking for you! Stop right there, O'Rourke!'

The busy sports department went quiet. Behind Connie stood Hype Hohenloe, the pixie-like sports editor, aside from Connie, Teddy's immediate boss. Behind the shy, self-effacing Hype stood someone Teddy had never seen before. Whoever he was, he looked nine feet tall. Dressed like a New Yorker but holding himself like a Texan, he was sort of down home and folksy. To Teddy, the guy could have worn white linen spats, carried a slim black cane with a silver knob, and tap danced up Fifth Avenue in shiny, patent leather shoes, he'd still look like he used cowflop for kindling. Besides that, he was chewing a toothpick. The rangy stranger, elfin Hype Hohenloe, and bald-as-a-boccie-ball Mezinger: bunched together they looked like a circus sideshow. Even more, Connie enraged reminded Teddy of 'Patsy Pig', the *Trident*'s homegrown cartoon strip. No one knew if Patsy was male or female; everyone knew whatever mess Patsy was in, was Patsy's fault.

Because he only came up to her chin, Connie had to stand on tiptoe to wave his Eskimo Pie in her face. 'Where the hell do you think you're going?'

Teddy looked right over the ice cream and his bald head. 'Down.'

'Down?'

'And out. I'm on a story.'

'What story?'

'*My* story.'

The elevator arrived, opening its steel doors on a surprised Sally. Sally, the elevator boy, who looked fourteen but was probably sixty, dressed like a hurdy-gurdy man's monkey; he wore his red hat down low over one jaunty eye. 'That was quick,' he said, gawping.

Connie caught at Teddy's arm. 'Say, you can't go anywhere. There's a hockey game at the Garden.'

Jerking her arm out of his clutch, Teddy got in the elevator. 'When you know the score, Mezinger, put it in big type and sign my name. All the way to the bottom, Sally.'

'You're not doing this, O'Rourke!' yelled Connie, making his point with the Eskimo Pie, spraying the open elevator and Teddy with melting ice cream. Sally ducked. 'Get out of that fucking elevator.'

'Yes, I am doing this, Mezinger!' yelled Teddy.

'You do it and this guy here – ' Connie's slapped the tall man in the stomach ' – Hopper is it?'

Flipping the toothpick from one side of his mouth to the other, the tall man gave Teddy a lazy amused smile. 'That's right, Harve Hopper.'

Teddy was amazed. The stranger drawled. And he had charm when he did it. Though somewhere along life's curious cattle trail someone had once been immune; they'd broken his nose.

'Hopper here', bawled Connie, 'is going to have to cover the story if you don't, and if Hopper covers the story – '

By now, Connie and Teddy had caught the attention of the entire sports department. All – except the mild-mannered Hohenloe; Hype had cut and run – staring without pretending they were doing something else. With a front row seat, Sally leaned against the bank of buttons to keep the elevator where it was.

Teddy glared at grinning Sally. 'Down, dammit.'

Sally pushed the button.

Teddy's elevator doors closed on the fat man's stick, squishing what was left of the Eskimo Pie. But not what was left of his sentence, ' – *you can kiss this job bye-bye!*'

In Sally's chrome and wood-panelled elevator, furiously struggling with her coat, Teddy whizzed down to Thorp's Art Deco lobby. Teddy hated elevators. Standing around in a tiny vibrating box, suspended hundreds of feet above God's good cement, putting her trust in the handiwork of man was nothing short of nuts. But she did it almost every day of her life. Spending each horrifying moment of the ride in prayer. Teddy O'Rourke had no church; elevators were the closest she got to God.

Sally kept his mouth shut until they got to the lobby. As the doors opened on freedom, he gave Teddy a brisk salute. 'From all the hurry, you got a hot ticket, right, Miss O?'

Teddy looked at Sally, who'd worked for the *Trident* as long as she had. Sally was the only person in the world who knew she was terrified in elevators. 'I hope so, Sally. Say a little prayer in there for me.'

Once out through the great bronze doors of Thorp's megalith, Teddy, now low and breathless on a New York City sidewalk, paused. Where to now? To find Jesse Bean, of course. But Jesse wouldn't be where she could be found until the slummers came to Harlem, and that wasn't until late in the evening.

Meanwhile, it was just after five. She'd had a cup of Dinah's tea and two Hershey Bars. Teddy was starving. She headed for Lindy's.

On Forty-fourth Street the temperature was dropping. New York's little heat wave, its false Indian summer, was over.

CD and Arch Durata pulled the small Studebaker sedan away from the kerb, followed the good looking redhead in slacks – both dreaming of pussy in the sky.

6

Blues for the Dying

With five hours' sleep, Jack Eagels's Sunday was one damn thing after another. Revving the Harley between police precincts uptown and down, in and out of dry back rooms and wet weather, trying to fit together the pieces of Bernt McTaggart's life – and death.

Every police station he set foot in – from West Forty-seventh Street up to 123rd – was hauling in suspects. Observed from dead centre in a senseless brawl, Jack figured the way they were going they'd have New York City behind bars by midnight. At the Harlem station, milling with petulant thugs and pushy police, he got a nice, off-the-cuff quote from the chief: 'If we scare 'em enough, somebody's got to crack.'

By noon, Jack got himself out of his last station for the day. By three, he'd met chorus girls from Forty-second Street to Fifty-ninth. A cattle call of sorrowful ladies. Jack was impressed. Alive and randy, Bernie McTaggart certainly made himself noticeable in old New York. Dead, he had the city spinning on the seat of its pants. Dead, he drove Connie rabid. And why not? Walker's cop knifed in an alley behind the Cotton Club just as Mayor Jimmy was facing up to the challenge of La Guardia (a nightclubbing mayor who might soon be as out of a job as Bernie), a crusading cop cut down in his prime, a young white hope slaughtered in the course of his solemn duty – Jesus! The murder of Police Lieutenant McTaggart was a gift to the papers; it had everything: bootlegging crooks, the scintillating lure of black Harlem, politics. It made a story that would burn up the front page for weeks.

Saying goodbye to his sixth weeping chorine, a sweet little chubby-knee'd blonde from George White's Scandals, Jack pulled up the collar of his leather jacket, pulled down his hat, swung his leg over his Harley, coughed for the umpteenth time. The temperature was dropping, the air blurred with a fine Scotch mist. Teddy was right. He needed his coat. The thought of buying a new one pissed him off. He'd had that greatcoat since Paris, 1916, winning it from a proper little prig of an English gentleman-officer. Maybe sometime during the long day ahead he'd find it. He must have left the thing somewhere. As it was, he'd hardly had time to eat. Three cups of automat coffee and a pack of Luckies wasn't eating. Taking a coin out of his pocket, he flipped it. Heads: *Vogue* magazine; Tails: go talk to Bernie McTaggart. Or look for Walker. The mayor was one of the items on Jack's list of things to do. In between cops and chorus girls – and now, on the turn of a dime, a corpse.

Bernt had been whisked from his slab in a Harlem morgue and was now resting in the Gold Room of Frank Campbell's Funeral Church on Broadway and Sixty-sixth Street.

In his time, Jack'd seen the inside of Frank's 'church' more than a sane man would want to. New York's élite usually made it their last call. Three years back, Valentino had launched the most hysterical Campbell's funeral of all. For Bernie, there was no hysteria. Just a lot of sombre cops and Tammany men keeping watch over a fallen comrade.

Smothered under floral tributes, no expense spared, McTaggart's heavy, silver-bronze casket lay on a classy marble catafalque. Under the cloying smell of flowers was a faint tinge of formaldehyde. Hat in hand out of deference, cigarette stuck in the corner of his mouth,

Jack bent over the open coffin. Accidental ash fell on the pale grey face of the dead man, landing in an eye socket. Jack checked out his audience. Fuck a duck, what if some cop in mourning saw that? A callous reporter would find himself sprawled all over Sixty-sixth Street. Bending closer, Jack blew the ash off. Then, slipping a finger under Bernie's dress collar and pulling gently, Jack peeked inside. Someone at Campbell's did a pretty good job. The wound was sewn neatly together, daubed with some kind of goo. But if Bernie had ever possessed an Adam's apple, it wasn't there now. Whoever stuck him had done a better job than Campbell's. Jack took his finger away.

To take a break from cops and chorus girls, Jack Eagels was studying the face of a dead man. Bernt McTaggart, born twenty-eight years before as a Tammany princeling, was the only son of the politician Cawley McTaggart. A renegade Scot in a borough of Irishmen, Cawley McTaggart was a Tammany patriarch, a sachem of sachems. It was his voice, still powerful, that was shouting the loudest for justice, his wounded bray of a voice galvanizing the press. The police, in fear and anger, were galvanizing themselves.

Cawley McTaggart's son didn't look as if he were sleeping; he looked dead. Very dead and very good-looking in an unremarkable way: no pimples, no wens, no warts, balanced of chin and brow – marred merely by a small bump on the bridge of the nose, large pores clogged with mortician's pancake and rouge, a mole on the upper lip. So dead, even his hair had died – lying lank across the unthinking skull. Whatever light once danced across this favoured cop's bland map, now it was as empty of character as a fashion sketch.

Dropping his butt in an urn where it went out with a *zzzt*, Jack stared at the man who knew the answers to all his questions – once. Who were you, Bernt McTaggart?

Who did you think you were going to be? And whose side were you on? Yours? So what in the fuck were you doing down behind the Cotton Club in a cold wet alley? Taking a leak? A kick-back? Waiting for another dumb broad? Did she come? If not, who did? *Who* did this to you, fella? Someone you knew? Someone in the pale and speeding car? A yellow car? Bernie said nothing. Just lay there in his best dress suit with a stiff little smile on his waxen face – Jack's cigarette ash tucked in his ear.

Jack's gaze travelled down the body until he got to the hands. Arms crossed at thin wrists, McTaggart's hands rested on the lapels of his dark suit like one of those carved, medieval knights – or like the slim white hands of a weeping angel. Jimmy Walker's angel. Bernie's fingernails were perfect ovals, their pale-blue moons peeking from the skin like – like what? Jack suddenly caught on. Bernt's nails were manicured. What's a cop need a manicure for? A cop with a maiden's hands? A young man with the hands of a woman. The hands of a woman?

Jack closed his eyes and a nimbus of fiery red hair formed in his mind. And another pair of hands. Softer, stronger hands, hands with purpose and a random scattering of faint freckles, Teddy's hands. One arm, tinted with the ruby blush of Roseland, flung across her face – her sleeping pulse tapping beneath the tender white skin on the upturned wrist. Somehow, from somewhere, a fist of depression reached down and gripped Jack's heart. He'd put last night out of his mind, tried to pretend it hadn't happened. Or, if it had, it was nothing. Another of Red's tantrums. It would blow over. Jack couldn't fool himself. It wasn't going to blow over. His redhead had left him. Drifting, dreaming, pained by thoughts of Teddy, Jack coughed. A long, dry, hacking cough that tore at his throat.

He was back in Campbell's again and the air was loud with the smell of white lilies, beeswax, and things that were once alive, and then were dead, and now were nothing at all.

Around four o'clock in the afternoon, Jack found Mayor Jimmy over a game of poker in a private backroom at Billy LaHiff's many-storeyed Tavern on West Forty-eighth. LaHiff's was frequented by every newsman in New York. Also by actors, Flo Ziegfeld's girls, Earl Carroll's 'virgins in cellophane', Shubert's dancers, cuties from the Scandals, Billy Minsky's burlesque Queens, artists' models, Broadway producers, Tin Pan Alley songwriters, top-dollar whores, politicos, boxers, ballplayers, and millionaire whisky runners. It was where Billy hung a portrait of every president America had ever endured, where booze was drunk from thick white coffee cups, and Jack hung out drinking it if he wasn't doing anything else. It was where Teddy hung out with him. Until last night.

Though his fellow card-players had their coats off and their sleeves rolled up, Gentleman Jim sat immaculate in jacket and waistcoat, an empty bottle of champagne at his elbow, a cigarette holder tucked between his teeth, and a handful of cards that couldn't lose. He hoped. Of the other three faces around the table – Roberts, his tall, glacial English valet, the scented and moustachio'd police commissioner, Grover A. Whalen, and a songwriter named McGruder – McGruder thought the same.

With a nine-high straight, the guy from Tin Pan Alley was right. Jimmy was wrong and McGruder raked in another pot. Which was what they were all doing when Jack Eagels walked in.

As gracious and – even in thick-soled shoes – as short as ever, Jimmy rose from the card table, extending his hand, thin cheeks so flushed they seemed rouged. 'Jack! You are precisely the one reporter I am most pleased to see.'

Jack shook everybody's hand, swung a chair around and sat in it. 'You're a hard man to find, Jim.'

Walker waved his cigarette holder. 'With what's going on, you think I'd be down at City Hall like a sitting duck? Your fellow newsmen have laid siege to the building.'

'So you hide in LaHiff's?'

'Last place they'd think of looking,' said Whalen.

Jimmy smiled at his police commissioner. 'I am here to help out a fellow songwriter. See how much I've helped him already.' Jack saw; most of the chips were on McGruder's side of the table. 'Grover is assisting me, giving of his time on this busy Sunday.'

Jack looked at Whalen. Mayors come and mayors go, even mayors of New York; but Grover Whalen was on his way to becoming a Manhattan institution. Before Walker made him his commissioner of police, before Walker was even mayor, Grover had already made a career of greeting bigshots passing through the city, had reduced welcoming to a science, raised it to an art. Now in 1929, and top cop, Whalen hadn't changed at all.

'Grover likes parades,' said Jimmy. 'A murder doesn't have quite the same effect on him.'

'Speak for yourself, Jim,' said Whalen.

'Deal you in, Jack?'

'Sure. From the top, please.'

'You flatter me.' Dealing ten fast cards – two for each player, one down and one up, Jimmy beamed. 'Now – go on, get it off your chest. Ask the questions you came to ask.'

'What other question would I have for a mayor and a commissioner of police? Who killed Bernt McTaggart – and why?' Jack looked at his hole card. He had a seven of hearts face up, the one face down was a two of diamonds. Nothing there – just like his day. The highest card showing was Jimmy's queen of spades.

Jimmy's bet. He threw in twenty bucks and sighed, 'I don't know who killed him. I don't even know why. Nobody on my side does.'

'Not many left of those,' said Grover.

The tip of Jimmy's pointed nose quivered. 'Excuse me, Commish? You were muttering?'

'If somebody doesn't get you out of this mess, and soon, likely your own cops'll shoot you.'

'You know something I don't know?'

'Damn papers are riling up the men, causing 'em to wonder what you know about all this, especially that bastard on the *World*. Sonofabitch never did like you, Jim.'

'Ah, you mean Sims Caffey. But that was only a minor tiff over a showgirl we both fancied. Still, we have the *Trident*, don't we, Jack?'

Jack scratched his jaw with the seven of hearts. 'I'm waiting till the dust clears.'

Jimmy smiled. 'Good fellow. Toots!'

Toots Shor, LaHiff's huge-bodied head waiter, poking his head round the door, hollered, 'What!'

'Brandy here, for everybody.'

'Brandy, sir?' said the stiff-necked Roberts. 'For lunch?'

Jimmy looked at his valet, said, 'Roberts, you're right – as usual,' thought for a second, called, 'Toots, make that more champagne!' then lowered his cards. 'Bernt's death is more than the brutal slaying of a New York policeman, Jack; overnight it's become a national cause. Governor Roosevelt sends his doleful rumblings down from Albany, from Tammany Hall Cawley McTaggart wails amid a chorus of raised fists, Hoover percolates in Washington, but guess who beats on a kettle drum?'

'I'd bet on La Guardia.'

'And you'd win. I'm in a helluva fix. The Little Flower is busy making political moonshine out of this sad and sordid mess, especially since it happened up in Harlem on

Owney Madden's doorstep. As a politician, boy, would I love to yell too, but – I can't. You know, Jack, conceited as it sounds, I still have to admit I often like being mayor.' Jimmy waited as the table covered his opening bet, then flipped out another round of cards. 'Part of me even wants to *stay* mayor. But everyone knows Owney is, and remains, a friend of mine. Madden's not such a bad fellow, and if he is, he isn't around me. I've persuaded him to pay for many an orphan or widow – most of which were none of his doing. Still, I suppose a mayor ought not to know such dubious citizens, which would make life rather dull. Perhaps I could learn to hide them under my skirts as all my colleagues do. What do you think, Jack?'

'You want my advice?' said Grover. 'You'll wear a dress from now on.'

'Thank you, Grover. Still, everyone also knows I loved Bernie like a son, Jack, that Grover and I were planning a fine future for him. We were under the quaint, outmoded impression that young Bernt McTaggart was that rare thing, an honest policeman. Weren't we, Mr Whalen?'

Grover grunted. 'Well, you were.'

In surprise, Jimmy paused for a second. 'Weren't you?'

'Jim, you like everybody.'

'I saw a lot of good in Bernie.'

'Only by squinting.'

Jimmy laughed. 'Grover, I've never for a minute regretted asking you to be my commish of police. I just wanted you to know that.'

'Thanks.'

'You're welcome – where was I? Ah yes, as Grover has just pointed out, Bernie made a patsy out of at least me. But that does not detract from the tragedy of his death. If you think I'm affected, you ought to see Cawley. His whole *block* is draped in black.' Jimmy raised his sweet blue eyes. 'I can see none of this is news to you, Jack.'

'No.'

'I thought not. Before dying, Bernt McTaggart, God rest his soul, was busy throwing away a fine future for a fine present. Pity. Perhaps it was a mistake to introduce him to some of my less savoury friends.'

Jack didn't really know if Jimmy loved Bernie, but the odds were, he had. In Gentleman Jim there was no malice, no intolerance, no sham. Jack couldn't help loving Walker. No one who knew Jim could. But he had a weakness, a soft spot he shared with that dear departed boob of a president, Warren Gamaliel Harding. Walker trusted his friends. Jack, hoping it wasn't his weakness as well, trusted Walker. Whatever Bernie was up to before his date with cement in a Harlem alley, he hadn't shared it with Jim.

Another round of cards, another of bets: as he lay his hard-earned money down, Jack said, 'His fine present seems to have included every feather-shaking female in New York.'

Jimmy smiled a smile of such sad fondness, Jack wondered who they were really talking about.

In Walker lived the spirit of the times; Jim was a New Yorker's New Yorker. Gay, happy-go-lucky Beau James, a rare moth in the flame of the burning twenties. Elected mayor in 1925, the year the *New Yorker* was born, he was state legislator and state senator before that – and a damn good one. But in his heart of hearts, Jimmy was a Tin Pan Alley man, a writer of popular songs. If he would change places with anyone, it must be the Gershwins – both George *and* Ira. But now the twenties were turning – and what would the thirties bring? To Jack, the onrushing thirties were beginning to look like a West Virginia miner's wife; grim, haggard, life and love and laughter sucked dry. Unless she suddenly lifted her tattered skirts, showed legs in silk stockings, whipped out a pot of rouge, what would the new decade bring to a gorgeous gadabout like Gentleman

Jimmy? The thought saddened Jack – the future didn't look good.

'Who am I, of all people,' Jimmy was saying, 'to deny a man his pleasures – or the pain they bring him? As in all of us, from Al Smith to poor dead Bernie to yours truly, there's a little bit of good, a little bit of bad, and a lot of day-to-day just making do.'

'Say, what's happening here?' said McGruder. 'We playing poker, Walker, or are we playing harps?'

'Excuse me, of course we're playing poker.' Jimmy flipped out the last cards, bets went down, and Jack, as he knew he would all along, lost.

Bluffing on nothing took nerve. The best he'd ever seen was Bluff O'Rourke riding a pair of threes into a thirty thousand dollar win. The next best: Teddy O'Rourke pushing Herbert Bayard Swope up to – damn! Jack grit his teeth. Where was that crazy redhead? What was she doing? Missing him? Coming to her senses? Coming home – ?

'Speaking of pleasures, Jack – how is Teddy?'

Jack jumped. Could the guy read minds? 'Teddy?'

Jimmy leaned back, stuffing a new cigarette into his holder. 'Last night at the Garden, she stood out as a pearl does among swine. Present company included, of course. And does she know her stuff! I'll say she does. Strictly between you and me, I cleared over a thousand on her Dancing Joe. My God, a girl like that – what am I saying? – there isn't another girl like that. Nothing beats an ace. From my heart, I envy you, Jack.'

Jack stood up, rocking the table. 'See you around, fellas. If it matters, Jim, *I'll* be voting for you.'

Walker flushed. 'But Bernie won't, will he?'

Jack stopped, turned back. 'Damn it all, Jim, who killed him?'

He'd asked Jimmy, but Grover answered. 'Whoever it was, it was probably a friend of Jim's. I hope that friend sorts himself out soon. The elections are nine days from now. Jim and I can't play poker at Billy's forever.'

'Speak for yourself, Grover,' said Beau James.

Jack rode his Harley to *Vogue*. Found the magazine in a state of shock. Its owner and publisher, Condé Nast, believing the market would spiral up in glory forever, invested everything he had, including his magazine – and lost it all. A mere sixteen million bucks. But that couldn't stop *Vogue*. *Vogue* and its editor, a severe old dame with lilac hair, went sedately on with the December issue.

At *Vogue*, Jack found Marlo. In a room hectic with flesh, he was looking at women with bold eyes and long necks, women juicy with youth and healthy self-regard. Women who chatted and languished and yawned and bitched. Jack could have reached out and pinched one. He certainly gave it some thought but in the end kept his hands to himself. He had enough trouble already.

Marlo was the bitch in blue. Her eyebrows were painted on, her black hair was twisted back into a Spanish dancer's bun, up close she snapped perfect flamboyant teeth, smelled like a mothball and smoked like a prude – pinching her cigarette between thumb and forefinger. Pointing the hot end at Jack, she told him to get lost. Who cared about a dead cop, anyway? Who spoke to lowlife like newspaper reporters? Especially about scum like Bernie, the double-dealing heel.

In his time, Jack Eagels had been pushed around by a lot of tough cookies. Take O'Rourke, for instance. This one couldn't be tougher. Besides, who could get rattled by a rude broad who'd borrowed a pair of Joan Crawford's eyebrows? Jack stood his ground – and found out who Lulu was. Aside, that is, from a man-stealing little gold-digger. But that was only Marlo's opinion. Lulu Leroy was a bit player in one

111

of those curious plays written by a phenomenon called Mae West.

Meanwhile, if he didn't eat something, his stomach would start singing the Gut Bucket Blues.

Everybody ate cheesecake at Lindy's; everyone walked through his doors. Leo Lindemann, once a busboy, now the proud proprietor of one of New York's landmarks, fed and watered Broadway, plastered his windows with photos of his favourite customers. Al Jolson, Jimmy Durante, Ruth Etting and her hood of a husband Moe Synder (also known as the Gimp), Groucho, Chico, Harpo and Zeppo Marx, and every mobster in town who'd let someone get close enough to take his picture. The night Arnold Rothstein began his two days' worth of dying in the Polyclinic from a terminal case of lead, he'd been sitting in his favourite booth at Lindy's. Lindy told Arnold he had a phone call – the phone call lured Broadway's biggest high-roller to the Park Central Hotel. For such a reputed 'brain', a friend of Tammany Hall, the owner of two gambling dens in the West Forties and a classy casino up in Saratoga Springs, for the man who'd fixed the 1919 World Series, Arnold died stupid. People who owed him money could get an awesome case of the jitters if they were slow on repayments, but money Rothstein owed made a permanent home in his pockets. So much for the brain. Arnold was a victim of Broadway's Golden Rule: 'Do it unto others before they do it unto you.' And he didn't get his picture in Lindy's window.

But down in a corner by the front door, between a potted Boston Fern with dusty fronds and a ceramic poodle, was a photo of Jack Eagels and Teddy O'Rourke. At the time it was taken they were smiling. Like the date of Arnold Rothstein's death, that photo was exactly one year old.

The moment Jack walked in, Lindy bustled up and winked.

112

'She's in a back booth.'

'Who's in a back booth?'

'Fooey to you. Who you trying to kid?'

'Lindy, knock it off. Who?'

'Who do you think? Teddy, who else? Why's everybody so grouchy tonight?'

'Red's here?'

'All alone. If you ask me, she looks down in the dumps. What you been doing to her?'

'Me!'

'Again, who else? Go make her feel better. I'll bring you a pork chop.'

'I don't want a pork chop. I want clam chowder.'

'Tonight, we gotta lotta pork chops. You'll eat one. Back booth on the right, the one you two always sit in. And Jack?'

'What?'

'You don't make her feel good, cook'll spit on your chop.'

'I don't want a chop.'

'You don't know what you want.'

That got to Jack. Lindy was almost right. He *didn't* know what he wanted, that is – not until his visit to Bernie McTaggart, biding no time at all on his cold slab in Campbell's. Since then, well hell, maybe he'd wised up a little. At least enough to know one thing anyway. He wanted Teddy O'Rourke.

Sitting with her chin propped on her hand, a cigarette burning unsmoked in an ashtray, a bowl of soup untouched on the table, Teddy had her eyes closed. From ten feet away, Jack had a sudden case of the jitters. What if she opened those gorgeous, gold-flecked grey eyes, took one look at him – and screamed? Well, what if she did? No risk, no gain.

Eagels slipped into the booth and coughed.

'Jack!'

'Red?'

'What are you doing here?'

'Looking at you.'

'Go away. I'm busy.'

'Not what it looked like to me.'

'I don't care what it looked like to you.'

'Yes, you do.'

'No, I don't.'

'*Yes* – you do. I'm the best thing you ever had.'

'And the worst.'

'That's not the point.'

'That *is* the point.'

'You're an idiot, Red. Nothing comes without faults.'

'Faults? With your faults, we'd lose California.'

'Cute – and glib. But that's why I love you.'

'You don't know what love is.'

'OK, I'll bite. What's love?'

'For one thing, Jack, loving is, it's like, love means – '

Eagels took Teddy's cigarette out of the ashtray and smoked it. 'Well, that's settled anyway.'

Sidling up to their booth, Lindy held two sizzling pork chops on a huge plate over Jack's head.

'Teddy, you feeling better?'

'Better, Lindy?'

'When you come in, you look sorta sad.'

At that, Jack sat back, smiling one of his rumpled smiles – the kind Teddy usually found endearing.

Teddy sat forward; she wanted to slap his rumpled smile off his rumpled face. 'Why so smug, Jack? You think this has something to do with you?'

'It occurs.'

'Does it also occur that I hate your smug guts? You want to know what love means? Love means asking if the person you love is getting anywhere with the scoop of the year.'

'The scoop of the year? *What* scoop of the year?'

'Love also means knowing what the person you love is talking about.'

114

Jack ground out Teddy's cigarette. 'I'll tell you what love means, O'Rourke. Love means getting stuck with a fruitcake.'

Lindy, looking from one to other, walked away saying, 'These chops, Jack – cook says they're not finished yet.'

'Dammit, Lindy, I don't want pork chops! I want what Teddy has – a bowl of chowder.'

'Cook don't like spitting in chowder. It sinks.'

Jack gave up on banter. Banter was getting him nowhere. Maybe sincerity had a chance? But first, he needed food. 'You want your soup, Red?'

'Yes.'

'God*damn* sonofabitch! Will someone give me one thing I want! Just one!'

'Name it, redman.'

'Gimme that soup!'

'It's yours.'

Teddy stood up, scooped up her bowl of chowder –

And Jack ducked.

'Don't be stupid, Jack Eagels. One of us here is all grown up. One of us does not throw food.'

'Thank God. I'm so hungry I could eat something *you* cooked.'

'One pours it.'

Tipping the bowl over Jack's head, Teddy walked out of Lindy's.

7

Falling Up

Jack Eagels now knew what he wanted and it wasn't Teddy O'Rourke. He wanted a blonde, a brunette, an albino – anything but a goddamned redhead.

When Teddy walked out on him, Lindy took pity. Not much, but enough to have his wife Clara lead Jack into the kitchen, rub his big curly head with a towel, feed him hot soup. From Clara Lindemann, Jack finally got his New England clam chowder – in a bowl.

After that, he went back to 1600 Broadway, bathed, changed his clothes, and drank two quick shots of bourbon. The bourbon calmed him down, but not as much as punching Teddy's pillow until the bedroom was downy with swans' feathers. Jack threw himself on the bed and lay there, staring at the ceiling.

Connie Mezinger knew what he was talking about when he said redheads were unreliable. Unreliable? They were fucking unstable. Not to mention gaga. The scoop of the year? She was working on a scoop? What kind of a scoop did sports writers pick up? Dempsey wasn't eating his Wheaties?

If O'Rourke wanted a scoop – Jack Eagels would show her a scoop. Next time he saw her, he'd show her a shovel.

In his head, Jack boxed with Teddy, *biff, biff, pow*, stunning her with a beauty of a left jab, *baff, biff* – boxed until he began coughing. Dry spasms that wracked his body, curled him up on the bed.

Goddamn feathers.

He must be allergic.

*   *   *

After stunning New York with a stage show called *Sex* – a name that summed the piece down to a T – getting tossed in the Jefferson Market Women's slammer for a full-frontal assault on public decency, and tossed out again (every shake of her hip, every flip, delicious remark, every trip in a Black Maria buried under the bliss of headlines), Mae West went on to knock 'em dead on Broadway with *Diamond Lil*. In *Lil*, Mae toned down her act a couple of watts, from a klieg light to a flood; there was less to shock and outrage, more to laugh along with.

Lil was about a tasteful ring of white slavers. Madams, hookers, dope pushers, junkies, shoplifters and uptown slumming parties did all the singing and dancing; Mae, of course, was Diamond Lil. For herself, she wrote all the show-stopping one-liners; cracks she tossed off like cherry bombs in an old folks' home.

West won Eagels's heart when George Bache, who'd given Lil a rave review in the *Trident*, told Jack how she'd described it. '*Diamond Lil* is like *Hamlet*, honey, but funnier.'

Now *Lil* was playing the Subway Circuit. A kind of a whistle-stop run through Brooklyn, Queens, Yonkers, New Rochelle, Flushing, Great Neck, the Bronx; anywhere there was a theatre with enough seats, enough nerve, and the local yahoos and yo-yos could get there by subway.

On his Harley, Jack caught up with the show between its matinée and evening performances at Far Rockaway, a town on a spit of land like the bony lower jaw of Brooklyn. Squeezed between Jamaica Bay and the Atlantic Ocean, Far Rockaway was nothing much more than a string of family homes braving the sea. Following directions from the Rockaway Shuttle, Jack rode bent by a wind straight in from a tour of the tossing Atlantic, a tough wind bearing exotic bits of foreign vegetation, spare feathers, idle sand from Rockaway Beach, and the chill

117

breath of onrushing winter. The wind had teeth; it bit through his leather jacket, nibbled his neck, chewed at his nose. Once off his bike, Eagels kept chasing his hat but the rest of him felt better. He had a pocketful of aspirin and, to wash them down, a flask of bonded bourbon on his hip.

When the toothsome wind shoved Eagels through the door of the Far Rockaway playhouse, his press card meant nothing. In fact, it meant even less than that.

One look at the *Trident*'s embossing and the guy patrolling the lobby in a long coat stiff with gold epaulettes snarled, 'Beat it, buddy.' With an expression set in shellac and a pair of bristling sideburns, he slapped a handy billyclub against his beefy thigh to make his point.

Jack stood his ground, watching him do it, loving the sideburns.

Placing the butt of the club against Jack's breastbone, the doorman pushed. 'Miss West is up to here with noosepapers.' 'Up to here' meant hitting himself on the forehead with his free hand.

So Jack went back out into the biting wind, snuck down a side alley, and slipped through the stage door when no one was looking. Took a wrong turn in the dark, and wound up doing a walk-on as an extra in a whorehouse.

Striding out between the show curtain and the red velvet traveller, Jack stopped dead. Not six feet away, Mae was in the middle of auditioning a new leading man. Caught in the lights, frozen by his blunder, Jack Eagels felt like he'd been dropped through a trap-door in the floor of time. He was ten again, going on twenty. Wearing braces and kneepants, dragging his drunken old man out of a Wyoming whorehouse. Over the shoulder of the hopeful young actor, the infamous Miss West was staring right at him.

Mae was tiny. My God, was she small. Jack could have picked her up with one hand and thrown her across the footlights. Squeezed into Lillian Russell drag – a tube of

118

tabernacle pink satin, an explosion of lobster-red ostrich feathers at both ends – her hair bone-white cotton candy and her eyes an intense blue, Mae looked like old Charlie Eagels's favourite lay.

Gaping and dizzy, Jack was suddenly, overwhelmingly, homesick. Huck Finn's life wasn't so bad, not at this distance.

Planting her hand on her ample hip, placing her forefinger, heavy with flashing stones, to her lips, Mae looked him first up, then down. The skin on the back of Jack's neck stirred. 'Ummmm,' she finally said in a slow, adenoidal drawl. It was the lewdest thing he'd ever heard. 'Another good one. Back off, honey, an' wait your turn. I ain't through with this one yet.'

A quick exit stage left and Jack was back where he didn't belong. On the right side of the footlights looking for another of Bernie's women.

Dotted around the darkened auditorium, watching the stage where West led another young man through her paces, were unneeded actors and actresses. With Mae hogging the brilliant box of light, scaring the pants off a trembling novice, this was obviously not their scene. Picking an empty aisle seat at the back of the house, Jack sat himself down next to a plump blonde. From the way she was dressed he figured she was meant to be a fallen woman. Short of the word 'whore' branded on her soft shoulder, there wasn't much more she could do for the part.

Eagels began politely enough. 'Excuse me, but – '

That's as far as he got.

The blonde turned her head and hissed, 'Scatter, wouldja?'

Before he'd really settled in, Jack was up again, backing into the aisle. Calling even more attention to himself wasn't what he had in mind.

'Don't mean to scare ya, sweetie,' she said, lowering her voice from a hiss to a wheeze and adjusting a buckle in her corset, 'but I'm hoping to attract me some company and from the look of your assets it sure as heck ain't you.'

Crouched down, not sure whether he'd just been dismissed for the state of his face or his pocket, Jack kept his voice to a whisper. 'Do me a favour before I go? Is there a Lulu LeRoy here?'

'Sure, two rows back of the orchestra pit, the little brunette. Now buzz off before you scare away my dinner.'

Lulu sat alone, bare feet propped up on the back of the seat in front of her, buffing her bitten nails. There was no single empty aisle seat next to Lulu LeRoy; she sat right in the middle of the row.

Moving along it as quietly as he could, Jack settled down next to her.

'Hi,' he said.

No pause in the buffing, Lulu turned, stared at him with candid hazel eyes, eyes like a clear, fresh-water pond in the middle of a deep wood, smiled, and said, 'Hi,' right back.

Jack smiled. Lulu smiled. And that was it. Jack liked her. She reminded him of Clara Bow. If Clara ever popped a black wig on her curly red head.

Lulu LeRoy was small and pert and probably Jewish. To Jack, she looked fragile and tender and sweet. She might turn out as fragile as a steel girder, as tender as a pork chop in a beanery, as sweet as she wanted to be when she had to. And that name – Lulu LeRoy! A coin minted in pure lead – but damn, she looked the business now. The exact opposite of Teddy O'Rourke. He'd be willing to bet his last nickel that what Lulu appeared to be, she was. Childlike, saucy, happy in a selfishness that thinks of itself as giving, sexy as only a kid in a woman's body can be, fragile, tender, sweet – and delightfully stupid. It did his heart good.

Mae must have noticed all this as well. Lulu was dressed as an innocent, like one of Charlie Chaplin's leading ladies – a lamb to the slaughter. A little straw hat on her head, a cluster of faded violets on the hat, white fingerless gloves on her small hands, buttoned to her dimpled chin in a plain wool dress the colour of thick pea soup that finished off with a white Peter Pan collar, and those bare feet. Lulu's feet were small and pink, the bones delicate. The baby toes curled over, tucked themselves under the foot like shy, newborn mice. Those toes charmed the hell out of Eagels.

He took off his hat. Things were finally going his way. He'd been fed, he hadn't coughed for two hours, and Lulu LeRoy wasn't a redhead.

Lulu, still looking at him, still smiling, her buffer poised over her glossy pink nails, said, 'I'm sure I haven't seen you before. You come for the part?' She had a voice with bubbles in it.

'No, I've come to see you.'

'Gosh,' said Lulu, shaking her shining cap of bobbed black hair under its sad little hat. 'Me! Why me?'

'Because a little blackbird told me you were with Bernt McTaggart two hours before she tripped over his body behind the Cotton Club.'

Lulu stared at Eagels, drowned autumn leaf eyes growing wider. Now was when he lost her – or got what he came for. Jack held his breath.

Lulu shivered, said slowly, 'Jeepers, you're right! Of course I was! Think of that!' Then plunged ahead. 'I was wondering if anybody was going to ask me any questions – but until you, nobody's asked me a thing. You a policeman?'

Jack showed her his press card. To Lulu LeRoy, it meant something. She held it in her small, half-gloved hand, turning it over to read the back, saying, 'Gee, a reporter,' with a satisfying wonder.

121

Jack decided it was time to live up to his reputation. In his jacket pocket was his flask and in the flask was bourbon. Tipping back just enough to make his eyes water, then wiping the lip, he offered a pull to Lulu. Lulu took the tiniest sip. Wrinkling her Jewish nose, a nose a little too large to be cute but small enough to stay out of her way, saying, 'Mae doesn't like us to drink in the theatre but – heck, just a little. Who could it hurt?' Then she belted back enough to make Jack gasp.

With that, Jack now knew three things: one important, one that might be, and one he'd have to think about. First. Lulu had something to tell him about Bernt McTaggart. Second. She liked her liquor. Third. He liked her even more.

After a day of sharing a dead man's life, Jack Eagels finally had something in common with Bernie. Because of the skirt-chasing cop, Jack had talked to a lot of women, a lot of women he could imagine himself playing pitcher in a game of night baseball with, but of them all – short, tall, blonde, brunette, quick on the uptake or slow in the corners, he *liked* Lulu LeRoy. Which made him rethink Bernie for a moment. Why would a guy like McTaggart hustle a little girl like this? Little Lulu broke the mould. In comparison to the rest, she was sweet, innocent – not Bernie's style at all.

'Bernie – ,' sighed Lulu, handing back Jack's flask, 'I recognized his picture straight away from the papers. Bernt McTaggart, they said his name was. Though me, I called him Bernie Miller. I didn't know about the police lieutenant part either. That was a new one on me. When I read that, I thought, jeepers, so that's why no one's come looking to ask me questions. I expect I don't much matter, not really – him being a policeman and all and me being just a girl he came calling on. I expect he got killed all in the line of duty, don't you?'

Jack thought about that. Anything was possible – so he shrugged. Hoping he looked sympathetic, grateful

122

for men who died for the good of the city of New York.

Lulu picked up her buffer again. 'But really, it's too bad about his being dead. He was a swell spender. Lookit this!' Lulu rattled a watch on her delicate wrist. To Eagels, it looked like solid gold.

'Tiffany's! He gave me that only last week. Wednesday? I'm sure it was Wednesday. Even with the terrible crash and all and people getting ruined left, right and centre. He was always giving me things – even though I thought he was a real squirt.'

Jack sat up. Had he heard right? 'You thought he was what?'

'A squirt, a creep, you know – creepy. Maybe I shouldn't say that about a real policeman – and also a person who's dead.'

'No, say what you like – be my guest.'

'Really?'

'Honest Injun.'

Lulu took a deep breath – and let rip. 'You know, Bernie wasn't, well, Bernie wasn't much, not really – only what you'd call a smart guy on the make. Even though he was awful good-looking. I have to say that for him. Girls like me, girls in shows and such, meet guys like that all the time. But this one, well, he wouldn't give up, you know? Cold shoulders didn't mean a thing to him. Kept coming back, following the show everywhere we played. Always bragging about who he knew, things like that. But I said to myself: Lulu LeRoy, if he wants to give, you don't mind getting. He'd just give it to some other girl if you turned him down.' Lulu lowered her pond-water eyes. Under the stage make-up a flush spread over her cheeks – turning a peach into an apricot. 'Of course, what I mean is, gee – I mean I don't mind giving so long as it ain't even-steven. You understand?'

Jack took pity on her. He patted the back of her hand.

Which made her smile again. 'Guess what my mother told me?'

'Haven't a clue.'

'She said, it's OK to fall, Gilda Tannenbaum – that's my real name, by the way, but I thought Lulu LeRoy would look better, you know, better in lights – anyway, she said, falling's OK, it's movement, ain't it? But a girl must be sure to fall *up*. And when and if she ever lets herself go, you know what I mean – ?'

Jack nodded. He knew what she meant. By now, he not only liked this refreshing, talkative kid – what was she? twenty-four? twenty-five? – he was half in love with her. Well, perhaps love was a little too strong. Real love for Jack was a boxing match with Teddy O'Rourke. But love in some sense wasn't totally wrong; Jack Eagels was a man, and men were what men were – led astray, confused and betrayed by the husky perfume of casual sex. Besides, dammit, by her own stupid choice, Teddy was past – Lulu was present. He knew he would love running his tongue down this child's belly, that is, if she'd ever shut up. Lulu was what George Bache would call a delighted idiot.

' – well, Marie – that's my mother; she lives in Florida – Marie says when a girl lets herself go, it better be serious. Say! I just remembered! You're from a newspaper. Is it the *Mirror*? Walter Winchell's my favourite.'

'No.'

'Too bad. So what paper is it?'

'The *Trident*. Remember the card I showed you?'

'Oh, yeah, that one. Kinda serious, isn't it?'

The *Trident*'s name disappointed Lulu. Jack watched her change. Emotions ran across this girl's face like sunlight and shade across a field of Wyoming wheat. Disappointing people never bothered him, but this time it mattered, not much, but it mattered. Why? Because it was like letting down a child? No time to wonder why;

like paper in the wind, Lulu rushed on. 'You know, I used to read the *Graphic* but since Walter's moved to the *Mirror*, well heck, I have to read the *Mirror* now. But the *Graphic*'s still my favourite, more pictures, more stuff about the movies.'

Eagels knew why millions read Bernarr Macfadden's *Daily Graphic*; it had all the excitement of a gruesome accident. One glance and you couldn't take your eyes off it. Connie called it, 'That scrap, that filth, that – ', sputtered, wheezed, and let it go at that.

'Speaking of the movies, I let Bernie pay for my lessons at the Empire – I take tap dancing. Me, I'm double-jointed. You want to see?'

'Here?'

'Sure.'

Jack looked up at the stage. Mae had the oiled novice at her feet, feeding him what looked like a raw turkey leg. 'Better not.'

Lulu caught on. 'Too bad. But you're right. Miss West would holler at me.' She turned in her seat and a wave of glossy narcissus scent washed over Jack. 'Though, personally I've been getting awful tired of this game, the theatre, you know. Miss West is awful nice and I learn lots from her, you know, tempo and stuff like that, and her show, well, her show is really something, but – you staying to see it?'

'I might.' Jack was a talker but Lulu could talk for the World Series. If he could just listen long enough, she was bound to say something important. Those were the odds – at least, those were the usual odds. So he added, 'It's not a bad idea.'

At that moment, Lulu was taking her first long, *silent* look at the man she was talking to. Big, with a headful of lovely dark curls, the face sort of beaten-up, but nice – a lopsided smile, that was nice too, good teeth, though maybe he was kind of old. But there was a light in his dark brown eyes she didn't often see. Not in the eyes of the men she'd met: actors, stage-door johnnies, hoods, ponces, half queer, half in love with themselves. If she could tell her mother about the light in this man's eyes, her mother might ask, 'And what was behind the light, Irena Josepha? A house, a home, children, safety?' And Lulu would have answered, 'Whatever it is, mother, it's *mine*.'

'Say, you're awful cute. You want me to tell you what I'd really like? More than maybe getting in the movies? What I'd really like is a nice guy with a real job and a couple of kids and a little white house with green shutters and some cabbage around the door. So you can see, right off, I knew Bernie Miller didn't want anything like that. But even if he did, I wasn't interested. As I said before, he was a squirt. Say, you want to know about Bernie the way I knew about Bernie, try any theatre from Columbus Circle to Forty-second Street.'

'I have, only I went the other way,' said Eagels, but thinking about a guy with a real job and a couple of kids and a house with cabbage round the door. Cabbage?

'There, see? You know already. There isn't, I guess I should say, there wasn't, a girl in New York he didn't try himself out on. Young, old, black, white, pretty as a picture, ugly as one of Cinderella's sisters – he didn't care. And the papers saying he was some kind of an undercover cop – jeepers! Only time you could call him that, far as I knew, was when he could argue a girl back to his place. Actually, me, I thought he was some kind of gangster.'

Ah, sighed Jack. Here it comes. 'Gangster?' One word was all he allowed himself. When an express train passes, a reporter would be a fool to wave flags.

'Well, sure. What else was I to think? That's all the people he knew. That's why he took me back to Rockaway so early Saturday night. He said he had to see one of them – that, and I had a show to do, of course.'

126

Up on the stage, Mae was pushing her way out of a clinch with the eager actor, a steaming connection that had gone on almost as long as Lulu could talk.

'Not bad, not bad,' growled Mae, patting her hair into place. 'In fact, you could be almost as sensational as me.'

Lulu touched Jack's shoulder. Her touch was as light as a leaf falling into his hand. 'Good thing you didn't really come here for that part. I don't think Miss West is going to see anyone else.'

And then, for a moment, there was silence. On the stage and from Lulu. Jack used it to think about that touch. So light, yet he'd felt it as a hot wire singing from his solar plexus to his knees. To his knees? Was that a lie, or was that a lie? *That* was a lie. Jack felt the heat stop right where he'd decided to live – at the tip of his cock. When had he decided that? When he'd seen the girls at *Vogue* – the ones with the impossibly long necks? Or when Teddy poured clam chowder over his head? He was sure it was the soup.

'You know,' said Lulu, breaking into his breakthrough, 'I'm sitting here thinking about why Bernie bothered chasing me for so long, taking me to places like clubs up in Harlem and introducing me to guys he knew like he really *knew* me, you know what I mean. And you know, I'll bet it's because I thought he was a creep. Guys are funny like that, aren't they? You don't want 'em, they want you. You want 'em, you don't see 'em for dust. Ain't life a pip?' Lulu's little face suddenly had an idea. 'And then again, maybe I was part of one of his undercover jobs? What do you think? Oh, gosh!' Lulu tapped Eagels with her nail buffer. 'There's two of the guys Bernie knew right now. The short one who looks like Mayor Jimmy is always sniffing around; he owns most of Miss West's show. I seen Bernie around them both plenty. Don't they make you nervous? They sure make me nervous. Especially that tall blond guy with Mr

Madden. I know him, you know, well, so to speak – in a funny kind of way is what I mean, kind of.'

Jack slowly turned. Thank God he was in the middle of the aisle, that Mae had the stage so lit up the rest of the theatre was in gloom, that Lulu hadn't screamed out a greeting to a gunman she kind of knew in a funny sort of way.

Lulu was right; except for the weak chin, Owney Madden *did* look like Gentleman Jim. Jack had never noticed before. Matching Madden step for step was Tom Channing. In the footlights, Channing's hair shone like gold foil. Sleek as an Egyptian cat, he looked like a man who knew women. He also looked like a smug sonofabitch.

What in the world was Tom Channing doing in Far Rockaway with Madden?

As Owney and Tom passed the plump peroxide blonde she gave them a sick little smile. Neither one of them noticed. If they noticed Jack Eagels, neither one of them showed it.

Sitting beside Lulu LeRoy, Jack made up his mind. He was staying to see a show in Far Rockaway. For more reasons than one.

8

Mama Be Blue

After chowder with Jack, Teddy changed her clothes at the Dakota.

From slacks and her old grey hat into the only evening gown she'd ever owned – bought for the grand opening of the casino in the park with Gentleman Jimmy Walker – but never worn. At the very last minute, Connie sent Jack off on a murder, gruesome and strange enough to make him go. Because the lady at Gramercy Park had been beaten to death with a baseball bat, Teddy went too.

The gown was black velvet, its skirt a long slim drop to the floor, its sleeves bloused to the elbow then tight to the wrist, its shoulders wide and dropped, its neckline plunging. A small black velvet cloche hid her red giveaway hair; large brilliants tucked over her right ear matched those clustered on the velvet between her freckled breasts. Unaccustomed kohl around her wide grey eyes, Teddy threw a raincoat over her black gown, hooked an umbrella over her arm.

On only one side, the velvet was cut to the thigh. Working a story, a reporter uses all the skills she has. Ignored under slacks, barely thought of for months at a time, were two of her finest assets. Coyly called limbs only a decade ago, Teddy had great legs.

George stood in the doorway eating a fat kosher pickle on a fork.

'I assume you know what you're doing?'

'Dixie Fiske promised me an exclusive.'

'An exclusive what?'

'That's what I intend to find out. He hasn't come to me – I'll go to him.'

'Dressed like that?'

'Before I can find Fiske, I have to find Jesse Bean.'

'I love the name. Anyone I know?'

'Dancing Joe's woman. She works up in Harlem at the Savoy.'

'I'm afraid to ask as what.'

'As a dancer, George. Just a girl who dances for a living.'

'Thank God for that. You want company?'

'Oh, wonderful. Me on the strong, Jewish arm of a tall, lanky drama critic. Nobody would notice us at all.'

'So what if they did? Who are *you*? Deadeye Dick?'

'George, get the fuck out of my way. I'm going alone.'

'No Jack either?'

'Fuck Jack.'

'Teddy, is it Connie who's done this?'

'Done what?'

'Given you such a foul mouth?'

'Hell, no, I got my foul mouth all on my own.'

'That's all right then. Go alone – and may your mouth go with you.'

Teddy O'Rourke climbed out of a dark green hole in the ground to find the skies over Harlem bruised with more damn rain. Rain that fell so hard it bounced a foot back up from the pavement.

Hiding in an uptown hole at the corner of Lenox and 135th Street, O'Rourke was far over the borders of the land of topsy-turvy, a city within a city. Black was white – and she was the odd girl out. Though Runyon's slick Broadway types were all here – the sharpies and pimps, pickpockets and snowbirds, the flashy gamblers and con men, his ladies of the night – they were heightened, out-of-whack, horses of another colour. The feet skimming over the pavement, hands gripping the chill metal rail of the subway kiosk, the faces under umbrellas moving past in the rain, rich, poor, mean, blessed faces – etched with the virtue of vice or vice-versa – were shaded and shadowed and black.

None of the mighty white voices that boomed and brayed through New York – Cornelius Mezinger's, Bernarr Macfadden's, William Randolph Hearst's, Herbert Bayard Swope's, not even the pervasive Walter Winchell's – were listened to north of 110th Street, New York's Mason-Dixon line. Like the passing faces, the mastheads were black: the *Amsterdam News*, *New York Age*, the *Dunbar News*, *Negro World*.

Before today, the closest she'd come to the bittersweet mecca of black America was tagging along after Jack Eagels on one of his frequent jazz-seeking jags. Whenever he could – if he wasn't covering something for the *Trident* or sitting in on a game of poker at the Algonquin or writing one of his stories – Jack took her up to 133rd Street. From dusk to dawn, they'd dash from speak to smoky speak, down into dingy cellar joints, through the backrooms of crowded cafés, anywhere – just as long as there was stride music playing. Jack sat at the bar, hat down low over his face, nursing a bourbon, his brown eyes full of black jazz.

Knowing only the sweet, happy faces of jazzmen, Teddy assumed Harlem was happy. Negroes danced on the rooftops, conjured up the Devil's music, sang the blues. The stuff of SNAPBACK – major league baseball, collegiate football, the guys who rode high on the necks of fast, skinny-legged horses – was as white as the paper it was printed on. What Teddy didn't know about Harlem could fill the *Trident*'s Sunday editions for a month. What she didn't know made what she thought she was doing easy. What she thought she was doing was dropping in on Jesse Bean, who would take her to Dancing Joe, who would in turn dig up Dixie Fiske – and Dixie would come up with the promised exclusive. A story which had everything to do with a front page gangster, and something to do with Bernt McTaggart. After all – and straight from the horse's mouth – hadn't Tom said, *'I'll take care of Bernie'*?

With the rain still bucketing down, Teddy scanned the front page of the *Age*. Bernt McTaggart was below the fold, one column. Up here, Bernie the cop's death was a passing shiver.

But, my God, O'Rourke, look at this! Dancing Joe Bright's come-from-behind victory over Max Schuldner was a three-column headline.

With a smile Connie would have choked on, she quickly read the copy. The unknown writer spoke of Bright as if he were the second coming. She knew it! Whatever that sleek little fat man down on Forty-fourth Street or that skunk of an Indian she'd left dripping at Lindy's might think, up here in Harlem Dancing Joe was a hero. The *Tattler*, a pictorial weekly of 'Society, Theatricals, and Sports', gave him a two-page spread. Grinning, Teddy bought both, ripped the articles from each, folded them, tucked them in her purse, checked on the rain – now a lazy drizzle – popped out of her hole and ran.

Teddy O'Rourke saw the bright lights of the Savoy Ballroom from three blocks away; she heard it from two. All down the length of night-time Lenox, jazz floated in a jumpy blue haze. Out in Harlem's wet air, the lights of her cabarets and theatres, nightclubs and sporting houses shimmied and shook.

Still a football field away from the Savoy, a wide tongue of dirty street spray – sent sideways by a speeding butter-yellow Cord with whitewalls – just missed drenching her from hat to shoe.

The neon sign running over the Savoy's canopy danced with musical notes, boasting in rain-miraged blue: 'The World's Most Beautiful Ballroom'. Under the canopy and out of the wet, Teddy shook herself down like a spaniel and looked the place over. It wasn't all that beautiful from the outside. In a building that ran a full city block from 141st to 142nd Streets, the Savoy itself was up on the second floor. On the first was Madame Walker's beauty salon, a grocery store still open and doing good business, Melba's Frock Shoppe, closed and dark, and a pharmacy having a sale on Ex-Lax. Running down the length of the building, north and south side, was the name of Chick Webb's Chicks, the Savoy's resident band. And on a dripping canvas banner it said: '*Tonight!* **MAMA B. BLUE!**'

In front of the Cotton Club, a block further north on Lenox, limousines were setting down a chattering, excited throng of slumming whites. With a fresh death on its doorstep, the Cotton was jumping.

Here where Teddy stood, long, lean, loam-coloured bodies descended from the back seats of long, lean cars. Girls in warm brown skin, talking low and laughing, tripped by Teddy and up the marble staircase to the Savoy. Girls in their changing hats – fashion turning now as the decade turned – brown girls in black shoes, ebony girls in ivory courts, copper girls in red satin pumps, high yellow girls, feathered and furred and fey, clinging to the arms of straight-backed men with slicked-down hair and brazen, boulevardier eyes.

As they passed, Teddy imagined them naked and unashamed, sons and daughters of the Congo striding through dense and dappled leaves. The image baulked at the edge of her mind. These people weren't exotic primitives. These people were the sons and daughters of New York's haughty Harlem, sophisticated children of an intoxicated age. Finding themselves suddenly nude, they'd do what any New Yorker would do. Dive for the nearest bush.

Slipping on the pavement's fermented leaves – late autumn leaves lashed into sodden drifts by the storm – dodging the cover charge, Teddy charmed her way past the doorman and entered the Savoy, following the laughing girls of colour.

Once past the hat-check girl, the Savoy might not be the most beautiful ballroom in the world but Teddy decided it had to be the goddamn biggest. Two thousand people were jumping around in here, a thousand more clicking glasses of Prohibition booze at tiny, packed tables.

The whole thing was orange and blue – not her favourite combination; it had two bandstands, a disappearing stage at one end, a couple of bars and, just for fun, a soda fountain. The burnished floor under her feet shivered and shook like Park Avenue when a train pulled out of Grand Central Station. Under a cut-glass chandelier big enough for an Alva T. Thorp lobby, she was almost immediately flattened by a herd of hoofers, all heading her way in high-stepping glee. Teddy kept moving.

Coming to a stop at one of the bars and ordering anything, she got a 'Top and Bottom'. Whatever the guy put in her glass was pink and smelled like dimestore cologne. Teddy took a tentative sip.

'My God! What's this?'

The barman grinned at her. 'Gin and wine, Little Eva. Drink it down, it'll send you sailing.'

'Oh yum.'

Taking her revolting pink sludge along, O'Rourke went to work. How was she supposed to find Dancing Joe's Jesse Bean – the lady with the unremarkable face – through all these dancing shoes?

Ask – the reporter's stock in trade.

Since Bean worked here, who better to ask than the manager?

Young Charlie Buchanan wasn't a hard man to find. It helped that he was standing on the edge of one of the two bandstands, beaming over the heads of his income. Behind Buchanan in his shiny shoes, wing collar and satisfied smile, the band raced through 'Doin' the New Low Down' as fast and as loud as they could.

'Jesse?' he yelled, cupping his hands around his mouth so he could be heard over the music – looking down at Teddy with her white skin, elegant velvet dress, and lack of escort with interest.

Back at the Baches', Teddy had dressed down – or up – for Harlem, not wanting to reek of newsprint. Instead, she radiated the strong perfume of a lady alone. An exciting, inviting infusion that was leaking through the Savoy like the musk of a stray bitch in heat. Not what she'd intended – she'd merely hoped to blend in – but, hell, it would have to do.

Teddy stood below him and yelled back. 'Jesse Bean. She's a dancer here.'

'I know who Jesse is, sister.' Buchanan tipped his head towards the far bandstand. 'Backstage. What do you want her for?'

Jesse was coloured. Teddy couldn't claim to be her sister. But sporting a long black dress with its cluster of brilliants and a pair of wet shoes on the end of long, lovely legs, she figured she could get away with saying Jesse owed her money. Buchanan looked like he believed her.

'She's got to do a number now. See her after. But don't take up too much of her time, time's what I pay her for.'

The band at Teddy's end of the Savoy came to a close in a crash of timpani. At the other end, Chick Webb, hunchbacked over his drums, rapped out a solo drumroll, and a moveable stage slowly slid out from the wall. Over it hung a gilded cage on an enormous curved stand. In the cage perched a woman on a golden swing, her body cloaked from head to foot in ostrich feathers of cerulean blue.

Uninvited, Teddy sat in an empty pretzel-backed chair at an occupied table near the footlights. No one told her to leave. But of the three she shared it with, only one made her welcome. Two light-skinned women in red made room in sullen silence. But the man – his shirt candy-pink silk and his suit electric-green – moved closer. From a gold case, he offered her a hand-rolled cigarette. The diamonds embedded in the case matched the diamond in his front tooth.

Crossing her silken legs under black velvet, Teddy smiled and took the cigarette. Then, sipping more of the nasty pink brew, she turned her back on all three.

Whatever Teddy expected to find when she came looking for Jesse Bean, a blackbird in a cage wasn't it. Washed in a smoky blue spot was the woman who was in the back seat of the steel blue sedan as Bright and Fiske sped away from Madison Square Garden on Saturday night. This was the woman with the funny face Dancing Joe took with him wherever he went. Good God! This was the Savoy's star dancer, Mama B. Blue.

To the hiss of the high-hat, Jesse Bean stepped out of her cage and onto the mirrored stage. To stand and slowly open the floor-length cape of blue feathers. Two or three stray wisps around her hips, feathered at the ankle and wrist, bands of silver wound round her upper arms – nothing else. The black and shining thighs of Dancing Joe's woman shivered to the drums, only the tips of her long fingers dancing.

Though Jesse's face was still plain, though the little mouth was turned down, the lines around the eyes tired and bitter, though she could have been thirty-five, maybe even forty – which made her years older than Dancing Joe – though among many of her own she was too black, the rest of Jesse Bean was magnificent: iridescent, proud and hard and predatory. Fine and fit as her boxer, oiled and coiled, exotic with musky sex.

Teddy thought the woman with the face of a black Jane Eyre had the body of an Amazon Queen.

Chick Webb and his Chicks played something mean and lowdown, a slow drag Jack would have called 'put out the lights and call the law' music. And Jesse could dance. Lord, could she dance. Lost in the lure of Dancing Joe's tap-dancing lady, Teddy lost track of time.

Until the stage began to disappear, sliding back into the wall. Caught off guard by applause, almost tripping in her unaccustomed skirt, Teddy jumped up to stop her. 'Jesse!'

Mama B. Blue froze in the middle of a triple wing, shaded her eyes against the glare of the footlights – and stared at her audience. Saw Teddy – and jumped right over the blue wash of lights. It earned her a rippling chorus of ooohs! and aaahs!

Whatever Jesse Bean felt about Teddy O'Rourke, it wasn't scared.

A foot from Teddy's table, Jesse landed with the grace of a cat, gripped Teddy's astonished arm, fierce fingers digging through velvet, and pulled her up out of the chair.

'You with this "sweet papa do little"?'

Jesse's jump threw Teddy; her question confused. 'Sweet papa what?'

'This pimp you sittin' with?'

'Hell no. It was a front row seat. I just sat in it.'

Jesse shoved her face into the face of the diamond-toothed pimp. 'No luck tonight, Sandman.'

Digging her nails deeper into Teddy's arm, Jesse pulled her away from the table, all the way to the soda fountain – the sweet papa do little watching them go with anger, the girls in red with triumph.

Jesse snapped her fingers for attention from a passing waiter.

Regrouping her scattered wits, Teddy turned on the tap-dancing Amazon. 'You can let go now.'

A glance at her Irish face and Jesse uncurled her nails. But she stayed close. 'You bring Joe's money?'

Teddy didn't answer that. She didn't even listen to it. 'Listen, before we get around to money, where's Dixie Fiske?'

'Don' know an' don' care where that white trash is.'

'Then, where's Joe?'

'My Joe's sick. An' I wouldn't even be here in this dump if we didn't need what they pay me. Where's his damn money?'

'Sick? How sick? Fiske said he was taking Joe to a doctor.'

Jesse snorted. 'A doctor! Fat chance. That man made us stop the car two blocks from where we started, ran lickety-split down Forty-seventh. *I* been Joe's doctor.'

Jesse's waiter waltzed up with a tray. On it was a bottle of house whisky and two shot glasses. Jesse lifted the whole thing off him and set it on the soda fountain. 'Miss Ofay's payin', Sticky.'

Sticky, the waiter, held out his hand.

Sighing, Teddy paid. There went another fifteen hard-earned bucks. When Connie got her bill for expenses – he'd spit. 'I came for a story, Jesse. I'm not leaving without it.'

Pouring out two shots, Jesse took one for herself, left Teddy to work out who the last glass was for – and shrugged. 'You leave when you leave. Ain't my business Harlem's no place for you. An' I ain't got no time for makin' up stories. That man Groat down at the Garden said you had Joe's money. Just hand it over like you promised.'

'I promised Fiske. He gets the money when I get the story.'

'If Dixie touches my man's money, that be the end of it. You don' get no story an' we don' need no help.'

'Help? I've already helped. I want to see Joe, talk to him. You owe me.'

Jesse laughed, shaking her cerulean blue feathers. 'Jesse owes you? How do you figure that?'

Already irritated, O'Rourke got angry. 'I'm holding money for you you couldn't hold for yourself. If it's dangerous for you or for Fiske, it's dangerous for me. As I said, you owe me.' Teddy picked up the last glass and dropped the whisky neat. If no one else, the tall man working the soda fountain was impressed.

Sighing at the stubbornness of this Irish bitch, Jesse pushed her plain face up close to Teddy's. 'You say you see Joe, we get the money?'

'That's what I'm saying.'

'Shit.' Jesse spent some time thinking. When she finally made up her mind, she moved fast. 'OK, you see him. But it don' make me happy, an' if it don' go well, or you don' hand over the money after, Jesse Bean'll put a whammy on you, girl. You'll be seein' things make your skin do the shimmy. You hear me?'

'You'll get the money,' said Teddy. 'It's Dancing Joe's, isn't it?'

'Now you lissen – ' whispered Jesse in the slanted rain, leading Teddy down dim wet alleys, through dark doors leading to darker doors, back out into alleys leading to more alleys, ' – where we're goin' they ain't partial to white. They ain't too partial to women neither. You keep yourself small.'

Jesse Bean, still in her Mama B. Blue tap shoes and feathers, had thrown a white coat over her spectacular self. The coat was baggy at the back, tight at the knees, and its monkey-fur collar was flattened in the wet wind. 'This here's King Tutt's place, where you shut up.'

Shivering, Teddy found herself standing behind Jesse in front of one more door – this one unpainted, a dim light bulb above it – the one Teddy hoped was the last. It was the kind of door that felt the thud of unfriendly boots in its time.

Jesse knocked twice, paused, knocked again.

The door clicked open, the space behind it suddenly filled with the smell of lavender, followed by a sleek black head. 'What you want?' it snapped.

'It's me, King, Jesse Bean, come to see Joe.'

The lavender head saw Jesse, grinned, caught sight of Teddy behind her and snarled. King Tutt flared his nostrils, batted his beaded lashes, but he let them in.

Clutching the collar of her raincoat, Teddy followed Jesse Bean down cold stone steps, guiding herself by touch on clammy walls. The steps ended in what looked like subway tunnels and felt like hell.

Hissing an underground music, steampipes crawled over two barrel vaults, each fifty feet long and ten feet wide. The vaults were lit by bare red light bulbs and joined by three low archways. Here and there were kitchen tables and a scattering of straight-backed kitchen chairs, a small scuffed bar in the corner, and an old piano against a steamy brick wall. In all her ramblings with Jack, Teddy had never seen anything like it. Everything was black. The walls, the furniture, the piano, the people. And everywhere – white stars painted on the rough black walls, giving the place a pathetic glitter.

Decked out in their finest: tux and tails, the sparkle of sequined gowns, ebony beads, high-heeled shoes, the boys of King Tutt's danced to a slow, ragged tune from the piano player. Each fey and shrill and furious at the sight of Teddy O'Rourke, the whites of their eyes as white as the painted stars.

'Joe's in here?' said Teddy, keeping her voice small and her head tucked in.

In answer, Jesse Bean clucked her tongue in disgust. Then turned and walked to a far door set into the starry wall, Teddy right on her heels. Jesse opened the door, stuck her head into darkness, whispered, 'Joe, honey? You awake?'

Caught up in her little drama of alleys and doors and dancing men with beaded lashes, Teddy almost jumped out of her skin when a hand clamped itself down on her left shoulder and squeezed.

Teddy flipped her head round. A big white man stood behind her, smiling a big friendly smile, holding a big finger to his pursed lips.

'Sssh,' he said.

Except for the gum and the lurid red light, he looked like a bulky Wall Street banker: conservative suit, a dark melton overcoat, hair turning silver at the sides, a tidy paunch. But one hand was now shoved deep in the melton's left pocket and the other, enormous, tufts of dark hair on the finger joints, kept its hold on her shoulder. The man who looked like a banker was pulling her towards him. Teddy, her back pressed against the fine coat of a stranger, was swamped in the odour of tutti-frutti. She could feel the beat of the big man's heart. Whoever was getting excited here, it wasn't him. Inside somewhere, Teddy groaned.

'Who's your new friend, Jesse? The boss told me to keep track of your friends.' Like his smile, the guy had a big friendly voice.

Jesse spun round, slammed shut the door she'd just opened, opened the mouth she'd kept shut since the last alley, and screamed. It should have brought the house down.

Not a soul in the steamy vaults could help her. The big man brought friends and the friends brought guns. 'Mr Rosenbloom!' moaned Jesse when she finished screaming. 'What you want?'

Huge hairy hand still clamped to Teddy's shoulder, Solomon Rosenbloom pushed – gently. 'For starters, this little girl's name. How about that? She a hoofer too? With those legs, she looks like a ballet dancer. Or maybe even something better?' Mr Rosenbloom kneaded Teddy's shoulder.

Out of the Savoy and into the shadow of big Sol Rosenbloom, Jesse was no longer Mama B. Blue. She was plain Bean again – and scared. 'A ballet dancer? This ofay couldn't be no – '

Before Jesse could make a mess of things, Teddy cut in. Getting felt up by a gum-chewing stranger was the last straw. A night of Eagels, a day of Mezinger, an hour of lippy Jesse Bean, went right out of the top of her head like steam. Reaching down, Teddy got a swift solid grip on the nice man's balls. Squeezing, she put everything she had into what she said next.

'If you don't take your hand off me, Mr Rosenbloom, you'll lose something precious.'

Sol laughed, a kind of choked-off gurgle, but he let go. 'Whoa there! What have we got here?'

Teddy stepped away, putting a few feet between them. 'You want to know things, you ask politely. I don't dance and I'm not anybody's friend. I'm a card player. Miss Bean owes me. You *do* owe me, don't you, Jesse?'

With no way out, Jesse had to nod, yes.

Sol Rosenbloom was looking at Teddy with a new light in his eye.

'A card player? I caught me a lady gambler? That's swell. God, how sweet that is. And won't it tickle the boss pink.' Sol gave Jesse a little shove. But he kept a good few feet between himself and the white girl with the quick hands. 'Hot down here, ain't it? What say we leave the rest of the ladies to their hole and go have us a little talk with a friend of mine?'

Jesse looked at Sol and Sol looked back. Teddy could almost hear them thinking. She didn't like the sound of it.

Under Sol's friendly, gum-chewing grin, Jesse's bitter mouth drooped. 'You don' mean Joe no harm, Mr Rosenbloom? He's sick, I don' want him hurt.'

From one second to the next, the big man with the paunch was through being nice. 'Who cares what you want? Who'd care a tit about a doxie with a mug like yours? CD, Arch! Gather up what's left of our coloured hero, get him up and out of this purple pit.'

Propelled forcibly up from the vaults with one black girl and a huge white goon, Teddy had one consoling thought. She was going to get her story after all. Or *some* story. Whatever it turned out to be, she hoped she was going to like it.

Outside, it had stopped raining. Which helped; Teddy left her umbrella at the Savoy. Parked in front of the unpainted door were two waiting cars, one a black four-door Studebaker sedan, the other a low snazzy cabriolet. The guy behind the wheel of the cabriolet – a guy Sol called Zipper – didn't bother looking up as Sol escorted his ladies into the front seat. Sol took the rumble.

The car whisking Jesse Bean and Teddy into the night was a whitewalled Cord. The Cord was as yellow as store-bought butter. Packed between the dead-eyed driver and a terrified headliner at the Savoy, Teddy suddenly knew where she was going. To see Tom Channing.

The thought rocketed through her like the finale at the Fourth of July.

Jack was drunk. It was no excuse but it was a damn good reason. Where the hell was he? In a pink room full of pink girlish things somewhere in Greenwich Village off Eighth Avenue, that's about all he knew.

Back at Rockaway, he'd kept an eye on Channing and Madden as they closeted themselves with Mae, watched them leave an hour later in Madden's black Packard. Then, after discovering that Lulu LeRoy – up from her seat and standing – was no more than five feet tall and weighed a mere ninety pounds, he'd fed her pancakes on the boardwalk at Rockaway Beach, stayed on for Mae's show, and loved every minute of its sassy honky-tonk wit. Lulu rode home behind him on the back of the Harley, and now here he was, in Lulu's bed – drinking too much. In order to keep up with how much she was drinking.

Lulu was lying on top of him, but that was OK. He'd been on top of her. They'd changed places so many times in the last two hours, Jack lost track of which end was up.

Little Lulu chattered away the entire time. Jabbering, giggling, screeching – and most of it sailed right by him. Stuff about West, about Hollywood, cabbage-covered houses, Bernt McTaggart. That Bernie Miller was always talking about his pal, Jimmy Walker, his pals, Owney Madden and Frenchy DeMange, his pal, Dutch Schultz, his pal – had she said hers as well? – Tom Channing. The bundle Bernie was going to win on some fixed fight. Babble babble in Jack's busy ear. Too drunk to listen, he'd shut out her voice, heard only the sound of her blessed little body. Hiding from crazy Bluff O'Rourke's crazier daughter in pink Lulu flesh. *That* was OK too. Jack felt fine, he felt righteous, he felt like that great jockey Earl Sande shooing in winners, he felt – actually, by now he felt dried up, sucked clean, vacuumed. And his cold, which had snuck off hours before to gather strength, was back bearing a blowtorch and a hammer. Aside from that, he now knew why Bernt McTaggart spent so much time and money on Lulu Gilda LeRoy Tannenbaum. A week of this gilded Christmas cracker and Jack would be holding down a neighbouring slab up at Campbell's.

Exploding a kiss in his ear and throwing back the covers, Lulu popped out of bed hot and naked. Jack grabbed the blanket back fast, but not before he'd seen his own bruised cock, sad and flattened against his thigh, KO'd in the ninth.

'You need something to eat?' she said. 'I could get you a sandwich, or maybe you want a cream cheese on bagel? Gosh, sweetheart, you certainly are some kind of lover. Feel like I could run a mile, ten miles! What about you?'

'Oh, swell,' said Jack, clutching a small satin pillow like a drowning man would throw his arms around the thick red neck of a Rockaway lifeguard. Stitched in vivid orange on the hot pink pillow was 'Atlantic City, New Jersey'.

Running in place, stretching up on her baby mice toes, hands on her hips, twisting to the left, then to the right – Jack couldn't believe what he was seeing. Lulu, exercising. Now? When she ought to be curled up beside him, slipping off into the sweet, satisfied dreams of childish sleep – finally shutting up? Over his tented toes, there she was at the foot of the bed, the beautiful little sixty-inch body planted firm on its short, sturdy tap-dancing legs, heart hipped, wasp waisted, uptilted breasts with their big chocolate nipples winking at him, round, soft, heavy breasts bobbing up and down on her narrow chest, the little blonde triangle stretching, shrinking – one, two, one, two, one –

Jack was getting seasick. 'Lulu?'

'Yes, Jack honey?'

'There's something wrong here.'

'What?'

'Your hair? What are you? Half Jewish and half Harpo Marx?'

Lulu giggled, patting her little blonde bush. 'You mean you just only now noticed? I dye it.'

'Which one?'

'The stuff on top, silly.'

'That makes a switch. So you're not Jewish?'

'No.'

'And your real name's not Tannenbaum?'

'No. It's Zaleska. That's good old Polack.'

'So, why pretend to be Jewish?'

'Because all the big movie guys are Yids.'

'Lulu, sit down.'

Lulu sat. Right next to his head, her pert little butt crushing some of the pillow. The pillow he was using to balance his weary brains on. His head rolled off and landed in her lap, nose first. Jack coughed in her hot Polish muff.

'Wow!' squealed Lulu, giggling. 'Do that again!'

Jack couldn't do anything again. He'd passed out.

9

Black King, Red Queen

Through torn and scattered storm clouds, the moon hung
low over Harlem. Up here the buildings weren't so tall,
up here architecture knew the fear of God. It hunkered
back on its basements, sending out simple stoops, plain
iron railings, rose to a humble height of no more than
four or five storeys. Like Harlem, architecture knew its
place. Over Harlem the stars could burn, the moon could
sail across a wondering city sky. No soaring fists of stone
and glass, no glimmering envelope of electric arrogance,
shut out the night.

On Harlem's highest point stood a casino. The casino
was in a mansion and the mansion – proud and
unchanged for seventy years, at least on the outside –
was squeezed into a row of johnny-come-lately apartment
houses, new homes for Harlem's rich. The old mansion,
flanked by black finery, stood on the giddy rock crest of
a wild outcrop of upper Manhattan called Sugar Hill.
A guest, idly glancing through a tall, scoop-curtained
window on the casino's east side, would see over the
Harlem River – and across its black waters – the new
Yankee Stadium and the old Polo Grounds. From the
west look down into the dark geometry of Harlem itself,
its neon streets glimmering in the November rain.

Set back from Edgecombe Avenue in the five hundred
block, the mansion still had its front garden and through
the garden ran a path of worn, moss-marked stones. It still
had its elms, stately trees that a half century ago screened
the great house from the Avenue, trees now tall enough to
tap on the tiles of its mansard roof. Winter roses rambled
over the gabled door. Outside, there was no neon, no
doorman barked his wares. Inside, the casino wasn't

enormous; no chubby cupids flapped their tiny wings across its high ceilings, which weren't painted an eggshell blue; it had only one band. But whoever in Harlem might be gifted or famous or rich or unusual gambled in the house on Sugar Hill.

Teddy O'Rourke had a motto – *when in doubt, strut*. Before it was hers, it was Daddy's.

Sucking her thumb in another strange bed in another hotel, a little girl growing up waited for Bluff O'Rourke in every fast town in America. Fast meant the place had a track, a poolhall, a red-light district. After dark, Teddy got left in hotel rooms – until she turned seven, and Bluff let her in on some of the action.

A life lived with her gambling dad meant a life lived on the hop. Meant travelling light. Meant hotels – grand if the O'Rourkes were in the chips, seedy if they weren't. But always close to the train station – handy for a fast getaway. Meant bags that were never really unpacked. Life with Bluff was spent on the rim of a wheel of nerves and laughter.

A little girl with a cloud of red hair, hotel sheets smelling of starch pulled up to her freckled chin, read the Gideon Bible by gaslight. Even then, Teddy found wonder in words. The Bible had some great lines. *Whatsoever thy hand findeth to do, do it with all thy might.* It wasn't so hot on the subject of women, but what could she expect? The Bible was written by a bunch of old men.

If Bluff O'Rourke's kid was going to get herself abducted, carried off, stolen away into a wet Harlem night, she'd be abducted with style. Do it with all thy might, indeed.

Gripped by her black velvet elbow, marched across uneven stones, slipping on moss, and into a mansion at the very top of the isle of Manhattan, Teddy was guided across a parquet floor and up the sweep of a curving stair. Stared at the whole way by men and women of the night, she kept her chin up, her grey eyes level, her shoulders back, her soft mouth with its short upper lip still, her mind open, and every freckle on her wide white cheekbones composed. Jesse Bean skulked beside her, heels dragging, her bag clutched in her hand, taps that had sung on the Savoy stage and the clammy stone steps of a descent into a starry hell now singing on parquet.

O'Rourke was jerked to an abrupt halt at a shadowy back table.

Behind a lit candle in a fluted silver holder sat a man with his back to the wall – a man who could charm rats out of holes, dollars out of misers, a bright girl out of her senses. In a shoulder holster under his unbuttoned dinner jacket gleamed the butt of a high-calibre pistol. This was the man who was talking about Bernie the night he was killed, this was the man who owned a yellow car.

How many yellow cars were there in Harlem? The only other one Teddy knew of was Babe Ruth's custom-built Packard. But Babe had told her one of the Minsky Brothers bought that for his wife. Did Mrs Minsky speed away from the body of a dead cop in an alley behind the Cotton Club? Oh, sure. Mrs Minsky did it every other day. Teddy was almost sick with the need to get back to the *Trident*. To lay this fizzing yellow time bomb on Mezinger's desk. What would the two sons of bitches say to that? She was dying to hear the sweet racket.

But meantime, swept up by Sol Rosenbloom with Jesse Bean and Dancing Joe Bright, Teddy could only be a clam in a lobster pot, a mistake, an afterthought, something extra. No need to confuse things by letting folks with guns know who she really was. Play a few hands with the boys, then get the hell out of here. And yes, the guys on the press got it right – Tom Channing was pretty.

'Look what I caught.' Showing Teddy off like a carny prize, Sol shoved her into a chair. Then, holding Jesse by the collar of her coat – a ruff of glossy black monkey fur – Sol screwed the dancer down next to Teddy. 'This ugly black mama you already know. But I thought, what the hey? I'd bring her along anyway.'

Rosenbloom took off the expensive melton, hung his jacket over his arm – Teddy was sure it was there to hide his gun – and looked less like a banker now, more like a faithful ape. The back of the big man's shirt stuck to the fat of his back with sweat. Out of the red underground light, she noticed Sol had green eyes.

'Guess where this sappy blackbird was keeping our boxer? Holed up in the back of King Tutt's pansy parlour, for chrissakes.'

Behind Sol, the driver of the flashy yellow Cord sniggered. It was the first sound Teddy heard Zipper make since the Savoy. Zipper – though dark, so like Channing in many ways: quick, hard, good-looking – had nothing in his eyes, nothing at all. But he had another damn gun. That made three Teddy knew of in this room alone. Sol sat himself next to Teddy, Zipper went back to the bar where he could keep an eye on the door, Bean slumped. O'Rourke sat straight and slim as a larch, breathing in a man who was fast becoming a legend in her old hometown.

Channing's table was on the second floor of the Sugar Hill casino. He owned the table he sat at, he owned the guns and the guys holding the guns; he owned the casino.

A casino jumpy with the sound of spinning roulette wheels, the nervous laughter of high-rollers, the tinkle of full glasses carried on upheld trays, the low, throaty wail of a saxophone. Well-dressed people of all colours were seated at small, white-clothed tables, were propped along the curve of an ebony bar, posing by the crimson swagged and festooned floor-length windows, glasses of Prohibition hooch in their hands. Behaving themselves, keeping their voices down and their eyes open; everyone aware of Tom Channing. The very air near him snapped, charged with a reckless vitality, an amused, casual danger. Tom was New York's bad boy, a comet that lit up its starry sky, burned for a moment, would die – would crash and bleed and die. And how they loved the thought. Like a wolf in a sleepy hamlet, a grenade in the front parlour, poison in only one glass of Park Avenue wine, Tom quickened their lives with risk. They all wanted to be there at the kill. Until then, ah! until that certain heady day – they basked like belled cats in front of his fire.

Not immune and a hell of a lot closer, Teddy felt the heat. Looking at Tom Channing was a little like looking at the Chrysler Building from street level. It made her dizzy. But she lit her own cigarette with her own steady hand, blew out the flame, and – without looking – flipped the spent match into the ashtray. Where she hoped it landed. She couldn't look to find out. Looking was cheating. Then she put her velvet elbow on the edge of the table, rested her chin in the cup of her hand, kept tabs on her heartbeat, thought of yellow cars, and smoked. Waiting. It couldn't have been done better. Thank you, Daddy.

The man across the table could be as impressed with this slim-hipped, grey-eyed lady in a soft black cloche, brilliants glinting at her breast and ear, as she was with him. But if he was, it didn't show. He played with his glass of mineral water, watched the bubbles rise. There was a slice of lime in the glass.

'A lady gambler?' Tom raised his startling blue eyes and smiled. Tom smiling held more heat than Tom not smiling. Teddy, warding off spells, lowered her own. 'That's pretty good, Miss – excuse me, but what do I call you?'

If Bluff could give a little girl a dog's name, the little girl grown could take the name of a racehorse – the one she'd won her first bet on. A long ago filly the colour of a bone in the sun. Teddy exhaled, watching the thin blue smoke billow and spin, and said, 'Silky Sullivan.' Liking the sound of it, she gave the name a husky lilt.

At that, Tom stopped smiling. 'When I was a kid, there was a filly running with that name. Ran like the wind when she felt like it. When she didn't feel like it – she

150

came in last. Funny thing, the guy who owned her? He got tired one day of all that independence – and put a bullet through her brain.'

Teddy met Tom's eyes. 'My father thought better of her than that. It must be why he gave me her name.'

'Your father liked horses?'

'Let's just say he believed in them.'

'A betting man?'

'Only when the odds were long.'

Tom Channing laughed, a fine, genuine laugh that touched Teddy but left Jesse Bean cold. Seated on Teddy's right, Jesse would not be tempted out of the mood she'd been dragged in with – sullen. Almost ugly, yet proud as a Roman matron, the dancer was defended from the spell of Tom Channing by a clean head of fear. Slumped in her coat of monkey fur, Jesse sat herself sideways to the table; it was as close as she could get to turning her back on Tom. In her lap was the small beaded handbag. If Jesse was looking at anything, she was looking at that bag.

CD Durata and his cousin Arch came up to the table like two bantam cocks, stiff-legged, shoulders hunched and rolling, hands shoved in pockets – Arch imitating every move CD made. When they got close to Channing some of the starch went out of their stride. CD got shorter.

'We did everything the way you wanted it, all nice and tidy,' said CD, taking a stand behind Tom; next to CD stood Arch.

'Sure, boys,' said Tom. 'That's fine.' He was talking to CD but he'd turned the full force of whatever he was on Teddy, saying without speaking: there was no Jesse Bean beside them, no Sol sweating next to Jesse, no dead-eyed driver at the bar, no dark-faced Durata cousins playing the room like a henyard. There was only this man and this woman and this time.

Whether he meant what he wasn't saying or whether he didn't, Teddy suddenly loved the game she was playing. It made her nerves sing, it woke her up. It wasn't about sports, and it sure as hell wasn't one of those smartass exchanges with Jack.

Channing smiled at her with the kind of smile no one but Bluff O'Rourke at his devious best came up with. But the man behind the gambler's smile, the man behind the man who was beginning to make her feel she might be the most desirable little thing in New York City, who was he? How old? How young? What did he want? Though the hair was a soft ashy blond, though the eyes were the blue of the sky over Times Square at twilight, Tom looked like a riverboat gambler, the man Edna Ferber must have been mooning over when she wrote *Showboat*. But he talked like someone out of one of Jack's stories, cool and hard and sure of himself. In other words, less than real. If she touched him, would he ripple like an image in a Broadway puddle?

Teddy shocked herself. Touch him? Under the jacket of his dark double-breasted suit, under the green tie, the natty gun holster with its high-calibre gun, Channing had a boxer's body, a hard, graceful body that could be used as a, well, for one – as a weapon. Or a target. A body that had been shot up so many times the press was losing count: once in a upstate hotel by rival rumrunners, once by a sore loser in a restaurant on Flatbush as he was toasting his own birthday, once on the corner of Bleecker and Barrow Streets as he walked a lady home. A body that had been beaten with lead pipes in some labour dispute, cut with broken bottles in a lower East Side alley, knifed in a fight over a woman – or by a woman? A body that must be a road map of scars; the scars like blind streets leading to a kind of crazed and grinning death. But each time veering off, cheating the odds. The scars not yet ending in a morgue, but becoming the stuff of tabloid myth. A hard body that could also be used as a, as a – God! Where was this going?

Stunned at the effort it took, Teddy drew her runaway thoughts up and away, held them there, felt her heart beating in her loins, felt heat run down the inside of her thighs, silken heat from a silken tongue.

'Hello, Tommy,' said a voice like bittersweet chocolate. 'You gotta light?'

Tom's eyes left Teddy's, fixed on someone above and behind her. A scented blonde head lowered itself by Teddy's shoulder as Tom lit the blonde's cigarette with a Dunhill lighter. As Silky, too cool to turn and stare, Teddy couldn't see the woman's face, but she felt her. Teddy knew that heat.

'You coming up later, sweetie? I been so lonely all day.'

As Channing laid the lighter on the table, his smile for the woman with the cocoa voice was as fine and as sweet as it had been for Teddy. Noticing the inscription on the Dunhill – *'For Tommy, all my love, Sophie'* – seeing that easy smile, Teddy died a little, began sinking into a shame so deep it was like drowning in salt water. Where the hell had her brains gone? For one of the few times in her life, she'd been sitting on them. Falling for the charm of a rake, mistaking a net that snared minnows for a golden hook. Which made her what? Another poor fish. It made her remember what this was all about. Some cute game, O'Rourke. Dicing with a gunman who'd just snatched Dancing Joe. Maybe killed Bernt McTaggart. And *where*, goddammit, was Dixie Fiske? Teddy pulled up her sagging morals, got a tighter grip on the man with the chemistry set stirring things up across this fishpond of a table.

'Course, Agnes – soon. Now beat it, OK? This is business.'

Agnes! Not Sophie. If Teddy could have felt worse, she would have.

'Oh sure, Tommy. Anything you say. But you know I'm always waiting.'

'I know you are, and you know I'll be there when I can.' Without missing a beat, Channing turned back to Teddy, said, 'As a gambler, Miss Sullivan, maybe you've heard of a guy named Dixie Fiske?'

Dixie Fiske! Teddy know Dixie? Because of Dancing Joe Bright, someone like Silky Sullivan would know Dixie. As a shady lady around town – every city is a small town to vested interests – Silky would know all the lowlife. 'Fiske? I've heard of him. He manages boxers, doesn't he?'

'Did. One boxer. Once.'

'Once?'

'There's a rumour Fiske got found in an abandoned car over in Hoboken early this morning. Could have been suicide. What do you think, Sol? Was it suicide?'

'Could be.' Sol was popping a fresh stick of tutti-frutti in his mouth. 'I've known a few guys go like that, hosepipe through the window. I hear guys like that turn red as a cooked beet.'

'Funny thing, though,' said Tom. 'Why would someone like Fiske want to kill himself? Maybe because he felt guilty owing me money? So much money he doped his own fighter for the side bets? Maybe he killed himself because when he doped Bright he almost killed him. What do you think, any ideas, Silky?'

Jarred, Teddy didn't know what the hell to think. Did Fiske kill himself? Or did he get help? A rumour, Channing said. Was Dixie even dead? Or was Tom just trying to scare her? And if he was, why bother? Why scare some poor fish like Silky Sullivan? And, dammit anyway, there went her exclusive.

The only thing she was sure of at that moment was that as Tom Channing spoke of Fiske, he reminded her of something Bluff O'Rourke said when she was a raw-boned fifteen-year-old. This while they were watching a group of fellows in chaps and spurs toss pennies into someone's new ten-gallon hat on the porch of a dust-bitten hotel in Santa Monica, California. The penny-pitchers were all real pistol-packing cowboys playing themselves on a William S.

Hart movie called *Hell's Hinges*, spending the last years of the old Wild West whooping it up for the hand-cranked cameras of the Inceville studio. One, a lazy, slow-talking ex-wrangler, tossing nine pennies in a row dead-centre into the hat, had turned to collect on his bet. But the loser, slope-shouldered and cheesy with loss, suddenly whistled. A huge mangy dog appeared out of nowhere, chomped down on the hat, and ran off with it, pennies and all. The slope-shouldered man spat at the wrangler's feet, said, 'Bet's off,' and sauntered away. Bluff, rocking and watching and laughing, said, 'Never bet with a guy who keeps fangs up his sleeve.'

Tom turned his blue eyes on Jesse, smiling with a big brother's indulgent warmth. 'Miss Bean here thinks I'm out to hurt Bright, but Silky, believe me – nothing could be further from the truth. It was Fiske who hurt him at the Garden, who doped up his own fighter so he'd lose, Fiske who was the tick, the hustler, looking for the main chance. It's Joe who beat the odds, came back like he did, even sick – and it's me who's going to make Joe champion.'

Teddy listened to all this, thinking – *perhaps, but it's you who kills people. Is that how you take care of things, how you'll take care of Joey?*

Tom slipped the lighter from Sophie in a pocket, began buttoning his dark suit jacket, straightening his green tie. 'It's a pity we got to stop chatting – but I got a casino to run and a boxer to see to.'

Teddy almost bounced out of her chair. The interview was over. Time to go. She could practically taste the look on Connie's face when she brought him her scoop. Read her own front page banner: *Ace Sportswriter Leads Police To –*. Until Sol Rosenbloom's heavy hand pushed her back in her seat.

Fishing the lime out of his glass, Channing nibbled on the pale green flesh. 'You know, Sol,' he said, his voice now dropping in tone, becoming harder, meaner, honed with an edge like the blade on an ice-hockey skate. 'Having this chat with our little friend, I've been thinking. I always wanted to talk to a writer off the record, writers come up with the goods – '

'Yeah,' said Sol, snapping his tutti-frutti. 'They got some funny ideas, writers.'

'If I wasn't so busy, maybe I could find out where they get all those ideas.'

Listening to this, Teddy froze. A writer? What were they talking about writers for? Did they mean her? Of course they meant her. Who was fooling who here? The charade of cool Silky Sullivan curled up and promptly dropped dead. Teddy O'Rourke would be thirty in December, she paid her own way, she was the girl who'd made a name for herself in a man's game. She was Bluff O'Rourke's daughter; she'd cut cards with the best. And for the last half hour she'd sat at a shady table getting played for a sucker, watched Sol run off with the ten-gallon hat. If Bluff could see her now, he'd have swotted her butt with a horse whip.

'What do you think, lady?' Tom held up his hand before Teddy could say a thing. 'No, don't pop any more brain cells. It's been a treat listening to you but time's running out. Sol here tells me you took the suitcase into Grand Central Station, but didn't come out with it.' He leant across the table, his face lit from below by the light of the wavering candle. 'You finally figure out what you're here for, sports lady? I want Joe's money, Miss O'Rourke.'

'How did Sol know where – ?' she began, but stopped. Of course the big man would know – he'd followed her. How else? Teddy suddenly noticed something she'd seen all along – but hadn't noted. The glass, Channing's tall thin glass of mineral water with its thin slice of lime. Speaking or silent, he'd never stopped touching it, turning it in his hands as it sat on the table, running a finger around its rim, tipping it, rocking it. There was a kind of love in the way the fingers tapped the glass, traced patterns on its dewy sides.

Beside her, Jesse Bean began stirring; her close-set eyes narrowed, the thin lips working until she finally got out a word. And the word was, 'Wha – ?'

'Miss Bean?' Tom's blond voice grew soft again, gentle – caressing.

Half turning, Jesse finally laughed. Unlike Tom's, Jesse's laugh wasn't fine – it was flat and harsh and it lay on the table between them like an ante. 'You been followin' this fool?'

Sol answered that. 'Ever since the Garden.'

CD Durata snickered. 'So close I coulda punched a hole in 'er with an icepick – anytime.' CD was idly picking at a scab on his beaked nose. 'Anytime at all. Shit, she almost beaned me with a shoe.'

'An' she led you to my Joe?'

'Sure. Why else was we dogging her?'

As swift as thought, Jesse kicked over her chair, whipped a knife from the beaded bag, the blade seeking Teddy. Teddy jerked back, pushing away from the table. And Sol's big hand flipped out, caught Jesse's wrist and held it, stopping the tip of the blade an inch from Teddy's stomach. He twisted Jesse's wrist until the dancer dropped the knife. CD, darting forward to pick it up, said, 'Ooo! Nasty.'

Laughing, Tom stood up. 'Ladies, ladies. Not in front of my guests.'

Spittle flecking her lips, Jesse's thin mouth was ugly with rage and hate. The colour drained from her black face, leaving it a sick, pulpy grey. 'It's your fault, you bitch, your fuckin' fault this murderer's got my man – '

'Murderer?' sighed Tom.

' – white girl comin' up here to do her dirt, white girl comin' up here, her an' her motherfuckin' story!'

Tom was still smiling his sweet, sad smile. 'Story, Jesse? What story?'

A great blossom of sudden panic opened its hateful petals in Teddy's heart. Hurtful *yellow red orange*, like the

157

huge paper flower a circus clown thrusts in a child's face. Her story! Jesse was going to screw up her story! She'd lost every hand here, but not that. Teddy was thinking of screaming, stomping on Jesse Bean's foot, anything to shut her damn mouth.

But Jesse was out of control. 'She thinks there's somethin' to tell about Joe, goin' to get a gold star on her paper if she tells it. I told you, bitch! Jesse put a whammy on you!' This time too fast for Sol, Jesse ducked under his arm, raised the beaded bag, and hit Teddy so hard her jaw hit her shoulder. Bright, black shiny beads cut open the corner of Teddy's mouth. Sol caught Jesse from behind in a bear hug, lifted her struggling body from the floor, held her there.

Raising painted masks, opening hungry mouths, craning powdered necks, Tom's guests smiled, pointed, said, *See! Isn't this something? What did I tell you?* Gathering up second-hand violence for after-dinner chats, but not one of them lifting a hand to help a spitting, helpless black girl.

'I'm getting tired of knives,' snapped Channing, moving around the table. 'Get rid of this stupid gash, Sol, lock her up until she calms down. CD, you and Arch take our new friend down to Grand Central, watch her claim that suitcase, then bring it back. And this time, CD, do it right.'

'You got it, boss,' said CD.

Tom stood near Teddy now, looking at her, smiling, working his magic with those Times Square eyes.

Teddy fended it off as her blood followed the delicate curve of her torn lip, gathered in the corner of her mouth – until it fell to her chin from its own red weight – then ran in a hot, salty-sweet line down the firm white flesh of her neck.

Tom touched the blood between her breasts with the tip of a tender finger. 'You want a story, little writer? You keep on with that Dancing Joe stuff you're so good at. His story's what it always was, only now Mr Dixie Fiske is out, and I'm in.' Tom lifted the finger to his lips, licked it. 'I'll be seeing you, Teddy O'Rourke. You're a gambler – put a bet on it.'

Tom Channing stepped into a darkened upstairs room. 'Is he all right, Sol? How's he feeling?'

Sol shrugged. 'See for yourself. That beating he took? It woulda killed some other guy. I got that Jesse Bean down the hall, called for a doctor.'

By the light of the Sugar Hill moon, Tom moved quietly across a floor of polished matt glass, stopping at the foot of his own bed. A gentle smile crossed his face. Looking down at the sleeping shape of Dancing Joe Bright, Tom felt a stirring of excitement, a stab of melancholy.

'You weren't at the fight, Sol. You really missed something. This guy lying here, he won all right – but it was how he won made a man's heart sing. Doped and down, he came back. I'll never forget it.'

Joe's left eye was swollen and bruised, the eyebrow bisected by a taped cut. Gently Tom put his hand on the fighter's forehead. 'No fever, that's good. If Fiske really hurt him bad, I'd want that bastard done all over again. Sol, you know what the best thing in life is?'

'Screwing a broad?'

'After that.'

'What?'

'Beating the odds. I'm going to make this kid champ. Me, I own the next heavyweight champion of the world. I'm going to stuff a big, beautiful black buck down this fucking country's fucking throat.'

'Sure you will, boss. No doubt about it.' When big Sol Rosenbloom said this, he meant it with all his heart. Back when they both ran with Madden, back when Tommy was just off the boat, Sol knew even then he had the right stuff, was a guy they couldn't put down. How far up could he go? As high as he wanted, higher, so long as little Joey stayed down.

'Sol?'

'Yeah, Tom?'

'That redhead, what's the odds on her?'

'You mean for you?'

'Maybe.'

'Like she said about her daddy betting on the ponies – long.'

Tom grinned in the light of the moon. 'That's what I thought.'

Silently closing the door on Joe Bright, Tom stood for a moment and dreamed. A redheaded, freckle-faced newspaper hack with grey eyes, eyes with gold flecks – a flame of a girl. Was she the broad who'd make him forget? A smart sassy dame – sitting in his casino like some kind of Irish queen, lying through her teeth. A tough Irish cookie with hair like flames – like fire and flames and dying.

Tom closed his eyes as a sudden dull pain throbbed behind them. Since Saturday night the fucking memory was back. Here it was all over again: the heat of the fire, his own drunken uselessness, his pain, his loss, his rage –

'You gonna stand there all night, boss?'

Tom opened his eyes. Sol was lighting a cigarette.

'Go on, get some rest, Tom. I'll wait for the doctor.'

CD Durata loved cars, knives and women. And money, of course. But money meant cars, knives, women. In that order. Working for Tom Channing got him what he loved. But not the best of it. Channing got the best. CD got the leavings when skirt was dished out, got handed what was left of any pile of hardware, drove the Studebaker instead of the Packard, the Caddy, the Cord. Zipper drove the Caddy; Tom the Cord. Except that one time on Saturday night, and for that Channing almost got sore enough to kick him. CD thought taking the yellow cabriolet was a good idea. It had a rumble seat. Rumble seats were pretty good for hiding things in. So what happens? Tom hits the fucking roof. His anger hurt CD's feelings. I mean, who was the one cleaned up the mess? Who was the one saw it coming in the first place and made sure it happened in one of the backrooms where it wouldn't spook all those slicked-back college kids and gambling shades? Who was the one thought of taking the wallet, making it look like the guy got robbed? And dammit all, who was the one almost got it in the neck himself a couple of months ago? (But he was smart – not like that dead cop. He'd brushed off Tom's bug-in-the-works like a guy brushes off lint.) Anyway, it was CD Durata, that's who was the one. Of course, there was a problem about it being his knife. And about his not getting it back after. But that ought to turn out all right. Tom said he'd take care of the knife.

CD grinned, pushing the Studdy up to eighty.

As a novice, Arch should have been driving the Studdy, CD should have been in the back seat holding a gun on the redhead, but they were going the fast way – straight down Central Park. No traffic lights, no cops at two in the morning, CD behind the wheel now doing ninety, showing off for the broad in the back seat.

Arch was the one holding the gun. And Teddy the one doing the thinking.

As their headlights picked out and passed bare dogwood trees, sped through the enchanted gloom of Central Park, she leaned her hatted head against the Studebaker's back window, its glass frosted with city dew. A scoop! A beautiful golden scoop. Tom Channing involved in the murder of Bernt McTaggart for certain. How or why was a problem for tomorrow. Now it was enough to know that much, to bring it to the boys back at the paper – and gloat. But if Channing got the money, she'd lose her ace-in-the-hole. With Joe Bright's seventy-five grand, there was still an in to Tom Channing; without it she was Silky Sullivan and that was less than zip. So – he couldn't get it. But how to pull that off? Make Tom's goons stop the car, let her out. Play sick? Fat chance. Open the door and jump? At ninety miles an hour? Shit – forget that. But they had to slow down when they left the park. So where? Who cared? Anywhere.

CD gunned the engine, running up through the gears, while Teddy remembered silken tongues, saw Tom Channing lick her blood off his fingers, felt that heat again – oh God! Go away! Channing killed people. Poor old greedy Dixie Fiske far from the red clay of Georgia, dying beet-red in a tomb of a car in Jersey.

Suddenly she wanted to see Jack Eagels, have him hold her, tell her everything was all right – show her how to jump out of a moving car. Jack could stop this feeling because with Jack – it was better. It was hotter and deeper, and damn it all, funnier. With laughter, everything was better. Fuck you, you rotten redskin. What the hell's the matter with you? Can't you see when I'm hurting?

Shooting out of the park, the speeding black Studebaker veered onto Fifty-ninth Street, squealing as CD hit the brakes for Broadway. Arch, leaning forward, was pounding CD on the back, the hand gripping the gun waving all over the back seat. 'Beat 'em to the lights, CD! Cut them crawlers up.'

Teddy slipped a hand around the door handle. Counted as they passed Fifty-third Street and Broadway, Fiftieth, Forty-ninth, the speedometer needle quivering between forty and thirty-five, dropping to thirty – Forty-sixth Street, Times Square. She hit the handle, tucked and rolled, saw the speeding asphalt leap up to meet her, heard Arch holler, 'CD! The stupid cunt's jumped! Stop the car, goddammit!'

10

Dreaming in Chinese

'Mar-vinnnn! Maaa-arvinnnn! Whaddaya want for break-fast!'

Jack Eagels opened one eye. Pink light, shot through with exploding white rosettes, drilled into his head.

'You hear me, Marvin!'

The voice was coming from the other side of the wall.

Jack shut the eye. He knew where he was, he just couldn't face it yet. So he lay there, hiding somewhere inside his own miserable skin. Whoever this Marvin was, he was only five feet away through the crummy apartment wall – and getting up before dawn. Which made him any number of things: baker, bus driver, garbageman, how about ratcatcher? The unseen early-rising Marvin dragging himself out of bed, bare feet thumping onto the floor, yawning, smacking his lips, slapping his belly – Jesus! Jack could hear the guy fart.

For Jack Eagels, *whatever* time it was, was time to go home.

But very quietly.

Jack couldn't know how hard that was going to be until he sat up. Clutching his head. The Cotton Club on a busy night was in there, Duke Ellington on the low keys, Sonny Greer and every one of his drums. Holding his head with both hands to keep it from falling off, Jack slid his legs away from the feral warmth of sleeping Lulu LeRoy, leaned over – and did a slow roll to the floor. Landing on his knees on a scatter carpet. Where all his clothes were. Kneeling at the side of Lulu's bed like a little boy saying his prayers: Hail Mary, mother of God, help me now. Cold bare knees slipping on the graceless covers of Lulu's magazines: *True Story* and *Photoplay* and *Moving*

163

Picture World; her theatrical papers: *Billboard*, *Variety*, *Zits Weekly*. Squashing girlish debris: rolled stockings, a hairnet, wadded-up tissues.

By the dim pink of Lulu's nightlight – a rubber Kewpie doll in a hula skirt with a tiny bulb poking out of the top of its raindrop head – Jack went looking for pants, shirt, shoes. Searching for socks, he stuck his head under the pink flounce of Lulu's bed. More magazines. Hundreds of them. Also a whole warren of dust-bunnies. And a box of Webster's 5¢ cigars. Pulling the sweet-smelling cedar box from beneath the bed with curiosity, he flipped it open. Expecting to find Lulu treasures, mementos. Cigars instead. At least half gone up in smoke. How much 'falling up' did Lulu LeRoy Tannenbaum Zaleska do? Unfair assumption, Eagels. Mean and newspaper masculine. Maybe she smokes them herself. Why not? Lulu out-drank him, out-talked him, she surely out-fucked him, why not out-smoke him too?

He spotted his brown leather jacket, motorcycle goggles and battered hat on the back of a vanity chair. Using the chair to stand up with and the vanity table to balance by, Jack swayed in the unearthly pink light, held his breath against the stink of hair gel, used cigarettes, the slow-blooming reek of guilt. Fighting down his own stomach. Making the table shake, clinking the empty bourbon bottle against the two empty glasses. Jack let go of the table and knocked into a cage draped with a Spanish shawl. 'Beep,' beeped whatever was in it. Jack held onto the cage until it stopped rocking.

Over on the bed, Lulu was nothing more than a bump. No Jewish hair on the pillow, no tiny Polish feet peeping from under the covers. Jack went round where he figured her top-end ought to be. Buried deep inside a fold of pink blanket, the fold like a nun's wimple, was Lulu's sleeping face. Lulu was curled into a tight, hot ball, sucking her thumb. He would have bent over, would have tried to kiss her goodbye, but if he had, Jack was sure he'd throw up.

So he left a note. Short and sweet. And a phone number. The *Trident*'s.

On the corner of Bleecker and Perry Streets, as the first flakes of cold white trouble to come dusted his hat, Jack kicked the Harley awake – while ten feet and a wall away from Lulu in her pink bed, Marvin in boxer shorts looked through yesterday's late edition of the *Trident*. While he read, he ate four fried eggs, six link sausages, and half a loaf of toasted bread thick with oleo. After whipping through the pages, back to front and back again, he threw the whole thing on the wife's new kitchen linoleum.

'I'm thinking of changing papers,' he told his other half, who, busy with her own breakfast, wasn't listening. 'That O'Rourke fella that writes the SNAPBACK stuff? he ain't in it again.'

Lulu woke up the minute Jack's bare knees hit her floor. Playing possum, she lay still, nibbling her thumb, listening to him leave. When her front door closed with the barest hint of a click – was that courtesy or caution? Well, little darlin', in a minute you'll know – she flipped back the covers and leapt to the window. No head-holding for Lulu, feeling just fine, if more than a little nervous – she hitched back her net curtain the barest half inch. There he was, down on Perry Street in front of Erlinger's candy store. Look at that! – He got that awful machine of his started. Jeepers, that's what she'd call luck. The kind of luck a girl like Lulu could use in a town like this. Still dark, starting to snow, and her new man – gosh, Lulu, a newspaperman like Mr Walter Winchell! – roars off on a motorcycle. Lulu made a face at her reflection in the windowpane. Icky! Ugly, greasy, nasty: that stupid old bike was the only part, so far anyway, of Jack Eagels she absolutely did not like. Maybe, if things went well, she could change that little bitty part of Jack, make him ride around in a nice warm car. Not much of a car, golly, not expensive, just a Ford, that's all she'd ask for. But first, little darlin', did things go well? Well, of course they did, silly. Of course they did. After last night when she used every trick she'd ever learned? And she'd learned plenty – easy as pie.

On her way to the window, she'd seen the note. What she found in that note could be an answer to everything. Though, of course, and naturally, there were other answers: like her being in an office in Tin Pan Alley the very exact minute some hungry songwriter brought in a new song, a song that would be just right for Lulu. Or having Earl Carroll or George White, heavens – what if it should be Flo Ziegfeld! – notice her. *Her*, Lulu LeRoy. Lulu chewed the nail on her little finger. That name, Lulu LeRoy? Was that a good enough name for a star? Even if LeRoy was like royalty or something like that. Maybe, it was time for another change? Lulu LaSalle? Lulu Lorraine? Lalapalooza Lulu? Lulu giggled. Stop that, Irena Josepha, you're getting too silly. And really, if it was time for anything, it was time to tell old Mr Stuck-up she wanted a better part in Miss West's show. Or maybe even a better show. But, crumbs, that was so easy. So easy to get him to do things for her, give her almost anything she wanted. Except what it was she really wanted. Now, that was hard. Getting what she really wanted wasn't so easy. But she would, oh gosh, would she! She would! Even if Lulu LeRoy had to light up all New York.

But now there was that real, honest-to-gosh reporter! There was an answer so much warmer, so much closer. Lulu, child of a thousand lies and a dozen names, had set her heart on Jack Eagels.

Back in bed, pushing a stray strand of black hair from her eyes, the downy skin of her cheeks crimped with anxious hope, she read his note. 'I'll be back. If I take too long, call me.' Then a telephone number, midtown exchange. Lulu kissed the paper. Call him? Would she call him? On her mother's life, Gilda Goldie Lulu LeRoy

Tannenbaum Zaleska etcetera, etcetera, etcetera would call him!

His face bitten by wind-driven pellets of snow, Jack flipped the Harley down, shaving the pegs as he turned onto Eighth Avenue. With a view down Horatio Street to the shipping piers and choppy waters of the Hudson River – waters yet to be harried with Monday's lighters and tugs, tankers and ferries, side-wheel Albany steamers and the dipping beaks of seagulls – he discovered he'd run out of cigarettes.

Which left Jack fuming as the city of New York rushed towards him, riding the back of its hump of an island like an Iroquois Indian myth – as the newly created earth rode the back of a great turtle. All those bristling towers rising up through a tangle of drifting snow, waving, *Here we are! Look at us! Gotcha*. Jack, betting this was one pissed-off turtle, remembered the two-decades-past words of a bitter bard, *'Crazed with avarice, lust, and rum, New York, thy name's Delirium.'* There was a billboard tacked to the side of a five-storey building as he passed Fourteenth Street. The sign, less than a week old, said, *Forward America! Nothing Can Stop US!*

Growing up in eastern Wyoming, Colorado was Jack's idea of beauty. New York was Jack's idea of speed. Put them both in a race and New York would have galloped home a length in the lead. But Denver would have looked better losing. The Harley's sharp nose pushed north. Astride it, Jack rode tormented by the stinging snow, lack of a smoke, the cold he couldn't shake, sudden hunger, and thoughts of Teddy O'Rourke.

Intending to ride straight to Alva T. Thorp's skyscraper, Jack changed his mind. He turned right, right again, then circled Chatham Square, looking for Doyers Street.

On impulse, Jack was going to have breakfast in Chinatown. He hadn't done that – not breakfast, not dinner, not even an egg-roll – for over two years. Not since he'd holed up with Teddy over a Chinese bakery for a naughty Chinese weekend.

Late September, 1927. Teddy, just back from Chicago and the Battle of the Long Count, heartsick over the Dempsey/Tunney rematch. Still stunned that Dempsey could lose the heavyweight title on a technicality. Jack, sickened by the splitting of America over a couple of small-time anarchists, a shoemaker and an odd-jobber – Nicola Sacco and Bartolomeo Vanzetti. Everyone he knew, people he admired – writers, artists, historians, playwrights, poets – joined their shrill clever voices in denouncing America. The same people who'd stood by and let Woodrow Wilson – like Lincoln, a man of ideals and honour – die. Turning their backs on an ill and embattled president, a president so true to his vision of perpetual peace, he'd given first his health, then his life, to achieve it. These same people made Sacco and Vanzetti heroes. Two Italians – not citizens, yet both avowed subversives; who'd surely robbed and killed a shoe factory paymaster and his guard – captured their hearts. Jack shook his head in sorrow over the logic of his friends: Sacco and Vanzetti were 'little people', therefore they must be innocent. If they were innocent, someone or something big was guilty. Hence, the guilt of America itself.

What was America, after all? America was US. Like a fox caught in a trap, Jack's clever friends were chewing off their own paws.

And what was everybody else doing? The rest of the good, decent *little* folk? They were screaming that on general principles alone all radicals should be shot on sight.

Almost a lone voice, Eagels of the *Trident* cried in the wilderness for something so simple as common sense. There wasn't even an echo. Except for the single shining fact of Connie Mezinger's letting Eagels have his say. For that, Jack could forgive Connie all his multitude of sins.

As Teddy stepped off the Chicago train, Jack had taken one look at her face, hailed a taxi – and took her to Chinatown. It was as far from the world of sports and the radical Left as they could get in New York. For two days they'd had Chinese dumplings sent up to their Chinese room from a restaurant on Doyers Street, burned incense, drank fiery *samshu*, and fucked themselves back to laughter.

No laughter now. Popping into a Chinese grocery, Jack bought a pack of American Luckies, shook snow off his hat, and was back out on the narrow street – more an alley as all of New York's Chinatown was more of an alley. Wheeling his bike for less than a minute, Jack found what he'd been looking for – the restaurant on Doyers Street: small, dark, already open at five in the morning and still almost empty. Its only waiter a waitress, a young Chinese flapper, her black hair blunt cut with low bangs, her skirt short and her rolled stockings the colour of dry straw. In two years, things *had* changed. Now, it was just a restaurant.

His stomach cramping with hunger, a hangover hammering between his eyes, Jack ordered everything.

When the food came, when it lay steaming on the table before him, he thanked the waitress with the only Chinese phrase he'd ever learned, '*M-goy. Nee-dee cha ho ho yum.*' And she, startled, then pleased, rattled off a great battery of Chinese back at him. Holding up his hand to stop her, embarrassed, he explained that was all he knew. The girl backed away, smiling, and Jack was left facing a meal that now he had, he no longer wanted.

Life in the big city wasn't going well. Not Jack's life anyway. Just what had he come to New York for? What finally lured Chicago's best reporter – all modesty aside for the moment – to the newspaperman's mecca, a mecca he'd resisted for years? Had he really been running from women? Or did Jack want to mix with the big-time?

Link his name with Runyan's, Gene Fowler's, Heywood Broun's, Franklin P. Adam's – become as his hero, Richard Harding Davis? He bet his suffering ass he did! Stories breaking broke bigger on the spiked and spinning isle of Manhattan. When stories broke around Jack Eagels, any kind of story: shoot-outs, fires on the thirtieth floor, well-planned heists that cleaned out the diamond district, tracking the killer of a bad cop, Jack ran on pure oxygen, was filled with a crazy levitating joy. He needed the shenanigans of his fellow man like a junkie needs dope, a doctor needs illness, a cop needs crime, a politician needs stupidity, a con man needs greed, and a man of the cloth – any cloth – needs fear. Without basic human nature, everybody'd be out of a job. For Jack it was worse; he'd run out of his reason for living. Good news was no news. New York's news was bad, and for a man whose blood was half Arapaho and half printer's ink, that was all he needed.

Seated at the back of a Doyers Street eatery in a Chinese booth coated in ancient blistered varnish, sipping perfumed tea and a butt on the go, Jack wondered for the very first time if how his life was panning out might not be his own fault.

Take his scrappy hooligan. Where was Red O'Rourke? No getting around it, one thing was for sure – wherever she was and whatever she was doing, if anything was his fault, last night was. Nothing Teddy had done warranted Lulu LeRoy. Not really, not yet. Or did it? (Pardon me, Jack, old fellow, but was that what Lulu was? Something for Teddy? Is that where things have come to? Screwing the ass off a child to punish Teddy O'Rourke? Of course not, you were drunk. That child wanted you. And God, but you wanted to be wanted. Besides, Lulu wasn't a child, she was a full grown woman – sort of. Well, parts of her were.)

Was Teddy staying with George Bache and his mother, Dinah? Of course she was – where else would she go?

Her friends were male. Comrades or not, old pals, sportswriters or sportsmen all, things could turn tricky if their redheaded, long-legged chum stayed with any of them. She couldn't go home either. With Bluff O'Rourke for a father, there'd never been any home. Bluff might have been a great way to grow up, but if she ever needed to go back, it wasn't there. The old man himself? Christ knew. Bluff could be anywhere – and always was. Blowing poison darts over the prow of a sinking canoe up some Amazonian backwater, leading a bloodthirsty band of *badmashes* across the Hindu Kush, screwing some delicious brown thing on the white sands of Pago Pago, beating Hitler at a hand of cards. Who the hell knew? So – Teddy was obviously staying at the Dakota. The question was – was she sleeping with George Bache? And the answer – Jack lit his second Lucky from the stub of his first – the answer was none of his business. Not after Saturday night, it wasn't. When she'd told him to get lost and he hadn't grabbed her jaw, clamped it between his fingers, made her look him in the face – not after he hadn't told her she wasn't going anywhere, that he loved her. Even after she beaned him with a bowl of soup, he still loved her. And worse, not after last night.

What was he going to do about last night? Maybe he wouldn't have to do anything. Maybe it would just go away, maybe Lulu cared as little for him as she'd cared for Bernt McTaggart. Sure, and maybe he'd write the Great American Novel. Jack knew he was kidding himself. He might not remember much of what sweet, idiotic Gilda Tannenbaum – or whatever her real name was – said, and God, she'd said plenty, but in all that thick bourbon fog, one clear, unnerving sentence came to him, remained sweet and shaming as when she'd whispered it into his ear. 'I love you, Jack Eagels,' she'd said in that voice with bubbles in it. 'I know it's quick and maybe even it's dumb, but I love you.'

Shit! Did he love Lulu? Of course not. Did he like Lulu? Oh Lord, he liked Lulu.

But now, sitting over a bowl of steaming won ton soup, his dark, aching head in his hands, Jack knew that whatever she'd done and whoever she'd done it with, he loved that damn redhead. It took him two years to find out, but he finally knew.

'I love you, Teddy O'Rourke,' he said to the Chinese wall, then began coughing. He coughed so long and so hard the girl with the beautiful slanted eyes and the short skirt came back on her jazz baby legs and slapped him on the back.

'You OK, mister?'

'No,' said Jack. He wasn't.

At seven thirty in the morning, Jack was standing by Teddy O'Rourke's desk. All around, the *Trident* was waking up. But Teddy, sound asleep, was slumped over her Remington. By the side of her typewriter lay a crumpled velvet hat and a few pages of print. Jack read the one on the top, something about Dancing Joe Bright. Of course it was good, Teddy was always good – the writing passionate, the style all her own. Why was he always forgetting how talented she was? Did he ever tell her? Praise her? No, guess not; he'd been too busy getting passionate about his own stuff. Maybe that's what this was all about? If so, things were changing – right about now.

Quietly, Jack pulled over Teddy's only spare chair and sat in it. Put his elbows on his knees, propped his chin on a fist, kept his hat on, and watched her sleep. Thinking that his love for Teddy was a constant which he constantly forgot. Thinking that if it mattered, and it did, Teddy was good in bed – but what mattered so much more, Teddy O'Rourke was good out of bed. Thinking that Teddy was honest and game, that the line of her jaw was heartbreaking in its gallantry, that her hair in the

172

thin November sun was the colour of a brand new copper penny, the one with Abe Lincoln on it, his all time favourite president.

Thinking – Holy shit! What the hell happened to her? Red looked like she'd been rolled in a gravel pit, chewed by rats; she looked like Lillian Gish after a few quick rounds with Max Schuldner. And what was she wearing? Whatever it once was, it wasn't now. Something velvet, black and slinky, busted out at the elbows, ripped at the shoulder, shredded from the waist down. Jack leaned over, looked under the desk. No shoes on her feet, but ripped stockings on her legs, her left scraped raw from ankle to knee. Legs? Teddy was wearing legs? No trousers?

Worried, concerned, dumbfounded, Jack was reaching over to shake Teddy's shoulder, wake her up, when a dry hacking cough ripped through his chest. A cough that startled Teddy out of sleep, made her clear grey eyes snap wide, made Jack double over with pain.

Red put her hand on his arm. 'Hello, Jack Eagels,' she whispered. 'That's some cough.'

'This little thing? It's nothing. I've had worse.'

'Maybe you ought to take something for it.'

'Any suggestions?'

'Well, I've heard that orange juice and aspirin work wonders. Then, of course, they do say staying warm is a good idea.'

'I've tried them all. Nothing works.'

'Not a thing?'

'No, not a thing . . . except maybe warmth. But have you ever noticed how hard it is to keep warm all alone?'

'Even in bed?'

'I've tried that too. It's hardest of all in bed.'

With her baby finger, Teddy drew a tiny, electrifying circle on the back of his hand. 'Perhaps . . . if you tried again? – and I peeled the orange?'

'Ain't this fucking cute?'

Jack lifted his head and groaned. Oh shit. Not Mezinger, not now. But it *was* now and it *was* Connie and love wasn't in Mezinger's dictionary.

'If you're trying to butter me up by getting here early, O'Rourke, forget it. I had that Harve Hopper cover the hockey game and I'm goddamned if he's ever seen a hockey puck in his life; I got a stack of mail already complaining. Sweet fucking Jesus, girlie! What the fuck happened to you? You fall off the Chrysler Building? Don't bother answering that. Once a dame, always a dame. Dames do screwy things.' Connie turned his Patsy Pig eyes on Eagels. 'I thought I'd find you in the sports department. What's new on McTaggart? Anything we can print?'

Neither Jack nor Teddy moved. Teddy kept her head on her typewriter, Jack kept his cupped in his hands. Connie was a very large gnat. If they waited long enough, he'd buzz off.

'Nothing new,' answered Jack, smiling at Teddy, in love with the red unhurtful sleep welt on her cheek where it had rested on the Remington, the freckles scattered over her nose, her dark lashes, the way the light burned in the tangle of her red hair, the three small cuts scabbing over in the corner of her lips, full lips that even while she slept had a delicate upward curve at – wait a minute. Who gave his redhead a knuckle sandwich? 'Madden thinks Schultz might have done it and arranged for it to look like Madden did it, though he doesn't say why. I'm seeing Dutch today to ask if Madden's right, and if Madden isn't, to ask Schultz who *he* thinks did it. Meanwhile, it's for certain Bernie McTaggart was Madden's man – but, don't get excited, that's not in writing.'

Connie's eyebrows went up, bunching the skin of his forehead into folds of happy fat. 'McTaggart worked on the side for Madden? Terrific. So where's the write-up?'

'On your desk. I called it in last night.'

Sometimes being short wasn't fun. Connie couldn't look over Jack's shoulder, couldn't read the copy he could see on Teddy's desk. 'That better be good stuff you got there, O'Rourke. Your job is hanging by a noose.'

Teddy and Jack said, 'It's good,' at the same time.

Not much Connie could say to that, nothing to yell at anyone about. No way to begin the day. Connie went off to find Leonard Lamont. Lamont was always screwing up. The simpering fathead had written a smear on O'Rourke. Mezinger didn't mind that so much as he minded what it might do to Eagels – take his mind off his work. Though, judging by appearances, neither O'Rourke nor Eagels had seen it.

Teddy was still smiling at Jack. 'You read what I've been writing?' she said. 'But, it's not finished, I wrote it half asleep, there's still a lot of – '

'Forget all that, it's good. It's even more than good. First things first – what happened to you?'

A look of surprise widened Teddy's eyes, her hand came up to her wounded mouth. 'That?'

'That – and the legs and the dress.'

'Oh, that. I promise, I'll tell you all about it later.' Teddy slid the black velvet hat into a drawer, her head full of yellow cars and Mezinger, of aspirin and oranges, of a bloodthirsty gangster with Times Square in his eyes, of her share in her redman's front page story.

Teddy's typewriter between them, Jack got up and came around her desk. Saying as he circled, 'I've always liked looking at you when you're asleep. Especially when the light is low and the hour late – sometimes a little half smile plays around your lips and I wonder what you're dreaming about. I figure it's me. What do you figure?'

Looking up at him, Teddy smiled a little half smile.

Avoiding the split lip, Jack touched the corner of her mouth. 'That's the one. Listen, little hooligan. Let's call this off. Whatever I said Saturday night or at Lindy's, I didn't mean a word of it. I love you – you love me. Why

175

gum it up?' Jack pulled Teddy out of her chair. 'Come home, Red. Your cactus needs you.'

'And you?'

'Oh yes, me too.'

Teddy reached up, slipped her hand behind his curly head, pulled his face towards hers, and whispered in his ear. 'Promise me, if I take you somewhere and I do something, you won't cough.'

Jack kissed the pale cluster of freckles on Teddy's nose, thinking, *do something?* Here? Why not? With twenty-seven floors, the *Trident* was full of private places. His reaction to that possibility was his first reminder of what Lulu LeRoy – speaking of doing things – had done to him. Where it counted, he felt raw – but ready. Also guilty. But bygones were bygones. It wouldn't happen again.

'I promise.'

Teddy took his hand, led him out of her cubicle, through the sports department, pushed the elevator 'up' button for the twenty-third floor. Her fellow sports writers stared at the ravaged black velvet dress and the bare feet. Jack, giddy with hope, followed. So far it wasn't what he'd expected, but at the touch of her hand, it was just fine.

Until they walked into Mezinger's office.

'Sit down, Jack,' said Teddy. 'I've got something for you you're going to like.'

'Not in my office, he ain't,' snapped Connie, who'd just booted Lamont out of the door a minute before O'Rourke and Eagels walked in. He was sitting back in his swivel chair, tapping a pencil against the baby-butt pink of his shining skull. Aside from Connie's tiny feet in their tiny shoes propped by their stacked heels on his blotter and an Eskimo Pie stick in his out-tray, most of Connie's desk was covered with opened mail and copies of rival newspapers, foremost among them the *Daily News*. Arms behind his head, glasses low on his enormous nose, George Bache was stretched out on an old couch by the window, startled by the sight of Teddy.

Teddy parked her tattered velvet butt on the edge of Mezinger's huge mahogany desk and swung her dirty stockinged feet. 'Shut up, Connie. If you'd listen for a minute, you'd like it too.'

At that, Jack kissed the kind of surprise he'd been hoping for goodbye, shoved George's legs off one end of the couch, and sat down.

O'Rourke opened the cigarette box on Connie's desk, took one, and lit it with Connie's desk lighter, saying, 'I've been waiting here for hours, since two in the morning at least, right after I jumped out of the car – '

Always quick on the uptake, Jack said, 'Jumped out of a car?'

'A black Studebaker, going thirty.' Teddy stifled a yawn. 'I've been snatched from a steaming Harlem vault where men dance with men, put through a wringer by a great-looking gangster in a Sugar Hill casino, almost got stabbed – then belted in the mouth – by a good black dancer with a bad black temper, taken for a ride through Central Park in the dead of night by two giggling, gun-toting brothers or cousins or whatever the hell they were – that's when I jumped, picked myself up from Broadway, and brother, let me tell you, Broadway's a hard street – that's when I lost my shoes, got chased up Forty-fourth Street in the dark – '

Jack looked at Connie. Connie looked at Jack. George looked at them both. They all said, 'You have?'

'You think I'm making this up?'

Jack and George rode over Connie's 'Yes', with firm, 'No's'.

Teddy stared Connie down. 'And I've been hiding here ever since. In case those two crazies are still down in the lobby waiting for me.'

Connie yawned so hard he almost cracked his jaw. 'OK, OK already, O'Rourke, so I listened. Where's the part I'm supposed to like?'

'Tom Channing owns a yellow car.'

Connie Mezinger's eyes lit up like Coney Island on a summer's night and a little quiver rippled the fat of his cheek. 'He does? Eagels, you hear that?'

Teddy hopped off the desk. 'Wait a minute, Mezinger, not so fast. I tell you the rest, I get a part of the story.'

'What part?'

'Half. I follow it up. I get a by-line with Jack's.'

'Like shit you do. You trip over a scoop, you share the whole story – you crazy? Where do you think we are, Russia? Butt out, O'Rourke, go back to Hohenloe and make the little guy happy. Eagels, fill up the holes.'

Jack, as eager as Connie, came off Bache's couch in one bound, lifted Teddy's hand, kissed the curled fingers. 'Thanks, Bricktop. You just saved me days of crap.'

Teddy didn't pull away, just stepped back a little, tossing her unfinished cigarette in Connie's out-tray. 'Say that again, Jack.'

'Thanks – '

'No, not that. Just the last part.' Like a pitcher's fastball, Teddy's voice was low and steady, humming with something Jack couldn't quite catch.

'You mean where I say, you just saved me days of crap?'

'That's the sentence.'

Teddy had backed two steps further away, the hand Jack just kissed, clenching.

'Well, baby, you have. Who knows, maybe even a week?' Jack reached forward to pull her back, and Teddy, stepping into the punch, connected with one of Shucks Spooner's best – smack on the point of his unshaven chin. It knocked him off his weary, feverish feet and right on his weary, feverish ass. Even Teddy was surprised. But not enough to calm down.

Hands still up in a classic fighter's right-left, O'Rourke stood over a flat-out Jack, a Jack who needed the rest. 'Saved you days of crap! You rotten, selfish sonofafuckingbitch! I almost killed myself getting this story and you just say thanks? You take it and walk off?'

'Pipe down, O'Rourke!' Connie's voice was louder than Teddy's. He'd come around his desk just as she'd decked Jack and was now, like Rumpelstiltskin, hopping up and down on furious little legs. George lay on his couch, a lopsided grin on his devilish face.

Teddy whirled, fists up, her fine-tuned fury turning with her. 'Why?' she spat. 'Only *you* yell around here?' Throwing two short jabs at his chin, she missed by a deliberate hair. 'You pint-sized toad! You foul-mouthed, mean-minded chimpanzee! You don't let me work this story, *my* fucking story, a story *I* found, I followed up – I quit!' For the third time Teddy jabbed, catching the fat of his jaw.

Turning purple as a rotten plum, Connie went crazy. 'I got you on a five-year contract!' he screamed. 'You can't quit – you're fired!'

Teddy popped him right on the button.

And George – delighted in his corner – let out a whoop!

At that exact moment, holding his bloody nose, something caught Connie's eye. Something more riveting than O'Rourke, the red-headed psycho. 'Good God, lookit that!' he yelled, jerking open his window and sticking his fat head out between two of the gargoyles on the *Trident*'s twenty-third floor. Across the street was a building almost as tall as Thorp's. A thin man in a grey suit, grey homburg hat and spats, was teetering on the ledge of its twenty-fourth floor.

Eyes popping, Connie pulled his head back and squealed, 'Another jumper!' Waving his stumpy arms and spraying blood, he dashed out of his office and into the city room. 'Who's covering my fucking jumper!'

One of the three phones on Connie's desk rang. Unclenching her busy fist, Teddy stepped over Jack and answered it. Listened, went hmmmm and ummmm and ahhhhh, said, 'Oh, really? How nice. I'll get him for you.'

Then held the receiver down to Jack, still sprawled on the floor. 'It's a woman and it's for you. I'd be careful what you say, she sounds like she's asking for more.'

Rubbing his chin, Jack took the phone, a deep breath, listened, groaned, said, 'Lulu?'

And Teddy walked away. From Jack. From Connie. From George.

George Bache, holding on to his heart, watched her go. Eight years before, Teddy O'Rourke blew into his life with all the force of a line drive slamming into a glove. Two and a half years ago, Lindbergh was setting out to fly the Atlantic, Ruth was batting his way to sixty home runs in one glorious season, it was the two-hundredth anniversary of the cuckoo clock, and George was winding himself up to ask Teddy to marry him. He'd taken her to see Bela Lugosi as Count Dracula, then to the Colony for a late-night supper, bought her a single white rose, talked about everything, about anything, talked with an intense beauty of language that dazzled them both, and – dried up. The moment passed. Before it could come again, Jack Eagels breezed in from Chicago, hit Teddy O'Rourke like a home run smashing out the lights over Yankee Stadium, and that was that.

Now? George had one Sunday of soaring hope; on Monday, Jack Eagels, mighty journalist and practising dope, looked set to sweep the field in the insensitive stakes; Teddy O'Rourke laid out Jack as neatly as George M. Cohan once had Broadway hits; and George S. Bache gave up. Eagels and O'Rourke were crazy about each other. Once again, George lowered his sights. But not his heart. He was so proud, so foolishly fond of Teddy, he thought he might cry. O'Rourke had chutzpah. Maybe even more chutzpah than his grandmother, Minnie Bache, and Minnie'd almost swum to America.

George stood up, picked Teddy's cigarette out of Connie's tray before it burnt down the *Trident* building, and handed it down to Jack – who, still on the floor with the phone, was listening, not talking.

'Here, pal,' said George, 'smoke this. You deserve it.' Then he walked out too.

11

Girls with Long Necks

Before organized crime, there was chaos. Too many gangs split up the takings; too many trigger-happy punks, spraying rivals with real bullets, hit Joe Schmo and his missus. But the soaring success of the smart guys down on Wall Street had given America's brighter thugs an idea.

Look at them guys, they said to themselves; why, they're nothing more than crooks in homburgs. Talk about a nest of thieves! But did they have the right idea, or did they have the right idea? Boy, did they! Fleecing the whole goddamn country and they call it 'business'.

So – choosing Jersey's Atlantic City as neutral turf – they held a convention in May. (Coincidentally, though the width of a continent away, Hollywood held one too. The movie moguls called theirs: the First Annual Academy Awards.)

Everybody who was nobody came. Nig Rosen from Philadelphia, Longie Zwillman from New Jersey, Al Capone from Chicago, Charles Solomon from Boston – Dutch Schultz, Johnny Torrio, and the Broadway Mob from New York. New York was strongest in numbers: Meyer Lansky, Joe Adonis, Frank Costello, and a guy called Louis 'Lepke' Buchalter. Together they fixed prices on booze, established quotas for each gang, arranged to pool supplies in times of shortage, and organized a clearing house for accounts. They called it the Combine.

Lucky Luciano, an observer for the Mafia, watched and was amazed. Mobs outside the Mafia had come to a working alliance. That a scattered group of free and greedy outlaws could come to such complex and organized deals stung Luciano into thought, shortly followed by action.

The Honoured Society would move with the times as well – or die as an underworld power.

Then there was Owney Madden. Slim, dapper, handsome, English: until New York – beginning when Owney stepped off the boat only eleven years old – rubbed all the Englishness off. A graduate of pre-Prohibition teenage gangs, an expert with guns, slingshots and lead pipes, Madden maintained his position in New York City as a respected 'independent'. In 1923, Owney earned his release from Sing Sing just in time to get in on the ground floor of the booze business. Working quickly, dealing with both the Combine and the Mafia, he'd cornered a piece of that brand new market with elegant skill. Now he controlled New York's booze, its nightclubs, its politicians. Nobody messed with Madden, not even Arthur Flegenheimer, aka Dutch Schultz, who'd carved an empire in Harlem. New York called Owney its second mayor – the one who didn't have to count votes.

Until three years ago, Tom Channing worked as muscle for Madden. Until one year ago, he worked for Arnold Rothstein and Waxey Gordon – whose concerns involved dope, shakedowns, the renting of women and the lending of money. As for money lending, it was the collecting that could turn nasty. That's where Tom came in. But now, all that was past. When Arnold died 'game' at the Polyclinic, Tom jumped in fast. Grabbing at gambling and boxing, Tom Channing worked for himself.

Madden had the midtown sewn up, Channing was pushing west from Brooklyn – between them they could squeeze Harlem. It was a thought. But, so far, just a thought.

At nine o'clock in the morning, Channing was eating breakfast in his private suite above the casino on Sugar Hill. Across the table sat the woman with the cocoa voice. The woman wore a loose wrapper the thin green colour of a sliced cucumber, satin high-heeled slippers, her blonde hair looped and held in a hairnet. She was ripe, though still young enough to get by on her looks; she spent all of her time and what was left of her dead husband's money at Sugar Hill; and she was trying too hard to please.

'You want jelly on that roll, Tommy?' Sliding his plate away from him, tearing open a hot roll with busy fingers, spreading a thick curl of butter on one piece, on the other. Arranging the salt, the jam pot.

Tom, wearing a dark green camel's hair robe, his face hidden behind a copy of the *Trident*, reached out and seized her wrist. 'Aggie, don't fuss. It ain't worth it.'

Knowing exactly what he meant but refusing to accept it, the widow stopped fussing anyway. And sat there watching Tom read his paper. Her netted blonde head heavy with endless schemes to win this man, a man she wanted but couldn't, for the life of her, have. For Agnes, her dead husband, Harold, would have melted like the butter on Tom's roll. For Tommy, Agnes did all the melting, for Tommy she'd put up with anything – hadn't she always? Whether he knew it or not, Tommy needed her. Whether he knew it or not, if she walked out of his life, Tommy would fold up and die. That's what Agnes thought. So Agnes stayed.

Without knocking, Owney Madden and Frenchy DeMange walked in on her cosy breakfast for two. Agnes held on to her seat.

Tom put down his paper and smiled.

'Pretty early for you, ain't it, Owney? You two want something to eat?'

'Sure. Hiya, Agnes,' said Owney, seating himself on Tom's right.

The blonde barely looked up.

Frenchie lowered his great butt into the chair on Tom's left. They both took off their hats, but not their coats. The hats went in their laps.

Tom tapped Agnes's arm. 'Say, kid, where's your manners? Move yourself. You want to keep my guests sitting here starving? Go down to the kitchens, order some more – say, what you fellows want?'

'Don't matter,' said Frenchy. 'What you're having.'

'Tell them bacon, eggs, toast, grapefruit, coffee, tell them to put those cherries on the grapefruit – and Agnes?'

'Yes, Tommy?'

'Don't come back with the food.'

With the widow gone, her slippers' frustrated heels clicking on the silvered glass floor, Tom said, 'OK, Owney. What's up? It's not like you to come calling.'

'We got a problem, Channing. I thought I'd ask you to solve it.'

'Whatever I can do, I'll do. What problem?'

'My pet cop, Bernie. I got Grover Whalen's boys sniffing my ass; every fucking one of them beating their meat over McTaggart. I got Jimmy asking me with those sad eyes of his to sort all this out – hell, Tom, you want that pushy little Italian asshole La Guardia running around our town calling himself mayor? The thought makes my hair hurt. This town's already got an honest mayor, what it don't need is a guy without a sense of humour. Anyway, I got the press with their hands up my trousers, squeezing my balls; the way they're telling it, Bernie was Mary Pickford, America's sweetheart.'

Frenchy, turning his hat in his huge hands, laughed at that. Madden paused to let him do it.

'It's no big deal to have the cops thinking I killed him, it's no big deal that everyfuckingbody in town from District Attorney Isidor Force Tuttle the fucking III to frigging Archbishop Cardinal Hayes is screaming their heads off – say, who the hell are they? And what kind of name is Isidor Force, for fuck's sake? What's a big deal, Tom, is my friend Jimmy's getting called names for something he don't have nothing to do with, and what's a bigger deal is now the Combine's getting pissed off. They don't like this kind of trouble. It's turning into a circus. You know that crack about something being bigger than its parts? Well, that's what we got here with Bernie. Stupid cocksucker, getting himself stuck like a pig. I told him, but you remember Bernie – too damn cute to listen.'

Listening quietly, Tom sipped his coffee. 'I warned him too, Owney. The first time I knew he was playing with too many queens and no ace.'

'I know you did, Tom. He shoulda listened, saved himself a trip to the morgue. But what's done is done. Now, we gotta deal with the mess he made. Like that asshole, Schultz. I'm the first to admit it was me and my crack Saturday night at the Cotton got Schultz all shook up. I guess I shouldn't of said what I said about him maybe doing the job. It was a frigging joke, wasn't it, Frenchy?'

'It made me laugh, but I was forgettin' dat Dutch don't laugh at nuttin'.'

'You ain't shitting, he don't. But then, I still thought the whole thing was a tap dance, even with Bernie getting found on my back doorstep. Now, *that* was a dumb move.'

'I understand it was a mistake,' said Tom.

'Some mistake. It's gonna get somebody killed. So me, I come here to make sure it's the right somebody.'

A waiter with a face like a Borzoi skipped in with a silver tray. Set places for Madden and DeMange, laid out their food, and was gone so fast Frenchy said, 'Wow.'

Between forefinger and thumb, Madden picked up a piece of bacon and bit off a delicate bite. 'Didn't think too much about what it was doing to me, Tom, because I was still thinking about what it was doing to you. Not even by yesterday, when you and me paid our usual call on Mae. But then, I didn't know what holy hell was breaking loose.

'Today, I know. Today, I got word that Schultz is steamed, steamed enough to do something stupid.'

'An' when Dutch does sumpin' stupid, it's stupid,' added Frenchy, playing with the cherry in his grapefruit.

'So,' said Madden, popping the rest of the bacon in his mouth, 'I come to ask you for the last time, do something about it. You owe me.'

186

Tom put his face in his hands, rubbed his eyes, combed his blond hair with restless fingers, stalled. The weight he was carrying, that he'd carried for years, had just gotten a few pounds heavier. No reason to ask Madden why he was asking him; Tom knew why. Madden was right. He owed him. Why in the hell did CD put the body behind the Cotton Club? Dumb shit! Why take the yellow Cord? CD's reason: because a body fits nice in a rumble seat! Tom had come close to plugging him. Maybe Sol was right. Italians, like women – and Dutch Schultz – were stupid. Tom raised the hard blue of his eyes to Madden's, and held them there. 'When a friend asks a friend for a favour, a friend gets it.'

Chewing bacon, Madden smiled. 'You're like a brother to me, Tom, a fucking brother. So I know what I'm asking and I know it ain't going to be easy.' He picked up another piece of bacon. 'Mae's show, it's pulling out for Frisco in a few days, right?'

'Three.'

'And everybody's leaving with it?'

'They will be.'

'So that's great. We'll give the broad a party before she goes. That West's a pip. And if the party don't do nothing else, it'll show Schultz what he's up against. You and me together, right, Tommy? Meantime, I'm counting on you.'

'Give me a couple days. I'll sort it out.'

'Sure you will, Tom. What's a brother for? By the way, I heard you dug up Joey Bright. Next fight, I'll put a bet on him.'

'Solomon!'

Sol Rosenbloom – behind a door ever since Madden and DeMange showed up – stepped out. 'Yeah, boss?'

'What's Durata and his idiot cousin doing?'

'Sleeping. They been up all night since they lost the redhead, staking out her newspaper building. When people

187

started showing up for work, CD gave it up and came back. That place ain't never deserted.'

Tom stood, walked to his tall window, stood looking out over the Harlem River. 'How could anybody lose a skirt? That's two mistakes in two days. *My* mistakes.'

'Yours, boss?'

'Who chose dummies for the jobs?'

'You did.'

'I did. What do you think, Sol? Am I turning into a chump, losing my touch?'

'You, Tom? Never, not you.'

Tom stepped away from the window, clapped Sol on his beefy back. 'Listen to me. I sound like some old woman – fuck that.'

Like a dog, Sol grinned from ear to ear. 'Right, fuck that. So, what do we do about the girlie reporter? She's still got the money.'

'Her? We don't do anything about her. She'll do it all herself. It's what I've got to do for Owney that worries me. This time it shook up the Combine. This one they're not letting me sweep under the rug. You were right all along, Sol, it's something I should of done long ago, God help me.'

'You talking about who I think you're talking about? You thinking of Joey?'

'Yeah, Sol. It's time.'

'Been time for years. You want me to help?'

'Couldn't do it without you, not this one.' Tom smiled, snapped his fingers. 'But hell, it had to happen someday. Enough of the sad talk. Come on, Rosenbloom, let's go see Joe. See if we can pry Miss Bean off him, get him on those dancing feet.'

Though George Bache had returned to the fifteenth floor, Jack was still where Teddy left him – up on the twenty-third. Lying flat on his back by a dead receiver at the foot of Mezinger's desk, thinking that just when they're loving each other again, Teddy hauls off and hits him. She was certifiably nuts. Teddy O'Rourke, through with him? Jack Eagels was through with her. Though he wished Lulu hadn't called. That wasn't on the cards at all.

Having sewn up the jumper story (another poor sap who'd been worth a million bucks on October the 20th, a half million on October the 24th, and *owed* fifty grand the moment he'd stepped off his ledge and landed five feet away from a slack-jawed housewife buying two tickets for *Animal Crackers*), Connie was back, bloody hanky to his wounded nose, spitting. 'Women! A pain in the butt. What's with that girlie? She crazy? Hitting me like that.'

From the floor, Jack sighed. 'Don't ask me.'

'Don't ask you? Why shouldn't I ask you? I'm speaking to the guy who's shtupping her, aren't I?'

'Nicely put, Connie.'

'Fuck it. What else would you call it?'

'I no longer know.'

'So, I'm right. You are.'

'I was.'

'Was? Was? You aren't going to get personal on me, are you, Eagels? Shtupping her, not shtupping her? Shit, what do I care? O'Rourke! When a dame gets ideas, you take it on the light side, like musical comedy.'

Jack held up a droopy hand in protest. 'Ah, come on Connie, she's more than – '

'No she ain't. Did you believe that crap she was selling? Jumping out of cars, for chrissake. If you can believe that, you can believe a clam would get down on bended knee and sing Swanee. It's mostly for that, I fired her. Firing her fanny is something I dreamed of for months. I'm giving Hype Hohenloe's new man her column. What's his name? Jumper? No, Hopper! Course, he'll have to come up with a new name to call it. What do you think? Behind the Plate? No. At Bat? No. Hell, that's his problem. He may not know his ass from a hole in the ground, but he'll learn. Besides, and goddammit, he's a man and a man is what the

189

job calls for. What are you lying there for, Eagels? You got the tip on the yellow car. Break open that McTaggart story. If the *News* beats us to it, I'll break every bone in your foot.' Connie turned away, changed his mind, turned back. '*Both* feet. And if what you find turns out to hurt Walker – hell, I like the guy, *everybody* likes the guy, but if Jim's fucking the city, fuck him.'

Jack crawled to his unsteady feet. 'This city's a whore, Connie – what else would he do with it?'

Back on the snowy street, hunched in his jacket against a Monday that was growing colder, hat on the back of his aching head, a fine mist of faint fever beading the hollow of his unshaven cheek, Jack gazed, first up and then down the long lick of Forty-fourth Street.

To Jack, Manhattan was like a boat with a great wallowing hull, its blunted prow pointed south to the sea. If one day it should slip its bridges, raise its tunnels, sail away across the grey, too-charted Atlantic, what then would America be? Still fed, still clothed, still housed, still governed for better or for worse, but along with this mad hullabaloo of an island would go America's dreams. This might be Teddy's town but it was Jack's city. New York was one big eight-column headline with three exclamation marks, now tipping up at the Battery, falling into the Bronx.

Colours ran – the swirl of traffic; sounds blurred – honking, squealing, hooting – horns, brakes, cop whistles; faceless drivers hung out of their cabs shaking impatient fists, their bawling language complex with crudities – a thousand cruising Connies. The pavement was a million shoes, shuffling, skipping, skimming, wearing away their soles. Shivering with energy, New York City looked as if it went on forever. Racked with a dry cough he couldn't shake, Jack heard the god-almighty roar of the city, up from Wall Street where the people worshipped Mammon, bucketing down Broadway where they gaped at spectacle.

New York rocked to the rhythm of rivet and hammer as punch-drunk skyscrapers were flung up in midtown – fevered flaunting of the money boom. A boom! that had echoed around the world, only now dying, only now dying, only now dead.

'You want somethin', fella?' asked a voice full of the choppy music of Brooklyn. 'You been standin' there thinkin' about it long enough.'

Brooklyn whipped Jack back to where Broadway joined Seventh at Forty-fourth Street – all of it Times Square. 'What?'

'I said, you wanna dog or you wanna shuffle along? Coughin' like that, you're scarin' the customers.'

Jack noticed the city smelled like mustard, like relish, like boiled and salty meat, that he was standing next to a hotdog stand. He also noticed he was hungry. He hadn't eaten his Chinese breakfast.

'Sure, two, with trimmings.'

Slopping everything onto Jack's second breakfast, the hotdog man jerked a thumb up and east. Five and a half crosstown blocks away, the Chrysler Building slipped a silver splinter under New York's nervy skin. 'Ain't that some baby? Makes you proud to be an American, that does.'

At that moment, not sure he was proud of anything, Jack craned his head back to watch workers walking on steel in the sky – and suddenly thought of Laurel and Hardy. The last movie he'd seen with Teddy had them clutching girders, weak-knee'd with hilarious fear. Red in his head again, Jack was struck by a simple dazzling thought. Above his head – all those windows. Windows rising above windows, the windows of Manhattan, and behind each – how many girls with bold eyes? How many girls with impossibly long necks? New York was full of women. Not all of them had known Bernt McTaggart. There must be a few out there who would like to know Jack Eagels. What did he have to lose? Teddy was gone. What did he

191

have to gain? Who knew? Bold-eyed women, women who chatted of this and that, women who couldn't box? Bring on the chattering ladies. Starting with Lulu whatever her last name was. Lulu could do more for Jack Eagels than lead him to Tom Channing and a yellow car.

Coughing, Jack kicked the Harley into life.

Seventeen floors above Jack, Teddy, heart in a slow looping burn, was back in sports. Shaky, the thin skin under her eyes jumping, her legs buckling, needing to breathe. Opened the window. Was startled by the roar of the city. The icy blast of city wind. Stuck her head out and sucked in gulps of New York's crisp morning. Up here, it was clean. And freezing. She slammed down the window, shivering the glass.

My God, who was Lulu? Whoever she was, Jack, the bastard, sure knew her – and knew her well. One night after she walks out of the apartment on Broadway, one goddamned night, and Jack knows someone called Lulu. He was with Lulu while she was getting bundled in and out of cars, socked in the mouth, getting chased barefoot up Broadway. If she was going to cry about anything, she was going to cry about that. It hurt. Listening to that sweet girlish voice on the phone, practically *breathing* Jack's name, asking if he made it to the paper all right, if he was feeling well, after all, he hadn't had much sleep, had he? Then the voice giggled. She'd handed the phone over to Jack before she screamed. No scene then; she wouldn't make one now. But it was hard, Lord, was it hard.

Teddy turned from a view that was no longer hers to face a desk that was no longer hers. Now that the redman was out of her life and into Lulu's, now that she'd thrown her job in Mezinger's face and he'd caught it on the hop, what did she have left?

Homerun baseballs signed by Babe Ruth and Lou Gehrig? The casing of Ruth's ball split open, loose case flapping like the skin of a scalped Indian (if only it were Jack's)? A worn mitt from Dazzy Vance? A scuffed football from Red Grange? Was that all?

Photographs? On her walls, a jumbled gallery of framed snaps: the splendid 1927 New York Yankees, football players from Harvard, Yale, Notre Dame, the New York Rangers hockey team, Sir Barton – the only horse to win racing's Triple Crown, Gallant Fox – the only horse that looked likely to do it again, and the greatest of them all, Man O' War, with Teddy O'Rourke up in the saddle and laughing. Gertrude Ederle, the twenty-year-old Amsterdam Avenue butcher's daughter who'd not only swum the English Channel a few years back but had done it faster than any man had – ever. From boxing, Gene Tunney and Jack Dempsey, from tennis, 'Big' Bill Tilden, golf, Bobby Jones and Walter Hagen – Teddy O'Rourke's vivid world of sports pinned down in grainy shades of grey. Over her desk a photo of the impish Tex Rickard in a bowler hat, arm flung around the shoulder of Bluff O'Rourke, the picture taken the year Bluff was cooking up another scheme that blew up in his face like a bubble of sticky gum. About which Bluff only laughed, and dreamed up something else twice as dicey.

Mementos of ten years of breathing the inky, oily, sweaty air of a big city newspaper. Ten long years since her first job on the *Morning Telegraph* – working out of an old brick building catty-cornered from where the new Madison Square Garden was soon to be, a building that started life as a car barn: low, dingy, sinister with rats.

Teddy at twenty ran errands for seasoned newspapermen, pulled them out of low smoky bars when a story was on the boil – and so were they. Made them coffee, prised open their drunken mouths to pour it down their throats, took to writing copy when that didn't work, got better and better at it, better than they, begged to cover sports when people began to listen. A few years later, her best stories in a Woolworth's folder, she finagled a minor post on *Ring*,

Nat Fleischer's boxing magazine. Then, just when she'd won Nat's trust, even admiration, she left. Just like that. Lured by a newspaper she'd heard was going to rival the *World*, even the *Sun* in its heyday. Walking with a bigger folder into the *Trident* when it was new and struggling and hungry for talent. Of course, first she had to face Cornelius Mezinger. So she brought Bluff O'Rourke along. Bluff got her in the door, made Mezinger shut his flapping mouth and listen – but it was Teddy O'Rourke who got the job – and kept it.

Now, steaming in her own juices, counting pictures on a wall, why had she ever thought writing for a paper was writing? Writing for a newspaper was like writing on ice. A few hours later and all you had was a puddle.

O'Rourke took a last look around, threw her raincoat over the mess the night had made of her gown, dug out a spare pair of low-heeled shoes she kept in the bottom drawer of her desk – and walked out on everything. Except Man O' War. His photo she slipped from its hook, tucked under her arm. And Hype Hohenloe. Hype, she ran into. Hohenloe must have been standing right outside her door. Fidgeting, embarrassed to see her, but waiting anyway.

The little man was a gentleman. Connie's sports editor was as thin as Connie was fat, as hairy as Connie was bald, as soft-spoken as Connie was a loud-mouthed sonofabitch, and knew more about sports than anyone Teddy ever met. He also thought Teddy O'Rourke was the best sports reporter in New York. Barring Damon Runyon and Grantland Rice. Those two, Hype thought her equal. Tripping over her sports editor reminded Teddy there was at least one thing she'd miss at the *Trident*.

Rolling his close-set eyes to heaven, Hype said, 'The word came down, and the word stinks. You know what that man is? That man is a schmuck.'

'Thanks, Hype.'

'Me, I wouldn't lose a reporter like you, not for all of the Babe's home runs.' Hype shrugged his tiny shoulders. 'But what can I do? In a word, nothing. Though anyone asks me, you get a recommendation from Hype Hohenloe with gold edges. All the stuff you're leaving? Don't worry about a thing. I'll get someone to box it for you, keep it safe.' Hype touched Teddy's arm. 'You OK?'

'I'm OK, more shaken than stirred. I'll get over it.'

'Sure you will, Teddy, sure you will. But, if you don't mind my asking, what you going to do now?'

Teddy couldn't tell Hype what was running through her mind, making her thoughts race like the bone white filly on a good day. Though she wanted to. Wanted to? Dying to, was more like it. What did she have left? She had the answer to the story that all New York was agog over, that's what she had left. Teddy O'Rourke was going to bring Tom Channing down all by herself, spread him and his yellow car over the front page. She would do that because of Dixie Fiske, gassed like a weasel in a car in Hoboken, for Bernt McTaggart, not all he was cracked up to be, but surely not bad enough, mean enough, to get knifed in an alley behind the Cotton Club, for Dancing Joe – and what had Joey to do with all this? She'd know soon enough. Even without Dixie and Bernt and Joe, she'd run Channing down; the gorgeous gunman had made her feel like a fool. But more, much more, Tom was going on the front page with an O'Rourke by-line because of Cornelius Mezinger and Jack Eagels. Let them eat that!

But whose front page? When the time came, that would take care of itself. For now, if she told Hype, he'd tell someone else, and then God knew, Connie would hear about it and Jack would hear about it, and right there, you had one hell of a mess. So she sighed, looked as defeated as she could, and said, 'Take a bath and get out of this damn dress.'

'I don't know; I kinda like it. But you ever need anything, you call Hype, right?'

'I ever need anything, you'll be wishing you hadn't said that.'

The little man laughed, rocking back on his heels. 'So, OK, Teddy. You take care of yourself.' Then he slapped himself on his own forehead. 'Say, I was forgetting. That fighter you were looking for, Joe Bright? – I hear he's been booked into Spooner's Gym for the day. I sent Hopper to check it out.' When the name Hopper came out of Hohenloe's mouth, he looked embarrassed all over again. 'Sorry, Teddy, but that's the breaks.' Assuming what he said next would perk her up, it perked *him* up. The words danced off his tongue like a happy jingle. 'So, you see, he wasn't lost like you thought, after all.'

'Guess not, Hype.'

Playing at the Rialto down the block from 1600 Broadway was *The Trespasser*, Gloria Swanson's first talkie. Standing out in front of the shuttered picture palace on an early morning pavement glittering with thin snow and mica, littered with fast walking New Yorkers, Teddy O'Rourke was trying to get across the traffic of Times Square. Unlike celluloid Swanson, Teddy was in full living colour.

Teddy O'Rourke was still the kid she'd been with Bluff for all those years – a nervy, fast-talking, flame-haired little girl with darting grey eyes. A breathless girl who was trying to see everything, read everything, do everything, be everything. For a kid's good and glorious reason: because they were there – to be learned, to be seen, to be done. It wasn't the want of money or the need for fame or power that spurred her. It was curiosity. Curiosity was Teddy's greatest gift. A monkey-pure interest supported by vivid energy, made sweet by humour, spiced by an intellect so quick it seemed like a sixth sense, or like good guesses in the dark – but was really reasoning at a dazzling speed. Nothing – not pain or love or the call of common sense, not even Connie Mezinger – slowed her down. The greed of others, the lying, the cheating, the manipulation, the killing, their blindness to beauty or wonder or grace, made up the raw stuff she wrote about. Teddy's slant on the world, the way she wrote, changed over the years; though it was still bursting with youthful delight in the chaotic state of her fellow man. But the blindness remained theirs, not hers. If Teddy was blind to anything – and she was – it was to limitations. To rules, like stop signs, that said: don't do this or don't do that. But most of all to a sign as big as a billboard that said a flat, defeated, 'It can't be done.' All Teddy didn't do was read those signs. What she couldn't do, she'd yet to discover. So she'd lived her life as she was living it now. Dodging traffic.

Carrying her photo of Man O' War, keeping an eye out for a black Studebaker sedan, Teddy was on her way to the 'A' Train that would take her up to George and Dinah Bache's for a bath and a change of clothes. She was also going to the gloomy Dakota to choose a gun. George had a terrific collection. Any calibre would do, so long as it fitted in her purse.

Then she was paying a call on Shucks Spooner.

If Jack wouldn't share the story, she'd take it all. Time to stop playing a man's safe and ordered game, time to play by Daddy's rules – wade in and bluff.

12

Skipping Rope

Dinah Bache took one look at Teddy's once lovely black velvet gown – and grabbed it. 'I take dot. Luffly pillows it makes.' She took one look at Teddy nude – and screamed, 'Vot! You bin ina accident! You're lucky you ain't dropped down dead already!'

The bruise covering Teddy's entire left hip was so purple it was black. Welts, scrapes, abrasions, and more bruises ran down her left leg. The right was in better shape – but it'd seen its fair share of cement. Dinah fussed Teddy into the bath, smeared salve over everything, and forced chicken soup down her throat. All the while bleating about germs. 'Liddle t'inks, you kin't see dem – but dey kin see you.'

When Teddy got away from George Bache's mother she felt like she'd swallowed the Red Cross.

Down on Seventy-second Street she was safe again in her long drill coat and grey slacks, her hair was shoved under the old grey hat, and in her purse was the envelope she'd mailed herself from Forty-second Street. In the envelope was the receipt for Groat's suitcase.

Still no black Studebaker, thank God – nothing on either side of the street, no hook-nosed Durata twins loitering behind trees in Central Park – Teddy went for a fast, wall-hugging, four-block walk on the Upper West Side.

Now, skimming under a sign that said, SPOONER'S COLUMBUS AVENUE ATHLETIC CLUB and under that, 'Boxing Lessons', Teddy O'Rourke was back on her own turf.

The sign ran the width of a thin four-storey building stuck between two fat eight-storey buildings on Columbus between Sixty-eighth and Sixty-ninth Streets. If Dancing Joe was working out at Spooner's – and of course he was, Hype was never wrong about things like that – then Tom Channing might be as well. If Channing was there, Solomon Rosenbloom with the big hands would be right by his side. That was what the .22 calibre nickel-plated revolver was for. The little gun wasn't one of George's favourites; he shouldn't miss it. But when she took it, she'd made sure George's mother was fussing in another room. Dinah would have called the cops.

The front of Spooner's Athletic Club was painted a deep, unpeaceful pink. Aside from the pink paint, Spooner's wasn't much different from any other professional gym Teddy ever walked into in a lifetime of walking into gyms. There was the same scuffed cement floor, most of the once terracotta colour worn away by hopeful feet, the same speed bags against a far wall making that racket only a speed bag can make – *whackata whackata whackata*. The same row of busted lockers, a couple of toilet stalls, one lone shower, the same bare light bulbs hanging from the ceiling on frayed cords, the same ring – sixteen feet square – taking up at least a quarter of the space, the same smell. Vaseline, cheap soap, oil of wintergreen, sweat, and the stink of desperate ambition, a *need* to punch a way out of back alleys and into the limelight.

What Spooner's gym had that made it different from a hundred others was the quality of the air. At Spooner's, boys drew success into their lungs. Shucks Spooner trained winners.

'Say hey! O'Rourke!' yelled a guy waiting for the shower, a towel held loosely around his waist and a thick scar, running like a twisted rope from right collarbone to left hip, curling down his chest. The rest of his skin was so white it was painful.

A dozen heads came up as Teddy snapped a hello. If a man had walked in, the fighters – would-be, up-and-coming, and has-beens – would have slapped him on the back. If a woman, they would have made googly eyes. Because it was Teddy O'Rourke, who'd once thought the ring was a play pen, she got the same kind of welcome they'd give to Damon Runyon. No wolf whistles for Teddy, no sham horror – sham on outside, real on the inside – over a lady choosing a door marked 'men'.

In Spooner's, Shucks provided a pretty decent shower but he neglected to provide a door. An old fighter – old meaning past thirty – stuck his dripping head out of the cloud of steam and hollered, 'Looky here, O'Rourke! Get a load of this!' Then replaced his head with his hips. Water streamed down his flat hairy belly, made interesting designs in the thicket of his springy black pubic hair, and ran like hot piss off the tip of his waggling tool.

Teddy glanced over and smiled. Every time she walked into Spooner's she saw the same old prick. 'Hiya, Spud.' Spud was called Spud because when he got hit he went down like a sack of potatoes.

At Spooner's there were fighters of every weight and size: fighters going up, fighters coming down. There were half a dozen cocky young street kids hanging around the ring smoking roll-ups, aping their betters. Two guys with their hats down low over their faces were passing each other tips and a wad of bills not thick enough to tempt a mugger. Spooner's was bulging with masculine pursuits – but no Dancing Joe. Teddy kept on going anyway.

Shucks Spooner was talking to another hopeful kid by the heavy bags. Both Shucks and the young fighter – a lightweight for sure, skinny, sinewy, hair the colour of Lindy's mustard hanging in his eyes – looked serious. But at the sight of Teddy, Shucks stepped away, crooked a finger and croaked, 'You! You, I wanna see.'

Teddy grabbed Spooner's cauliflower ears, pulled his mashed face towards her and gave him a big sloppy kiss.

'Hiya, Shucksie.' Then took his arm and led him to a quiet corner by the row of lockers, saying, 'Same with me. I heard Joe Bright is here.'

'Was. With that tap-dancing dame of his and a bunch of shady types never been here before. He's coming back after they all eat their lunch over at Reubens. Some geezer from your paper went along with 'em, a tall, loopy fellow I never seed before either.'

'Not my paper, Shucks. I quit.'

'Nah, you didn't.'

'Sure, I did.'

'What'd the Indian say to that?'

'I don't know and I don't care.'

'You two fighting again?'

'You could say that.'

'You two guys! You're both crazy. I never seed two so crazy as you. So, what're you gonna do now that you ain't on the paper?'

'Become a reporter.'

'That makes sense.'

Spooner, who'd known Teddy when she was still sucking on a bottle of cow's milk and sharing a Gladstone bag with a fresh deck of cards and Bluff O'Rourke's laundry, took whatever came out of her mouth without batting an eye. Bluff's little girl was like his daughter or his niece or – well, whatever, Shucks loved her like he'd love his own. Wasn't he the guy that come up with the dough when she was just four years old and Bluff, being Bluff and broke, used the kid as his marker for a two thousand buck debt? It took Shucks a week – but he found the two G's. By the time Bluff and him went to claim the marker, the shifty sonofabitch didn't want to hand over the little redheaded kiddie. Told Bluff she was lucky to have around. And kept on saying it until Shucks gave him a little talk. Back then, Spooner's 'talks' meant something, back then he was in his prime, a bare-knuckled fighter who could go twenty rounds without pausing for breath. A couple of stiff jabs and he'd persuaded the guy to take the cash and let Bluff's motherless kiddie go.

When he told Runyon about that – how long ago now? Three years? Five years? Anyway it was over a few beers at LaHiff's – the little man's newspaper eyes lit up. No wonder. It made a good story.

But Teddy in a travelling bag was almost thirty years ago. Now, she was all grown up and standing on her own two feet; not only that, she was asking him something. 'You heard about Dixie Fiske?'

Shucks rolled eyes that looked like fertilized eggs – each had a knot of angry blood swimming next to the iris. The ex-fighter's teeth were more orange than yellow, and he held a little pot belly high up under his ribs. 'Dixie Fiske?' he croaked – someone, in some long gone fight, almost crushed his windpipe. 'Sure I heard about Dixie Fiske. By the way, who hitcha, Red? Was it Jack? That why you quit the paper?'

'Forget that.'

'So, OK, don't get pushy, it's forgot. As for that Fiske geezer, forgetting's not so dern easy. I lost a lotta money what with somebody pulling his plug.'

'I'm told it was suicide, Shucksie. In a car in New Jersey.'

'That so? Ain't the story I heard.'

'What did you hear?'

'It's going the rounds he was bumped off.'

'How?'

'That wasn't part of the story.'

'By whom then?'

'Not that either. But hey, one way or the other, it ain't the point. The money's the point. Though, good riddance to bad rubbish, I'd say. It'll only do Joe good for Fiske to be gone permanent. Excuse me a minute. Say you! Yeah, you. Getta outta that ring. What's a little girl wanna climb in a boxing ring for?'

Curious, Teddy turned her head to see who Shucks was yelling at. Over by the ring, a little girl jumped back down from the canvas. Dirty dishwater hair in messy braids, her skirt too long – hanging uneven beneath what looked like a very old coat – she skittered across the cement floor and darted out of the door. A few of the fighters were laughing, but the young street punks were outraged.

Shucks shook his head. 'Comes here all the time. Throw her out, she's back. Throw her out again, she's back. Can't make heads or tails of it. Now, what was I saying? Oh yeah, Fiske. Ever since that no-account brought Dancing Joe to me – you know, Red, that was some name you give the boy – anyway, I been trying to tell the coloured kid Dixie Fiske was nobody anybody'd want to know. I mean, who else did he manage? Who'd he ever managed? Where'd he come from? Some sharecrop way down south in the land of cotton? Who the hell knew? The guy was bunk. Just shows up one day leading in this big rangy boy like some bashful black colt to a starting gate. But loyal, damn, was Joe loyal. You know me, ordinarily I like that in my fighters, but for Joe it got in his way. Like how Fiske was handling all the money they was starting to win.' Shucks got a starry glint in his eye. 'Jeez, that kid has a reach on him. Seventy-seven inches. Long as Tunney's, long as – ' Shucks almost crossed himself, ' – Dempsey's. Tall, broad shoulders, strong thighs, strong calves, wants to please me all the time, please the crowd, and hotdog, if he don't want to hurt as well. So it hurt me to see him in the hands of a horse's keester like Dixie Fiske. A know-nothing nobody into that Tom Channing for plenty. Lost a bundle, a real bundle over at Channing's casino.'

At the mention of Tom, Teddy sat down on a hard, three-legged stool. It was Channing she was chasing. Channing, not Dixie, who drew her on. 'How much did Fiske owe him?'

'A lot more'n his share of Joe's Garden winnings was gonna cover. Thirty per cent of seventy-five G's ain't enough. What's that now?' Shucks held up his stubby hand and started counting the stubby fingers.

Teddy helped him. 'Twenty-two thousand five hundred bucks. He owed more than that!'

'Sure, lots more. Fifty grand.'

'Wow!'

'You bet. So he was expecting to pay it back from some sure deal on the stock market. But was he surprised when the market went blooie? I'll say he was! Speaking of surprises, it wouldn't surprise me one little bit to learn Dixie wanted Joe to throw the Schuldner fight to pay off Channing. Sly cracker woulda had enough side bets going to more than make up for what he owed – say, Red, come to think of it, before he got iced, did Dixie get his share?'

'Not that I know of,' she lied. For Teddy, this was where things got tricky. Nobody had their share because everybody's share was still snug in a locker at Grand Central Station. That locker was her hole card. It kept her in the running for the story she'd spent two days on, a story she quit her job for, that earned her a punch in the mouth, a tumble from a moving car, and brought her turbulent life with Jack Eagels to an end. A story that had become a paper chase with an Indian; it was all of Jack she had left. A surprising pain near her heart came with that thought. Teddy shook it off with an angry toss of her head.

A sudden cast in his eggy eyes, Shucks wheezed, 'He musta got his share, else why was he killed? Speaking of which, I am owed ten per cent as it is. Fiske steals from Joe, why, this means he steals from me.'

'Maybe he did,' agreed Teddy, and side-tracked fast. 'But Joe didn't throw the fight, did he?'

'Throw the fight!' What there was of Spooner's nose after a career of using it as a target, quivered. 'My Joe! A fella Shucks Spooner would train! He's a hundred per cent, an up and up fella, a gentleman – though I wouldn't cross him anywhere over that funny looking woman of his. Or her neither, for that matter. People don't stay out of that tough little mutt's way for nothing. I'll let you in on a little secret – Joe's got the talent, but Jesse's got the balls. You know what I mean? As for throwing a fight – never, not Dancing Joe. That kid's on the level. So someone, and you can figure out who for yourself, drugged him up the night of the fight.'

'Channing?'

'Maybe.'

'What do you mean maybe? Who else would?'

'Who needed the money? Who knew Joe was too game to throw a fix?'

'You mean Dixie Fiske?'

'Sure I do. It's doing that that got him killed.'

On a hunch, Teddy threw in a wild card. 'And Bernt McTaggart, what about him? What's he got to do with boxing?'

'McTaggart? The cop who got knifed in Harlem?'

'Yes, him.'

'Nothing I know of. What's he got to do with anything?'

Teddy, getting nowhere on that one, veered off. 'Shucks, do you know who's got Joe Bright's contract now?'

'No, but from the way you ask, you do. So who?'

'Channing.'

'No?'

'Yes.'

Teddy thought Shucks was going to cry. But what he said next almost knocked her off her stool.

'Now, that is very great news! So that's who those geezers work for!' Spooner threw a punch at a locker, leaving a dent near the peeling paper name tag – Tiger Bink. Then he reached down and pulled Teddy up, knocking into her hip. Teddy yelped with pain. 'You wanna go a few rounds? I ain't give you a lesson in weeks. Come on, throw your best punch.' Shucks was dancing around Teddy, thumbing his nose, dukes up, shoulders hunched. 'Come on, Red – hit me! Right on the beezer.'

Teddy stood there, amazed. 'Are you crazy? What's going on here? Tom Channing's got Dancing Joe and you want to fight *me*? Shucksie, Channing's a gangster.'

'A gangster?' croaked Spooner. 'Course he's a gangster! So what? You know what it means, Joe with Channing? It means we're gonna go all the way! Young Joe don't know how great he is, which is why Dixie got hold of him. But Shucks knows, that's why I trained him – even with Fiske in on the action.' Abruptly, Shucks stopped dancing, looked over his gym with a scornful eye. 'Look around you, Red. You see any coloured boys in here? No, no coloured boys. Except Joe, I ain't trained any in years. And why? Well, we all know why – bunch of shitfaces out there. But Channing don't care about that, not a fig. OK, so he's a tough guy; that's why he'll make sure nobody else cares either. He'll shove that southern crap right down their throats. With Channing, Dancing Joe'll be heavyweight champion, and me? – I'm gonna train him to do it!'

When Dancing Joe Bright came back to Spooner's, he came back in a crowd. Not only Tom Channing, Jesse Bean, Sol Rosenbloom, and the terrible Durata cousins, but Zipper, Channing's silent, vacant-eyed driver, two or three extra torpedoes for comfort, and a blonde woman wrapped from ankles to ears in a fur coat. Teddy had no idea what animal died to keep the lady warm, but whatever it was, it was huge. The furred blonde wore a diamond on her hand she could have used to warn ships off reefs.

Watching them all walk in under Spooner's sign, it occurred to Teddy that if boxing had existed in the fifteenth century, the Borgias would have been promoters.

Behind them strolled the lanky, toothpick chewing rube, Harve Hopper. That goddamn Mezinger wasn't wasting any time; he had his pinch-hitter out of the dugout and into the batter's box before her copy dried.

Spotting Teddy next to Spooner, the whole flying wedge headed straight for her, Tom at its apex. Teddy, hands in her pockets, the right curled around the butt of the .22 calibre gun, stood her ground, a sweet smile on her freckled face. The little gun wouldn't make much of a dent on seven or eight pistol packing goons, but it could blow a nice hole through Tom Channing's charming head.

'Miss O'Rourke!' Tom had that smile back on his face, the one he did so much damage with. The blonde in the big furry coat hung on to his arm like a fuzzy limpet but it didn't seem to slow him down. 'You never came back to see me last night. I missed you.'

At that, Shucks gave Teddy a very odd look.

'Sorry,' said Teddy, sending Channing volt for volt. 'I couldn't make it. I had another appointment.'

'That's OK, we got today. Say, Joe – don't you want to say hello to your biggest fan.'

Mumbling something, the gorgeous black boxer moved out of the pack towards Teddy. His huge body squeezed into a blue pin-striped suit, his feet into patent leather pumps, Joe Bright was a full head taller than everybody except Channing. Tom, he was only a half a head taller than. Teddy had to look up to see Joe's eyes. A butterfly bandage over his left eyebrow, Bright's eyes were clear, untroubled, empty of schemes, or for that matter, brains – but they were nice eyes. Sweet, gentle, anxious to please. Here was the same Dancing Joe Teddy knew and loved.

Joe picked her up, crushing her bruised ribs in a friendly hug. 'It's real nice to see you, sportin' lady. I wanted to thank you for all the write-ups and for what you've been saying about me. You done me a powerful lot of good.'

Teddy, set back on her feet, adjusted her grip on the gun. 'And now, Joey? How are you now?'

'Now, Miss O'Rourke? I feel great. Mr Channing says he's gonna manage me. That's swell, ain't it?'

'That's just fine, Joe. But what about Dixie?'

A line etched itself by the corner of Joe's mouth, drew it down, as he answered. 'Dixie killed himself. I don't know why he'd do a thing like that, not after I fought Schuldner like I did and won and everything.'

'He killed himself?'

'He sure did. Yesterday morning, Mr Channing and Mr Rosenbloom took me to a morgue over in New Jersey somewhere. It was Dixie all right.'

'I'm sorry, Joey.'

Joe shrugged his shoulders, almost ripping the seams of his tight blue suit. 'Yeah, well, you never know about people, do you? They can do just about anything. Even when he got me out of Detroit, you know, when I was working on Mr Ford's assembly line making those cars – well, even then, he used to get the blues. Still, I never knew he could get 'em so bad. I owe Dixie a lot, and I sorta liked him some – even though Mr Spooner kept telling me I shouldn't.'

Here, Shucks spoke up, his fried eyes popping. 'And was I right, or what?'

Solemnly, Joe turned his enormous liquorice head on his powerful neck and found his trainer. 'That doesn't mean he should be dead, does it, Mr Spooner?'

'That, kid, I can't answer.'

Joe gave Spooner's crack a moment's thought, couldn't pin it down, and forgot the whole subject. With one graceful movement he reached back into Channing's crowd, got hold of Jesse Bean's hand, and pulled her forward. 'But I still got my baby. You think I got muscles, Miss O'Rourke? You should see Mama's muscles.' Dancing Joe reached down and lifted Jesse's skirt. 'Look at that. A woman's body is the most beautiful thing I know of in this world.' Yanking her skirt back down, Jesse slapped him – but not a tenth as hard as she'd whacked Teddy. All she got for her efforts was Joe's ringing laugh.

With that, Teddy understood Jesse Bean's attraction for Joe Bright. Some women's bodies might not live up to Joe's expectations, but the body of Mama B. Blue did – and then some. Calling her 'Mama' instead of Jesse also gave a little colour to the picture.

'I'm intending to buy this woman a great big apartment with all the trimmings right on St Nicholas Avenue, maybe even as far up as Sugar Hill. Aren't I, Mama?'

Jesse dipped her bitter head. Teddy guessed that meant Jesse thought it was a good idea.

'With my Mama here happy, and with Mr Channing managing me and you writing about me, and me getting to do battle with Mr Sharkey, why heck, we're on easy street. By the way, Miss O'Rourke, Mama has something she wants to say to you. Mama, you tell Miss O'Rourke you're sorry you hit her. Go on.'

After a little nudge, Jesse Bean snapped, 'Sorry.'

'She was just worried about me.' Engulfing her head with his huge hand, Joe patted the springy black hair. 'But there wasn't nothing to worry about, was there, Mama? – *Was* there, Mama?'

Joe got another snap out of his Mama. 'No.'

'See.'

Teddy felt like laughing. With a gun in her hand and the money still at Grand Central Station, she thought she could afford to.

But Joe hadn't finished talking. 'I told Mama we could trust you. I told her you'd hold the money like Dixie asked. I don't know why she thinks so bad of folk, Miss O'Rourke, but I told her she'd learn different with you.'

At this, Jesse Bean almost laughed – but didn't.

At this, Teddy hadn't a laugh in her. There went another ace. Tom, watching for her reaction, smiled.

But Teddy, child of a man who played poker for a living, kept the loss off her face. 'I've only been waiting to see you're OK before I give it to you.'

Joe turned to Jesse, his face split by a huge happy grin. 'See!'

And Spooner, still beside Teddy, jolted her arm with a stiff finger, almost making her lose her grip on the gun. '*You* got all the money, Red?'

'Sure, I never said I didn't.'

'Why then, I've got my money! Hotdog!'

While all this was going on, Hopper had been chewing on his toothpick, that dust-eating grin never leaving his weathered face. 'Say, Miss O'Rourke?' he drawled.

Teddy turned on him, grey eyes flashing. 'What?' Daring him to say anything, to tell these people she wasn't with the *Trident* anymore.

Harve smiled, lowered his eyes. 'Oh, I don't know. Nothing, I guess.'

For an active gunman, Tom Channing had a lot of patience, but by now it was wearing thin. He pulled a cigarette case out of his pocket, snapped it open. 'So it's just one big happy family,' he said, lighting up with that engraved Dunhill she'd seen at the casino. *For Tommy, all my love, Sophie.* Dammit, who was Sophie? 'Let's bust it up, what do you say? Joe, why don't you get back in the ring, show this famous sports columnist what you can do?'

'Sure, Mr Channing, that'd be swell.'

'The rest of you, beat it. I want to have a word with the lady, private.'

Though everyone but the blonde drifted off, Sol hadn't budged. 'But Tom – '

'You don't think Miss O'Rourke is going to do me any harm, do you, Solomon? That she is packing a rod? You insult the lady. Go on, watch over Joe. And by the way, take Agnes here with you.'

The blonde cleaved to his side. 'Ah, Tommy,' she purred in her hot chocolate voice. Hearing it, Teddy remembered the casino on Sugar Hill, the blonde head dipping between hers and Jesse Bean's. So Tom Channing kept his promises. How considerate.

Tom peeled Agnes off. 'Scram, Aggie. You like sweaty bodies, go soak up some atmosphere.'

Now, it was just Tom Channing and Teddy O'Rourke. And Teddy had a fight on her hands. It should have been easy – as easy as dealing from the bottom – to hate this goddamn gangster. But, it wasn't. It was all she could do to dislike him. Channing was a hood who told women to scram, told men to hop through hoops, helped guys in his way commit suicide, and maybe he even cut the throat of Mayor Jimmy's favoured cop. And here she was, only a few hours after the scene with Connie and Jack, struggling with her own idea of who she was and where she was going; here she was, almost liking this guy. She had a loaded gun in her pocket and he had a loaded gun in his pocket and they were both probably swell shots and what she was thinking as her finger played with the trigger was – *Dear God, ain't he pretty*. Face it, O'Rourke – you're a poor fish after all. The man's reeled you in. Not your talent, not your brains, not even your pride can cut the line.

Reeled in or not, Teddy hadn't forgotten Bernie. No longer safe behind a suitcase of money that only she could get her hands on, Teddy was left with just one way to stay close to Tom Channing – her own sweet self. What else could she give him? But he wasn't going to get it on a plate. The lesson of Agnes went home.

So when Tom said, 'I've arranged Joe's next bout with a comer named Jack Sharkey,' Teddy said, 'Nice for Jack Sharkey.'

'You aren't going to keep this up all day, are you?'

'Keep what up?'

'The cold shoulder.'

'What the hell do you expect? I almost killed myself jumping out of that car.'

'Yeah, that was pretty good. When I heard about it, if I could have seen you, I'd have handed you a cigar. But that was business. What I got in mind now is pleasure.'

'You got to be kidding!'

'Me, kidding? Kid somebody as smart as you?'

'Smart? Who led you straight to Joe?'

'So? You're a beginner at this kind of stuff. You'll learn to look behind you next time.'

'I've been looking.'

'You like what you see?'

'Agnes does.'

'Agnes's a dumb cluck.'

'Agnes is a human being. It can't be too thrilling to get treated like less.'

'Mussolini's a human being. That don't mean I want him around.'

'Tom Channing, you have a point.'

Tom smiled his ravishing smile. 'I liked what that old guy called you. Red, that's a good name. Suits you better than Silky Sullivan.' Tom put his hands on Teddy's shoulders and looked her straight in the eye. 'You and me, Red O'Rourke – we're going to make the damnedest team, see if we don't. You're going to keep on writing up Dancing Joe Bright like he was already champ and I'm going to make sure he is. Say, won't that be something? A boxing promoter and a writing lady!'

Now wasn't the time to tell Tom Channing she'd quit her job or to ask him what else he was besides a boxing promoter, but Teddy took her hands out of her pockets.

'But first, let's take a drive over to Grand Central. Joe wants to spend some money on that dancer of his. Then Red, I'm gonna show you off.'

When Teddy walked under Spooner's sign again, it was an hour later and she was walking with Tom Channing. Right under their feet, the little girl with the messy dishwater braids was on her scabby knees, chalking shapes on the sidewalk.

'What's that?' Teddy stopped to ask, trying to make sense of a jumble of blue lines.

The girl looked up at Tom and Teddy with wide-open eyes, brown eyes, coca cola brown. 'That's a spider.' She lifted the hem of a dirty, too-long dress, wiping her nose with it. Under the skirt, her legs were as thin as a new born bird's and they ended in cracked leather hook and eye boots, the toes aiming in. Then she pointed at Teddy's mouth. 'Where'd you get the fat lip?'

'Present from a lady.'

'Yeah?'

'Yeah.'

'You're a girl, ain'cha? So why you get to wear trousers?'

'I don't know. Maybe because I'm not married to anybody.'

'Yeah, I get it. Who'er you anyway?'

'Teddy O'Rourke.'

'No kiddin'? You the person who writes that column about sports?'

Teddy was famous, but not that famous – and surely not to a little girl with a piece of blue chalk on the Upper West Side. 'You've heard of my column?'

'Sure. I read it, don't I? I read everybody who does sports. Gotta keep up, you know.'

'You do?'

'Sure. You dumb or something? I'm gonna be a fighter like them in there – only better.'

'But honey, you're a girl.'

'Cripes! Of course I'm a girl. What do you think, I don't know that?'

Both Tom and Teddy laughed, and the girl began skipping without a rope. 'See this? I can do this forever. I could play a piano if I wanted, I could dance good as Bojangles or do numbers like that Einstein, I could be as good with a bat as Mr Babe Ruth, I could ride a motorcycle if I could get aholt of one, I could play that!' The child stopped skipping long enough to fling a contemptuous arm at a mob of Columbus Avenue boys running a football through uptown traffic. 'But what I really wanna do, is I wanna be a prizefighter. That's for me!' She flipped a braid over her shoulder. 'I got character, that's what my mom says.'

Like letting go the string of a helium balloon, something in Teddy went suddenly up, sailing back through the years, to the time when she was Bluff's little girl. To remember what it was like to be young and unafraid and so sure. To say to a big, moony, grown-up face leaning down over hers, *You dumb or something?*

Was she two, two and a half, when she first saw a blade of New York grass? Bluff put her down near the pitcher's mound during a break in the Giants' spring training, him talking to a young man who would become Teddy's hero and later her friend, Christy Mathewson. Teddy sat and stared at the Polo Grounds between her chubby legs. What was this green spiky stuff? She reached down, dug her fingers in and came up with dirt. Stuck the fingers in her mouth and sucked. Good. Gritty but good. And while she sat there, savouring her dirt, a big black something came walking over the grass, stopped at the mountain of her ankle, thought about it, then began to climb, all eight legs working. Round-eyed, Teddy watched it come, laughing as the legs tickled her thigh. It looked like an olive, one of the black ones on a pizza, juicy and ripe. Teddy plucked it from her freckled skin, its long legs thrashing in flight, popped it in her mouth, and bit down. A crunchy, hairy olive.

'Kathleen Ellen O'Rourke!' yelled Bluff, his big red face swooping down from a bright blue baseball sky. 'What's in your mouth?' Big daddy fingers poking between her lips, forcing her teeth apart. 'Oh, Jesus,

Mary and Joseph! Spit that out, Teddy! *Spit it out –
now!*'

Teddy looked up into that red face, considered for a
second – then swallowed. Christy laughed and laughed
until Bluff had to slap him on the back.

That was the day Teddy found out she was Teddy
O'Rourke – and though Daddy knew a lot, he didn't
know everything.

Teddy took Tom Channing's arm and climbed into the
butter-yellow Cord.

13

Gasoline Wind

Jack Eagels and Lulu LeRoy were on Broadway. After *Diamond Lil*'s Monday night show – the last in its New York Subway run – they'd taken the train back to Manhattan from Far Rockaway, Jack coughing the whole way. And now, because Lulu thought it might be fun, were in Victor's Pool Hall. Because she found no fun at all in the Harley, it stayed propped up against the Silver Slipper.

Before the pool hall, Lulu, eating popcorn, tugged Jack into Hubert's Flea Circus – stepping over the two live pigs Hubert used to advertise his performing fleas; into a show of medical horrors where Lulu stared open-mouthed and wide-eyed at misshapen green babies pickled under glass; and then to a gypsy fortune teller in a penny arcade. The gypsy woman oozed sex like a peach oozes juice. She was curt and dismissive with Lulu, worried about Jack. 'Look to your health, mister,' she'd purred, tapping his fevered palm with a blunt nail. 'It don't look good.'

Offended by the woman's interest in Jack but more by her beauty, Lulu said, 'Oh, pooey.'

'Pooey to you too, shorty,' snapped the gypsy. 'Gimme a buck.'

Victor's had twelve tables, no other women customers, and a jukebox that Lulu fed with nickels for a solid hour.

'Those pigs we just saw? They remind me of Minsky's,' Lulu was saying, waggling her butt to great effect as she set up a pool shot – the nine ball in the corner pocket. 'Minsky's had this little round stage out front from the main one where a girl could do a real special

216

solo number. Mine was with this awful cute baby pig and an apple.'

At Jack's look she added, 'Well, it was a *big* apple.'

While Lulu set up her shot, Jack stood back and gave her room, leaning on his pool cue in mute appreciation of that waggling behind and listening to Al Jolson sing 'Toot Toot Tootsie, Goodbye' for the fourth time.

Lulu sank the nine ball, which surprised the hell out of Jack, and then moved around the table after the seven, still talking. 'And this little round stage, which was practically in the laps of the guys at the front tables, was really clever. They made it so it'd come up out of the floor with me on it, all of a sudden and real dramatic, you understand, and as it was doing that a microphone was supposed to drop down out of the flies, and there I'd be – all alone and spotlit.' Lulu missed the seven by a whole lot of inches, which didn't surprise Jack at all. 'Your turn! Anyway, so there I was, dancing with my pig on this tiny round stage and singing my heart out. And getting a lot of applause, right? Feeling like I was Fanny Brice wowing everybody with "My Man", except Miss Brice didn't have to take her clothes off while she was singing it, when – wouldn't you know – that microphone dropped straight down and kept on coming; it conked me right on the top of the head. Talk about seeing stars! And the sound! Jeepers, the sound was like the biggest hard-boiled egg you ever heard getting cracked.'

Jack, sighting down his cue for an easy shot, said, 'So then you quit burlesque?'

'Gosh no, not me. Not for that. I'm a trouper; I finished my act. Things like that were always happening. I quit because of all the jerks who showed up and sat there with newspapers covering whatever they were doing in their laps. Most of the other girls thought it was funny but, jeez, it made me sick to my stomach. Besides, I wanted to be in a real show, you know, something serious with ladies in the audience – so I got a part in Miss West's play.'

'*Diamond Lil*?'

'No, way before *Diamond Lil*. The one she did called *Sex*.'

Jack couldn't see any point in responding to that. He sank every last ball on the table, hung up his pool cue, and said, 'After all that popcorn, you still hungry?'

'You bet.'

'Come on then. There's a place a couple of blocks up the street serves the best blintzes in town.'

Their heels crackling the crust of the city's yellow snow, Jack was taking Lulu to Lindy's. Pulling her past the bright lights of what was once an Indian hunting track and was now Broadway, past a dozen dazzling marquees, past small-time bookies, tapped-out cardsharps, ladies in tight dresses who did what they could to make them a dime, past pickpockets and junkies – blinking in the white light like vampires who'd lost track of the time. Running a sweet, chatty dark-haired child up Broadway, Jack had a mild revelation.

If life is a film in the dark, if reality the unreeling of a never-ending talkie, then mankind is the guy who slumps in the cheap seats, smack behind the fat lady in God's haughty hat. By night, the Great White Way was like an artist who tapped on the fat lady's shoulder, some cheeky fellow leaning forward to say, 'Do you mind?' Sometimes the lady shoved over a little; sometimes, if the tap had force, she ducked – but nothing anyone ever said, nothing anyone ever wrote, could make her take off that hat.

There was the artist for you, thought Jack. Squirming in the dark, craning his neck, pounding on the fat lady's back, the artist never stopped trying to see the movie.

'Eagels!' Leo Lindemann came scurrying up as Jack and Lulu walked through his door. 'Where have you been? Who's this? Where's Teddy?'

218

'This is Lulu LeRoy,' said Jack, ignoring Lindy's first and last questions.

Lindy frowned, but he got the picture. Leading them to a high-backed booth – not the one Teddy and Jack called home – he swept crumbs off the table with a sweep of his hand, took Lulu's fur-collared coat, and snapped, 'There you go – privacy. What more do you want?'

'Two sour cream blintzes, two coffees.'

'I don't know why but you got it.'

Lindy glowered off.

Lulu stared after him. 'Of all the crust. What's the matter with that guy?'

'Probably something he ate.'

Lulu looked at Jack like he was loopy. Jack looked at Lulu like *she* was loopy. He wished she'd laughed; but with *her* ass – a man couldn't have everything.

'This Teddy? She's a girl?'

'Sometimes.'

'Who is she?'

'Someone I work with.'

'You mean at the newspaper? She the one who answered the phone when I called?'

'That was her.'

'She pretty?'

'No – ' began Jack and then went off into a coughing fit.

Jack's answer made Lulu feel better until he could finish his sentence.

'She's better than pretty – she's classy and she's smart.'

'Oh,' said Lulu.

Jack reached over and took her hand. 'As Winchell would say, we were an item but now it's gone *pffft*.'

Lindy brought the blintzes and coffee, gave Jack a nasty look and buzzed off again.

Lulu, happy once more, ate her blintz with her fingers. 'Isn't Winchell wonderful!'

Jack had many ways of describing Walter, but none of them included the word 'wonderful'. With care, he said, 'Well – '

Not one to let a good pause go unfilled, Lulu rushed on. 'I got in Walter Winchell's column once. That was when he was still working for the *Graphic*. Did I tell you that? Did I tell you I was married once?'

'No, Lulu. I'd remember.'

'Well I was. For eight hours.'

Coffee cup held to his lips, Jack looked at Lulu. Why bother saying anything like, 'How long!' After his second evening with this little brunette-on-blonde, Jack knew enough just to listen.

'It all started out really nice, me and Milt. Milt, that was his name.'

Jack took a bite of his blintz and gagged. Faced for the second time in one day with something else he'd ordered that he couldn't eat, Jack lit a cigarette.

While Lulu pattered on. 'Milt was a third banana at Minsky's National Winter Garden when I was a headliner, a real soubrette. I bumped into him backstage right after he got hired and when I did, well, gosh, I'd met a fella who could make me laugh right out loud. Not many guys could tickle a girl's funny bone like he could – probably because they were always trying to tickle something else. Anyway, after a week of laughing a lot, Milt started asking me to marry him in every way he could think of: on his knees, notes in boxes of Cracker Jack, singing telegrams, even from the stage, which confused the guys with the newspapers, you can bet. Finally I just gave up, said we could get married between shows. And with four shows a day, boy, that wasn't easy. But we squeezed the preacher in somehow, and then, after the last show, we went to his place on Hester Street for our honeymoon. Only one room and a real dump, but gee, I thought it was sweet.'

By now, not only Jack's stomach was feeling a little sour. 'Any storm in a port.'

'You said it. One hour later, I hated that room, but I hated Milt more. Boy, you can never tell about men until they get you alone. Besides everything else, Milt wore a cigar like it was part of his face, even in bed. Anyway, I told him how I was feeling at the top of my voice and also ran around putting my clothes back on as quick as I could, and got out of that crummy room fast. Milt just lay there naked staring at me.'

'What the hell did he do to you?'

'Everything! And it all hurt. So the next day I told Billy Minsky all about it and he says, "You want I should fire the guy?" and I said, "Well, I'd be a lot happier if you did, Mr Minsky." So he did; after all, Milt was just a comic and I was a specialty act. So what do you think happened next? What happened next was the following night, Milt came round backstage to my dressing room screaming I'd lost him his job, and beat the living heck out of me, gave me a black eye. But, fortunately, a bunch of the other girls heard what was going on and dragged him off me. Billy threw Milt in the street. So then I didn't see him for a couple of days and, of course, I forgot all about him.'

'Of course.'

'Can I have another coffee?'

'Sure. Lindy! Two more coffees.'

'So anyway, about a week later when I got home – back then I lived at the Peerless Palace Burlesque Hotel on West Forty-sixth – it was the middle of the night and I found this big cop and a bunch of news photographers and firemen with nets and a huge crowd waiting for me. The cop said, "There's a guy who says he's your husband sitting on a ledge." So I looked up and, jeepers, sure enough, there he was in this big searchlight, dangling his feet over the ledge all right, and looking down at me from the seventh floor. The cop said Milt was gonna jump if I didn't talk to him. And I said Milt didn't have the nerve and the cop said, well, he'd had the nerve to stay out there for four hours now. So me and the cop went up to the seventh floor and into this room Milt rented in the Peerless Palace without me knowing about it. You gotta understand, sweetie, Milt was a funny man and he had ambition too. He couldn't stand being just the third banana, being the brunt of the first banana's jokes – you know, pies in the face, being the one to have his pants fall down all the time – so I thought this was just a stunt of his. Why should he jump over me? Jeez, we were only married for half a day. So I walked into that room and said, "OK, Milt, here I am. You can jump now." And the cop got steamed, boy, did he. "Listen, lady," he said, "I didn't bring you up here to make this guy jump, I brought you up here to get him off that ledge." So I saw he didn't understand a person like Milt at all and I said, "You just leave me alone with him for a few minutes and I'll get him in." So he did. Walked right out and shut the door on the faces of all those other cops in the hallway. And I walked up to the window and I said, "You may have fooled these cops up here and all those people down there, Milt, but you can't fool me. You wouldn't dare jump."'

Lulu paused long enough for breath and a bite of blintz. 'Gee, I almost forgot, but I guess the important part of this story was when I got to the window – I noticed up on the seventh the wind was blowing pretty hard. Milt was sitting out there and he was having to hold on to his hat. The wind smelled funny too, like gasoline. Anyway, Milt started screaming at me and all the people down on the ground started yelling at him. "Jump!" is what they were yelling. And Milt said to me, "I'll jump all right and you're gonna look like shit when all the papers come out tomorrow." Pardon that word, but that's what he said. And I said, "Too bad you won't see it." And then Milt proved me right. He got so mad, he hopped up and tried to climb back through the window at me. But he slipped and I guess the wind took him. So he didn't jump after all, but, jeepers, he sure did fall. Straight down like a rock. And everybody down there said, "Ooooo!" as he fell and "Ahhhh!" when he was squashed flat as a raspberry pancake on Forty-sixth Street. So like I said, I made Mr Winchell. Walter Winchell had it in his column the very next day. A picture of me and everything.'

'Jesus, Lulu. When was all this?'

'Three years ago. When I was thirteen.'

Jack choked on his cigarette. 'You were married and stripping in Minsky's burlesque when you were thirteen years old!'

'Oh no. I was stripping in Minsky's when I was twelve. I got married when I was thirteen. But Billy Minsky didn't know how old I was until I told him a long time later. Milt never knew at all. After that, Mr Minsky started asking girls for their birth certificates.'

Lulu got a funny look on her face, one Jack hadn't seen before. This look was wistful and sly and much older than she was all at the same time. He wasn't sure he liked it. 'You know, while I was telling you that story about Milt, I remembered Bernie. He reminded me a little of Milt.'

'How so?'

'Well, I don't know how so really. Maybe it was the way they both used their hands. It's awful strange, isn't it? I'm almost seventeen and I know two dead people already – no!' Lulu stopped speaking, so suddenly it was like she'd walked into a sheet of plate glass. Jack watched her forest brown eyes widen in surprise. 'Gosh, actually, I know three. Milt Rabinowich, Bernie Miller, and my mom, Irena.' Lulu spoke the last name so softly she could have been praying. 'Irena was so beautiful men used to stop in the street and cry when she passed. But she died when I was eleven.'

Jack was bothered by what Lulu told him, but something else bothered him more than that. 'Wait a minute, Lulu, your mother is dead? You told me her name was Marie and she lived in Florida.'

'Did I? Well, I guess I did – but I lied. I didn't want you to think I had nobody looking out for me. A girl's got to protect herself in a town like this. The truth is, if you must know, she died on my eleventh birthday, burnt to death in a fire. After that I got farmed out to a family already had nine kids. And that's 'cause he loved my mom, boy! did he ever, but even so, well, no – actually, I don't think he really did sleep with her.'

'He? Who's he?'

'My uncle.'

'You don't *think* he slept with his sister! Who *is* this guy?'

'Just my uncle. Nobody really. Who never loved me, only Irena. Those people in Brooklyn he left me with? They lived on the Polish end of Grand Street. The papa worked at a factory where they made things like safeties, the mama scrubbed the floors of Gorling's Department Store, and the oldest boy, who brilliantined his hair and thought he was some kind of Valentino sheik, didn't do nothing but chase me. They all of them hated Germans, they hated Russians, they hated the Irish, they hated Jews, and they hated each other – but most of all, boy! did they hate me. I hated them back like poison from the moment I got there. So when I was twelve and the sheik wearing his papa's safety finished raping me for the second time, I ran away and got a job at Minsky's. Listen Jack, you wanna come to a party with me?'

Running around in his head, Jack missed that last sentence. His own unspoken talk with himself drowned it out. That last nickel he would have bet on his judgement of her at Far Rockaway? Jack lost it. This little girl wasn't as innocent as she looked. There was

224

more to Lulu than Jack Eagels had imagined in his rush to follow her lead to Mr Tom Channing – and bed. For one thing, it made her human, for another – it made her much younger. A *lot* younger. No wonder she talked like a kid, she *was* a kid. Not only was she half his age, he was twice hers. Either way, it made a man think. And for another, even with all her jeepers and gees, Lulu wasn't Lorelei Lee, a dippy, dumb brunette/blonde; she was no idiote savante of gold-diggery. But if she wasn't, what was she? He also noticed something else: Lulu LeRoy's beauty might be strictly rural, but her mind was feral. Jack suddenly felt old.

'Sweetie, you listening? You want to go to a party with me? Tomorrow night, Owney Madden and Tom Channing, you know those two guys you saw out at Far Rockaway?'

Still in shock over what Lulu had told him and told him so casually, Jack nodded: yes, he knew those guys. Owney was the guy about whom Gentleman Jimmy had said, *He's not such a bad fellow, not really*. Channing was the guy he was running around town with Lulu LeRoy for; he was the guy who'd killed Bernie. Know them? They were what he did for a living.

'*Diamond Lil* is going to San Francisco. Miss West's got us booked into the Curran Theater there. So Tom and Owney are giving the cast a going-away party and paying for everything, the food and the floorshow, and they're inviting a lot of interesting people. Jack, are you all right?'

'Why?'

'You look a little down in the mouth.' Lulu laid her cool hand along his jaw. Jack flinched; Teddy's punch still lingered. 'Gee, you're really burning up. Maybe we ought to go back to my place – I make a pretty good hot toddy.'

'Maybe,' said Jack.

'Jack?'

Something about Lulu's tone put Jack on his guard. 'What?'

'Miss West expects me to go to San Francisco with the show. I mean, anybody would want to see San Francisco, especially if they'd never been there before.'

'Makes sense.'

'A girl would be a sap not to see a city like that if she could, wouldn't she?'

'She'd be a sap for sure.'

'That's what I thought, so, of course and naturally, I said yes.'

'Good for you.'

'But when Miss West asked me it was a week ago.'

'So?'

'Well, a week ago I didn't have any better offers.'

Snap! went Lulu LeRoy's sweet trap. What should Jack do now? Telling Lulu she still didn't have any better offers would put the breaks on his going to a party given by Owney Madden and Tom Channing. On the other hand, telling Lulu he could think of a thing or two that might make her want to stick around New York would – would what? Who did he have to answer to? Teddy O'Rourke, the battling redhead? O'Rourke, the *Trident*'s Nellie Bly, who'd walked out on him, on her job, and as far as he could tell, on her senses? Lulu was cute, she wasn't a smart ass, she was only five feet tall, and he bet she couldn't punch her way out of a nursery. Though she was a little strange. Well, what about it? Who wouldn't be with a history like hers? Also, she did better things than make a pretty good hot toddy.

So Jack threw in his hand. 'Funny how a week changes things,' he said.

Lulu licked the last bit of sour cream off her fingers and hopped up to kiss him. 'I knew you were swell the first time I saw you. Let's go to my place.'

Before he knew why he said it or what it could really mean, Jack said, 'No, let's not. We'll go to my place. It's only a block away. I'll show you my etchings.' Besides, he didn't feel all that well. Maybe that gypsy knew something after all.

When Teddy woke up at the Dakota on Tuesday morning and walked into the Baches' living room, the place smelled like a Hollywood florist. Dozens and dozens of roses, all long-stemmed and all red, covered the furniture, the floor, Dinah. Teddy, wide-eyed in George's pyjamas, felt like she'd won the Kentucky Derby. Dinah handed her a note in a thick buff envelope. Teddy tore it open: ten crisp one hundred dollar bills fell out onto the Baches' thick oriental carpet.

'Dear Red. This is for the ruined dress. You'll need a new one for a party I'm taking you to tonight. Plus a little extra for all the trouble. With aces, Tom.'

Teddy glanced out of the window. It was snowing. Wearing her slacks, a pair of winter boots, a little red fox cubby and her slouch hat – though she left George's .22 calibre revolver under her mattress – Teddy went shopping on Fifth Avenue.

Knowing next to beans about fashion, Teddy, choosing names from Dinah's *Vogue*, went straight to Bonwit Teller's on Thirty-fourth. With nothing there to get excited about, she hoofed it on up to Henri Bendel's – passing the stuffy glitter and glory of Tiffany's, the lure of the New York Public Library, the gothic spires of St Patrick's Cathedral, and the banks – for over a week now, very nervous banks – of Fifth Avenue. Marched into Saks Fifth Avenue, and finally, Bergdorf Goodman's. By so doing, Teddy O'Rourke made a great discovery. She couldn't stand shopping. It hurt her feet, it confused her, and worst of all – she couldn't have everything. And if she could, where would she wear it all? At Spooner's? Down on her knees in a crap game? In a smoky Harlem speak with Jack? Oh! for the love of pete – Jack popped up everywhere. Jack Eagels was out of her life – when would he get out of her head?

Teddy bought her dress at Bergdorf's. But first she had to get past the receptionist. The girl had a pinched triangle of a face, her hair was a tight series of yellow, patent leather curls flattened to the sides of her head, her breasts were flattened to her ribcage, and she wore little white gloves on her little white hands. Now she was staring at Teddy's hat and slacks and wet, snow-stained boots as if she'd suddenly been beamed to the Bowery.

'Yiss?' she yipped. 'Can I do something for you?'

Teddy lit a cigarette. 'I came for a dress.'

Right behind Teddy's ear, a voice punctured the air. 'Young woman! Smoking is unhealthy, unsightly, unclean, and what is worse, vulgar. Caroline, is this person a friend of yours?'

Caroline of the curls was horrified. 'Why no, Miss Zingas, I – '

Teddy turned on her heel and found herself looking down into the hard brown eyes of a stiff old dame whose wisps of grey hair looked stuck to her tiny skull with glue. Toe to toe with uncompromising grit, Teddy ditched her cigarette in the decorative dish the nervous Caroline offered.

Here was another reason to dislike shopping. Teddy hated bullies. 'I'm a customer. I'd like a look at your stuff.'

'Stuff?' sniffed Miss Zingas.

'Evening dresses.'

'Come with me.'

Teddy bought sleeveless white eggshell satin, slim and snug as a second skin: very high at the collar, very low at the back, a row of tiny satin buttons from neck to floor. She bought long white satin gloves, white satin pumps, a dozen pair of Japanese silk stockings – a girl never knew when she'd have to jump out of a speeding car – and an evening cape of white maribou.

Though the bill for all this got warmer and warmer, Miss Zingas got colder and colder. Her parting shot to Teddy: 'You know, young lady, if you did something with your hair – which is admittedly quite a beautiful colour – stopped wearing those disgraceful trousers, and wore the right make-up, you might amount to something.'

Laden with classy boxes, Teddy got her hair done. Something that would wash right out.

By the time George came home it was eight o'clock in the evening. By ear alone, he found his mother and Teddy. They were in Dinah's bedroom, laughing like schoolgirls. Teddy, sitting on a vanity stool, was wrapped in something soft and white and clinging; seated beside her, Dinah wore something stiff and loose in a shade of powder blue. George knew that blue gown. It was a Worth from Paris and at least forty years old. Which still made it a lot younger than Dinah Bache. The last time he'd seen it on her he'd been six and standing in the wings of a Yiddish theatre on Second Avenue, also known as 'Knish Alley'. Ten feet away Dinah was swanning around in the footlights as Zara of 'The Amazing Zedik and Zara', a ventriloquist and magician act. His father, Samuel Bache, was Zedik. George hadn't seen that dress since Sam died. Seeing it now stopped him in his tracks.

Dinah's vanity table was buried under a sprawl of lipsticks, rouges, mascaras, powders, perfumes; Teddy and his mother experimenting with the lipsticks when Teddy caught sight of George in the mirror.

'What do you think?' she said, turning on the flounced stool to bat her eyelashes. 'Drop dead red or prissy pink?'

'With your hair and that lip? Avoid the pink.'

'Right.' Teddy turned back to the mirror and started filling in her lips with the tube of dark red. When she was finished, you'd never know she'd been slugged.

George waited a full minute, standing tall and lanky and lost in a thick herringbone suit, still wearing his hat, still holding the programme of the show he'd just seen and reviewed. 'OK,' he finally sighed, 'I just fought my way past all the red roses. One of you might tell me what's going on here.'

Dinah, pursing her ancient lips, painting them pink, said, 'Teddy, she goes on a date mit a crook.'

'Excuse me?'

Glancing up in the mirror, Teddy sent him a reflected smile. 'Tonight, Georgie, I'm hitting the town with Tom Channing. Isn't it something? He likes me.'

'You like him?'

'Like I like tigers. When they're in a zoo.'

'He's not in a zoo. You think going around with him is safe?'

'I'm all I've got left that can tell me if Channing killed McTaggart. I know he killed Dixie Fiske, and why – to manage Joe.' Teddy neglected to mention the only other thing she had: George's gun. That was out from under her mattress and back in her purse.

'You're beginning to make me crazy, O'Rourke. You know who Channing is – '

'I hope he's a killer.'

'I *know* he's a killer; *he* knows he's a killer. Who does he think you are?'

'A racehorse.'

'I'd ask you to explain that crack but I'm too nervous to listen. Who's my mother got a date with?'

Testily, Dinah put down the lipstick. 'Don't I vish. But, vot da hell, ve hed a leff. I ain't like George's grandmudder Minnie Bache – my Sam's mudder. At my age, dot voman vas beautiful even, vent to bet mit Napoleon da t'ird, Dumas, da bote of dem, Victor Hugo,

230

end da Empire City Quartet. Me, at my age, all I get to do is go to da toilet. Excuse, please.'

Dinah's bedroom window looked out over Central Park. Angry at Teddy, frightened for her, George took himself to the window after his mother left the room. Down on Seventy-second Street, snowflakes darted like fireflies in the butterscotch glow of globed street lamps. Across the street an old man scuffled through the snow that was gathering on the dark and dying grass, the dead and fallen leaves. He was bent over so far he hadn't much further to go to lie down, picking up stray butts from the path that wound its way through the stripped and shivering trees. Behind him trailed a child's wagon, a soap box on wobbly wooden wheels. The old man was all alone down there. Standing in the trapped warmth behind a window on the fifth floor of the Dakota, George watched the old fellow go into a coughing fit that brought up a sticky mass of shining sputum. Gathering it in his wrinkled, toothless mouth, he curled his tongue into a tube and shot the wad halfway across Central Park West.

Tracing a circle on the frosted pane, George said, 'I spent every Christmas over there when I was a kid.'

'Over where?' Teddy had her face an inch from the mirror; she was brushing her dark red eyebrows straight up.

'Central Park. While Dinah and Sam dressed the tree, I used to build snow forts.'

'You had a Christmas tree, George? You're Jewish.'

'My parents would celebrate anything. Dinah sewed; Sam cooked. So we had two trees: a Christmas tree and a Hanukkah Bush. And two feasts. Nobody cooked better than my father.'

'I wish I'd met Samuel Bache.'

'That's nothing to how much he would have wished he'd met you. Especially when we lived in Yorkville and

231

he was still The Amazing Zedik, America's only Jewish ventriloquist. Like mother Minnie, like son.'

'Sam vent to bet mit Dumas, da bote of dem?'

'*Avant* Dinah, *le déluge*. As I was saying, there was a girl, a little blonde cutie, used to live across the street at the Majestic, and she'd be out there every Christmas too. I'd build my snow fort and her chauffeur would build her snowman. She'd stand around in the snow in her blue coat and blue boots telling him how to do it. She had a little fur hat on her head and a little fur muff to keep her little white hands warm. Every Christmas it snowed, ah, God! I was in love. It got so I had to beg Sam to buy me a long coat to wear over my knickerbockers. If not, you could tell I was thinking about her.'

'What a lovely story, George.' Red hair swept up and held by a diamanté clip, Teddy stood in front of one of Dinah's tall mirrors in her shimmering eggshell satin dress – turning and posing and primping and wincing from the beauty of a bruise on her hip. 'Think of it. *Two* trees for Christmas. When I was a kid I never even had one. All I had for Christmas was Bluff – and he was never the same place twice, sometimes not even in the same place from Christmas Eve to Christmas Day. Of course, if Bluff was on a winning streak, I got a lot of presents: books mostly, I always wanted books.' Teddy began pulling on her long white satin gloves, first the left, then the right. George watched her do it with a lament in his heart. Only that afternoon he'd watched a girl at Minsky's do the very same thing – in reverse. Teddy O'Rourke putting clothes on was a much better show – but a lot more painful. George went back to his window where he could listen without the distress of looking. 'So, I never knew what I was missing until one year, guess I must have been five or so, and the liner Bluff was working over docked in San Francisco. You like this dress, Georgie?'

In answer, George merely blew a hole in the steam on Dinah's windowpane.

'Anyway, for another of the usual reasons, Bluff had to get off that boat fast and lay low for a while. We holed up in the room of a redheaded Jewish hooker in a Barbary Coast cathouse. So there we were on Christmas Eve, living in a magical place called Silver Street, all gilt and crystal and stained glass. And there was me, dressed up like an angel, sitting under an enormous Christmas tree, the branches glowing over my head with hundreds of candles and around me and it about fifteen gorgeous whores singing carols. Our Santa was an old guy named Appetite Ike who dribbled tobacco juice all over his beard and kept a bottle of rye down his pants. George?'

George, staring down into Central Park, said, 'Hmmmmm?'

'How's Jack?'

'Jack?'

'You know. Jack.'

George Bache's Christmas reverie spun away, melted like his snow fort. 'He dragged me off to Minsky's today for a matinée.'

'Oh yes?'

'Since I was there, I thought I'd review the show; Jack had a talk with Billy Minsky.'

'Just you two?'

'Just us and a stageful of what I'd swear were naked girls. I gave 'em a rave. Which reminds me: as we came out we were waylaid by a gentleman selling a very nice line in pornography. I didn't buy and you'll be pleased to hear neither did Jack. But when the fellow offered them to the man behind us, *he* said, "What for? I don't even own a pornograph."' When Teddy didn't laugh, George sighed, 'Well, I thought it was funny.'

'How is he, George?'

'Who?'

'Jack! Who do you think I'm interested in? The guy without a pornograph?'

'To tell you the truth, Teddy, Jack Eagels looks sick as a dog. But it doesn't seem to be slowing him down. Bernt McTaggart is making the both of you nuts.'

'Not nuts, George – dedicated.' Teddy turned, picked up the maribou cape and slung it over her bare shoulders in a flurry of soft white feathers. 'How do I look?'

George peered down his enormous nose and sighed. For all he could tell, she wasn't wearing underwear. 'Like snow in Central Park.'

'Teddy!' The sound of Dinah's voice made them both raise their heads. 'Dot man's here!'

George took Teddy's gloved hand, held it. 'Be careful, Red.'

Teddy slipped her hand away, took her loaded purse from the vanity. 'I can handle Tom Channing.'

George said, 'Sure you can. Easy as falling off the Chrysler Building.'

But he said it to himself. Teddy was already out the door. George was left with a vanity of powders and paints, stray wisps of maribou dipping and spinning in empty air.

14

Shooting Stars

For one brief moment, taking Tom Channing's gloved hand, Teddy thought he was luminous, saw him shine with visible energy.

'Hi, Red.' The collar of his overcoat up, a white silk scarf draped round his neck, Channing stood just outside the Baches' door looking – well, O'Rourke, what's the word? Pretty? God, no. Beautiful! As beautiful as a paper lantern in the dark – or a free-swimming shark. The coat was a dense heavy wool, as deep and as black as her lost velvet dress, his gloves were soft black leather, his tie bottle green, his tiepin a star sapphire, his hat a black homburg. The pale gold of his hair, the wild blue of his eyes – goddammit, here we go again.

Her white gloved hand in his, Tom spun her slowly round. Those blue eyes appraising, finally – savouring. 'You need more than feathers to top this off. How about fur? What's that stuff? You know, it's all white and costs a mint?'

So attracted to this man, warmed by his beauty, his effortless, almost eerie presence, she was dazzled, giddy – and silly enough to say, 'Polar bear?'

Tom should have laughed. Oh God, he should have laughed. But instead he said, deadpan, 'Nah, something Russian. I got it! Ermine. You need an ermine coat.'

That, she said to herself, was a very close call. If he'd only laughed, Teddy O'Rourke would have been lost in Tom Channing, New York's dashing desperado, forever.

Or at least until Christmas.

'Zipper! Bring the lady her fur.'

From around one of those dark bends in the Dakota's gloomy halls stepped Tom's chauffeur, holding something soft and white – and as dead as his eyes. *Now*, Tom laughed, took the coat from Zipper, held it out to Teddy. Who wasn't sure how to take it. How much was the front page worth? Or her virtue? Seeing no gracious way round Channing's present, short of making Zipper wear it, Teddy smiled, let Tom place the short white cubby over her feathers.

Down the Dakota's groaning elevator, out through its great arch, Teddy stopped in her white satin tracks.

If two was company and three a fur-bearing chauffeur, what was ten? A basketball team? Oh, wonderful! An intimate evening with Tom. In the elevator, Teddy had looked him over; no gun. But a gun was the only thing he hadn't brought with him.

Zipper slid behind the wheel of a custom Cadillac, a big smoky grey sedan. Beside Zipper, CD Durata rode shotgun. In the back seat was a new face – a huge goon with popeyes, thinning hair, and a cigar. Gunning its engine behind the Caddy was a big black wire-wheeled Packard and in the Packard were Solomon Rosenbloom and Agnes the cocoa-voiced blonde, Dancing Joe Bright and Jesse Bean. Arch Durata drove the black Packard.

The popeyed goon with the cigar pumped Teddy's hand. 'Hiya, toots. The name's Benny Magnolia. Boss wants ya in the back.'

Once inside, the caddy sounded like Madison Square Garden on fight night – and smelled like the back three rows. Teddy, squashed between Benny and Tom, felt as invisible as the guy who lost. No one told her that both cars had bullet-proof glass, armour panels and hidden pistol and rifle racks. She also had no idea where they were going; no one bothered to tell her that either. Following the Hudson River, the big sedan swept down the West Side to Greenwich Village, its back bumper hugged by the Packard, then swooped through the Holland Tunnel into Hoboken.

While CD punched holes in the Caddy's air. 'Joe'll

236

whup him,' he said, twisting round in his seat. 'You saw what he did to the Kraut. He ruined him. Like this – one two, one two.'

'Sure,' agreed the bug-eyed Benny. 'He don't even have to train.'

'Oh, he'll train,' said Channing with a slight touch of irony. 'He's got a week. I set up a meet with Sharkey on Monday.'

Listening as she gazed out of the Caddy's window, watching the squat, sullen town of Hoboken slide by – Dixie Fiske's Hoboken – Teddy smiled. The whole bunch of them were talking though their hats. Joe fight Jack Sharkey? The 'Boston Gob'? She gave the touchy Lithuanian a lot of credit – if he wasn't hitting low or busting out in tears, Sharkey was a hell of a boxer. Dancing Joe was good, he might someday be great; he still needed more time than a week. Tom Channing made a terrific crook, but was he a promoter? Teddy thought of Rickard. If Tex was alive, he'd chew Mr Channing like a plug of raw tobacco.

Ten miles from anywhere, the black Packard and the custom Cadillac pulled up to a huge two-storey log cabin set back in the snow-dusted woods off a dirt road. A small sign, flapping in the New Jersey wind, said 'Kitchen Monday's'. Zipper and Arch drove around the side and parked in the back.

Inside, Kitchen Monday's was as intimate as a beer garden: log walls papered in birch bark, acres of chequered red tablecloths, and a roaring fire on a huge flagstone hearth. Everywhere Teddy looked, dead dusty wildlife looked back – staring through dull glass eyes.

None of them there for the food, Zipper, Benny and the Durata cousins stationed themselves near the windows and doors, while Tom walked through Monday's like a crown prince, Teddy on his arm feeling out of place, out of step, and as embarrassed as a wallflower at her first dance. Wherever Channing went, he attracted attention.

Eyes shining, women nudged their men: 'Look! There's that gangster, the good-looking one in the papers all the time. Who's all the others? They gangsters too?' The men, barely shrinking but shrinking just the same, hissed back, 'For Christ's sake, clam up!'

Kitchen Monday himself was black. He had the hips of a hootchie-cootchie dancer, a rolling gait, and a smile as friendly as a vacuum cleaner salesman. Spotting Tom Channing and party walk through his door, Monday wiped his hands on his apron, shuffled out of his kitchen, and hollered, 'You all hurry now, get out of that cold!'

Sol Rosenbloom chose the chair at the end of the table nearest the closest fellow diner and sat in it. Dancing Joe fussed over Jesse, seating his bitter-faced, awesome-bodied lady while everyone else but Sol was still milling. Jesse was in no danger of freezing, not even if they'd taken a dog sled to the North Pole. Thanks to an epic shopping spree, she was wearing a brand new full-length Persian lamb coat. Tom sat Teddy in her feathers; the ermine cubby she'd left in the car. While Agnes, in silver-tipped fox, just stood there.

Monday marched right up and wagged a huge black finger in Sol's face, pointed at the sorrowful blonde. 'What's the matter with you? Pull out the little lady's chair. Heavens, I don' know what the world's comin' to.' Then marched over to Teddy. 'My goodness, child, wearing just this itty-bitty fluffy thing when it's coming on winter out there. I *said*! Where's this girl's chair? Is a gentleman deaf here?'

Teddy stole a look at Rosenbloom. He looked like an eight-year-old kid at his first cotillion. Zipper – sliding a quiet hand under his bulging lapel – looked like the anxious mother. Oh hell, there went a quiet dinner for ten. Suddenly smiling, Tom Channing scraped back his chair and stood up. Bowing from the waist, he showed Agnes into her seat.

'Thank you, Tommy,' thrummed Agnes, and behind her

Teddy heard a matron in bugle beads gasp. 'You heard her, Arthur? She said Tommy. I told you it was Tom Channing.' What Arthur said to that was lost to Teddy, but the matron shut up like a chicken shuts up when you chop its head off.

'That's better,' snapped Monday, then warmed at the sight of the women. 'You relax, sweethearts, warm yourselfs up, get real comfortable. Monday's gonna cook you somethin' special.' With that, he glared at Sol, then stomped back to his kitchen.

Solomon leaned over and whispered something in Channing's ear.

Tom shook his head. 'No, the guy's right.'

Now that it was over, Teddy'd loved every minute of Monday. She fished a cigarette out of her well-stocked bag. My God, there were still people who'd never heard of Tom Channing.

Teddy, sitting on her bruise, got her cigarette lit with that lighter of Tom's from whoever Sophie was, got her menu handed to her – and discovered she was in the damnedest poker game of her life. Almost always, Bluff's kid could count on holding three aces: enough beauty, enough sex appeal, and enough brains to ante. In this game, what for? Tom Channing assumed he'd already won. Why? Because *he* was holding four: *his* beauty, his brains, the business he was in, and the obvious trump – manhood. Reducing the men around him to pawns, a woman to no more than an audience, and later, the prize. Lesser men flattered; women fawned. Golden in the light of Kitchen Monday's leaping flames, Tom Channing sat across from Teddy drinking mineral water, holding the table with the power of his improbable self. Tom talked to Sol Rosenbloom, he talked to Joe Bright. Dames were here only for the feeding of, for the showing off of dead furs, for an audience of big eyes and little flutters of admiration. (Aside from Jesse Bean, that is. Jesse was here because Joe was lost without Mama B.

Blue.) Men like Channing supported flower shops and jewellers, furriers and cold people on foreign mountains who packed chocolates into heart-shaped boxes. Tom Channing bought women like long-stemmed roses, like diamonds, like mink, like bonbons.

Overdressed in white satin, Teddy ordered steamer clams, and settled back to watch Tom on display. Few people filled space like Channing; Bluff O'Rourke and Jack Eagels were two of them. Teddy made three. Usually. But for once in her life, Bluff's daughter sat out the hand. If she wasn't so annoyed, she'd be amused.

OK, O'Rourke, what now? End up like Agnes, the arm-clinging blonde? Where was the story in that? If she was to get the better of this man, winkle out his weakness, be more for him than the conquest of a brainy newspaper lady, she'd have to beat him at his own game. Since, like Jack, like most men, the only game he seemed to know was himself, that was the game she'd play. What she had to be was – nothing more and nothing less – the female flipside of Tom Channing. Could she? She could try. Remember what Bluff always said? 'Kathleen Ellen O'Rourke, you're a born crapshooter.' First: find an opening.

Sol Rosenbloom offered a peach.

Silver-haired Sol was holding forth on the history of baseball. Across the table, Dancing Joe's mouth was hanging open like a kid hearing ghost stories at midnight.

As she listened to this alfalfa, waiting for a natural pause, counting the errors, Teddy thanked God for a little knowledge and the conceit that went with it. If there was one thing Teddy knew about, it was sports. If there was one thing she could do, she could make a story live. If that's some of what it took to open a man up, tap her dancing shoes on his turf, no one could do it better than O'Rourke. Teddy could play that kind of man's game dead drunk and blind-folded. After all, she'd been doing it for years. The writer of SNAPBACK went to work.

Ten minutes later, Solomon sulked, Joe had sporting history in his eyes, Benny Magnolia, deserting his post, drifted over to listen, even Jesse and Agnes stopped posing – and Tom leant towards her. All riding on her voice like a high fly ball lost in the mid-summer sun.

An hour after that, Zipper was running the Cadillac east on a long lonely road that slipped under a ghostly vault of luminous white birches. The sliding glass panel between the Caddy's front seat and back was closed; Benny banished to the Packard. Snug in a white ermine cubby, Teddy O'Rourke felt like a sandlot pitcher who'd just faced Rogers Hornsby at bat – back in the days when Hornsby swotted a shattering .424 for the St Louis Cardinals.

Spitting in the dust, winding up on the mound, her arm coming round in a dizzy snap, her knuckles scraping dirt on the follow-through – and the third strike smoked past Hornsby in an arc of fire. Teddy had Tom to herself. If only George could see her now. She told him she could handle Tom Channing.

Somewhere far ahead in the moonlight was the Holland Tunnel; beyond the tunnel, the party.

The snow had stopped falling. Over Manhattan the sky hung like an ice rink and the skating moon followed Jack Eagels and Lulu LeRoy up Sixth Avenue. A ghost of a moon with a rag doll's face.

At the corner of Fifty-second and Sixth, Lulu stepped over a bundle of old clothes frozen to the sidewalk. Rattling a tin cup, an arm reached out of the huddled rags, eyes glowed from a face more ravaged than the moon.

'Eek,' eeked Lulu.

'Gotta dime, lady?' croaked the raggedy man as the skirt of her coat brushed his moonstruck face. 'Lost mine in the crash.'

Jack laughed – but Lulu pulled her coat away, drew it close to her legs. 'Ugh,' is all she said.

The bundle shook its cup at Jack. 'You, mister?'

Jack – noticing the beggar wore a pair of Van Gogh's boots – dropped a silver dollar in the cup.

The ragged man snatched it back out, sniffed it, then flipped it in a pocket. The dollar clunked when it landed.

Turning the corner onto Fifty-second, Jack and Lulu had come to the party. Jack wore his only really good clothes: a white tie, tails, and his second best dress shoes. Lulu wore red.

At Bootsie's Flim-Flam Club, anything went. Hidden behind a placid face of plain brownstone, Bootsie's was small, airless and ugly. But as popular as a ferris wheel. Black, white, big name entertainers, small-time hustlers: everyone threw money around at the Flim-Flam. Tucked under the sidewalk halfway down Fifty-second, the place was stuffed with New York smarts and sophisticates, booze, broads – and noise. Bootsie Basco was once a left fielder for the New York Giants but quit when Hype Hohenloe said, 'Bootsie, you couldn't catch your ass with both hands.' Now, Bootsie fielded free-wheeling fun, lit his joint with loud laughter and the danceable jazz of a six-piece band.

The bandstand was jammed in the corner. Which meant it was under the sidewalk. To get to the tiny stage, a musician had to walk up three stone steps and when he did, he – and whatever he played – spent the rest of the evening stooped. The ceiling above the bandstand was less than five and a half feet high. Embedded in the stucco ceiling was a milky glass grill. Sitting out a number, a jazzman could spend his idle time looking straight up, humming skat to himself and counting the shoes walking Fifty-second Street. If he played piano or string bass for Bootsie, he had it better. He could work down on the dance floor and count the shoes there.

At the Flim-Flam, spotting Mae West was easy. Her table for twelve was right in the middle of the room. The table was round; its surface a small city of bottles, ice-buckets, cocktail glasses, a pitcher of carrot juice, one tall glass with a straw. Six of its chairs were empty – but waiting. The tall glass was Miss West's. So was the carrot juice, pure and unspiked. Mae was hoisted into a confection of purple bugle beads that drove the light back hard enough to hurt. On her mass of candied blonde curls sat a hat like a heart. The hat was cerise. The ceiling over the cerise hat was much taller than the bandstand's, even lowered by a circus of netted balloons; like Mae's dress, every one of them purple.

At her table lounged a hunk of Italian beefcake in a shiny sharkskin suit, Frenchy DeMange with a woman who could have been his older sister – but prettier, and Owney Madden with his arm around a Persian cat of a girl, all soft grey fur and big blue eyes. At smaller tables, ringing Mae's like bleachers round a one-ring circus, caroused the entire cast of *Diamond Lil*.

Mae shook her beads with pleasure. 'Say, Owney, I like this place. It's sorta rough. You choose it?'

'Channing did. It's one of his joints.'

Mae stretched out the fingers on her right hand, arranging her rings. 'Tom Channing, huh? Him, I like even better.'

At midnight, as the fifth of November crashed into the sixth, Jack and Lulu walked in. Lulu strode straight across the Flim-Flam and handed Mae a flat box tied with a pink ribbon.

'For me, little Lulu?' said Mae, raising her painted brows.

'For going away, Miss West,' smiled Lulu.

By this time Jack had caught up with his Polish brunette. Seated, Madden and DeMange looked him over, saw nothing to get offended about – and went back to their women. Mae's Italian felt differently. He shoved his beefy torso closer to Mae's purple beads.

Mae shoved back. 'Don't crowd, Mario, there's plenty

243

to go around.' Taking the box in her tiny hand, Mae tipped back her honeyed head with its heart of a hat and peered up at Jack. 'Oh my! This yours, little Lulu?'

Her black hair held in place by a band of red sequins, Lulu nodded, said, 'Yes.' Then thought better of it. 'Well, not so much mine – '

Jack cut in. 'I'm mine,' he said. 'But I can be had.'

Mae let out a hoot. 'You, I like. What I always say is personality is everything, and like me, that's what you got, honey – personality. But say, you look familiar. Ain't I seen you someplace before?'

Standing in elegant tails, his white tie too tight, his arm gripped by Lulu, Jack hid a dry cough behind a hot hand. It wasn't part of his plan to have been seen before, not by Mae, not by Frenchy, not by Madden. Before they'd walked in and after they'd passed the ragged beggar, he'd said to Lulu, 'Let's keep it between you and me what I do for a living, OK?' And Lulu, dimpling, squeezed his elbow. 'Sure, sweetie, anything you say.' Now, grinning down at the tiny upturned face of Miss West, Jack said, 'Nope.'

Mae patted the seat of the chair next to her. 'Well, you're big and you're tall and you're dark, and though you ain't hairy enough – you're all-over handsome. Park yourself, curly, you look peaked. You sit too, little Lulu.'

Lulu was so thrilled to be invited to Mae's table, she vibrated.

Mae touched Jack's cheek with a hand that had a ring for every finger. 'What's the matter with you, honey?'

'The gypsy wouldn't say.'

'You saw a gypsy? Where?'

Picking up one of the empty glasses and smiling hopefully, Lulu said, 'In a penny arcade. Jack paid her a dollar for nothing.'

Mae moved closer to Eagels. 'The name's Jack, huh? Well, Jack, you got to go see Sri Deva Ram Sukul. He'll fix you up. Mario, pour little Lulu and her friend here a drink. Whaddaya want? It's all rotgut.'

Lulu chose champagne; Jack the house bourbon.

Mae sipped her carrot juice, said, 'Gimme your mitt, Jack. Let's see what the gypsy saw.' She pressed back his fingers, rotated her thumb, ran her blood-red nail down his heartline. 'Too bad, honey. I don't see no blondes in your life. There's someone there, though, someone kinda special. But that ain't all, not by a long shot. Say, handsome Jack, you know a lotta women, doncha?'

At that, Lulu shot him a hard look from under her sequined brow.

Before Jack could answer Mae – or Lulu – Bootsie's band launched themselves into a raucous rendition of 'Bye-bye Blackbird'. They played it hot. Not Harlem hot – Park Avenue hot. The music took Mae away. Took even Lulu LeRoy. The table forgot Jack. For which he was very, very grateful. It gave him time to think.

Staying close to Lulu so he could get close to the people she knew, which, of course, meant Tom Channing, was beginning to make him nervous. Especially after talking to Billy Minsky. *Before* Billy, he couldn't have said why. Just a funny feeling in the pit of his stomach, a reporter's hunch, a newsman's unstoppable urge to answer questions. Sitting in Lindy's the night before, listening to Lulu rattle on, left Jack with a headful of dead-end streets, back alleys, and stairs that ended in ceilings. *After* Billy? It was worse. For starters, Billy Minsky had never heard of Lulu LeRoy. Gilda Tannenbaum rang no bells either. So Jack described her. Billy slapped his forehead in astonishment. 'Oh, my God! She's dyed her hair! You mean Joey.' And Jack said, 'I do?'

'Sure, the kid who was only thirteen years old. The one I had to fire.'

'You fired *her*?'

'Of course, for how old she was I could get my theatre closed, maybe even get thrown in jail. Who needs all that grief for just a nipper in the pony line? We get raided for less.'

By now, Jack was getting the picture. Lulu hadn't been a soubrette, merely a chorus girl. She hadn't stayed with Minsky's while Milt got pitched in the street. What else hadn't happened?

'And Milt Rabinowich? What about him?'

Here, Billy got cagey. 'What'd Joey tell you?'

'That Rabinowich chased her around backstage until she let him marry her – '

Billy stopped Jack. '*Milt* chase *Joey*? You got it the wrong way round. Joey chased Milt. Drove the guy crazy. Until he married her. I told him it was a dumb thing to do, but he took to feeling sorry for her.'

Jack accepted all this better than he might have done. After half a life as a newsman, this kind of thing was as common as rice. Still, this was Lulu they were talking about, and Jack liked Lulu.

'Did Milt really beat her up?'

Billy looked glum. 'Oh sure, Milt kicked the shit out of her a couple of days after they got tied. I sent him uptown for that, made him work my Little Apollo Theater in Harlem.'

'Why'd he hit her?'

'Well,' said Billy, 'the way Milt told it, Joey knew things in bed no thirteen-year-old ought to know, which got him thinking. So he got her talking – this is right on their wedding night, you understand – and as soon as she told him a few things, he told her he was getting a divorce. And Joey went crazy. Before he beat her up, *she* beat him up. Stole the only thing he had, he wanted. A Tiffany watch, I think he said. When she wouldn't give it back, he came round and bounced her around a bit.'

'Is Milt dead?'

'Dead? You better believe it. Fell out a window over at Joey's hotel. I never could figure out how.'

Having trouble with his breathing, Jack excused himself from the table. Maybe if he loosened his tie? A half a minute on his own in the men's room and the doors banged open.

It was Madden and DeMange with their hands in their pockets.

Owney got right to the point. 'You a reporter?'

No point in denying it; Jack told the truth. 'Yep.' He sounded a lot better than he felt. Not knowing if Madden and DeMange scared him, or if he scared himself. Floating like flannel on aspirin and bourbon, he still couldn't shake this goddamned cold.

'Jack Eagels, the guy from the *Trident*?'

'That's me.'

Madden took his hand out of his pocket. Jack almost kissed him when the hand came out empty. 'Put 'er there,' he said. 'You're the only snoop in New York ain't calling me McTaggart's killer.'

Jack was proud of himself when he opened his mouth. His voice didn't crack or squeak, and better than that, he still had one. 'I like sticking to the facts. Fact is, there aren't many to stick to.'

Madden pumped Jack's hand; Frenchy gave him a wink. 'That's about right, Eagels, but I don't notice it bothering rags like the *Graphic* or the *News*. That was my policeman got killed. I feel terrible somebody cut him.'

'I can imagine.' Jack was beginning to feel awkward. Madden was still holding his hand.

Madden stuck out his receding chin. 'A guy in my line of work needs all the cops he can get. I'll miss Bernie. Hell, Jack, I always used to know when old Grover, even Gentleman Jim, was taking a piss. Now, I gotta read papers like yours. Come on outta the can. We got a party waiting.'

'Sure, Owney,' said Jack. 'But first I have to see a man about a dog.'

Walking out of the men's room a few minutes later – his tie loosened, his breathing easier – Jack had about three seconds to enjoy himself, when – escorted by a squadron of fussing waiters and followed by turning heads, Tom Channing walked into Bootsie Basco's Flim-Flam Club.

Fanned out behind Channing was a remarkable display of human flotsam and jetsam. A big man with silver hair, this guy as large as Frenchy DeMange and flanked by a drooping blonde flower with sad eyes, four dressed-up thugs, one slapped together out of asphalt, one almost as bald as Connie Mezinger, two who looked like the Katzenjammer kids, and Teddy O'Rourke's big black boxer, Dancing Joe Bright with his sour black lady.

But the most impossible of all – and only five feet away – was Teddy O'Rourke.

Red was a white cloud of feathers, her hair swept up on her head, and her gloved arm linked through Channing's. Reeling, curling his toes for a grip on the floor, Jack stopped where he was, took a quick halfstep behind a potted palm and a couple of Bootsie's customers, also potted. His redheaded screwball was looking up into Tom Channing's pretty-boy face – and laughing. Laughing?

Jack's heart lurched, shuddered in his chest. What was he feeling? Jealousy? Jack Eagels – jealous? The man with all those women in the palm of his hand? The hell he was! What he was really feeling was fury. What he really wanted to do was to stride up behind her, tap Teddy on her bare white shoulder, and when she turned, when that freckled, laughing face of hers swept up towards his, when it froze in surprise, pop her one right where someone had popped her before. But he contained himself. Not a good idea. Not a good idea at all. Why wasn't it a good idea? Damned if he knew.

Pull your thoughts together, Eagels. Figure this out. It's

not a good idea because you're on a story and the story is right this minute heading for Mae's table. Mae's calling for two more chairs, Madden's shaking Channing's hand, he's shaking Joe Bright's hand, then – Lulu! What the fuck is Lulu doing? LeRoy's little mouth's just popped open like a beached goldfish. Who's she looking at? Channing? Teddy? (Come to that, where is Teddy?) So who then? Oh Christ – wouldn't you know it – it's me. There she goes, hopping up in that fire-engine-red dress to squeak, 'Jack?' Better get back before she busts out in tears.

Two feet from his potted palm – the gold flecks in her grey eyes glinting in fury – O'Rourke blocked his path.

'Why were you hiding behind a tree, Jack?'

'What's any man do behind a tree, lady? I was taking a piss.'

'I'm not laughing.'

'Not now, you're not.'

'Meaning?'

'Channing. What is he, a laugh a minute?'

'He's as funny as a gun – but he listens.'

'Glib as ever, Red – but you lost me there. Listens to what?'

'Me, you idiot. Tom's a rogue, a killer, and a thief – but he wouldn't steal a scoop from a friend. What the hell are you doing here anyway?'

'Wondering what *you're* doing here.'

'I'm working.'

'As what? Muscle for Channing?'

'And you, Jack? Candy for children?'

At that, Red turned her back on him. But before she got a foot away, Jack tapped her on her bare white shoulder, she turned back – and Jack pinched her nose shut between the knuckles of his good right hand.

Teddy's 'Eek!' was more a short honk.

'Say, Red!' called Tom. 'Where are you? Come on over, meet Mae West!'

Jack let go. Taking a step forward, Teddy's hand flew to her red nose. Jack took a step back, keeping an eye on her free hand. With O'Rourke, you never knew what was in it. 'If you mess this up for me, Eagels, you'll never need a tree again.'

Rubbing her nose, Teddy walked off and Jack stayed where he was. Gulping for air. That settled it. Jack Eagels was making an entrance. Here goes.

Jack strode back to table, stopped on a flourish – and swept all thirteen faces with a gaudy grin.

'Hi, there,' he said. 'The name's Jack Eagels. Mr Channing. Mr Bright. I'm afraid the rest of you have me at a disadvantage – except, of course, for my colleague, Miss O'Rourke here. How are you, Miss O? Feeling good? You *look* good. That a new dress? Looks good with the nose. I hear you missed a great football game at the Polo Grounds. The Giants won. Mud and ice up to their knees. Hopper did a swell job on it.'

Impressed, but – Jack had to give it to her – not defeated, Teddy grinned back. 'Why, Jack, what are you doing here?'

Jack flipped back his tails, threw himself down on the one remaining chair, and shoved it closer to Lulu's. 'My friend brought me. Lulu LeRoy, say hello to Teddy O'Rourke.'

Jack noticed with glee that Teddy's eyes widened – not much, but enough – at the name Lulu. Watching Teddy's face, he almost missed Lulu's. If Lulu's name tipped Teddy, Teddy's shocked Lulu. But what Lulu said next rocked Jack. 'Oh! You're the girl from Jack's newspaper.' Her little hand flew to her mouth, her bright, childish eyes sought Jack's. 'Oh my! I wasn't supposed to mention that, was I, sweetie? Gosh, I'm sorry but – say! I hope Teddy doesn't mind I watered her cactus. You're just so terrible with things in pots.'

The high voltage that passed between Teddy and Jack could have burnt all the toast in Queens. Meanwhile,

Channing looked at Jack, at Lulu, at Teddy, at the sad-eyed blonde, then settled on Lulu again.

Lulu hadn't finished. 'Miss West, aren't you going to open my present? It's for your going away to San Francisco – Jack and me, we decided I'm not going with you.'

And right at that interesting moment, a moment when any damn thing at all could happen, the damndest thing happened.

Dutch Schultz and his gang of very unmerry men walked into Bootsie's Flim-Flam Club – and shot the place up.

Because it was a party for Miss Mae West, because Schultz had just gotten started, and because he wasn't angry yet, his men all aimed at the ceiling. Popping a lot of purple balloons. Bringing down sizeable chunks of dusty white ceiling plaster. Scattering waiters, barmen, cigarette girls, and the shrieking cast of *Diamond Lil* into all four of Bootsie's busy corners – bringing the band to a crashing halt two bars into 'There'll Be Some Changes Made'.

Every single one of the fourteen people at the centre table sat where they were like the stones on Easter Island, whatever they'd been doing when the rumpus began frozen in place. Drinking, smoking, mouths open to talk or closed to listen. Patting down a stray curl, Mae had just put her hand to the back of her cotton candy head. It was Mae who was the first to speak when the shooting stopped. The first to ask the obvious question when Dutch strolled up to her table, a tommy gun cradled in the crook of his arm – while his men ranged themselves around the Flim-Flam, herding Madden's and Channing's goons into the centre.

Picking a sliver of plaster out of her milk-white décolletage, she drawled, 'Dutch? Why the hell'd you do that?'

Dutch batted his bulging eyes as he answered. 'I heard about your little party, busty. Knew it wouldn't have that pep without me. So, here I am! Happy to see an old friend,

Owney? You, Tom? You wanna know if I'm happy? I'll tell ya. I ain't happy. Not since you sicked the cops on me for Bernie.'

Madden tipped his head towards Channing. 'Now you see what I mean? The guy has no humour. Being a gangster is like being a dictator; who's gonna protect you from your friends?'

Dutch stretched his lips in a grin. 'You got it, Owney. We're all friends here, ain't we?' Then waved the tommy gun at Mae. 'You! Get all these women up from the table. Put 'em away somewhere safe. Mrs Flegenheimer's little boy don't shoot dames.'

'Since when?' said Teddy, but no one was listening to her.

Mae rose with all the dignity she could muster, which was plenty. 'OK, girls. You heard the man. Let's go powder something.'

Of the remaining six women, five stood up: Agnes, Jesse Bean, DeMange's hefty lady, Madden's soft Persian, and Lulu – though Lulu came slowly, twisting her linen napkin, chewing her lip. Teddy stayed where she was, still smoking the cigarette Tom had lit for her – with that damn lighter of his, of course – when she'd first sat down. Her red hair littered with white plaster, shreds of purple balloon, her grey eyes cold and clear and monumentally pissed off.

Schultz tapped Teddy's shoulder just as Jack had, but Dutch did it with the hot end of a gun. 'What's the matter with you, sister? You wearing pants or something?'

If Jack hadn't decided this was all rather serious, he would have laughed. Then again, maybe he wouldn't. Schultz without his gun might have trouble with O'Rourke.

'Go on, Red,' said Tom. 'I like my women in one piece.'

Jack didn't feel at all like laughing at that.

'Shut up, Channing,' spat Schultz. 'I do all the talking here.'

Slipping her bag from the table, Teddy pushed back her chair. And stared at Schultz's flat baby face. That stupid face with its bulging eyes, eyes fringed with an albino's lashes, drove Jack and Lulu out of her mind. What was this? Another Douglas Fairbanks movie? Doug with a knife in his teeth and a limp blonde in his arms fending off hordes; some dime novel where the dippy heroine trips over a speck of dust just as the Indians ride up to scalp the shit out of her. Why not? What had anything like this to do with women?

O'Rourke was getting sick of it. It was Mezinger all over again. Scram, ladies. Stand in a corner and go eek! and ahh! Come back when they pass out the bandages. Teddy looked round the table. Already – and still seated – she wasn't here. Stern, grim, brave as hell, the boys were sorting out the odds. All except a large slab of beef Mae had introduced as her own. Mario looked ready to piss himself. But the rest: Madden, DeMange, Rosenbloom, Channing, even Joe Bright and Jack Eagels (here, Teddy ground her teeth – Jack! With his new friend Lulu – a friend who'd been in Teddy's bed; when she had time, she'd kill him!), who notices a dame when the blood is up? Who indeed.

You watching, Daddy?

Teddy stood up, stepped back three paces, stopped. For Dutch, the malingering redhead was out of the picture. For Teddy, the broad back of the flat-faced gangster was two feet away, but coming up rapidly on her right was the only man who seemed to know she was alive. Even dressed in rags, he was one of Schultz's punks, a guy with a ravaged face.

In one fluid motion, she moved up behind Dutch – close enough to breathe sweet nothings in his ear – opened her bag, gripped the .22 calibre revolver, and gently placed the cold barrel against the tender hollow of bone between his bulging eye and his oily hairline. Though it still took the distinctive rolling click of a hammer drawing back to get Dutch's full attention. But the punk with the ravaged face understood immediately. Raising his own hand with its own gun, he aimed it right at her white satin heart – and Teddy, twisting at the waist, shot him through the tattered mess of his tattered sleeve. Then slammed the .22 back where it'd been in the first place, up against the now rigid temple of Dutch Schultz.

Tom Channing's admiration was all over his beautiful face. He let out a long-held breath and grinned. 'Nice going, Red.'

As the raggedy man gripped his shattered wrist and sank moaning to his raggedy knees, Teddy, her voice husked, said, 'I'm not doing this for you, Tom, I'm doing it for me. Now, I guess we can all talk.'

Frenchy turned in his chair, looked up at Dutch, at Teddy, and laughed out loud. 'Dat's pretty good, I like dat.'

In the same glass, Madden poured himself a shot of gin, a shot of whisky, and a splash of Mae's plastered carrot juice. Then drank it.

'So that's settled,' he said when he'd finished retching. 'We all talk. Who wants to start? How about me? What I got to say is short and sweet and this is it, so listen up. I didn't kill fucking Bernie, Dutch here didn't kill fucking Bernie. Somebody better own up who killed fucking Bernie before we all fucking kill each other – and that's bad for fucking business.'

'If nuttin' else,' added a baleful DeMange.

Jack spent a moment wondering if he ought to invite Madden and Mezinger to tea. They'd have so much to say to each other – and in so few words.

Madden tapped Channing's arm. 'Now you, Tom.'

Tom Channing smiled, stubbed out his cigarette, leaned back in his chair. 'Nobody killed the stupid bastard – '

Under her breath, holding the gun steady, smelling the stink of the sweating Schultz, Teddy whispered, because *you* did, Tom. But even though she'd finished his sentence, she was still stunned to hear him say –

'Because I did. In a way.'

Jack didn't know what Teddy O'Rourke thought of all this but he knew what he thought. Holy shit! Give the girl a kewpie doll. Goddammit! He loved Teddy O'Rourke. He also needed more than he'd ever needed anything to get to a phone. Would anyone shoot him if he just got up out of his chair and strolled off to find one? Would the guy in rags get a grip on himself and find his gun? Would he aim it at a fellow who'd given him a silver dollar? Should he find out? And would Teddy be able to handle things while he called the paper? O'Rourke, handle things? Who was he kidding? The look on Dutch's face answered all those questions. As long as Teddy held that gun to his head, no one on his side was shooting anyone. Jack rose. 'Don't mind me, folks. I'll be back in a couple of minutes. Talk among yourselves.'

Dodging out of the clutch of women, Lulu threw her arms around his neck as soon as Jack, on very stiff legs, marched past her. 'What are they doing, Jack? What's Mr Channing saying?'

Jack prised her off, vaulted over the maître d's desk, then reached around, and yanked Lulu back with him. 'What do you care? Shut up.' Jack groped blind on the top of the desk, found the phone and grabbed it. Dialling his city desk, he asked for Mezinger, then waited, tapping his fingers on his nervous knee.

Lulu popped her dark head over the desk, sequins flashing. 'I wish I could hear what they're saying. Gosh, this is exciting, Jack. Is this what you do all the time?'

Digging his fingers into the hair of her head, catching hold of the red headband, he jerked her down again. 'No, this isn't what I do. This is what Teddy does. What I do is come along after they do what they're doing and write about it. Keep your voice down – hello, Connie? Listen,

255

I've cracked the McTaggart story. Lulu! Stop pinching! What, Connie? Never mind where I am and never mind who Lulu is. Dammit, I'm whispering because if I didn't whisper someone might shoot me. Jesus Christ, Connie, stop yelling.' Wincing, Jack held the receiver away from his ear. On his end, Connie was screaming. 'What the fuck's going on! What's the story! Get it in – now!'

'Can't,' whispered Jack.

'Can't! You sure as shit can – or you're as fired as O'Rourke is!'

'Baloney.'

'What!'

'I said bullshit.'

Forgetting Connie, Jack let the yammering phone sink into his lap. Thinking fast. If Channing killed McTaggart that put his redhead right in the thick of it. Could Jack Eagels go trotting off to his desk at the *Trident* and write up this story – a story that would stop the presses – leave Teddy all alone to deal with whatever happened next? Would he? Well, hell, he'd like to – but he couldn't. He loved his Irish gunslinger. Besides, he had to explain about Lulu. (He could swear the daffy Pole had said what she said on purpose. Water Teddy's cactus, Jesus!) Explaining Lulu wouldn't be easy but on his knees seemed a good way to start. And besides that, his girl was walking around New York on the arm of a good-looking gangster – and laughing. What the hell was so funny?

Jack, lifting the receiver, cut through Connie's spitting rage. 'I can't bring the story in, Mezinger. Not yet.'

Just as Jack figured, Connie screeched, 'You're fired!'

Jack hung up. Lulu was tugging at his arm.

'Jeepers, Jack. Did one of those guys kill poor old Bernie?'

'Not now, Lulu.'

Sitting for a minute, staring past Lulu's sweet baby burlesque face, Jack made up his mind. He was taking Teddy home.

Jack stuck his head over the edge of the desk.

Like everyone else at Bootsie's, Mae and her bevy of ladies were on their way back to the tables, DeMange was sweeping plaster off the seats of the chairs, Madden had his arm around Schultz, one of Madden's men had helped the raggedy man with the shattered wrist to his feet, and Tom Channing was gone.

So were Dancing Joe Bright and his lady.

So were the drooping blonde and silver-haired sideman.

So was Teddy O'Rourke.

'Shit,' said Jack.

'Jeepers creepers,' said Lulu. 'Miss West never did open my present.'

'What was it?' asked Jack absently, standing up and dusting his black tails.

'A picture of me. You want one too? I got lots.'

15

Houdini Hearts

Tom Channing, a New York original – charming, gutsy, and as wicked as immortal sin – had all the time in the world for women. But time for just one? Tom wasn't in love, but he was sure in something from the moment Red O'Rourke stuck the barrel of a .22 calibre pistol against the head of Dutch Schultz.

At the top of the Sugar Hill mansion, Red sat cross-legged on his bed in a chemise the colour of an Arizona sunset. A pile of Woodrow Wilson dimes in her lap, a cigarette dangling from her lips, in her hand a bottle of his casino's best hooch – right off an Irish boat and bonded – beating his ass at poker.

Red's clothes were all over the place; his were hung neatly in a wardrobe. The wardrobe was a huge piece of Macassar ebony set with lacquered leather panels; the whole thing smooth and rounded and hard as a flapper in a silent movie. Having a taste for the finer things in life, Tom had it valued before boosting it. The valuer, a little man with a lisp, said it was Art Deco, a genuine Pierre Chareau. 'Yeah?' said Tom. 'I like it. Rothstein, Luciano, Lansky, even Capone – I bet they don't have nothing French. Sol, you and CD, steal me some more.' As a result, Tom's bed was a shining scoop of black lacquer, his walls were lined with blue silk, the silk was embroidered with silver thread, his armchairs were tubular steel, his floor a slab of silvered matt glass – every bit of it Art Deco and all of it hot. In a corner his American radio, all sharp corners and scroll-work, was tuned to WEAF; in a brown voice black with despair, Ethel Waters sang 'Am I Blue?'

Lying back against his silk pillows, wearing a pair of emerald-green boxer shorts, Tom was looking at the cards Red dealt him. One more diamond and he'd have a flush. Another king and he'd have at least a pair. One more bright funny crack out of Red, another glimpse of sweet secret heaven when she moved those long tucked-up legs with their girlish scrapes and bruises, and he was in danger of losing his composure. Tom Channing didn't like it at all. With women, he never lost anything. Not for five years now, anyway.

Yet – here he was for Christ's sake: two in the morning, a great-looking, fast-acting, sharp-shooting broad in her underwear, he in his, both of them in bed, and he still hadn't got any nookie. For him, this was a first. Though for now, just winning a hand of poker seemed winning enough. Besides, the broad held surprises. If he wanted from Red what he could get from any other damn dame by crooking a finger, he'd have to play her like a Stradivarius – with feeling.

Tom flipped a silver dollar into the pot. For a dollar in a dime-stake game, he had the pleasure of seeing the corner of Red's lovely mouth twitch. 'I open for a buck. That newspaper guy at Mae's table? He important on your paper?'

Teddy, fanning her hand, didn't look up. 'He thinks so. Unfortunately, he's right.'

'So, this bigshot newsie, he a friend of yours?'

'He was.' Teddy called Tom's opening bet. 'How many cards?'

'One. Was? What is he now?' Tom picked up the card she'd flipped on his stomach. Things were looking up. By throwing his king, he'd picked up a diamond. Fucking hell, what were the odds on that?

'Now he's an ex-friend.' Teddy took two and another slug of Irish.

'So it's like that.'

'That's what it's like. You betting?'

259

Tom smiled. That settled the problem of the boyfriend. He threw in another dollar.

'Well, Red, you got any feelings for him left at all, you'll tell him to stay away from the little brunette I saw him with tonight.'

Teddy raised him a buck and a half. 'I don't think he'd listen, not to me anyway. Why?'

'Just tell him I said so.' Tom had a diamond flush. What in the hell could Red have?

'Like you told Dixie Fiske to let go of Joe Bright?'

Inwardly, Tom groaned. Hell, here it comes. The old third degree. After Spooner's gym, he'd bet Sol he could charm that reporter crap right out of Red's head. Find in those newspaper eyes what he always found in the dames he met – melted butter for his bread. OK, so he owed Sol fifty bucks; charm didn't work. In that case, fuck violins. See how a freckle-faced smartass handled cold truth. If he'd caught a mermaid, what did Red think she had on her hook? A blowfish? A Great White Sap? Maybe it was time for the lady to find out it was shark. And if he lost her? Hell, those were the breaks. Red was getting too close anyway. Women, when they got close, got in the way.

So he said, 'You could say that.' Then watched Red study her cards, smoke her cigarette, knew the exact moment she decided to reel in her line.

'People around you,' she said – he loved the way she fished, the way she dangled bait – 'they die sort of early, don't they?'

Lowering his hand, Tom stared at Teddy long enough to make her lower hers. 'OK, sportswriter, I got an idea. Let's you and me play something else.'

'Like what?'

'Like twenty questions.'

Teddy stared at him, caught by the rush of reality her question had blown into this poker game.

Tom settled into that look. It was the kind of startled bunny expression he'd seen a lot of in a lifetime of scaring rabbits. But he took his hat off to Red. No bunny here. He'd flushed a pissed-off ginger pussy cat.

'What the fuck you want from me, lady? You wanna know who I am and what I do and how I do it? You wanna hang around a bad guy like me so you can write about it? Give a bunch of dumb pricks out in the big wide world a few cheap thrills? Is that what I am, Red? Like Dancing Joe's tarbaby said: a big story where you get a gold star?'

Teddy couldn't answer any of that. But she had enough moxie not to flush or squirm or pretend that was not what she'd meant. Enough moxie to keep her grey eyes on his, to take whatever was coming. Tom loved that too.

'I'll tell you a story, you want one so bad. You can even put it in that paper of yours, see what it gets you. When I finish, get the fuck out of here or don't, it's up to you.' Tom hadn't sat up, hadn't moved a muscle in his body, but he held Teddy just the same. 'You got a pencil? You wanna take this down? No? OK by me, but I'm telling you only once. I figure, see, people get what they need in this life, not what they want. If some son of a bitch like Fiske, or that cop, McTaggart, needs to die early, then the somebody who sees he does it on time is doing no more than a tidal wave does, or an earthquake, or a fire. Guys like me, we're what you could call a – '

'Force of nature?'

'You called it. Other guys, they're like those lilies of the field, you know? Tractors run 'em over, sheep crap on 'em, they get stepped on by guys like me. So what's the big deal? That's life. You tell me why every time some weed gets shat on, all the other dumb lilies start wailing and weeping and calling on some dime-a-dozen God, phoning the cops, writing their congressman. Everybody making such a stink out of dying, trying to pass a law against it. Why newspaper hacks like you make a living out of sheepshit.'

Stung at the small injustice, Teddy took a small stand. 'I'm a sports columnist. I write about sports.'

'Oh yeah? You here to write about sports? Don't give me that baloney, you're here to write about dying. You wanna see me get mine? Get your picture on the front page with a dead guy? I'm nothing to you but a way to smell the rotten stink of death. People like you make me sick. Me, you, the Pope, we're all running down a road – and what do you know? It's a fucking dead end. You gonna sit right down in the dirt and bawl about it? I been dead a dozen times over. Take it from a guy who knows: being dead's just another thing to do. The only people who cry about it are the suckers left standing in the road.' Tom spread his flush on the bedspread. 'What the fuck are you holding? I call.'

All through this surprising speech, the skin on the back of Teddy's neck prickled with a fearsome clarity. Tom Channing had called more than her hand – he'd called the whole game. Now was the time to walk out on Tom – or turn up every card she was holding. Choosing, she laid out her hand. 'Dead man's hand, Tom. Full house. I don't work for the *Trident*; I quit two days ago.'

Tom laughed aloud at the sight of Red's aces over eights, at her news, at her choice. 'You wouldn't be floating the deck, would you, Red?'

Teddy dimpled. 'Who me? Cheat a force of nature?'

Throwing his losing flush in the Art Deco air, scattering dimes and silver dollars, Tom made a grab for the redhead with the luck of the Irish. Wrestled Teddy down and kissed her struggling face. 'Lie back, lady luck, and shut up. I got something you can't beat.' Slipping his hand under her back, he gripped the rosy chemise and pulled. His mouth, an inch from hers, whispered, 'Bill me later.'

In a room hot with the scent of winter roses, a room with long windows and still shadows, a room lit only by a lowslung moon, Teddy saw a little white hand water a small green cactus. The sunset chemise was ripped from rosy neck to rosy crotch.

When Red fell asleep in his arms, Tom Channing dressed and went wandering. Down all his silent stairs and out into the casino's back garden. He didn't give a fuck about green growing things, but at least they kept their mouths shut. To Tom, walking in the light of a ringed blue moon, feathered with blue Harlem snow, his garden looked like nothing at all. Except a good place to hide. But if there were enemies lurking, skulking behind bushes – he hoped they'd freeze their balls off. Day or night, the garden was where he did his thinking.

'People who cry over dying were the suckers left standing in the road.' That's what he'd told Red. Not bad. A pretty good way of putting it. And brother, he knew what he was talking about. Who was a sucker and who was left all alone out here? No need for three guesses – he was. It took only one special death, only a fire he couldn't put out. Even if he'd been sober, which, God help him, he wasn't. Since, oh yeah, *after*, but not then. Not when she needed him, not when she was trapped and screaming in the flames – and he stood helpless on the wet grass below her high window with the tears running down his face. Stood there with Joey, listening to all the balloons popping, knowing the balloons were exploding and the candy in the little pink paper cups was melting and the cake dripping with hot hotter chocolate and the wax from Joey's candles was running across her shimmering table, and it was so hot he burnt his hands, his face, before he even got near the door of her house, trying to bully his way back in. But he hadn't. Got back in. Ever. Not even through her door, a door suddenly sickeningly wavering in the heat like a mirage, like it was never real at all, like it was never the door to her house or even her, like she was never more than a movie burning on a flat white screen. And he hadn't even seen it coming. Sol had, good old Agnes, she'd seen it too – but not Tom, drinking his way through the good times.

Tom laughed in the dark, a bitter laugh that died under the Harlem moon. He'd told Red he was like fire. When people needed a match, he was the tough monkey who had one. So back then, when someone got in his way so bad he was left broken up inside – worse than all the bullets and knives and fists ever did – what did Tom Channing, tough guy, do? He stopped drinking. Now, *that* took nerve. And what did he do after last Saturday night, when time was running out?

Saturday night and Sunday morning there was Dixie Fiske to take care of, Dancing Joe to find, a border squabble to settle with a hot-headed rumrunner in Queens, a new still to set up in a small town deep in the Catskills. Sunday night there was Red O'Rourke, a dame who was getting under his skin. If that weren't enough, came the business with Joe Bright and the deal with Jack Sharkey's management: to get the dumb Lithuanian to fight a black kid, Tom had to offer – win or lose – a lion's share of the purse, plus ten per cent of his promotional deals for the next ten years. They also wanted the fight as soon as possible. A week! A week for Joe to train. The deal stank, it was highway robbery, but it was the only deal in town if he wanted the heavyweight title for Dancing Joe Bright. That's what Tom Channing did. And that was nothing at all.

Oh yeah, he was tough all right. A real hard guy, a bootlegger who couldn't drink, a killer who couldn't kill.

In the meagre light of dawn, a naked, juttery and very confused Teddy O'Rourke lay propped on her elbow.

Tom Channing was one stunning son of a bitch. And no more stunning than when he turned his hand to rape. Who was she kidding? Rape? If Tom hadn't made his play when he did, she would have jumped him. As it was, she'd been mistreated, abused, adored, aroused, fulfilled – then when Tom crept away in the night, abandoned. And she'd loved every goddamn minute of it. Teddy O'Rourke had just coupled with a werewolf. Tom was pure unedited passion: hearty, hungry, selfish – so selfish it turned on itself, became generous. With no vows of love, no sham, no shame, no conceit, it was a romp, a shag, an unholy thrill –

Teddy reached for a shaky cigarette – and, it would never happen again.

In Tom's lacquered French bed she'd done her own ecstatic 'little' dying – but once was enough. My God, she could develop a taste for his cold climate, his black and white landscape of violent joy, could lose her precious self in the snow. Would that be such a loss? Yes, it damn well would. Kathleen Ellen O'Rourke almost liked who she was, almost understood the self that had once fitted into Jack's like Cinderella fit her glass slipper.

Fear lit a match in her mind. Jesus! Jack!

Rolling over, she turned her back on where Tom had been, his side of the bed already cold, lay staring out at the elms that tapped their frozen branches on his window. What if Jack were to find out about Tom? After tonight at Bootsie's, he must be thinking something. Hope made a brief visit in Teddy's chilled heart – perhaps that was the reason he'd paraded his gilded child under her nose, only to hurt her.

Of course, O'Rourke, tell yourself another lie. Jack knew Lulu *before* he'd seen Teddy with Tom Channing. Lulu had come first. Anger seared away her confusion. Jack Eagels, Connie Mezinger, Dixie Fiske, Jesse Bean, Solomon Rosenbloom, now Tom. Teddy O'Rourke had had enough of being used – even if Tom's using made her feel like she'd taken that dizzy plane ride to Paris with Lindbergh. Being used, using. Who was using whom? Everybody, that's whom – who. She'd used Tom to erase Lulu's little face, the dark mossy eyes that slyly sought hers when the girl – oh, so artlessly! – let drop her remark about Teddy's bedside cactus, those childish fingers seeking Jack's arm, touching, saying, 'This is mine.'

Tom was gone, off doing whatever men like Channing did in the lost hours before dawn. Teddy was wide awake and sober. In her search for a story, her need to prove her talent, what, dear God, did she think she was doing? Grinning like a junkie, the truth was right at the edge of her nerves. It wasn't her understanding that was in trouble here, but her judgement. In anger and pride, she'd run away from the redman she loved, from jealousy slept with the first man other than Jack Eagels since she'd met that damn Chicago train. Letting herself play more games than a hand or two of poker with a man like Tom Channing, a gangster who'd probably bumped off Dixie Fiske, who said he'd killed Police Lieutenant Bernt McTaggart – in a way. She'd seen Jack's front-page face when Tom made his remark at Bootsie's. Noticed that Jack hadn't listened to the final phrase – 'in a way'. All he'd heard as he escaped to Bootsie's phone was a confession. But Teddy heard. Knowing what Tom's 'in a way' must have meant. Either 'by order', like the demise of Dancing Joe's unlucky manager, or by 'tacit wish', as England's Henry II had rid himself of that meddlesome priest, Thomas à Becket.

What was it Tom said as they lay curled up together, dimes and silver dollars and Bootsie's ceiling plaster stuck to their sweating skin? Teddy touched the golden hair of his chest, traced with a sated nail the puckered mouths of two scars just below his left collarbone. The bullets that made them could only have missed his scampish heart by inches. *What kind of bullet could kill Tom Channing? Only one made of silver?* She'd asked him then why he always wore green: ties, robes, even socks. Was he Irish? And he'd laughed. 'Irish? No.' Then why? 'Because, Red, green is the devil's colour.' With that answer, the ghost of the still living Jesse Bean made a faint shape in her mind. 'If things don't go right, I'll put a whammy on you, girl.' In Channing's scarred, death-defying arms, Teddy had shivered.

As Irish as Tom's bonded booze, Michael Francis O'Rourke believed in ghosts and fairies and all manner of supernatural folk. His redheaded child, leaning her freckled elbows on his knee between hands of poker, between races, between the throw of a die, listened to the Celtic music of her father's voice, soaked in his emerald tales – and grew up believing in them too. Here with Tom Channing, she'd met a mythic being, had sided with the King of the Underworld; not only met him, but fucked him. So – if Tom was Satan, what did that make her? One of the bad guys? Looked at a certain way, Bluff O'Rourke was a bad guy: a gambler, a drifter, a breaker of feminine hearts. Looked at Teddy's way, Bluff was the only really good guy she'd ever known. He hadn't fitted in, but damn – he'd stood out, silver in his laughing chicanery. He never said he was anything but a rascal, and he never was. Which made Daddy an honest man. Was Tom Channing any less? No. More? Yes. As far as Teddy knew, her father had never killed anyone, while Tom was the American dream: a slum kid made good. Tom Channing sewed lots of unwanted people into weighted sacks. But had the good grace to make sure they were dead first.

Three days ago Teddy O'Rourke had been doing her job, sitting ringside at Madison Square Garden watching two grown men beat the crap out of each other. Now what was she doing? What had she done at Bootsie's? Shot the raggedy man without even a 'Sorry', sure she would have put a tidy hole in Schultz's head at the first wrong twitch out of him. Who was the killer here? Who wasn't a killer?

Teddy was driving herself crazy. Jumping out of Tom's astonishing bed, she paced across his glass floor. Her chemise in shreds, she picked up Tom's green camel's hair robe, ran into his bathroom, stared at herself in the mirror – Jack suddenly back in her mind. With Jack, her fast-talking halfbreed, love was one long conversation, a kind of constant needling, shot through with humour – but so shaky. The first wrong word and they could both explode, scattering pain like buckshot. With Tom? Love was no conversation at all. As with Mezinger, it wasn't even a word. Tom love her? Teddy almost laughed in her own face. A man like Tom Channing couldn't love.

Tom. Jack. The little girl in red clinging to Jack's arm. A bolt of pure green flame flooded Teddy's heart. Jealous! Still moist from Channing, she was sick with jealousy. Lulu wasn't just hanging around Jack Eagels, she'd staked a claim on Teddy O'Rourke's big funny Arapaho, her newsman, her best friend – and the little bitch had done it in Teddy's bed.

Falling on her knees in front of Tom's Art Deco toilet bowl, Red threw up.

Jack Eagels had been thirty-two years old that May morning in 1927 when he'd first set foot on the island of Manhattan, not only running – but seeking. Come to a city whose streets once rang with the footsteps of the radiant Richard Harding Davis. Davis, the 'knight errant of the nineties', the most dashing, most glamorous foreign correspondent of them all. A handsome young man of honour, a newspaperman's newsman, who believed, as Jack believed, that 'the sun only rises that man may have light by which to read' his paper.

What Jack found was a city forty years on, a city besotted by itself. Insolent as a duchess – yet lovable as an ingénue; wicked and wanton – yet guileless as a guy who'd bet on a shell game; explosive, extravagant, desperate – and as irritable as caffeine. New York was a city for everyone – except the faint of heart. But its newspapers were still as Davis had described them: *'rising, one above the other, in the humorous hope that the public will believe the length of their subscription lists is in proportion to the height of their towers. They are aggressively active and wide-awake in the silence of the night about them. The lights from hundreds of windows glow like furnaces, and the quick and impatient beating of the groaning presses sounds like the roar of the sea.'*

While Teddy was shaking Bootsie's Flim-Flam plaster out of her hair in Channing's Art Deco bed, Jack Eagels was leaving Lulu at Mae's table – hoping he could keep her happy by promising to see her again, honest, really, as soon as he could – rapidly walking the eight snowy blocks down Broadway to the *Trident*, where he passed under Alva's stone scroll. It still read, 'Here Lives the Truth'. Pushing open Alva's great bronze doors, he got in the elevator and found himself sharing with Leonard Lamont. The *Trident*'s gossip columnist, smelling of sen-sen and cocktail onions, was smirking.

'How did you like my column, Eagels?'

Jack coughed. 'You talking to me?'

Disgusted, Leonard covered his mouth. 'Indeed, I am. It was my very own scoop.'

'What was?'

'Well, now – a certain someone was seen by a certain someone else, namely me, kissing another certain someone and since the first someone happened to be someone close to you, I was sure you'd enjoy reading about it.'

'Leonard, do you talk like this all the time?'

'Why yes, I do.'

'Does anyone ever laugh?'

'Well – no, they don't.'

'Curious.'

Leonard Lamont got mad enough to press his luck. 'Haven't you heard what I've been saying? Don't you

269

know what I'm talking about? I'm talking about your Teddy O'Rourke planting a very hot kiss on George – '

Jack coughed again, a mighty effort that propelled him into Leonard and made the whole car shake as it whizzed past the thirteenth floor.

' – Bache. *Will you stop that!*'

'The hell with your scoop, Lamont. Everybody kisses George.'

Pursing his lips, Leonard turned his back on Jack.

Four months shy of thirty-five, Jack had just bumped his nose against a dark and fearsome insight: Jack Eagels was all grown up; not only that, he wasn't immortal. Not Lamont, but a cough, was driving him towards age. A dry cough nothing he tried could control. The cough and the shivering, the fever and his breathing – which grew more rapid by the minute – and all this at the same time.

At two in the morning, Connie, for some reason, wasn't shouting. The phones weren't ringing, only a couple of reporters were clacking out copy on the *Trident*'s typewriters, Billy Brennan and the rest of the copy boys weren't dashing around waving paper and paste pots, the presses were more like a babbling brook than Davis's mighty sea. Not even one wide-eyed crazy haunted the city room demanding his say. It was very, very quiet. Too ill to care why, or to wonder if his last conversation with the fat man had meant he was really fired after all, Jack slapped the snow off his shoulders and waited for the editor to say something.

Connie's hello was the usual, 'Well, so you showed the fuck up. You think I should kiss you, or what?'

At that, Jack perked up. Not much, but enough to keep him from falling over. If things were going wrong at the paper, Connie would have thought of something new to say.

'That might be nice,' said Jack.

'I'm sick of how cute you are, Eagels, sick enough to throw you off the top of this building. What the hell was that fucking phone call all about?'

'Lots.'

Jack's usual hello was to sit on the edge of Connie's desk and fiddle with the first thing he saw. This time a paperweight, a small glass dome that snowed when he shook it. Under the dome were the galley proofs of Connie's Wednesday editorial. It took no more than a glance to see the editor-in-chief was telling New York that the *Trident* was hot on the heels of McTaggart's killer. Jack tossed – then caught – Connie's glass bubble. Inside was the *Chicago Globe* Building.

'Put that down. What's "lots" mean?'

Eagels put the bubble of snow back where he'd found it – holding down Connie's high hopes. 'Tom Channing said he killed McTaggart.'

Like a lit firecracker, Connie exploded out of his seat. 'What! Holy jumping Jesus! What time is it? Have we got time to – '

' – stop the presses?' offered Jack.

Something about the way Eagels said that checked Connie's mad dash for the door, made him park his oddly small ass back on the edge of his swivel chair. 'OK, spit it out. Why can't I replate the front page?'

'A feeling I have,' said Jack, picking up the bubble again, holding it up to the light, making the Chicago snow dance.

'A feeling?'

'Yep.'

'That's it?'

'Yep.'

Connie threw a pencil. It hit the wall, bounced off, and winged his own ear. 'Dammit, Eagels! What fucking feeling!'

'On my way over – '

True to his nature, Connie cut in. 'Which took you long enough.'

True to his, Jack paid no attention. ' – here, I had some time to think about what Channing said and how he said it, and now that I have, it bothers me. Something stinks. I think there's more to all this than shows.'

'You stay enigmatic two seconds longer, I'll mash your face. You think I'm too short to do it, Eagels, you try me.'

'OK, OK, keep your pants on. It's like this. Madden didn't kill Bernie, Schultz didn't kill Bernie, and Channing did.'

'So? What stinks about that?'

'The way Channing said he did it, I don't think that's the way it actually was. I think the guy knows how it happened and why it happened and who made it happen and somehow feels responsible.' Jack went off into a coughing fit and Connie waited him out, staring at his office wall – a wall covered with more plaques, testimonials and photos of American bigshots than O'Rourke's, a wall on which a huge blow-up of Alva T. Thorp's gloomy map took pride of place, its thin lips crudely inked in a luscious lipsticked kiss. When Jack could finally talk, he wheezed. 'The long and short of it is, I don't think we've got a story – yet. Although I can make a terrific potboiler about Miss West's going-away party. That was swell.'

Connie deflated. His fat little shoulders, little round belly, and puffy pink cheeks sagged. 'Shit. There goes my headline. So, hotshot, what's on the front page tomorrow?'

'Damned if I know. How about "Watch This Space?"'

Connie stood up so suddenly his swivel chair spun without him. Lunging forward, he shoved Jack off his desk. 'Get the fuck out of my office! Get out of my building. And don't come back until you find out for sure who killed that goddamn cop. I hate this story.

I'm beginning to hate you. Most of all, I hate this mucksucking city! There's a Babbitt a block! Everybody in it's a Public Enemy or a Catholic or a top-hatted slicker in spats, and if they're not any of those, they're a Republican or a communist or a poodle wearing perfume, or, Christ Almighty on crutches, they're Jimmy Durante or Jimmy Walker or Heywood Broun – or you! The *Trident*'s the only sheet in town waving a lonely halloo out in left field, the only one printing what I'm printing. And what am I printing? What you're writing, that's what I'm printing. I stuck my neck out for you all the way, Eagels, hung around until way past my bedtime three nights in a row. Now I want this story over, finished. I want a good night's sleep, and I don't ever want to hear the name McTaggart again. You got all that?'

'Every well-spoken word. But hold on a minute, Connie. Me, I should find out for sure? Jesus, I'm not a cop, I'm a reporter. You know where all this could put me?'

'Where else? In the shit! And stop that coughing, it's making me sick.'

Jack strolled out of Connie's office, went to a water cooler to swallow a few more aspirins. Lit a cigarette. Which tasted awful. But he smoked it anyway. Thinking about Jimmy Durante, remembering that wise man's immortal words: *Everybody wants ta get inta da act.* In the Bernt McTaggart Show, everybody was. Somehow or another. Channing and Madden and Schultz dodging cops and each other, Walker and Whalen dodging cops and press, La Guardia hogging both. And every other living soul in New York within reach of a paper brimming with slap-happy violence and wide-eyed wow. *He* was supposed to solve the whole mess, wrap it up for Connie in a big pink bow? Oh yeah? How was he going to do that? When he couldn't even find Teddy O'Rourke, who was, God knew, wherever Channing was.

Shivering, cold from the inside, Jack bent a little from the waist and retched. Nothing came up but fear. Was that what his redhead was doing, getting into da act? Or had her business with Channing gone further? No longer an act, but the real thing. And why had that happened? Well, for one thing, because Mezinger had elbowed her out of a story she'd busted her ass – almost literally – for, shoved her aside when the going got interesting. And who let him do that? Who stood there grinning like a goddamn fool while Connie walked right over her enthusiasm, her talent, her heart, then walked out and dallied with a child who called herself Lulu? *He* had, Jack Eagels from Wyoming, ace reporter, short story writer for two-bit magazines, dare-devil motorcyclist, and a really nice guy. Jack winced. He'd done that because she was a girl, a woman, because she was only a sports reporter – but more to the point, because he was a man. Like Harry Houdini, Jack Eagels could wriggle out of anything – especially responsibility. He was a reporter so caught up with his own headlong rush for the brass ring, his own needs, he'd missed hers.

Standing by a water cooler on the twenty-third floor of the *Trident*, Jack was losing track of time. Two gaudy days, or was it one? had spun by in vivid confusion since he'd last held Teddy O'Rourke. Living in the present, time was never easy for Eagels. He had trouble understanding how it worked. Forwards, backwards, sideways, up, down, where the hell did time go anyway? Maybe Prophet Martin, Harlem's barefoot Messiah, knew, but Jack didn't. Always covering one story or another, forever on the move, living on a ledge of language – words told him what time it was. Yesterday, tomorrow, soon, never. There was really only now, and now felt like it always did – plaintive with questions.

Now, Jack was having his first glimmering of what might be going on in Teddy O'Rourke's mind. To be good at something, really good – and not only to know

274

that you were, but for others to know it too. He ought to understand that kind of need – he shared it. If he'd lost Teddy O'Rourke, it was his own damn fault. If he gained Lulu LeRoy, it was what he deserved. And if he hurt Lulu? What could anyone expect from such a nice guy?

Jack shook his head until his brain rattled. Only to find one of Irving Berlin's old tunes quietly threading its way through his unquiet thoughts, Berlin singing badly in the key of F-sharp – 'I'd Love To Pick A Quarrel With You'. Fucking hell, it could be his and Teddy's theme song! Jack gritted his tired teeth, drove the song away – which only made Irving sing louder. Swaying on his feet, Jack squeezed Berlin to the back of his skull where Irving hummed and strummed and clattered along on his own.

'Mr Eagels?'

A hand was pulling at his sleeve. Irving buzzed off. The hand belonged to Billy Brennan. Billy's pink face, aglow with bumptious health, was peering up into his, the eyes watering with concern. 'You all right?'

'Why? Don't I look all right?'

'No, Mr Eagels, you look kind of terrible.'

'I feel kind of terrible.'

'Maybe you ought to go home.'

'Can't go home. Gotta come up with a couple of hundred words about a typical Broadway party, then I gotta solve a murder that baffles New York's finest, and at the same time there's a redhead to find – and a brunette to lose. Wanna help?'

This kind of talk made Billy suck in his suety cheeks, heave a sigh of moist admiration. 'Sure!'

'Good, go get me a cup of coffee, would you? No sugar, no milk. Ain't a reporter's life grand?'

'Boy, you said it!' Billy spun on his pudgy heel, took one awkward step, spun back. 'But, say, I'm supposed to tell you – you got two phone messages in the last hour. First is from some girl who said to say she was going home, and would you meet her there later.' Billy was struggling to get a grip on his amazing repertoire of nervous tics – and failing. 'The second is from the same girl who sounded like she wondered why you hadn't shown up yet. She said she's waiting.'

Jack took another aspirin. Little Lulu! Good grief. Jack didn't have time for that Christmas cracker right now. Maybe later, when things had quietened down. Maybe not even then; Lulu spooked him.

Her little horticultural speech at the table, the bit to Mae about quitting the show – cute touch to tell Mae and, of course, Teddy it was a joint decision – Minsky's story, her own over Lindy's sour cream blintzes. And damn, if it wasn't hard telling her so. He'd tried after the shoot-up at Bootsie's, in between asking where Teddy had gone and getting no answer except the obvious – with gunman-about-town, Tom Channing, of course. From Lulu, all he got for his trouble was a hard-baked smile, a grip on his arm, and a hiccup or two. Now, less than an hour later and in the middle of the working night, she was phoning his paper, leaving messages with Billy Brennan. Who, no doubt, was taking them down in ink. He was closer to the mark than he knew when he told Billy he was avoiding a brunette. *Hiding* from was more like it. Jack held his aching head.

'Billy, the next time the lady calls, tell her I'm on a long hot story – down in Chile.'

'Sure thing, Mr Eagels.'

16

Double Solitaire

In the casino up on Sugar Hill, O'Rourke padded down two flights of curved stairs on bare feet and found the kitchen by instinct alone. Listening to the muted hoots of Harlem River boats, one bird singing in Tom's late-blooming roses, her own breathing, her own hurried heartbeat, she made herself coffee by reheating what was left in an oversized percolator, then wandered out into the darkened gaming rooms, sipping the bitter mess. Stalked through high-ceilinged rooms in the hush of early morning, risky rooms with heavy red velvet curtains drawn against the coming light. Hoping to walk off the blues.

And walked right into Tom's husked blonde, Agnes. Agnes sat at a cornered roulette table under a cone of thin light, playing tiddly-winks with a stack of fifty-dollar chips. The silver-tipped fox hung from the roulette wheel, a cocktail shaker sat on number twenty-seven, a shallow, wide-lipped, thin-stemmed glass sat on thirty. A thick glass ashtray full of stubbed butts nudged her slumped elbow, every butt ringed with russet lipstick.

Agnes was drunk. Not out-and-out, falling-down drunk, but drunk enough to make sitting an effort. Before Teddy could turn, keep her blues to herself, the blonde kicked out a velvet-bottomed chair, pointed at it. 'Like two lost ships, right?'

Her unsteady cup and saucer in the palm of her unsteady hand, Teddy balanced on her heels, thinking: she'd beaten herself up for a couple of hours now. Could she stand a few more wild punches from the girlfriend? Why not? It might help. As Shucks always said, 'Does a young fighter good to take a few punches now and then, knocks some of the cockiness out of him.' Teddy and her already bleak heart dropped into the offered chair.

Agnes snapped a chip across the table. 'Tommy boot you outta that nutty bed a his? He's always doing that – he'll fuck 'em, but he won't sleep with 'em.'

Teddy winced. When Agnes came away from the ropes, she came away swinging.

'But say, I gotta give it to you, sister, you been up there a lot longer than most. So, what is it? Six o'clock in the morning?'

'Quarter to.'

'Not bad, Annie Oakley. What'cha do? Teach him a few neat new tricks with your gun?' Agnes snapped another chip. This one cleared the roulette wheel and disappeared in the dark. '*His* gun's already tricky enough.'

At Agnes's slurred words, more bitter than the casino's coffee, Teddy knew she had company. The chippy sent off to ogle the sweated male at Spooner's, the poor kid left standing at Kitchen Monday's, the cocoa-voiced woman sliding off her chair in Tom's casino was not only drunk, she was jealous. Who the hell could blame her? O'Rourke knew just how she felt: seasick – nine days from land.

With a bitter taste in her own mouth, Teddy was sure she saw Agnes in her lonely cone of light as clearly as she'd just seen herself. The blonde was slim at the waist, the wrist, the ankle, the hands were bloodless as veal, and the eyes – though hooded with hooch – were harried with a hope as fatal as cyanide. Agnes was as lovely as a gardenia. Too white, too scented, too waxen: she was something a man wore in the lapel of a dinner jacket – until it began to fade.

But she was smart enough to see Teddy's pity before Teddy knew pity was what she was feeling. 'Say, who do you think you are, anyways? Who needs you feeling sorry for 'em?' Flipping back her short blonde hair, Agnes laughed – a laugh that rattled like a handful of dice. 'So, maybe Tommy does fuck around from time to time and so maybe he does it right over my head, but he always leaves 'em lying there alone after, you bet, he always comes home when it's over – and you know what, it's *always* over. Therefore and so, Mrs Reporter, what does that make you?'

Teddy's pity sagged. And a vivid picture of Jack shimmied behind her eyes. Jack with Lulu. Jack with Lulu and Lulu with a well-watered cactus. Tom comes home . . . *after*? What kind of woman took that kind of crap from a man? Whoever she was, she had to deserve it. 'Honey,' she said before she could gauge her shot, 'what does that make *you*?'

Agnes flinched, stared at Teddy out of startled brown eyes. Then, raising a hand to slap, paused, said, 'Oh, God,' and burst into tears.

And Teddy's pity came flooding back, along with a strong surge of guilt. Sometimes, she wished she could just shut up.

By now, Agnes was shuddering all over with soft wet hiccups. 'You wanna know how long I've spent on that bastard up there? Go on, guess. No, can't? Well, why should you bother when you know I'll tell you anyway? Nine years. Ain't that funny? I guess you could call what I got an addiction.' Agnes drank straight from the cocktail shaker, bumping her nose on the long silver stirrer. Plunked the shaker back on twenty-seven and hiccuped some more. 'Nine whole years – and four of 'em when Harold was still pushing those corsets of his.'

'Harold?'

'My dead husband, Harold. Harold spent his life making a fortune out of ladies' lingerie. Me, I spent my life spending it. On stuff like this, see?' The widow flashed her diamond as big as Scott Fitzgerald's Ritz under Teddy's nose. 'You probably think that's pretty bad, you probably think I shouldn't be nuts about Tommy when I was still married to Harold.'

Teddy wasn't sure what she felt. But if Tom made a habit of loving this fading gardenia as he'd just loved Teddy, nine years of devotion made sense. For some women, that kind of loving was a life sentence.

Agnes took Teddy's busy silence for a yes. 'So, who cares what you think? A woman who'd steal another woman's man couldn't think anything I'd want to hear.'

Over the rim of her cup, Teddy looked Agnes straight in the eye. 'Before, I didn't know Tom was your – '

Agnes smacked the back of Teddy's hand with the wet cocktail stirrer. Which may not have hurt but it certainly startled. 'Oh brother! Don't make me laugh. You knew. You're smart and you knew, you just didn't give a good goddamn. All you cared about was whatever it was you come up here for in the first place.'

Teddy drew back her hand, licked off whatever Agnes had in that cocktail shaker, knowing every word she'd just heard was just, was no more than she should have been telling herself – but it still hurt like hell. If anyone was in the wrong here, it wasn't Agnes. Agnes didn't cut people out of old newspapers like paper dolls, she never – Teddy stopped right there. The phrase was too apt to let slip by. That's exactly what she'd been doing. Cutting a shape called Tom Channing from old headlines, stories she'd overheard in the city room or imagined in Tom's bed, fitting the shape over the man. Snipping away things that got in the way, didn't fit – like widows with hungry hearts. If anyone was in the wrong here, it was the lady from the *Trident*. She set her coffee down on red nine. Somebody had to stop hurting Agnes; it might as well be Teddy O'Rourke. 'You're right, every word, that's me – good God. And now it's too late, I'm sorry.'

Agnes stopped crying, wiped her nose with the hand that held the diamond Harold bought. 'Sorry? So, when you fucked Tommy you were working? Some girls call that working.'

Teddy gave the blonde another point. She was not only not dumb, she was smart. 'It started out that way.'

'Started, but not finished?'

'Oh, it's finished all right. I've already been dealt out of this game.'

'Your choice – or his?'

'Mine, but probably both.'

'You mean you don't want Tommy?'

'Not the way you do.'

Slamming her hands down on the numbered felt, knocking over her stack of chips, Agnes rose in her seat. 'Is that a crack? Because if it is, sister, I could rip out that red hair and stuff it right down your throat.'

'For pete sake's, calm down. I only meant, no, I don't love him and no, he doesn't love me. If there are any lost ships around here, Agnes, I guess you could say they were Tom and I.'

'Yeah?'

'Yes.'

Agnes sat down. 'I think you've got something. The only one who don't know it is Tommy. You got a spare cigarette? I smoked all mine.'

From deep in Tom's green pocket, Teddy pulled out her crumpled pack of Old Golds, took one for herself, slid the rest across the felted tabletop for Agnes. Then went searching for a light. She found Tom's Dunhill in the same pocket.

And Agnes seemed to go crazy. 'Oh my God!' she screeched, snatching the lighter away from Teddy before Teddy could get it lit. Jolted, O'Rourke jumped in her seat. 'This! You see this! This is why Tommy can't love anybody.'

Teddy looked, saw what she'd seen every time Tom lit her cigarette for her. 'You mean . . . *all my love, Sophie*?'

'You bet! Sophie! Goddammed Sophie, that's who Tommy loved. That's who Tommy *still* loves. He's stuck on the woman who gave him this lighter; I should know, I was there the Christmas he got it. And sister, not you, not me, not Marie, the Queen of Rumania, has a chance against a dead woman.'

'Sophie's dead?'

'As a dodo. Burnt up a month after she gave it to him. Christ Jesus, what a fire! Burnt down a whole block of real nice houses in Brooklyn, took eight people with it, and one of 'em Sophie.'

'Sophie was Tom's wife?'

The snort that convulsed Agnes startled Teddy. 'Wife! Are you kidding? His *wife*! Sophie was his *sister*, his *older* sister, pardon my Yiddish.'

Agnes was finally using Tom's Dunhill to light her cigarette. Too drunk to get it lit the first time, she got it lit the third. Leaned back and blew a smoke ring at Teddy.

Who was still struggling to catch up. 'Loved his own sister, you mean – ?'

'I mean what I mean.' Pouring herself another drink, Agnes smoked and sipped and sipped and smoked, and snapped ten-dollar, twenty-dollar, hundred-dollar chips over the fox-coated wheel and into the dark. 'I mean Tommy saves enough dough working for Madden that he goes over to Europe someplace and brings Sophie back here to the good old USA. I mean he brings her kid back too, this little brat Sophie'd picked up like a disease from some old dirt farmer over there, a guy who goes and ditches her for putting out in the first place – sweet Jesus! Don't Catholics make you puke? They sure make *me* puke. So here they are right off the boat and here I am, and you just gotta know nothing's ever the same after that, not ever. So, for this sister he hasn't seen in I don't know how many years, and who can't speak a word of American, Tommy buys a big house, a car, clothes, my God, he about does everything but marry her. So then what happens? *Then* what happens is some big goddamn surprise for Tommy, but Sol and I saw it coming all along, ever since they all got off that boat. Me and Sol, I guess you could say we smelled it; the stink of trouble coming off 'em was so strong.' Agnes stubbed out a cigarette; lit another, laughed without humour. 'The house Tommy bought Sophie? Well, it burns down, don't it? And Sophie? She dies in the fire – and Tommy almost dies with her. Not from the fire, not then; when that fire got its start he was already home from the party. No, he almost dies 'cause when Sol tells him what's happened, Tommy rushes back and there's nothing he can do to save Sophie, not even burning himself trying.' Agnes blew smoke down her nose as she said, '. . . and doncha know, all this happens on her kid's birthday, the day Joey was eleven years old.'

Leaning forward on her elbows, the blood hammering in her veins, Teddy caught sight of her coffee. Cold. Cold and scummed with cream.

When she poured it, she'd been absorbed in herself, mourning some loss of her own . . . Now? Now, all around her was loss. Loss and sorrow, sorrow and pain. People were always losing something: their jobs, their hearts, their lives, their minds. Lately, losing seemed to be what life was all about.

Agnes was touching her arm, gripping it. 'And after, who feels so goddamn sorry for Tommy she gets stuck with Joey. Who loves him that much? The perfect mug, me, that's who. For the love of Tommy Channing, I got Harold to let that kid stay with us. What a laugh! Me and Harold trying to raise Joey. Sweet suffering Jesus, it's a wonder we didn't die in some fire too. Say, you wanna know how she paid us back instead?'

Teddy nodded, yes, she did want to know, yes, she was grateful she came searching for coffee, that she ran into Agnes, that a Sugar Hill cocktail shaker had turned a woman with a chocolate voice into Leonard Lamont's 'Tattle on the Town'. Meanwhile the name 'Joey' chased itself round in her head. Joey? Tom's Joey? The Joey he was going to take care of on Saturday night? Not Joe Bright but his dead sister's daughter, Joey.

'Stole my best diamond bracelet, half my wardrobe, stuffed it all in my favourite alligator suitcase, and ran off with the greasy son of a guy down the block who made condoms, that's how. The boy came back a month later, scared right down to his toes, but Joey, we didn't see Joey for three. Tommy found her living over in Greenwich Village with a rummy painter old enough to be her grandfather. So what do you think I did? Took her back, that's how hot the torch was I was carrying for Tommy back then – and damn his soul, still am.' Agnes shook her cocktail shaker at Teddy. 'You want some of this? Suit yourself. I'm for anything can get you through the night. So, anyway, here we all are. Tommy's still watching over his sister's scary kid, I'm still watching over Tommy, and Harold's dead. Circles, huh? We're all going in circles.'

For five long minutes the two women sat at the roulette table, Agnes knocking back whatever was in the silver flask, both smoking.

Until Teddy broke the silence. Tom was right. Tom's blonde widow was right. She'd come for a story. Sickened by herself, chilled by the honesty of Channing, touched by the loyalty of Agnes, saddened by everything, still – she wasn't leaving without one. She wanted that front page. It was all she had left.

'Agnes, did Tom kill Dixie Fiske?'

The widow turned her dizzy head, focused her eyes. 'Tommy? Nah, he doesn't do that kind of stuff anymore, not since he stopped working for Rothstein and started working for himself. Things like Fiske are the wops' job now – '

'Wops?'

'That's what Sol calls 'em. You know, Italians: CD, Benny, now that cousin of CD's, Arch. Sol says Italians are dumb, but they make good hitters, says it's in the blood – that's what Tommy hires 'em for.' Agnes smiled, and what beauty was still hers softened her face. 'My Tommy's got a good heart, you better believe it; he'd hire anybody, even a Hottentot, so long as they did what he told 'em to do. And say, what the hell! What am *I* when you get right down to it? Me, I'm part Swede and some parts Kraut. And what's Tommy? A goddamned Polack, can you credit? Leszak Zaleska – ain't that a hoot? No wonder he changed it soon as he hit Brooklyn.'

'But why?'

'Why what?'

'Why have Dixie killed?'

'That wasn't Tommy's idea, it wasn't Tommy who made it happen. Dixie did that to himself. You gotta understand how it is. If Dixie'd done what he was told, let go of that coloured boxer and take the money like he was offered, he'd still be alive, nobody would of touched him. But Dixie was a born fool; he just wouldn't listen.'

'And Bernt McTaggart? He kill himself too?'

'Bernie? You know about Bernie?'

Here, Teddy needed help. A small lie, a little twist of the truth. 'Only what I heard Tom say.'

'Yeah? So you know Bernie was dumber than Dixie. But I bet you don't know why. He was dumber because everybody warned him, everybody told that dumb cop he was riding for a fall. Tommy and me and Sol, Madden, even CD – we talked until we was all blue in the face. But just like Dixie, Bernie wouldn't listen, nope, not Mr McTaggart. He just kept chasing all those women, laughing at what we were all trying to tell him. Oh, says he in that voice of his made you want to slap his face, he knew better. *He* was pals with the police commissioner, even the mayor, if you please; he was the son of some Tammany bigwheel, and on Owney's payroll, so he could do anything, act any damn way he liked. So he did – until he paid for it like we all knew he would. Saturday night, right here at the casino.'

'Agnes, please! Who were you warning McTaggart about?'

For the first time, the drunken blonde turned cautious. 'Say now, if I was to tell you that, Tommy'd *kill* me.' Tossing her head back, Agnes blew another smoke ring at Teddy. 'What's your game on that paper of yours, anyway?'

'Baseball, boxing, crap shoots.'

'Not crime?'

'No, not crime. Crime's for the boys.'

'Ain't that the truth.' Agnes reached for the cocktail shaker again, but this time before her fingers could close around the silvered flask, her whole hand froze. And her face set in a rictus of surprise – then bright and burning fear. 'Tommy! How long you been here?'

The widow's fear was contagious; Teddy turned her head.

Fully dressed and carrying his own cup of reheated casino coffee, Tom Channing had resolved out of shadows, was leaning on the oak panelled wall behind her. He smiled at O'Rourke. 'Morning, Red.' But not at Agnes. 'You been having a good time, Aggie?'

Harold's widow practically fell off her chair in an effort to get away from the ugly look on Tom's beautiful face. 'Say, maybe it's about time I got myself on home.' Swaying on her feet, Agnes stood up, whipped her fox fur off the roulette wheel – and slowly wobbled backwards.

Teddy watched her wobble. The poor kid had a long way to go if she was hoping for the casino's front door. The air sticky with blonde fear, it seemed a furlong away.

Tom caught the widow's arm, twisted her and her coat back into the chair. 'Stick around, Agnes. You like talking, so we'll talk, OK?'

286

Tears of pain filling her bloodshot eyes, Agnes pulled away. 'Let go, Tommy. I'm going home.'

Tom, getting a good grip in Agnes's hair, began pulling her head back. 'Go on. You're so hot to tell Red what you know, spit it out, let's all hear it.'

'Stop it, Tommy, that hurts. I hate it when it hurts.'

'Answer Red's question, Aggie. Did I kill McTaggart?'

And then – as Teddy sat two feet away from what was glaringly obvious had nothing to do with her, a matter of inches away from what was so close and so real it was also scaring the bejesus out of her – Agnes suddenly slipped Tom's hold and slapped him across his chilly Polish face. She did it as slick as Ty Cobb stealing second. The snap of the slap echoed through the empty casino and before the echo died, Agnes was screaming, straining her gorgeous voice. 'I said stop it, you fucker! Stop showing off for your new bitch, you stop taking your pain out on me!'

Astonished at the sudden change in Agnes, Teddy was shocked at the change in Channing. No longer lit from the inside with a clean violent light, now he was like a brash young boxer knocked on his rump for the very first time. Tom looked comically stunned.

Jumping to her feet, Agnes poked him in the chest with a furious finger, temper and diamond flashing. 'You wanna hear it? You wanna hear the honest-to-god truth! So, yes! The goddamn answer is yes! You killed poor dumb Bernie like somebody kills a baby when they leave it by its lonesome in a full bathtub. Sure you killed him, just like you killed all the guys she got rid of when they were through with her. Bernie wasn't business, Bernie was a mistake. Your mistake, Tommy – one that should never have happened, except you been mooning over Sophie for years, not doing nothing to stop her because you keep telling yourself she's all of Sophie you got left. So, you see now what it's got you? It's made you a garbage man, Mr Tom Channing, hauling a sack of garbage on your back.'

Teddy expected Tom to hit the blonde, at least clamp his hand over her mouth. But all he did was sit down. And stay there.

Agnes reached out, took Tom's hand. 'That's OK, honey. Agnes doesn't want to hurt you, she just wants you to let go. Sophie's dead. There's nothing left of her to hold on to. Nothing, baby. Except me.'

'I can't do it, Agnes. I've tried but I can't.'

'Sure you can, Tommy.'

Agnes curled herself on Tom's lap, wrapped her arms around his neck, stroked his hair.

Teddy, sitting at a roulette table as the cold November sun rose over Sugar Hill, turning a cup of cream-scummed coffee round and round in her hands, cigarette forgotten between her fingers and the juice of Tom Channing still warm in her body, knew she wasn't there – not for Agnes, not even for Tom. They were locked into a kind of love that had nothing to do with Teddy, or Fiske, or McTaggart. Though it seemed to have a lot to do with dying. But who, for God's sake, were they talking about?

'All you gotta do is let Sol do his job. That's what he's here for, what he's waited to do for over five years. Just waiting for you to give the word ever since the fire.'

'Nobody could know she started it, Aggie, not for sure. If I really knew – '

'You know. In your heart, you've always known. She meant to do it, Tommy. Even eleven years old, that kid knew what she was doing. You protect her, get her jobs with your friends, hide the ugly things she does, when all along, at least you should of locked her up in a loony bin. Not even that time she shoots you – '

Channing shrugged. 'Hell, just an accident.'

'Damn! You make me mad, Tommy. You're so smart, you're stupid. An accident on a dark street down in the Village and her with a pistol in her bag? Shit! – Some accident. She's not gonna stop, her own mother, guys that dump her – she's got a taste for it. The kid was *born* bad. All *you* do is help *her* do what she was born for.'

On the edge of her seat, jumpy white light going off in her head, Teddy's thoughts spun like a wheel-of-fortune. *Joey?* She wanted to scream, *you mean Joey!*

'You know she set that fire, Tommy. Let Sol have her. It'll be like stepping on a spider – that's all that kid is, believe me, baby, that's *all*. Don't let her go off to Frisco with Mae's show, step on her, Tommy. Please. For everybody, but honey, mostly for Sophie.'

Like getting hit with one of Christy Mathewson's spit balls, Teddy had the wind knocked out of her. Mae's show! Lulu! They were talking about Lulu LeRoy! Lulu was Joey and Tom was Joey's uncle and Joey – not Tom – killed Bernie.

The little girl sitting next to Mae West, the girl who'd watered her cactus, slept in her bed, that girl killed people she didn't like? My God, *that* girl was with Jack! Incandescent with sudden fear, if Teddy was the type to faint, she would have. Since she wasn't, she sat there and, without noticing, snapped off the handle of her coffee cup. The problem was no longer how much Jack liked Lulu – it was how much Lulu liked Jack!

What Teddy did notice was the light that danced around Tom's head again, that sly slanted light in his gangster-blue eyes as he wound his hand in the tangle of the widow's blonde hair, turned her face to his – and kissed her eager, hungry mouth. Even scared to death for Jack, Teddy was glad to see the steely gardenia's slap fade from that beautiful Polish face.

But the kiss was a slap in her own.

Teddy O'Rourke hit bottom. She'd thrown away her job, her own sense of virtue, and worst of all, her man – for this? For a scoop, a hot story? Chasing Tom Channing like McTaggart chased women, what had she caught? She'd caught pain and loss and confusion. Opening her clenched fist and peeking at the catch huddled inside, all she really had left was fear. Where was Jack? What was he doing? And God! Who was he doing it with?

While Teddy was propped on her freckled elbow in the snug rookery of a gangster and deciding she'd just slept with an abridged version of Satan, Jack was sleep-walking into a flat up in Harlem – seeking oblivion.

Finishing the tongue-in-cheek tale of Miss West's party (which he'd slugged 'The Mobster Quadrille', and embellished with altered quotes from Lewis Carroll), Jack had sat back, coughed for one long, unutterable minute, and come to a decision. To cure whatever was wrong with him – a new strain of New York flu? The bubonic plague? – it was either the Turkish Baths at the Pennsylvania Hotel or finish what he'd started at Bootsie's – going on a god-almighty spree. Getting drunk won. And what better place to booze away the flu than an all-night house-rent-party in Harlem?

Jack, who'd found the shindy by reading handbills tacked to Lenox Avenue plane trees, had no idea whose flat he was stepping into – but he sure knew who the piano player was. Willie 'The Lion' Smith's raggedy pounding hit him just as he turned the Harley onto West 148th Street. Jack, still in his tails, rode without a hat, without goggles, without a coat. Not something Jack would normally do, but Jack had stopped feeling normal a day ago. Under a jittering red light bulb, he paid his dollar admission – and tumbled into a basic black brawl. The kind of nightly uptown event that would start out nice and peaceful and wind up in a free-for-all. A smoky harum-scarum crammed into all seven rooms of a railroad flat that travelled from the front to the back of an old mud-brown building sagging into its own basement. Between walls bulging with dancing couples – with no room to swing, they just hung onto each other, closed their eyes, and shuffled their sweaty feet – Jack got offered red wine, egg nog, or reefers, pickled pigs' tails, chitterlings, collard greens or hog maws. He took a little of everything, set his heaped plate on a spare bit of floor, kept his glass in his hand, and followed the piano music, fine Harlem Stride.

Passing dazed on the way snippets of conversation: a grave young girl with a black Botticelli face quoting Marx; an excited young man in a tight blue suit, tight ebony skin, and a loose fuchsia cravat: 'I say it's hell to be an Ethiopian in America.' Two older women – black orchids in a garden of rampant sweet peas – patting each other's arms, shoulders, as one of them trilled, 'You hear? Joe Bright's going for the title! Every one of us on the *Tattler*, every single one's gonna be there to cheer that sweet nigger on.'

A happy liquorice voice bellowed from somewhere behind and to the left of Jack's aching head.

'Well, hey! Look see! Here comes one of the Lion's cubs! And all duded-up! My, don't he look fine!'

The room the piano was in had gone silent, all the dark expectant faces turned towards that bellowing voice.

Willie rose from his stool, slapped Eagels's back, and propelled him headlong. Jack fell in a heap at the foot of the piano, an almost peaceful grin on his wild western face.

Out of the ogling crowd a mocha girl in a vivid orange hat bent down, picked up one of his hands, then let it drop. 'Ooooweee!' she said, 'What's this honied yam done take?'

Willie reached over, got a good grip under Jack's limp armpits, and heaved. 'You come along, reportin' man, let the Lion sort you out. Fats, get on them keys and entertain the folks.'

Waller shimmied his huge behind onto the piano stool, gave Willie a toothsome smile, and broke into Ragtime.

Willie dragged Jack to the only room left that wasn't already occupied – the pantry. Willie sat on a barrel of cornmeal and propped Jack on a sack of potatoes. From

291

Jack's point of view, cock-eyed with dope, homemade wine, fatigue and the kind of cold that could make a man question the goodness of God, Willie looked just as fine in the pantry as he did on any stage in Harlem. A battered bowler hat tipped down over one eye, a cigar clamped between his pure white teeth, his shirt pistachio green silk, his tie ice-water blue, and his trousers off-white linen. Willie looked swell. He also looked sore. Handing Jack another joint, he said, 'You been messin' your woman around, reportin' man?'

Even now, fighting for breath, trying to get warm, so tired, so very tired, Jack managed to look surprised – then hurt. 'What?'

'You just listen to the Lion, boy. He knows things. When a man look as bad as you do, he's got woman trouble.'

'Jesus, Willie, spare me.'

Willie held up one brown finger and wagged it. 'See this? A woman's like a finger on a man's hand. If the finger works, the hand works, if the hand works, why, a man's got something only God can give him. And you, boy, you got yourself the right woman – so, if you been messin' her round, the Lion say, don't. Ain't you been told Irish folks have souls? Don't you know that redheaded mama is one of God's white niggers?'

Head swimming with another harsh intake of dope, Jack gave Willie a sick smile. 'I'm not messing the lady around, she's messing me around.'

Willie opened his big brown eyes. 'You tryin' to tell the Lion that sportin' woman, she's got another reportin' man?'

Jack tried out a laugh and got only a fragile croak from the back of his throat. 'It's the reporter she wants rid of.'

'So,' said Willie, 'It's like I say. You messin' her around.'

'How the hell, Willie, do you figure that?'

'Shee-it, boy, that's simple. If the lady ain't happy, it's the fault of the man every time. The women, they're weaker, and that's a fact. It's up to the man to strengthen them up. You gotta find out what they want and when they want it and how they like it and then give it to them. Gimme some of that weed. Reportin' folk all alike, greedy. They want all the good times and all the bad times and all the lovin' that's going.'

At that moment, Jack found the oblivion he'd come for. Falling sideways in a dead faint, he slipped off the potato sack, hit his head on a low-lying shelf, and ten cans of Heinz baked beans tumbled into his lap.

Willie took the chewed cigar out of his mouth and hollered, 'Fats! Come here!' The piano playing stopped, and a minute later the door to the pantry snicked open. In came fresher air, more light, a lot more sound, and Fats Waller's hatted head. The lipstick he was wearing wasn't his.

'What?'

'Give this man's newspaper a call, get us some help here.'

Jack woke to find George Bache's mournful mug leaning over him. Glasses propped on his pompadour, beautifully dressed even though he'd been woken from a sound sleep by a call from Hype Hohenloe after Mezinger's call had woken Hype, and Fats' call had woken Connie. Jack was still in his Harlem pantry, arms curled around the sack of potatoes.

Jack smiled up at George. Teddy was right. The *Trident*'s theatre critic looked like a demented moose. But George could have looked like ex-President Coolidge, like the Yankee's Babe Ruth, like Walter Winchell; Jack would still want to kiss him. He loved George Bache and George loved Teddy. It was all in the family. Wishing Leonard was there, he kissed George.

Horrified at the transfer of germs, but resisting the urge to scream, George took the last can of beans out of Jack's lap. 'Jack, old fellow, you need to be in a bed.'

'OK, but I get to choose which one.'

Jack chose 1600 Broadway. Where the bed was still mussed from Lulu's Monday night visit, Teddy's newly watered cactus was basking in Roseland's blushing red light, a letter for Teddy was waiting on the mat, and the window was still broken. Eagels had at least found time to tape part of a cardboard box over the shattered lower pane.

George manhandled Jack up all three flights of stairs, dumped him on the lumpy living room sofa, picked up and pocketed Teddy's letter, went around lighting the gaslog fires, making the bed. Thankfully for George, Jack undressed himself. Then flopped onto the covers in his sagging socks and undershorts. Which meant George had to wrestle the covers out from under him, roll him onto the sheets, and tuck him in. He picked the crumpled tails off the floor, noted the motorcycle oil stains on the trouser legs, but hung them up anyway. Teddy's clothes were still in the closet. For George Bache, the most painful of all: a pale grey dress shimmering with crystal beads she'd worn the night he'd taken her to the opening of MacArthur and Hecht's 'The Front Page'. That was only last year – where had Jack been? Where else? Three blocks south of the Times Square Theatre getting blood on his shoes down in the subway. Someone had forgotten to mend a faulty switch. Which meant that in a matter of seconds two trains had concertina'd into each other, leaving sixteen dead and over a hundred injured. Never an ill wind, thought George as he closed the closet door, went off seeking coffee and a bottle to spike it with. Gasped as he turned on the kitchen light – a million cockroaches ducked for cover. When he came back, Jack's teeth were chattering, his hands gripped the edge of the blanket he'd pulled up to his chin. Over it, Eagels's eyes glittered with fever and ice.

'Where's that redheaded idiot, George?'

'I don't know, Jack.'

'What's she doing?'

'I don't know that either. I thought I did, but I'm not so sure now. Drink this, it's one part coffee, one part cockroach, and three parts bourbon.'

Jack took the mug, gulped at it, coughed. 'She love 'im, George?'

'Love who?'

'That sonofabitch, that cheap gunslinger, Channing.'

'I don't think so, at least I hope not.'

'But she's sleeping with him, isn't she? Isn't she!'

George, remembering the calls from a girl named Lulu at the *Trident*, the state of the bed Jack was lying in before he'd changed the sheets, punched out an answer. 'Is that our business, Jack?' But pulled a little at the last minute. 'Teddy's on a story. You sleep with your stories?'

'She walked out on me, George. Told me to get lost.'

'I know. Saturday night, wasn't it? When was the brunette here, Sunday? Monday? Cutting it fine, wouldn't you say?'

'You made your point, Georgie.'

'Good. You look terrible. Maybe I'd better get a doctor.'

'For what? A cold?'

'This is a cold? Dinah would have you in an isolation ward at Bellevue by now.'

'By now, your mother'd be picking me out a nice headstone.'

'True. But a little cold, this isn't.'

'OK, maybe it's the flu. What's a doctor gonna say? Take aspirin, stay in bed, drink, that'll be five dollars? If I handed you five bucks, I'd be doing all that now. What time is it?'

'Six thirty. In the A.M.'

'Oh, my God, my Harley!' By now almost too weak to lift his arms, Jack struggled to throw back the covers. 'My Harley's in Harlem. Somebody'll kill my motorcycle!'

'Calm down. I asked Willie to take care of it.'

The panic left Jack's French Arapaho eyes. 'I love you, George. You know that?'

'I know that, Jack.'

'And you love Teddy.'

'I know that too.'

'Well, smart guy, what you don't know is I messed things up.'

'Surely not you, Jack?'

'Oh, it was me, all right, I lost her . . . all I hope, George . . . is that you won.' Jack fell asleep, still holding the steaming mug of hot-coffee'd bourbon, and dreamed of a little town in Kansas. Where he lived a quiet retiring life, sober and chaste – above all, chaste – and wrote for the *Emporia Gazette* and the best living newspaper editor of them all, William Allen White. An editor whose paper was a pane of perfect glass through which the truth, like light, passed unadorned, untinted, and undistorted.

George Bache prised the mug out of Jack's dreaming hand, set it down next to Teddy's cactus, closed the curtains against the dimming lights of Broadway. Lights that promised everything – even on a frost-scrubbed Manhattan morning. Just before shutting out the dawn, George glanced past Jack's half-assed attempt to mend the window. Across the street, Broadway's bustling buildings were apricot, silver, russet red. He turned his back on the Great White Way, looked around the room that had been Teddy's for as long as he'd known her. Her typewriter glowered at him from the top of a bureau, her books beckoned from shelves ranged against the far wall. Dorothy Parker's poetry, Radclyffe Hall's *The Well of Loneliness*, Gaston B. Means' *The Strange Death of President Harding*, the collected works of Emerson, Longfellow, Twain, Sax Rohmer, new books in shiny covers: Fitzgerald, Hemingway, Willa Cather, Ring Lardner's short stories, a half row of horse-racing forms dating back ten years, and a dandy example of popular trash, Elinor Glyn's *It*. George smiled at her choice; good, bad, hilarious – there was no method in her madness. Then remembered the letter in his pocket. Propping it on her typewriter, he noticed first the San Francisco postmark and then the slapdash scrawl. The latter made him chuckle. Teddy'd got a letter from Daddy Bluff.

Walking out on Jack, George took his hat from the sofa, stuck it on his head, his heavy overcoat from the chair in front of Jack's cluttered desk, threw the coat over his slouched shoulders, glanced once at the cartoons of Eagels and O'Rourke on the wall, swallowed the vision of Teddy sleeping with Channing – and opened the door.

Holding a cage in her left hand, a confused canary inside clinging to its swinging perch, a small trunk propped against her leg, Jack's little brunette had her right hand in the air, pink index finger an inch away from the doorbell. Her mouth made a little 'o' of surprise as she stared up at George. Her nails – at least on the hand George could see – were bitten to the quicks. The top of her head barely made the height of his Adam's apple.

'Lulu, I presume?'

'Gee, that's right.' Lulu assembled a quick smile, piecing it together from her varied collection of hellos for men. 'How did you know?'

'Intuition.'

'What's that?'

'Magic.'

'Really? Jack here?'

'His body is.'

'Oh.' Lulu's fixed smile went out of focus. 'Well anyway, he invited me here, so here I am. Would you mind helping me get this trunk inside? You'd never believe how long it took me to get it up all these stairs after the taxi driver wouldn't help. Don't you think that was mean?'

'Depends how much you tipped him.'

'Tipped?'

'I see,' said George. But, ever the gentleman and his mother's own son, he prodded the trunk with his foot, shoving it into Teddy's living room. From the effort it took, George figured Lulu had her own library in there. He longed to see *those* books.

'Thanks. Say, who are you, anyway? I guess you must be a friend of Jack's, huh?'

'I must be. This very night, Jack said he loved me.'

'He said that?'

'And sealed it with a kiss.'

Lulu got more confused than her canary. 'Well gee, well gosh, that must mean you're going to be a friend of mine.' The brunette dimpled. 'Doesn't it?'

If there was one thing George was used to, it was a woman's smile. In theatre lobbies, restaurants, backstages, nightclubs, the *Trident*'s first-string drama critic was swamped with women; the fairer sex almost crawled to him on their silken knees: actresses, playwrights, potential backers in the form of divorcées, dowagers, married women on the prowl. George soothed them, petted them, fed them with oysters and the heady wine of wit, and finally – and with feeling – explained why it could never be. They were too good for him, too pure, too *something*, in any case. He was too coarse for them, too sullied by the brutal world of a daily newspaper. Eventually even the most persistent went away – feeling loved, elevated, touched by genius. And all this fending off because, when the chips were down, Bache's loyalties lay with the redhead. Though it didn't stop him from getting laid.

Lulu's smile disturbed him. Beyond the obvious and intense desire to please, there was something even more pathetic than that, a kind of gentle, helpless pleading. But behind the pleasing and the plea, what else was there? George shrugged. That would be Jack's good – or bad – fortune to discover. He tipped his hat. 'Only time will tell. Happy hunting, Miss – ?'

'Ah, it's – say, you're Jewish, ain't you?'

'As Calvin Coolidge.'

'That guy who was president?'

'None other.'

Lulu's shock showed up on her nose. It looked like someone had reached out and pinched it shut. 'The president was a Yid? I never knew that.'

'Not many do. He kept it a secret, except to certain friends such as myself. Dear Calvin was afraid of all those poor relations, you see; uncles and aunts and nephews and nieces who'd come swarming out of the East Side and down to the White House looking for hand-outs. You know how Jewish relatives are.'

'Gee. Sure, I getcha.' Swinging her birdcage in one small white hand, Lulu thought for a moment – thoughts that were as visible as the cartoon Ko-Ko's bouncing ball. George watched while Lulu's little mind bounced from Jews to presidents to power. It came as no surprise at all when she made the final leap. 'Say! You got anything to do with the movies?'

'As little as possible.'

Lulu frowned, putting a tiny line between her pencilled eyebrows. A child's frown. 'Oh. Then – my name's, umm, I guess, LeRoy.'

George clicked his heels, bent over her free hand, kissed it, and strolled off down the hallway, whistling Dixie. Making a mental list of things to do when New York woke up. One of them was to have someone fix Teddy's bedroom window. Another to find a spare moment to ponder the state of Jack's mental health. After two years of Teddy O'Rourke, inviting home little Lulu umm LeRoy would be like burlesque after Ibsen, Elinor Glyn after Flaubert, water after wine, popcorn after a meal prepared by the gifted Oscar in that little French restaurant on the Upper East Side whose name George told no one.

George Bache was exhausting his comparisons without getting close to what he was trying to tell himself. Lulu after Teddy? There was no comparison.

Watching his lanky loping back disappear down the stairs, Lulu tapped on the canary's cage. 'Jeepers, Jews! I guess they come in all colours, Walter.' Walter lost two golden feathers beating his wings against the gilded bars.

Irena Josepha Zaleska quietly shut the door on the third floor of 1600 Broadway, turned – and surveyed her new kingdom. It wasn't the Sherry-Netherland at the Plaza or a penthouse on Park Avenue, but it sure beat the hell out of Milt's one room dump down on Hester Street.

17
Bye-Bye Redbird

Sober now, belatedly biting her runaway tongue, Agnes
stared at one of Tommy's blue silk walls, out his long
low-silled window into Edgecombe where the Avenue
was coming alive with dark-skinned sophisticates, at the
wardrobe of Macassar ebony, the tubular steel chairs, the
silent scrolled radio – at everything, at *anything*, except his
lacquered scoop of a bed. Where Tommy had jazzed the
newspaper reporter. But eyes weren't everything; Agnes
still had her sense of smell. Tommy fucking the redhead
husked the air she was trying not to breathe. Nothing
could have induced her up to this room, nothing but
Tommy telling her to stay with Teddy O'Rourke, not to
let the newsie out of her sight. Where she went, Agnes
went. But damn, if some things about Tommy didn't hurt
worse than others.

Electric with nerves, Teddy was back up in Tom's
French room because that's where her clothes were. Ten
feet away from the penitent blonde and just drawing on
one of her dressy white gloves, she paused – looked with
turbulent dismay down the long length of tight white satin,
at all those buttons, at the tips of the flimsy white shoes.
'Agnes, I can't wear this.'

'So?'

'Couldn't you lend me something?'

'I'm wearing it all,' snapped Agnes, tweaking the knobs
of Tom's radio, waiting for its tubes to warm up. 'What do
you think, I *live* here? You think I ain't got class enough
to pay my own way? Anyway, why? What's wrong with
what you got on?'

'Run around town at six-thirty in the morning in white
satin and feathers?'

'Why not? Everybody else does it, all them rich college kids. What about the ermine Tommy gave you? Wear that.'

'I can't keep that. You take it.'

Agnes struck a pose. 'Oh gee, sister, thanks – but you can shove it. Besides, where're you going? Tommy told me to keep an eye on you, said you weren't leaving until him and Sol got back.'

'Got back? From where?'

'None of your business.' The radio, gathering volume, came on with the news. Neither Teddy nor Agnes heard a word the announcer was saying. 'You just park yourself and wait.'

Teddy, reaching out to pick up her loaded bag from Tom's side table, was getting angry. Almost angry enough to mask the jump of her nerves. 'Hold on a minute, Agnes. Tom told you to keep me here?'

'You better believe it.'

'Who the hell does Channing think he is? I go where I want, when I want, and what I want right now is out of here. Where's the phone?'

'What for?'

'What do you think, for crying out loud? To warn Jack Eagels about your little friend, Joey.'

'To warn Eagels? He's the reporter from your paper?'

'Yes.'

'In that case, no phone.'

'What!'

'You heard me, no phone, no telegrams, not even a messenger boy on a bicycle.'

Strike three, thought Teddy, looking at her own hand nestling like a dappled pigeon on the edge of Tom's night table. Though her nerves sang, though her heart gained weight by the second and her mind raged, her hand looked contented – and bird stupid. She snatched up the purse and turned. 'You expect me to sit here doing nothing? What about Jack?'

'You're a writer. Write him a poem.'

'Agnes, this is crazy.'

'It's what Tommy wants, and what Tommy wants, I do.'

'Good for you, Agnes. I don't.' Sweeping the maribou cape off a tubular chair, Teddy strode to the door.

The widow lowered her powdered voice. 'I wouldn't, if I were you.'

'I *am* me and *I* would.'

Without moving from the spot, Agnes threw back her blonde head and yelled, 'CD!'

With her own head blazing with red hair and red fear, her face frantic with freckles, Teddy felt like Suzy Speed, Girl Detective – long legging it out Tom's bedroom door, heading for his curving staircase, that candy-bar voice of Agnes's following her down every rushing step. 'Ceee-Deeee! Zipper! Where is everybody! Benny! Archie! Dammit all! Wake up!'

Holding her canary cage, giddy Lulu whirled round in the middle of the living room rug at 1600 Broadway. In her mind she quickly rearranged the furniture, especially the awful rolltop desk taking up a whole wall, got rid of the pictures, the cartoons, most specially the ones of that reporter friend of Jack's, threw out the books and the cardboard boxes full of junk, painted everything pink, wondered where to hang Walter's cage. So far, it looked like nowhere. Until she caught sight of the gramophone. With a proprietary flourish, she shoved the pile of typed pages off the top, kicked them all under the sofa, then replaced them with Walter.

'There, sweetie,' she whispered. 'You stay here, OK? But just until Joey gets her stuff moved up from Perry Street.'

Walter glared at her through black BB eyes, beeped once, and hunkered down in an irritated ball of yellow feathers.

Lulu went exploring. First peeping in at Jack. Who was just as George had left him: covers up to his chin and dead to the world. Lulu sniffed. What was that smell? Whatever it was, it wasn't her smell. Never mind. She'd change that too.

Lulu giggled. On her first visit, she'd spent all her time in the bedroom, of course, well, naturally, where else? But now – jeepers, now, let's see what's what and where's where. On tiptoe, Lulu crept across the living room. The kitchen? What was that like?

Like George a half hour before her, Lulu woke up the cockroaches. Like George, she ignored them. In New York, cockroaches came with the rent. In a corner, the icebox grumbled, vibrating the stained linoleum under her feet; over the sink, with its dripping faucet, the only window was gritted with city dirt. No food in the cupboards except a box of stale Grape Nuts, a can of Log Cabin syrup, a half-full bottle of bourbon. Nothing on the counter except the warm dregs of coffee in a cracked pot. Not much in the icebox: a hunk of bologna, two bottles of cream soda, one lonely egg, and an opened can of condensed milk. Lulu sipped from the can.

'Yuk,' she said. 'How long's that been in there?' and left the can and the kitchen to the cockroaches. Jack would have to take her to that Lindy's of his for breakfast. And this time, the guy who waited on them better not ask where someone called Teddy was.

Aside from the bathroom, there wasn't much left to look at. And the bathroom she'd already seen, of course, well, naturally – where else does a girl wash up? Especially after she's been with a man?

Lulu had another giggle. Which made Walter go into a rapid series of shrill tweets and high-pitched toots, ending on an impressive run through his scales. 'Walter, you shut up! It's me who's gonna wake up Jack.'

Lulu opened her trunk. Everything that could go in a travelling trunk was in it. Aside from every stitch of clothing she owned, she'd packed her latest issues of movie magazines, the Tiffany watch she'd borrowed from Milt (but heck, as his widow, it was hers for keeps now), and a small bundle of twenties. After Saturday night up at Uncle Tommy's casino, the bundle wasn't as thick as it usually was – but jeepers, Tommy was always doing that after she got angry with someone. He must keep thinking if he cut down her allowance, she'd behave. Oh sure. As if it was *her* fault. Why couldn't Tommy understand? Jeez, who made her do all those things anyway? What was he, dumb or something? Why ever did he think she was always calling her own dead-as-a-doornail mother Irena? When everybody knew Irena was her *own* first name, Josepha her second? Well, really. It was as plain as the nose on CD's face, for goodness' sake. So Tommy'd see she was Sophie. So Tommy would love her like he did Sophie. Which, of course, and naturally, was why she had to burn Sophie up. So Tommy would stop loving Sophie and start loving Irena. With all that heat coming from *her*, why, heavens! you'd think the heat would burn *him*.

Lulu felt around for the pocket in the lining of her trunk. There it was, the sweet little gift from CD, the one he gave her right before she met Bernie. Even with that big nose of his, CD was cute. And there was the red silk nightie, the one she wore for Bernie. Bernie was cute too, until he wasn't. Which, of course, he deserved, three, no! four-timing her like that. And getting her so mad she'd almost missed the last show of *Diamond Lil*. Good thing Zipper could drive so fast.

She set off for the bathroom: washed her face, scrubbed the taste of condensed sour milk out of her mouth, brushed her hair, daubed perfume on her neck, her wrists, in the hollows behind her knees, between the swell of her breasts, then slipped on the red nightie.

Thought about it, and pulled the hem of the nightie up. Shook two drops of perfume onto her golden bush. Stood looking at her reflection in the mottled glass. Pert, pretty, perfumed and young, Joey's face stared back at her. She drew her lips back from her teeth. Perfect. Every tooth glowed. At the last minute, she pulled the nightie back up and splashed her breasts with cold water, a trick she'd learned from the girls at Minsky's. Boy! Little darlin', now they'd stand up. Lulu LeRoy hugged herself. And boy, was Jack in for a surprise – or what?

Shedding white feathers, Teddy made it out the front door of the Sugar Hill casino a good minute before she heard the rattle of racing shoe leather on the stairs behind her. And found herself too frantic to freeze.

Now what? One thing was certain, though neither CD nor Benny, probably not even the dead-eyed Zipper, and surely not CD's Turkish twin, Arch, would shoot Channing's new redheaded catch, they'd sure put a cramp in her style. Locked up in Tom's bedroom, no use of a phone, what would happen to Jack Eagels? Teddy dug her nails into the palms of her hands, fighting the urge to throttle Jack, not warn him. Jack Eagels, the stupid sap. Right out of the starting gate, the first female he bumps into is Tom Channing's niece. Was he with Joey right this minute? If he was, where were they? Watering Teddy's cactus together?

Meanwhile, a minute's lead on Agnes's galloping wops, and nothing in her purse but a compact, one tube of lipstick, three cigarettes left in a crumpled pack, book matches from Bootsie's, the key to 1600 Broadway, and a gun. Money? Forty-three cents. Enough for the subway, if she could *find* the subway before Benny or Zipper or either one of the cousins found her. All her winnings off Tom, all those Wilson dimes and shiny silver dollars? Everywhere but in her purse. And where was she? Fleeing on slippery white satin pumps down a frozen avenue on the edge of a Harlem cliff. Both sides of Edgecombe lined with new apartment houses and old mansions, most of the mansions and all of the apartment buildings manned by liveried black doormen, but between the houses on her left she got heart-stopping glimpses of sheer drops off the ragged edge of Manhattan – straight into the Harlem River. Where a girl could drown. If she couldn't fly. Feathers or no feathers, Teddy O'Rourke couldn't fly. But she could run. After a lifetime of baseball players and jockeys, after sparring with Shucks Spooner and catching trains on the fly with Bluff O'Rourke, dear God, could she run.

Kicking off the satin shoes in mid-stride, holding her bag tucked under her arm like a football, Teddy veered right onto 158th Street, glanced back once to determine her lead – great, none of Tom's armed baby-sitters had even made it to the corner of Edgecombe yet – and darted up the stone steps of a promising building. A jaunty young Negro in a tidy grey suit was just coming out. Teddy gave him her best – and fastest – smile, helped him down the rest of the steps with a shove, and closed his own door behind her. Inside, the back of another early riser was just disappearing down the hall.

Teddy beat the woman collecting the morning milk and newspaper to her open apartment door and dashed inside.

'A phone? You have a phone? Please – shut the door, quick.'

It took Teddy a minute or two to catch her breath, rip off what was left of her silk stockings, and charm this astonished black woman in a flowered organdy wrapper into believing her story. It wasn't too hard. How many white women in eggshell satin gowns were running barefoot in the Harlem snow? But it was her mention of Dancing Joe Bright as a chum that really turned the trick.

On the second ring, the phone was answered at 1600 Broadway.

'Yeah?' said Joey's breathy voice. 'What?' For some reason, she was whispering. In the background, Teddy heard the trill of some kind of bird. A canary? Jack had a canary? Joey's whisper got harsher. 'Who is this? Say, you think phoning people at this time in the morning and not saying anything to them's a joke? Shut up, Walter.'

Her heart in her throat, Teddy hung up.

Phoned George.

Who wasn't there. But Dinah was.

'Dot you, Teddy! George? He vent out in da middle a da night. Vot for? For dot Jeck of yours, dot's vot for. But vhy? I don't know. Sure, you tell me vot you vant me to say, I say it. Soon as he gets beck.'

Hanging up for a second time, Teddy just sat there, expecting any minute to hear a pounding on the door of her hostess. A woman who was so black she was purple, so trusting she'd made a breathless white stranger on the lam a cup of sweet tea, given her a plate of ginger snaps on a paper doily, and was now bouncing on flapping slippers from window to window, wringing her hands, moaning, 'Oh my, oh my.'

Jiggling in red silk and reeking of Black Narcissus, Lulu put down the phone. The nerve of some people, calling just to breathe, stirring up Walter, maybe disturbing a sleeping person. Lulu draped a sweater she found lying on the floor over Walter's cage. And continued on her interrupted way to the bedroom. Slipped her sweet heavy-breasted body under the sheets on Teddy's side of the bed, dipped her dark head and kissed Jack's flushed cheek. Giggled when Jack stirred, made room when he tried to turn over. 'Morning, sweetie.'

For a second, Jack's eyelids fluttered. For less than a second, he smiled, 'Teddy?'

Taking half the covers with her, Lulu reared back. 'Teddy? You think I'm that stupid Teddy!'

Even opening his eyes was an effort of will, but Jack did it with all the energy he had left. 'Jesus Christ, it's you!'

'Golly gee, you're right, it's me, Mr Jack Eagels.'

Here she was, Teddy O'Rourke, the respected New York *Trident*'s ex-sports columnist, famous friend of Jack Dempsey and Gentleman Jimmy Walker, best pal of the city's leading drama critic, chummy with all of its baseball teams, its hockey squads, its tennis and golf players, a girl who'd had the honour of taking Man O' War for a morning run at Faraway Stud Farm, occasional cocktail-sipper and wise-cracker at a big round table in the dining room of the Algonquin Hotel, terror of backroom poker sessions, corner pool halls and floating crap games, here she was – nibbling the edge of a ginger snap and sitting on a wingbacked chair in a Harlem parlour. While the lady of the house wrang her pretty purple hands and kept looking out the window.

'Anything out there?'

'Two white boys with big noses ringing doorbells.'

CD and Arch, of course. Who else? 'What'll you do when they get to yours?'

'Not answer.'

'Lady, you're a pip.'

Teddy's benefactor turned her tailored head. In the light from the window, her skin was amethyst, her smile simple and direct. 'Mrs Claude Larson, Junior. Mr Larson is a teller at the Dunbar National Bank. But please – call me Louise. Louise is my given name.'

Both Louise and Teddy almost squeaked when Mrs Claude Larson, Junior's buzzer went. And kept on buzzing. Until it stopped.

Teddy sat poised with her ginger snap for a full three minutes after that. Louise kept a low profile by the window.

When Teddy finally said, 'Where are they now?'

'Moving on down the street. They're stopping people, everyone's shaking their heads. White boys like that don't get a lot of answers around here.'

From somewhere in the back of the apartment came the healthy holler of a healthy baby. Louise's head snapped away from the window. 'That'll be Blanche. Excuse me a minute.'

Sunk back in her armchair, Teddy sipped tea, her mind dipping and dodging. Tom's crazy little Joey was with Jack. While she was safe for the moment – but still stuck in Harlem, a good five miles from midtown Manhattan. Still in silly white satin but now without shoes, a .22 calibre nickel-plated pistol but little money in her purse. Forty-three cents wouldn't buy her a five-mile cab ride, but it would get her on a bus. The bus would take her to the subway stop on 135th Street. If she knew *which* bus. A bus! Buses were slow. Buses were forever at rush hour. By the time she got to Lenox and the subway, by the time the subway got to Forty-second Street, she'd still have to hoof it a couple of crosstown blocks and then uptown six and a half more – unless she caught another goddamn bus. Damn! Forty-three cents was a pain in the ass. Forty-three cents was no money at all – and no money at all would mean getting to midtown in time for lunch. But in time for Jack? Come to think of it, what the hell was she supposed to do when she got there? Kick Joey's butt? And all this in white satin and barefoot?

Teddy had three bent cigarettes left. She lit one in an apoplectic tizzy, her tangle of small change and subways and buses only a way to stop her thoughts from repeating a single sickening sentence: *Joey's with Jack! Joey's with Jack! Joey's with!* – enough! enough! Jack could steal every scoop she'd ever have, never say thanks; he could stay out on stories for months, never phone; he could fuck every little girl on the island of Manhattan – and do it right on top of Mezinger's desk; just let him be alive! Don't let Tom's lethal many-named niece hurt him – not Jack, not her redman. Jack Eagels was hers; he was all she wanted. Agnes floated into her head, Agnes in her lonely cone of casino light, flipping back her hair, saying, *Wherever my man goes, whatever he does, he always comes home when it's over.* She'd laughed at Agnes then, now she understood from the heart. *Let Jack come home.*

'Say hello to Teddy, Blanche.'

Teddy swam back from the rim of a whirlpooling panic.

Louise stood beside her chair, holding the hand of a toddler the colour of a cinnamon bun.

Blanche said nothing, just twined herself around her mother's legs and stared at Teddy out of coffee-bean eyes.

'Hello, Blanche.'

'Gah,' said Blanche, and ran behind the couch.

'You'll have to excuse her. My baby doesn't see too many white people.'

'In the poetic sense of the word, neither do I.'

Teddy smiled at Louise; Louise smiled back. Mrs Larson glanced away first. 'Lord, look! It's really snowing now.'

Outside the Larson's window, fat white flakes as delicate as Louise's ginger snap doily were cradling down from a hard, white sky.

That capped it. Teddy wasn't hopping on buses, bounding down the metal stairs of subway kiosks, tripping up Broadway without shoes.

'Louise, please. Do you think I could borrow a pair of – ?'

'Honey, you can borrow anything but money. I've got exactly nineteen cents in the house.'

Fifteen minutes later, Teddy was catching her first bus in Mrs Claude Larson, Junior's best wool suit, shoes with sensible heels and ankle straps, a small cloche hat and a warm winter coat – all loden green. Cramming herself between people in black and white dread, all reading newspapers, their noses buried in the tumbling stock market quotations. In temporary exchange, Louise was left the Bergdorf Goodman gown, the cape of white maribou, the location of the matching satin shoes, and Teddy and the *Trident*'s address and phone number. But O'Rourke kept the little white clutch bag – and the gun. While her Lenox Avenue bus crawled, jerked, got stuck behind overloaded trucks, cars, taxis, even a horse-drawn wagon, slid in the slush of big city snow; stopping, starting, few folk getting off, more crowding on. Hot and cold breath down her neck, elbows in her ribs, the corners of lunchboxes, purses, umbrellas snagging the borrowed coat, she sent a fervid message to whatever god was listening. *Please, I'm begging – couldn't we miss just one red light?*

Hanging by a strap and burning with nerves – above her head no Dempsey ad for SNAPBACK. What? Connie'd already cancelled the space? – dipping to see out the fogged windows, counting the cross-streets, the minutes, Teddy ran a jerky unsilent film in her mind. *Jack is wearing that rumpled grey suit of his, the tie she'd bought him one week after the quarrelsome cab ride at dawn, Lindy in the mud, and love-at-second-sight – dark grey with black splodges, a pair of co-respondent shoes, shoes he kicks off as soon as he can – his Indian feet hate shoeleather. He's taking his hat off, throwing it into a corner of the small room he's just entered, he's turning his dark curly head and laughing. It's late afternoon. The light through the window is old amber, lacquered light. And there she is, lying on her stomach on a Chinese bed in a Chinese hotel room, her red hair spread out on a pillow in Chinatown. She's wearing nothing but a silk sheet – and a halo of laughter. She's twenty-seven years old and she's in love for the very first time and whatever she does, whatever*

312

Jack does, they can't stop laughing. Love is so much fun.

The film hurts so, it makes Teddy's eyes water.

At the top of Central Park, her bus changed – but not the ride. Evidently the gods were off shooting a little pool.

On the Great White Way, right across the hustling street from 1600 Broadway, Tom Channing and Sol Rosenbloom were in the front seat of CD's black Studebaker. Tom, hat down over his eyes, hunkered back in the passenger seat; Sol, chewing gum, pockets full of pistols, elbows propped on the steering wheel, watched the women of Manhattan going to work in the November snow. Girls with bold eyes and impossibly long necks. Every other one earning a remark; Sol's remarks finally prodding Tom to sigh, 'Solomon, if you ever got all of that you wanted, you wouldn't get nothing else.'

'A man can dream, Tom.'

Tom wasn't dreaming; he was remembering the last time he saw Red O'Rourke. Sitting down on the floor of the casino, tiny in his green robe, listening to goddamn rummy Agnes shoot her mouth off, probably taking notes. He could see the front pages now, all about Tom Channing's sixteen-year-old niece killing that stupid cop, saying that killing people must run in the family. Stuff about the other guys she did, about Sophie. The press would go wild, drive him crazy. Red probably thought she'd win some kind of fucking prize for 'inside' reporting, cover the trial; Joey's trial! What a circus that would be! Every day more crap about Joey – about him, about Sophie – smeared all over the fucking papers. Damn! Was he going to let Red do that to Sophie? Hell no, he fucking wasn't. But just what he was going to do instead he still hadn't figured out. Stashed up on Sugar Hill, O'Rourke was a problem for later. Too fucking bad though. Red was a firecracker – a goddamn rocket. Too bad Agnes had to have her little scene when she did; too bad Red had to see it. Hell, easy come – easy go. Red and him, they'd burn each other. But still, but still – she hurt him a little. In a place he'd thought seared away by that long ago fire in Brooklyn.

On the other hand, old Agnes now. Agnes was a good old broad; like Solomon, he could always count on Agnes. And sometimes she even packed a surprise or two, sometimes the sappy dame had spunk, backbone. Maybe he'd take her to Paris for Christmas, or to the new place he was building up in Vermont. She'd like that.

Tom's stomach cramped. Not hunger, no, it wasn't hunger. His stomach was bursting with bile, with bitter hate. With fire and dying. Fire and dying young was all Sophie got for her years of waiting for him. In America, that fucking fire was all that was waiting for her.

'Sol?'

'Yeah, Tom?'

'You sure she's up there?'

'Sure I'm sure. Ever since Bernie, I've had a man day and night on her. She's ain't been doing nothing except that show of Mae's and running with the newspaper reporter.'

'Who the hell are all those people going in and out of the damn door?'

'They got a factory up on the sixth floor makes cartoons. You seen Ko-Ko the clown at the movies, right? Those are the people that draw him.'

'They need that many! Fucking hell, don't lose her in the crowd.' Tom edged up in his seat, tipped back his hat. 'Listen, Sol, I've been thinking. When she comes down, I want you out of the car.'

'You want what? Jesus, Tom, I'll do it, you're saying I won't do it good?'

'Good? Sure, Sol, you're the best. But that's my own little darlin' up there. I'm doing the job. You think I forgot how?'

Jack Eagels couldn't get warm. Banked in heavy blankets, the gas fire burning on high, a soft body stinking with hot perfume squirming beside him, and he was still cold. He was also making a valiant attempt to sit up. Which got his head raised a full dizzy inch from what was left of Teddy's swan's-down pillow after he'd beaten the shit out of it. Woken from all he wanted in this world – sleep – to a dry mouth, an awesome pain running down the left side of his chest, and a worrisome effort just to draw breath.

'Lulu? For God's sake. How did you get in?' The length of that sentence sent Jack's head back to the flattened pillow with a whumph.

'Your friend, that tall funny Jewish guy? He opened the door and let me and Walter in.'

'Walter?' Jack's Walter came out as a breathy wheeze.

'Walter Winchell, my canary.'

'You brought your canary?'

'Sure, you don't think I'd leave him in an empty apartment, do you?'

'Lulu, slow down. I'm missing something here. What do you mean by an "empty apartment"?'

'Like in empty, silly, like, you know, not lived in any longer.'

When the import of what Lulu was telling him hit home, Jack coughed. But this time, the cough went on and on and on, ripping through the pain in his chest, and finally – bringing up a sticky mass of bright red blood.

Not only Jack, but Lulu, stared at the red mess in his trembling hand.

'Gosh, Jack, why'd you do that?'

'Because, Miss LeRoy, I think I'm dying.'

'Really!'

'Beats me. I've never died before. Do you think you could get me a towel.'

'Sure, Jack.' Lulu ran for the bathroom and when she did, Jack knew for certain he was sick. The sight of bouncing Polish buttocks under opaque red silk did nothing for him at all. Lulu came back and threw the towel on the bed, then kept her distance – like a child does from something icky.

Wiping his hands, Jack thought of Florence Nightingale with longing. 'When you say "not lived in", Lulu, you mean you've moved out?'

'Sure! The idea came to me in the middle of the night while I was waiting for you down on Perry Street.' Lulu hopped up and sat on the bed, poked Jack's chest with a playful finger. 'I thought, why am I waiting down here, when I could be waiting up there? You know, like waiting every night for you to come home from work and I'd of cooked us a nice dinner, I mean after I learn how, and then we could go to the movies or something, I mean look at all the movies you live in the middle of up here right on Broadway. Gosh, it could be swell, couldn't it, Jack? So I packed my trunk, grabbed up Walter, slipped the key in the landlord's mailbox, and took a taxi right over. And here I am! So far it's been just perfect, except for when you thought I was that Teddy. That part made me kinda mad – but I forgive you, so long as it doesn't ever, ever happen again. Anyway, I don't know about you, sweetie, but I'm hungry. The cockroaches ate everything you got, so why don't you get up now and take me to Lindy's, OK?'

Jack listened to all this in growing horror. As she spoke, Lulu was walking her fingers up and down in the hair of his chest. Jack shivered with more than fever. It wasn't hard to remove Miss Lulu LeRoy once she'd grabbed hold – it was impossible. 'Get up? Listen, kid, maybe you haven't noticed, but I'm not feeling too well here. Besides, who ever said you could move in on me?'

Lulu's little fingers stopped in mid-stride. 'Well, nobody, but I thought – '

Sick, a little scared, more than impatient, Jack went for broke. If there was one thing in the world he didn't need, it was a goofy little girl bouncing around on his bed. Not *this* little girl. This little girl was just a wee bit nuts. It hadn't needed Billy Minsky to convince him; Lulu of the numerous names had done that all by herself. So, if it took hurt to finally get through, that's what it took; Jack resigned himself – he'd probably hate himself when he beat this cold, but right now, it was either her or him. 'What about what I thought?'

'Well, I – '

'And what about what Teddy would think?'

'Teddy?'

'This isn't my place, it's hers.'

'Teddy? You mean that awful girl from your paper, that stupid old thing hanging off my Uncle Tommy? She lives here!'

'I hope she does. I hope so with all my heart.'

Lulu opened her mouth and shrieked, a thin, keening blood-curdling shriek of pain and rage. Jack, backing into his pillow, watched her do it with no real surprise; he knew she was nuts – but with a great deal of concern; just *how* nuts was she? In the second before she leapt at him, hands crimped into claws, Jack got his answer. In those forest brown eyes he caught a glimpse of Lulu's soul; just beyond a cute kid with an unstoppable mouth lurked a furious chittering thing that could sink its teeth in – and hold on.

At the same second, he was rapidly sorting pieces. *Uncle* Tommy. Tom Channing was little Lulu's uncle. Channing was the guy who hadn't fucked his own sister, at least Lulu didn't think so. One more piece like that one, Jack might go as crazy as Tommy's niece. Which was what he was worrying about when Lulu landed with her knee in his groin. Jack couldn't even gasp from the pain; for now, it was all he could do just to breathe. His hand came up to shield his face from her nails, his legs automatically curled, and his balls got out of the way fast.

Spraying him with spittle, Lulu screamed an inch from his suffering ear, 'You, I don't like! I don't like you at all!' Then stared at him, her little pink tongue poking through her little white teeth. Staring back, Jack felt tears sting his tired eyes. A fully grown half Indian, a front page reporter, and he was crying – from pity, he hoped. Where had Clara Bow gone? His happy little Christmas cracker, his delighted idiot – was insane. For keeps. Little Lulu Joey Gilda was five feet tall, four years old, and fucking crazy. She was the kind of crazy four-year-old who'd crack another kid over the head with a grown-up hammer to get its way. This must be how she looked to a comic with baggy pants on the seventh floor of the Peerless Palace Hotel. This mad light in her eyes – once the brown of a falling leaf, now black as charred flesh – was the last thing Milt Rabinowich saw as he clung to his ledge in a wind smelling of gasoline. The famous ledge that made Winchell's column, a hundred and fifty famous feet up from all those gaping mouths down on West Forty-sixth Street. Worse, was this the last thing Jack Eagels was going to see? Because if it was, he couldn't do a damn thing about it. He couldn't even lift his own head. 'Lulu, you couldn't get me a doctor, could you?'

Froth in the corners of her mouth, Lulu's teeth were chattering faster than his were and she was whining. 'You don't think I got feelings! Irena has feelings all right! But you! I thought you were so swell. So important working for a newspaper like Mr Walter Winchell, I thought you were lots more important than that Bernie, and almost as funny as Milt. But was I wrong! I was as wrong as a person can be.' By now, Lulu was hissing in Jack's face. 'You just wait right here, Mr Smartie-pants, don't you move. I'll get you something better than a doctor! I'll show you what Bernie saw.' Then she spun, scrabbled on her cute knees over the side of the bed, and took off for the living room. As she went, those feet with their little mice toes kicked his shrinking scrotum.

Jack made an effort to follow, fell back on the bed. Bernie? Oh, suffering Christ! What Bernt McTaggart saw!

Teddy had a peach of a run in one of Louise's chiffon stockings, a bitter stitch in her side, and Louise's ankle-strapped shoes were killing her. But, holding on to the borrowed hat, the dark green coat flapping like bat wings, she was rounding third, heading for home base in the slow and easy snow. Spooking Times Square pigeons, scattering early New Yorkers, she tore across the triangle of cement and confusion where Broadway crossed Seventh Avenue. Bolted up the Great White Way. Two blocks, now one, now passing the Silver Slipper, less than ten feet from her own door. Noticed there was no motorcycle, but so intent on whatever she thought she was doing, she missed the parked Studebaker – its nickel trimming glinting in the cold white light like all those dimes she'd won off Tom in the night.

Waving away the hellos of the guys who came down for coffee and stayed long enough to draw the cartoons she hung on her walls, Teddy took the stairs two at a time. To stop dead on the landing. Panting, holding her side, favouring her feet.

What would she find when she opened her door, what would she see? Joey? A spatula in her hand and an apron round her waist, flipping pancakes? Jack, his arm curled round Joey's warm and willing waist, reading her one of his ghost stories? Or three in her bed: Jack and Joey and Walter, the canary? Or worse? – much worse.

Fighting to recapture her breath, Teddy took her key from her bag, slipped it into the lock, and turned.

What Teddy found was a small trunk open in the middle of her living room, its contents thrown all over the carpet, what must be Walter in a sweatered lump on the gramophone, Jack's stories tossed higgledy-piggledy under her sofa.

What she heard came from the bedroom.

The chattering sound of Sophie's little angel – and no sound at all from Jack.

Teddy took George Bache's gun from the bag, dropped the bag on the floor, ran towards the unnerving sound of Joey's unnerving voice. Which was toneless, flat as stale Coca-Cola – and repeating itself: 'Here it is, sweetie, here it is. You like what I brought you, you like what Irena has for you?'

On the bed, Jack lay coiled and coughing in a mess of tumbled blankets, one shaky hand held up, the other covering his mouth. On the bed, Joey, up and standing over Jack, sweat gleaming on her quivering pink body, running down the soft curve of her tensed back, the dyed black hair flattened to her sweated neck, red silk flattened to her heavy breasts. In one hand she gripped Teddy's pillow, in the other, a knife. Joey began hopping, her feet coming down on either side of Jack's ducked head. 'Bernie did, he liked it; jeepers, you should have seen how he smiled. Bernie thought I was cute. Don't you think I'm cute, Jacky? Really cute? Just about everybody thinks I'm cute, everybody except Uncle Tommy – but I fixed that, Irena fixed that all right. *That* was cute, wasn't it? Uncle Tommy watching my fire and nothing he could do about it. You should have seen Tommy when I fixed her for good.'

Jumping, Joey was jabbing the knife at Jack – and by the way she held it, blade down, Teddy saw Joey knew nothing about handling knives, but knew all there was to know about what could be done with one. By some strange trick of the light, Joey looked enormous, Jack – so big in every way – looked tiny, shrunken, almost helpless. Teddy saw all this in one sharp intake of her own shocked breath, but not why the once cocky Jack

320

Eagels just lay there, why he wasn't slamming the crazy bitch into the wall, slapping the knife out of her hand. Since Jack wasn't, Teddy would. Or someone was going to die in this room.

'Joey!' From ten feet away, Teddy levelled the .22 at Joey Zaleska's mad Polish heart.

Joey twisted her head, ducking so fast, quick turn and turnabout, George's gun was pointing at nothing. The next Teddy knew the little pistol had spun out of her hand, skittering – where? Oh my God, where! And Joey's teeth were sunk in her wrist, the knife jabbing through Louise's woollen skirt, stabbing at Teddy's white thigh.

'Jack!'

At Teddy's cry, Jack could only groan, force his shuddering body an inch from the bed.

Teddy beat at Joey's dark head with her free hand, kicked Joey's short bare legs with Louise's sensible shoes. Panicking. Trying to remember what Shucks always said. But boxers don't bite. And they never use knives.

Teddy dug her thumb into Joey's left eye, pressed until the girl moaned, and let go. Teddy leapt for the bed; Joey right after her. They both came down on Jack in a thrashing tangle of arms and legs and teeth and CD Durata's switchblade.

'Jack!' screamed Teddy. 'Jack, will you do something! Get the knife off her!'

Jack Eagels did the only thing he could. He bit Joey's finger. Bit like a rabid dog until the tiny bone snapped between his teeth – held on until the knife fell between his face and the mattress. With the only fight he had left, Jack rolled over on it.

Spitting in fury, Joey squirmed out of Teddy's grip, crashed to the floor, crawling over the carpet like a ninety-pound baby in red. Gathered her legs under her and bolted out the door. Leaving Teddy with a handful of dyed black hair.

Sucking her badly bitten wrist, Teddy let Joey go. Leaned over Jack instead.

'Jack, what's the matter with you?'

Jack Eagels, breath coming in spasms, smiled at Teddy, a sad weak mess of a smile. 'She killed McTaggart, Teddy. See, I solved it after all.'

'Sure you did, baby. Lie still.'

'I can't do anything else. Teddy?'

'Yes, Jack?'

'If we had the time, I'd tell you how crazy about you I am. See what she's doing; Lulu could be coming back with a cannon. But first, please, Red, get me a doctor.'

Teddy kissed Jack on his dry cracked lips, levered Joey's knife out from under his shivering body. Where was George's gun? No time to find it now. Holding a switchblade like a switchblade should be held, Teddy followed Joey. The child with the body of a woman and the mind of a maniac wasn't in the living room, the kitchen, the bathroom. Where was she? What was she doing? The answers: anywhere; anything at all.

It took Teddy less than a minute to dial for Jack's ambulance, then she was down the stairs after Tom Channing's hell of a relative.

Solomon jerked upright. 'There she is, Tom! Christ Jesus, what's she been doing now!'

On the other side of Broadway, Irena Josepha Zaleska had just slammed open the door of 1600, run straight across the milling pavement and out into the shrilling street. Traffic screeching around her, horns blaring protest, Joey whirled, started north, changed what was left of her mind, darted south. Right down the middle white line of the busy Great White Way.

'Get out now, Sol!' Tom slid into the driver's seat, gunned the Studebaker's engine – and left Sol standing. Backfiring, the black sedan took off after Joey the moment Teddy reached the pavement, a pavement vibrating with the underground to-ing and fro-ing of passing subways, glittering with mica.

Teddy saw Joey, saw Broadway bumping into itself to get out of her careening way, saw the familiar dark sedan. Watched as the Studebaker, gathering speed, struck Joey as she ran, tossing her small ripe body in the red nightie over its hood like a bull tosses a red rag, Joey's arms and legs as jerky in flight as a dummy in Macy's store window. Heard the sound of impact on dingy grey asphalt. A horrid liquid thud. Saw the sedan swerve, skidding in the snow, come sweeping round, tyres burning rubber – cutting through braking buses, taxis, drays, Model A Fords, low limousines. Rushing back to run over the too-red huddle that had been little Lulu LeRoy a moment before, the tiny body catching in a back wheel, dragging, rolling into the gutter in front of a news-stand – the face of the guy selling papers reflecting Teddy's in horror. The car then screaming past O'Rourke – and away up Broadway.

Teddy also saw who was driving. Not Zipper, not CD, not even Sol Rosenbloom or Agnes. Tom Channing was driving. For one second in this mad slice of shivering time, Teddy saw Tom Channing's face. Wicked, charming Tommy. And Tom saw her. Tom Channing was a gangster, he was a force of nature, he was the devil on wheels – but Leszak Zaleska was crying.

She turned her face away – just as a truck, swerving to miss a braking bus, the bus braking to miss the pathetic red bundle of Joey, jumped the kerb and smashed into the blue metal box of the US mail. The back of the tipping truck sprung open and out tumbled dresses, summer-pink frocks floating through falling snow. Modelling themselves in the blood on Broadway.

Over the hubbub of people running, the sound of a thousand voices shrill with excited shock, came the wailing siren of Jack's ambulance. For Teddy, the air smelled of burning rubber, of early snow, of blood. The wind reeked of gasoline.

Then a traffic cop's shaky voice – how long after? One minute? Ten? – asking, 'You see anything, lady? What the hell happened here?'

Slipping the switchblade into Louise's coat pocket, hiding her throbbing wrist in the torn green sleeve, Teddy focused on the face of the cop. A single snowflake fell, melting in the corner of his mouth. A big mouth, a big face, as big as Jack Eagels's, as friendly as Kitchen Monday's, but the eyes in shock, shocked brown eyes. In his hands: a notebook, a pencil – both waiting.

Late of the *Trident*, Teddy O'Rourke was an eyewitness to a story that could bring that half-pint Connie Mezinger to his chubby knees, hellzapoppin' New York to its senses, could bring her an exclusive explosion in print. What she knew, what she'd seen, could make Kathleen Ellen O'Rourke a reporter of note overnight – a front page reporter in New York City.

'Pardon?'

'I asked, you see the accident, miss?'

'The accident? No, no, I didn't see anything. I guess I got here too late.'

18

Stealing Home

Teddy O'Rourke put her elbows on her knees, her face in her cupped hands, kept her hat on, and watched Jack Eagels sleep.

Thinking that her love for Jack was a constant she constantly forgot. Thinking that Jack was clever and honestly dishonest, that he was a wonderful fool; that his face, pale and thin in the late afternoon light from the Polyclinic's window, was as dear to her as Bluff's rough Irish map.

Thinking: most men were many people, a bit of borrowed this and a touch of stolen that. One face for one friend, a second face for another, a third face for strangers, a fourth for their wives. Very inventive, perhaps, but not straight, not true. But Jack was Jack, all his own. God, how she loved him.

Teddy sneezed. Aaah! Chew!

Jack groaned, slowly opened his Arapaho eyes and smiled. 'Hello, Bricktop,' he whispered so softly she could hardly hear him. 'I missed you.'

'Hello, Jack Eagels,' she whispered back, 'I've been here all along.'

'You have?'

'Every day, twice, three times, hell, I live here. Guess what?'

'What?'

'Leonard Lamont's caught pneumonia.'

'Yeah!'

'Yeah, and from you.'

'Good for me. Where'd they put the little rat?'

'Right down the corridor. He hates the oxygen tent, but he hates his room more.'

'Why? No poison pens in his desk set?'

'Arnold Rothstein died in it.'

For the first time in three weeks, Jack's laugh came out like the original – loud, full-bodied, and joyous. That laugh filled the white hospital room, made Teddy jump up and kiss his pale laughing face.

'You're really alive, Jack!'

'You thought I wasn't?'

'I thought you might not be.'

'That close, huh?'

'That close. Jack, you read my story?'

'Sure. It's on top of all those cards and candy boxes. Christ, I didn't know I knew so many people. There's stuff from everybody – Runyon, Fowler, Walker, Hohenloe, Billy Brennan, Gene and Norma Goetz, Willie the Lion, flowers from Leo Lindemann, a joint card from Madden and Frenchy – '

'How sweet.'

' – even Mae West. *Even* Winchell, for pete's sake. How much did Lamont get?'

'Gladioli from me I signed from you – and a newspaper cutting service from Walter.'

'A cutting service?'

'So he could read Walter's column whenever he felt like it. As far as I can tell, he hasn't felt like it once. Jack?'

'What?'

'Well, what did you think?'

'About what?'

'My goddamned story, that's what!'

Jack grinned. 'Red, you're a peach, and what's more you're a writer.'

'Honest?'

'Honest.'

'Of course, you noticed I played with it a little? It's not exactly what happened. I threw in a few lies for colour, left a few facts out.'

'Left out? Left out what?'

Remembering a bed scattered with silver dollars up on Sugar Hill, Teddy felt uneasy enough to lower her eyes, but not enough to blush. If Jack noticed, he let it slide. 'Nothing important, not really. Joe's all there, Channing, Dixie Fiske, even Shucksie. I think I finally worked out what I think about boxing, why I like it.'

'You certainly do that. Who bought it?'

'The *New Yorker*. If you can call what Ross is paying "buying". Thurber convinced Harold a piece on sports and the mob could be funny – even if it *is* written by me.'

'What's wrong with you?'

'I'm a woman. Around women, Harold gets a bad case of hay fever.'

Jack spent a moment or two inspecting the hem of his hospital sheet, finally saying, 'Ross is a dope. He doesn't know what he's missing.'

'Thank you for that, redman.'

'What're you thanking me for? You're looking at an ex-dope.'

Teddy bent quickly, kissed him on the top of his Indian head. 'Speaking of dopey men, Bluff's back.'

'Oh God.'

'I've got him sleeping on your old sofa. For him, after where he's been and what he's been doing, it's a suite at the Ritz.'

'Where's he been?'

'You got six hours?'

'Are you kidding? Look at me. Lying here, I've got six days.'

'One. The doctor told me three weeks here is long enough. They're kicking you out tomorrow.'

'They are! Terrific!'

'Of course, after that – you get to stay in bed and rest. You'll love it. You can lie around, count cockroaches, finish your ghost story, get started on a new book.'

Jack drew himself up, looked horrified. 'A new book? Hell no. To write books, a guy's got to sit on his butt all day long. I'm too old for that intense literary shit; deep down in my bones, Red, I'm a newspaperman. I like the action.'

'So, I guess we're back where we started.'

'Where's that?'

'Never home.'

'Eagels! When the fuck are you getting out of that bed!'

Bearing the latest edition of the *Trident* and a small bunch of violets, Connie Mezinger barrelled into the room. He shoved the flowers in Jack's hand, dropped the newspaper on his chest. 'Take this! Give you something to think about.'

Jack sniffed his violets. 'Which one?'

Behind Connie loomed George Bache. George carried a cake on a plate – chocolate, gooey and huge.

'Happy Thanksgiving to Jeck from Dinah. It's her best, a *Schwarzwälder Kirschtorte*. Don't eat any, it'll keep you here for another month. Hello, Teddy. I hear Bluff's in town. Is he coming with us tonight?'

Squeezing his violets, Jack's eyes narrowed. 'Us, George? Going where?'

'Not you. You're staying right where you are. I mean Teddy and I. We're dining at a restaurant I know of on the Upper East Side, then to see Cantor in *The Nervous Wreck*, then going to the casino with the mayor – '

'Mayor? Which mayor?'

'Jimmy, of course. Beat La Guardia by a landslide.'

'So Walker's still mayor and you're chasing Teddy?'

In answer, George tipped his pompadoured head, let his glasses ride down his nose, and smiled.

'Bache, when I get out of here, you'd better lay low.'

'What? No more kisses?'

'The both of you, dry up.' Connie, coming up to the height of the water jug, poked at Jack's forearm with a stubby finger. 'You ain't gonna cough in my face?'

'Haven't coughed since I turned back into me, a whole day now.'

'Good. I hate sick people; they make me puke. The docs, they told me two weeks ago you just might die on me, but I told 'em if you did that, I'd dig you up and fire you. Nobody quits on Connie Mezinger.' Connie's Patsy Pig eyes hooked into Teddy's. ''Cept her. You read what that jackass Hopper's been writing, O'Rourke? It's enough to make a grown man heave.'

'You offering me my job back, Connie?'

Mezinger puffed, drew back, offended. 'When people walk out on me, they stay out. Say, what's this?' He'd been snooping through Jack's cards, eating his candy, sniffing his flowers, now he was reading the first page of Teddy's story in growing agitation. 'Is this what you've been doing in here, Eagels?'

'What?'

'This!' Connie flapped Teddy's typed pages. 'This is great, gets you in the heart. But I hope you don't expect me to print it. It's good – but it's not fucking reporting.'

Teddy reached out and snatched the papers from his hand.

'That's mine, Connie. You keep your mitts off.'

Connie snatched them back. Stuck them under Jack's nose. 'I thought you told me right after you got here there wasn't a story behind McTaggart, Eagels? On your death bed you swore it turned out to be no more than a guy being in the wrong place at the wrong time when somebody was looking to rob somebody. When I put that in the *Trident*, Tammany buried him like a fucking hero.'

'That's all there was to it, Connie.'

'What's all this then, goddammit? It doesn't say nothing like that in here. You're a reporter. Reporters don't hide stories from their newspapers.'

'What that is, Mezinger, is a story of Teddy's. It's a work of fiction.'

Connie narrowed his eyes, looked from Eagels to O'Rourke to the paper in his hand. 'And I say bullshit. When a woman writes like this, I quit the business.'

George, who'd been standing behind him, reading not over his shoulder but over his bald and shining head, said, 'Shall I phone the paper, Connie? Have them clear out your desk?'

Jack suddenly yelped. 'Shit, Mezinger, listen to this leader!' Holding the *Trident* at arm's length, he punched the front page with Connie's violets. ' "Sources on Wall Street today say the country is in for a short depression." Who's writing this stuff? It sounds like the *Times*, for crissakes. Where's the colour, the heart, the human interest? Where's the goddamn breadlines? Teddy told me they're forming all over the city, all over the *country*!'

Diverted – as Jack had intended – Connie squealed, 'Sounds like the *Times*? Are you out of your fucking mind! Gimme that!'

Teddy drifted away – both in body and spirit. Somehow, her ex-editor's fat rantings no longer rattled her. There were no vivid scenes of professional death – this time Connie's – raging through her mind. She'd moved away from Jack's busy bed, was quietly standing by the big hospital window that looked right into the top floor of Madison Square Garden. Albert Groat was over there, cleaning his glasses, shoving pens around on the top of Warren G. Harding's desk.

Down on Eighth Avenue a sudden gust of Thanksgiving wind picked up stray paper, snatched candy wrappers, bus tokens, theatre tickets, pigeon feathers – trash; tossed them spinning into the air. A single sheet of newspaper, folding and refolding in mad origami, cartwheeled up the wall of the Polyclinic, winked past Jack's window – and disappeared.

Forehead touching the chill windowpane, flattening the brim of her old grey hat, Teddy leaned against her own freckled reflection.

Across Eighth – Madison Square Garden. Two weeks and four days ago Dancing Joe Bright lost his fight with Sharkey. Harve Hopper, not Teddy, covered the match. But Shucks Spooner gave her a blow by blow. Spooner spitting as he said, 'That Sharkey, he hits below the belt. Nobody but me saw, the morons. Also he opens up Joe's eye again. The cut Schuldner give him hadn't all healed. But for Joe that wasn't the worst. Nah, the worst got saved for last.' As Shucks led Joe from the ring, guiding the fallen boxer out the back way, Jesse Bean had walked out of the Garden – through the front. 'You know what that woman said, Red? she says: "Win the next one, Joe, or adopt yourself another mama." And I said: "Sure, he's gonna win the next one. He's a dead cert." But I tell ya, Red – it was all I could do to stop myself decking that black jelly bean right where she stood.'

Where was Joe now? Channing had hidden Joe somewhere up in the Adirondacks. Was sending Shucksie along to get him in shape for a rematch with Sharkey in the spring. Jesse hadn't left. She'd gone along with Joe – but she'd made Joe buy her a round-trip ticket.

What had Teddy been doing? All she'd done since Joey died was sit at Jack's rolltop at 1600 Broadway and write. Or visit her redman. Both talking of Tom and Joey – both leaving out what neither needed to hear.

But not until she'd bought Louise Larson another green suit, another coat, delivered them in person. Brought a gift for Blanche. The little coffee-bean eyes lit up when her mother opened the door on Teddy. Walter, singing his heart out, now hung in a Harlem window overlooking 158th Street.

Not until she'd done something about the little travelling trunk in her living room. Without a glance inside, she'd shut it, snapped the lock, given it to the Salvation Army.

The day after Joey died, Teddy O'Rourke took a cab to the Manhattan Bridge around nine o'clock on a rainy evening, made the driver nervous by asking him to stop halfway across – with a bandaged wrist, who could blame him? – climbed out of the back seat and stood by the rail. Below the bridge, a wind sharp with the tang of oysters whistled over the river, lifting the hem of black rain. A slender white yacht, its decks lit with Japanese lanterns, drifted by on the cold waters. As it passed, she heard a woman's voice singing low, listened until the song faded in the oyster wind and rain –

Someone to watch over me? As Tom tried for so long to watch over Sophie's little Joey. As Agnes watched over Tom. As Teddy watched over Jack Eagels on that first day as he lay so close to his own death in a white bed in a white room – in a city hushed in snow. Snow that only lasted until late afternoon, melted and ran through city gutters, washing the asphalt of Broadway.

Teddy threw Joey's knife in the East River. Watched as it flipped in a silver arc, cut into the flowing black water, and vanished.

No trunk, no canary, no knife – but on her wrist Teddy would wear Joey's bracelet of scars forever.

Tom Channing buried Irena Josepha Zaleska. Except for the surprising presence of Billy Minsky at the graveside, Tom and Agnes and Sol were the only ones who came.

And Bluff O'Rourke showed up on her doorstep, not a penny in his pocket but with such wealth of mind and humour Teddy curled up in his presence and purred.

With Bluff – and Jack Eagels – in the world, the world was fine.

'A dime for your thoughts?'

'A dime, George?'

'You want more?'

'Get Connie out of here, please.'

'Easy. I'll tell him no one's covering the Macy's Thanksgiving Day Parade. By the way, though he'll never say so, he wants you back at your desk. Hopper is driving him to six Eskimo Pies a day. Since you've been off the back page, circulation's dropped by thousands, hate-mail addressed to Mezinger is stacking up in the mailroom. On top of that, Hohenloe is threatening to quit if Hopper spells "ball" wrong one more time. Connie told him that's nothing; the man's so illiterate he can't even spell "fuck". But Hype's still about to walk.'

'George, after five years of Connie, I'm not sure I could stand any more. He hates me.'

'Hates you? Cornelius Mezinger's opinion of women would have earned him a hug from St Paul.'

'My point exactly.'

George adjusted his glasses, scratched his nose. 'Connie's a pain in the heinie but he's as democratic as an avalanche – he'd fall on anyone. So what? He's the only editor in town that nurtured a rare bloom like Teddy O'Rourke. Any other paper would have thrown her to fashion without looking twice.'

'OK, all right, you win, George. I'll think about it.'

'What if I can get him to pay you what he pays me?'

'You think you can?'

'Ah, interest at last! Did I say I want you back too?'

'In that case, maybe.'

George turned and gazed with great fondness on his tiny editor. Connie was spouting at Jack, flapping his arms, waddling from candy to bedside to window to Jack, his voice booming through the clinical air.

George snapped his fingers. 'Mezinger! Let's go get in the way of some department store floats.'

'Why didn't you tell Connie who Lulu LeRoy was, Jack?'

'After I read your story, what was I supposed to tell?'

'It wasn't an accident.'

'But you told the cop it was.'

'That was my choice.'

'Not telling Connie was mine. Not everything's front page, Red; some things shouldn't even make the paper.'

'You're kidding? Is this *my* newsman talking, the guy who dressed up like a Rabbi for a dying Rothstein? The guy who works for a guy like Connie, who says people who read the *Trident* have a right to know?'

'A *right* to know? If it affects their lives, sure. If not, fuck that. Bernie got told like he should. Everybody's happy.'

'Jack?'

'Hmmm?'

'I'm crazy about you.'

'The way I look, who wouldn't be?'

'After catching every bus, every subway, after running down Manhattan the long way just to save your red skin, I wonder I still am. Jack! Good God, I just realized what I want most from you in the whole world!'

'Is it something I can afford?'

'I want you to teach me to ride a motorcycle.'

The words 'Women don't ride motorcycles' almost popped out of his mouth before Jack could catch them. Clamping his jaw shut, he remembered who he was talking to. 'I suppose I could. Say! I know – if you still want to by spring – '

'Crap. You'll teach me as soon as you're better.' Teddy clapped her hand to her mouth, hopped up from his bed. 'I almost forgot.' From his closet she pulled out an old English greatcoat. 'Look what I found!'

'My God, my coat. Where the hell was it?'

Teddy brought the coat back to Jack's bed, laid it over him, then sat on it. 'One of the upstairs cartoonists, you know, the one who's always drawing me – he borrowed it and forgot to give it back.'

'Jesus, you can't trust an artist.'

Jack turned his head and for one long moment gazed out of his window, watching rain fall past the clean glass.

'What's it like out there, Teddy?'

'Raining.'

'I don't mean the weather. I can see the damn weather. I mean, what's happening? Who's shooting who? Who's stealing what? What's that grim son of a bitch doing down in the White House? How much is the dollar worth now? How much is *anything* worth now? What's Germany up to? How are women wearing their hair? I've got to get out of here, Red. There's news out there – and I'm missing out on it. Things are passing me by. People are losing their jobs, people are beginning to get hungry, little kids, old folks, everybody. Guys selling Fords two months ago are on street corners selling apples, families are pitching tents in Central Park. Holy shit, America's cracking up. I've got to be there to see it.'

'Tomorrow, Jack. You'll be back on Times Square tomorrow.' Teddy stood. 'I guess it's time I went home. I'm meeting George early.'

Jack gave her a grimace. 'That's nice.'

'Isn't it, though?'

'Teddy?'

'Hmmm?'

'I've been doing a lot of thinking lying here these last three weeks.'

'Oh, good.'

'It's about us.'

'Yes?'

'You want to get married?'

'Married? As in "married"?'

'Right.'

'What'll I do then?'

'What do you mean by that?'

'I mean, when you're a husband and I'm a wife – what am I supposed to do?'

'What you always do.'

'You mean run around the country chasing baseball teams and boxers and fast horses?'

'No. Yes. Hell, Teddy, you want to get married or not?'

'I don't . . . I never thought . . . well, actually – no.'

'No! What do you mean no? You mean, you don't want to marry me?'

'I didn't say I didn't want to marry *you*. I said I didn't want to get married.'

'What's the difference?'

'God dammit, Jack. I don't want to be a wife. Do you want to be a husband?'

'I – forget that. So, what the hell *do* you want?'

'I want to be a writer.'

'You *are* a writer.'

'I want it to stay that way. Just like we are.'

Jack gave Teddy a beautiful smile.

Of relief? Teddy wasn't sure. It looked like relief.

'That's fine with me, Red O'Rourke. What more do we need? I love you, don't I? As much as a newspaperman can love a writer.'

'I love you too, Hotdog.' Teddy shoved her hat to the back of her head, grabbed Eagels by the top of his hospital gown, yanked him upright, and looked him right in the eye. 'As much as a writer can love a newspaperman.'